The Gifts

Cathy Hemsley

Book cover by Beck Hemsley

Also by Cathy Hemsley: 'Parable Lives'

ISBN: 9798595860857

DEDICATION

This book is dedicated, with many thanks and
much love, to my great friend and fellow novelist,
the late Edwina Mohtady.

ACKNOWLEDGMENTS

Acknowledgements and thanks go to my wonderful family: husband Phil, children Lizzy and Beck. Especial thanks go to Beck who first thought of the Hued, their gifts and the original plot, and who designed the cover.

I'm very grateful to Izzy Jarvis for reviewing the manuscript and for all his insightful and helpful comments. Thanks also to my friends who have encouraged, supported and commented on this and on my other writing: to Trevor Boyes, Sheila Bridge, Debbie Hibberd, Hilary Iredale, Nick Marsh, Sarah Menary and Steve Orton, and to all the Rugby Writers.

CHAPTER 1
THE MARKING

Rain drenched the city. Sarielle watched it streak the window panes, blurring the outlines of the slate roofs and balconied windows of the houses across the square, as she twirled a lock of her purple hair between her fingers. It's foolish to be so anxious, she told herself. Hundreds of children were marked every year without any problems. Her daughter would be gifted, she was sure of it. She looked at her palm, and the scar of her own marking, a pale diamond on her violet skin, reassured her. Turning away from the window, she paced around the room, adjusting ornaments and re-arranging scented freesias in enamelled vases. Dernham stood and watched her while their daughter sat on the carpet nearby, humming as she piled wooden bricks into walls and towers around her dolls.

"I wish this was over," Sarielle said. "I hate the suspense. I want to know what Berrena's gift is. I want to be sure that she is gifted!"

Dernham went to her and put his hands on her shoulders.

"There is no need to be so apprehensive," he said.

"I know. But I can't help it! You know that people are saying that she is - she is different! That she is a," she gulped. "A freak!"

He took her symbol from where it nestled in her curls and put it into her hand. The amethyst glinted in the light from the window. Then he gestured to his quill symbol on his lapel.

"Sarielle," he said, taking her hands. "Calm yourself. We will know soon."

She traced her finger over the feather-shaped scar on his dark-blue palm. They were both powerfully gifted Hueds. Of course their daughter would be gifted. But the tiny doubt remained.

She knelt next to Berrena.

"Come here, darling," she said. She put her hands on either side of Berrena's face and gazed at her eyes and skin, as dark and intense as ebony. If she looked hard, there were hints of blue, deep emerald and purple in the child's inky-coloured eyes and hair, but that was the only trace of colours she could see. She pulled the child to her, held her and caressed the child's soft dark curls.

There was a knock on the door and the butler came in. "Madame Thera Redstone," he announced.

A slender woman, with frank eyes, a confident air and tangerine colours in her face and her short, neat hair came in, her hand raised in greeting. Sarielle ran to her and kissed her cheek.

"Thera! Oh, I'm so glad to see you!"

"Sarielle - I'm dazzled!" Thera said, staring at the gold and orange swirls on her dress.

"Well, one of us has to wear something bright," Sarielle shrugged and gestured towards Dernham's dark grey jacket. "For the celebration. If there is one."

"Of course there will be one."

"Yes, but this waiting has been horrible. I'm so pleased it will be you that does the marking. And you've won your council seat! Madame Redstone - doesn't it sound well!"

"Yes, I have my seat at last!" Thera said, putting a leather case onto a chair. "How is your daughter? Is she nervous?"

"No, not at all, though I am. She is as quiet and calm as ever, while I have hardly been able to sit still all morning! Berrena, darling, come here, make your greetings to Madame Redstone."

The child smiled at Thera and murmured a quiet salutation to her.

Thera smiled back. "Greetings. I am glad to see you,

Berrena. You know that I am here to do the marking for you. I am here as a witness as well, Sarielle, now that I am a member of the council. Not just as a doctor. You need to have friends with you for this." Thera placed her hand on Sarielle's shoulder and rested it there for a moment.

The butler announced, "Cairson Watergiver and Sir Jeiran Sabusson," as two more of the Hued entered. They raised their left hands, and Cairson, a square-shouldered man with deep gold skin and a matter-of-fact manner, kissed Sarielle and Thera on the cheeks, and nodded affably to Dernham.

"Greetings and congratulations on Berrena's second birthday," he said.

"Greetings, Lady Rochale," Jeiran said. His wrinkled turquoise face was serious as he kissed Sarielle's hand. He bowed to Dernham. "Lord Sapphireborne, greetings. Madame Redstone, greetings also. I assume you are here to perform the marking?"

Thera nodded.

"This child is an unusual case," he continued. "If she is not gifted she will be subject to the city laws, as you know. But we will be impartial."

"Of course we will be impartial!" Cairson said. "Berrena is unique. You know, as deputy secretary, I have access to the archives. I've searched back through them, back for hundreds of years, and I've found no mention of any black Hued."

"Of course not," Jeiran said. "No one has ever heard of one."

"Precisely. And so no one has any idea what the ceremony will reveal. I remember witnessing my eldest niece's, six years ago," he said and touched his own leaf-shaped golden symbol complacently. "Brown Hueds are rarities as you know, and we were intrigued when her bird appeared. It was wonderful to know that she would be able to turn into a bird and fly. But black – it is completely unknown. It will be fascinating to see what her symbol is. I am sure that those who hint that she's not a Hued will be proved wrong."

"There can be no doubt about that," said Dernham.

"Also, I suspect, given the depth of her colouring, that she will have a powerful gift. She cannot be ordinary."

Dernham turned as the butler came in again. "We are not expecting anyone else. Who is it?"

"My lord, Sir Ferard Mavretan of Peveque. He insists that he can attend the ceremony."

"What!"

A tall, slightly-built Hued, with cropped hair standing in dark red spikes on his head, entered. Instead of lifting his hand to show his mark in the usual greeting, he tossed his cloak onto a chair and looked around with a disdainful sneer on his thin, ascetic mouth.

"Mavretan!" Dernham snapped. "Why are you here?"

"Lord Sapphireborne, believe me, I have no particular desire to be here. But I have the right to attend. I am a councillor now, despite your efforts."

"Despite Dernham's efforts?" Cairson exclaimed. "We all opposed you!"

"I had noticed your little clique ganging up against me. Shame you failed."

"A shame?" said Dernham. "No one with any wisdom or integrity would want you on the council. Not with your known warmongering intentions."

"My intentions, Sapphireborne," Mavretan hissed, a frown on his sharp-featured intelligent face, "are to keep the Hued safe. Have you forgotten that my brother was butchered by those dullard savages fifteen years ago? I will fight against your liberal views, your weak appeasements, with every breath I have, remember that."

"Raiding the treasury and increasing taxes so we can double the size of the City Guard? Folly!"

"Gentlemen," said Jeiran, stepping forward, his hands raised. "Let us leave politics for now. This is hardly the time or the place."

"True," said Dernham. "But I strongly object to your presence here, Mavretan. You were not invited, and – as you hear – you are not welcome."

"So I find. But I have the right to be a witness to any child's marking. Any child – even yours, Sapphireborne."

"Even mine? Well, I suppose I should apologise that you have had to interrupt your busy schedule of coercion, bribery and speculation in order to grace our daughter's marking!"

Mavretan's deep-set red eyes narrowed. "Apology accepted. I must also point out that the entire city is talking about your child and whether she is a dullard or a Hued. You might also show a little gratitude that I'm here."

"What!" Sarielle exclaimed. "Gratitude?"

"Yes. The more witnesses who can confirm that your daughter is legally allowed to remain in the city, the better for you. And I don't want the ceremony to be - let us say - incorrectly reported because only your cronies were present."

"How dare you, Mavretan!" Dernham snapped. "That suggestion is outrageous. I am not even going to discuss an accusation like that, not with you!"

There was a pause then Jeiran said, "Nevertheless, Mavretan is correct. He does have the right. The law gives all council members the right to witness any marking ceremony. Madame Redstone, my lord, my lady, we should proceed."

Sarielle took her daughter to a cloth-draped table at one end of the room. She laid her daughter on the table, her head on a small pillow, and whispered, "Lie down and keep still, dearest." For a moment, as she looked at her daughter's contented expression and wide eyes, she wished that she could delay this. But it could not be postponed nor avoided: the city laws were adamant. And when it was done, at least she would know her daughter was gifted.

At the ceremony for Thera's son his symbol had formed instantly, a glossy emerald stone that left a clear oval mark

9

on the child's palm, like his mother's. Hopefully Berrena's would be revealed as quickly. Any gift, any symbol; round, square, fish, apple, butterfly, whatever; Sarielle did not mind, as long as it was incontrovertible.

Thera unclasped a chain, holding a pendant orange stone, from around her neck. She took Berrena's left hand, the ebony of the child's skin dark against her bright amber colouring, and placed the stone on the child's wrist. Sarielle stiffened and her husband put his arm around her shoulders.

Thera glanced up. "Sarielle, there's no need to worry. I've done this many times, for many children. I won't hurt her."

She stared at the child for a few moments. Berrena's breathing deepened and her eyes closed.

"There. Her arm and hand are numb now and she is asleep. She won't feel anything."

"My lord, will you say the invocation?" Jeiran asked.

"Powers above and Virtues around us, by the blood and the life, gift this child," Dernham said, and Sarielle, Cairson and Thera echoed, "Gift this child."

Thera took a steel knife from her case, lifted Berrena's hand and swiftly made a long, deep cut across the child's palm. Sarielle winced. The adults watched and waited as Berrena's jet-black blood seeped out.

The blood swelled and gathered into a shimmering ebony patch that grew on the child's palm. It trembled, swirling patterns appearing on its surface. Sarielle thought that it would rise up and solidify into the symbol that she so longed to see. But the rising blood dropped back and rippled over the child's hand and fingers. It flowed along her wrist in ribbons of liquid then sent dark tendrils along her arm and up to her shoulder, like sinister tentacles reaching for her face and head.

Sarielle gasped and went to pick up her daughter, but Thera held her back. "Wait!" she said.

Faster than a spider could run, charcoal threads bloomed from the tendrils and spread across the child's skin and tunic, until a dark grey cobweb of fine lines enveloped her head and body in shadows. Sarielle stared in horror. Suddenly the shrouding mesh faded. It melted into the child and vanished. All that was left on her palm was a faint blotch. It was grey against her ebony skin, and had blurred and ragged edges.

"Oh no!" cried Sarielle. "There's nothing! No symbol, no shape! Oh, my poor daughter!"

"By the city walls!" exclaimed Cairson. "What was that? What happened? Do you think that was a gift?"

"I'm not sure," Thera said. "Whatever it was, it happened too quickly and it's left nothing. I've never seen anything like that. Not in all the children I've marked. It seemed to me that the blood did something. That there is something special about the child."

"You're biased," Mavretan said, his dark red eyes narrowed in contempt. "There's nothing special about her! Look at her hand - there's nothing. No symbol and no mark. She is clearly a dullard and she should be exiled."

Cairson and Jeiran bent forward to examine the child's palm. They shook their heads.

"I can't see any shape," Cairson said. "It is a patch of dark grey, that is all, with no clear edges. I've never seen a mark like it."

"But it is there," Thera said. "There is something."

"I'm not sure. It has no shape. It is too vague."

"That is not a mark and there is no symbol," said Jeiran. "The blood has gone. My Lord, my lady, I regret to have to say it, but she is not gifted."

"Hmm, I am very surprised," said Cairson. "And grieved, very grieved, but I have to agree. Whatever the blood did, it has passed and left nothing. Dernham, with no visible and solid symbol, and no clear mark on her hand, she cannot be said to be Hued."

Sarielle swept the little girl up into her arms. Berrena woke and stared at her palm and then at the solemn and disappointed faces. When she turned to Mavretan and saw him, Sarielle felt the child shudder. Berrena started to sob and buried her face into her mother's dress, holding her palm out at him as if to push him away. Dernham put his arms around them both.

"Do I have no say in this decision?" he said.

"No, of course not. How could you?" Mavretan said. "The freak must be exiled from the city. Or killed. You will have to accept that. You should have had her killed at birth."

"You barbarian!" Thera exclaimed. "No one would do that to a child!"

"Don't be so naive, Madame Redstone. You know as well as I do of those who have quietly disposed of a dullard runt."

At this, Sarielle could not stop her tears. She shuddered and clutched Berrena closer.

"Disposed of? Runt?" exclaimed Dernham, stepping forward, his hands raised as if he would strangle Mavretan.

"Threatening violence, Lord Sapphireborne?" said Mavretan. "How unlike an ink-stained book-obsessive like you. But I doubt your arms are strong enough to lift anything heavier than your beloved quill."

"My quill?"

Dernham stepped back and folded his arms. His symbol suddenly rose from his lapel and flew towards Mavretan. It hovered, its nib lunging towards him. He stepped back as it came closer, until his back was against the mahogany panels of the wall. He hit out at it. It dodged his flailing hands and darted nearer and nearer until it was a finger's breadth from his face.

"Dernham, for the Powers' sake!" exclaimed Jeiran.

The quill quivered in the air, then its steel point jabbed forwards until it almost pierced the red iris of Mavretan's wide, staring eye. He flinched and shut his eyes. The quill retreated then hung poised in the air in front of his face. Thera gasped, and Cairson put his hand on Dernham's arm.

"That's enough, Dernham," he said.

"You can leave," Dernham said to Mavretan, turning

away and smoothing the creases from his jacket. "You have seen and said all you want." His quill drifted back to settle on his lapel.

Mavretan stood up straight and glared around at them. "I leave with pleasure," he said softly. "And I won't forget this. I look forward to seeing my name on the records as a witness. To Berrena Rochale's marking: ungifted and to be exiled. My most sincere condolences to you, Lady Rochale." He seized his cloak and walked out, emphatically shutting the door behind him.

Sarielle, still clutching Berrena, walked to the window and stood with her back to them, looking at the rain drenching the street below and letting her tears fall freely too.

"Dernham!" exclaimed Jeiran. "That was disgraceful, attacking Mavretan like that. As if you were brawling in the streets! The city will not tolerate violence like that!"

"I must apologise," said Dernham. "But his comments, his cruelty, his gloating... They goaded me beyond endurance."

"Apology accepted. Understandable, in the circumstances."

"Most unlike you, Dernham," said Cairson. "But to return to the main issue. Berrena... She is not Hued. I am sorry. You know the law."

Sarielle turned back. "The law?" she exclaimed. "The law can go to ... to hell! This is our child!"

She wanted to scream, but she bit her lip to keep the cries within, held the child closely and buried her face in her daughter's hair. There was nothing they could do. Dernham came over to her, lifted her face, gently touched the tears running down her cheek, then took them both into his arms.

"Sarielle," he whispered. "We must bear this. Our child will be safe. It is only exile."

"She can live in the country," Thera said, taking her hand. "You can find a dullard family to take her. And you will be able to visit her."

Sarielle clung even closer to Berrena. The others stood in silence. Eventually Cairson said, his face grim, "We have no choice. As deputy secretary, I have to record the ceremony, the witnesses and the decision. She has no mark and no symbol, and she has to leave the Coloured City. As I said, I am bitterly sorry. I will insist that the council gives you time to find a suitable home for her. In Langron, your town, perhaps?"

CHAPTER 2
THE TALTHEN

Clouds and autumn mist blew across the plain, obscuring the landscape. The small group of travellers on the road from Langron could not see their destination until they came over a slight rise. Then, through breaks in the mist, the grey and white walls of Hueron, the Coloured City, appeared: over a hundred feet high with many-coloured flags fluttering on the battlements, and dark gates guarded by sentries in black uniforms.

The older man on the cart looked up at the sun's pale blotch in the cloudy sky.

"Tis early," he said. "Lord Sapphireborne said he'd meet us at the gate at noon. We'd best rest for a while. Anyhap, we won't be allowed into the city without a Hued with us."

They pulled the cart and horses over to the side of the road. The two younger men riding next to Laithan Veorne stared, open-mouthed, at the glimpses of the distant city. His wife, sitting by his side, clutched his hand and stared too.

"Tis huge!" one of the young men exclaimed.

Laithan nodded. "Aye. Huge, beautiful..." he said, and added in a whisper, "And foul."

Three years ago, after his election as town chief, he had visited the city for the first time. Until then he had lived among ordinary people all his life; some might have swarthy, brown, freckled or sallow skin; some red, chestnut or blonde hair; but that was all the variation he knew. Never had he seen anyone like the Gifted People that he had seen inside Hueron. He had been dazzled by the glorious colours: brilliant magenta, grass green, bright scarlet, pale yellow; men and women with orange eyes, lilac hair, turquoise faces. He had realised why, despite its name, the city had walls, buildings and towers of plain white or grey. Such rainbow colours needed the foil of simple walls. He had thought it was beautiful.

But since then he had visited often. The contrast between the city's conspicuous richness and the grimy poverty of his home, with its shabby thatched cottages and crumbling houses, galled him like a strap rubbing on an old sore.

"Look at that! Look at the height of those walls," said the other young man. "Coloured swine. Hiding behind their walls. Powers above, wish I could pull the whole place down."

"Aye, plagues take them!" said the other. "Raid it, cut the brutes open, see if their blood is the same colour as their skin or if tis red, like ours."

"Course tis red. Ain't it, Chief?"

"Nay. Tis the same colour as their skin and hair," Laithan said. "But don't talk like that. Not inside. You don't want the City Guard overhearing you say things like that. Remember, they're the Gifted People, not us."

"Have you ever seen any of their gifts?"

"Nay, only their symbols."

"I ain't never seen a Hued's symbol," said the first lad. "Is it true that they're made from their own blood? What're they like?"

"They're shaped, like jewels or leaves or fishes. And, aye, they are made from their own blood."

"Someone told me that they can turn into birds or animals. Ain't true, is it, Chief?"

"Some of them can, and some can heal, and some can make stuff from nothing, like silver or bread. And some can fight."

"Like the cursed City Guards," said the second lad, and spat into the dust.

"What's Sapphireborne's symbol, then?" asked the first.

"Lord Sapphireborne! He's a Hued Lord. Call him by his title, for Powers' sake! His symbol - tis a dark blue quill, like a pen. When you meet him, you'll see it. Like many of them, he wears it on his jacket or pinning his cloak."

"Showing it off."

"You'd do the same, if you were them."

"Wish I were! I'd give my right arm to be in the City Guard and be able to fight like them."

Laithan turned to his wife.

"Ingra?" he said. "You're very quiet."

"Aye, I am, I guess. Tis just... Like you say, the city - tis wonderful. But I've been wondering. Laithan, why did Lord Sapphireborne ask for me to come as well this time?"

"I don't know," replied Laithan. "And I don't know why he's asked that we bring bodyguards. Tis odd. Anyhap, let's move on. When we go into the city, don't stare at them. Keep your eyes down, give way to them, show respect."

At the gate, the City Guards gestured for them to stop and dismount. Laithan saw, through the open archway, Lord Dernham Sapphireborne walking down the street towards them. As usual, he wore grey, and his quill symbol rested just below his shoulder.

"Greetings, Laithan. I see you got my message," Dernham said, raising his left hand to show his mark. "We will go to my house to talk".

"Aye, my lord," Laithan said, bowing. "As you asked, I've brought my wife. My lord, this is Ingra Kessenor."

She curtseyed. Dernham nodded briefly at her then turned to the two lads.

"Men from the town, coming with us as guards, my lord," Laithan said.

The two young men stared at the Hued Lord; at his indigo hair, at his dark blue eyes, their whites gleaming palely against his deep blue skin. Laithan nudged the lads, and they started and bowed.

"Very good. I am glad you brought guards with you," Dernham replied. "I have a particular reason for wishing you to be safe on the journey back."

Dernham spoke to the City Guards, who told them to leave the cart and horses outside the walls, then took their swords and knives to be stowed in the guardhouse.

"Why can't we ride?" muttered one of the young men.

Dernham turned.

"The law forbids dullards to ride in the city. I am aware it is inconvenient. However, my house is less than a mile away and it is a pleasant walk."

He strode ahead into the city and they followed.

"How is the situation in Langron?" Dernham asked Laithan, as they came to a wide square. Snatches of music came from open doors, the scents of flowers and spices drifted from nearby shops. "What are the harvests like this year? I would like to know what taxes I can expect."

"I'm sorry to say, but tis bad again, my lord. The yield's down to less than two-thirds of what we hoped, and some of that's been ruined by overmuch rain. We need a visit from the Magi."

"The Magi? Remind me."

"The wizards, sir, the Magi - they travel round and heal people, bless the harvests, bring good crops and weather. They only visit the Talthen, not the Hued. But we ain't seen them for several years."

"Ah, I remember. There's an old Hued law about them, I believe."

"Aye. There is. It says that every forty years they can take six Talthen lads to be their apprentices. If they choose someone the boy has to go, or his town will be punished by the Hued."

"Talthen lads? So the Magi are not Hued, but dullards?"

"Nay. They ain't coloured, sir, and they ain't exactly Talthen either. They don't have special gifts like the Hued, they're different, but they're powerful. They're far more powerful, by all accounts, than the greatest Hued."

Laithan paused, conscious that Dernham looked offended. Well, he thought, I can't help what he thinks about the Magi. Tis not as if the Hued need them, unlike the Talthen, desperately hoping that the Magi would heal their children, cure their herds, and make the crops grow.

Dernham glanced at Ingra and the two young men as they continued up the main street of the city, past the white marble columns of the City Hall, past chatting groups of friends and families, past glimpses of market stalls down side-streets. Ingra and the others gazed with wide eyes at the tall buildings, the broad streets and the rainbow colours of the people, but Laithan noticed how the Hueds looked at them with hostile or scornful glances.

"The city is new to you, Ingra," Dernham said.

"Aye, sir. I'm sorry to stare so much, but tis so strange to me," she murmured, red blood visible in her cheeks.

"I'm sure it is," he said.

As they passed a shop, with a window display overflowing with fruit, bottles, bunches of grapes and garlands of vines, a young woman came out and put a basket of lemons on the trestle table outside. She wore a striped skirt of green and white, with a green blouse. Her hair, like her skin, was a rich and glorious red, worn pinned up with flowers and a large ornament of grapes. She stared contemptuously at the Talthen, and said loudly to someone inside, "Come and see these dullard idiots. Gape-mouthed peasants staring as if they'd never seen civilised people before."

Dernham stopped. His mouth hardened, he whirled round and strode back to the woman.

"Joulette Iverna, is it not?" he snapped.

She nodded, leaning arrogantly against the door frame.

Dernham turned to Ingra and the others. "You have had a long journey. Doubtless you would like some refreshment."

Ingra blushed and stuttered and shook her head.

"Nevertheless, some plums, I think," Dernham said to

Joulette. "And show this woman - this lady! - how you use your gift."

She raised her eyebrows. "What? For dullards? I don't think so!"

"I believe you know who I am. And I believe you supply my household with wine and fruit. So, a dozen plums for my companions. If you would be so good!"

She stared at him measuringly, then shrugged. "Of course. Whatever Lord Sapphireborne wishes," she said with heavy sarcasm, then picked up a small basket from the trestle table and handed it to him. She took the ornament of grapes from her hair and held it in her out-stretched palm. It looked as if it had been made of deep-red crystal. She closed her eyes. The ornament shimmered on her palm. Laithan saw a faint outline of round objects, like a reflection in a glass, appear in the basket, then the objects darkened and solidified into a dozen ripe plums. Ingra gasped in surprise, and the two lads looked with awe at the fruit and the scarlet-skinned woman.

"You can add them to my account," Dernham said, passing the basket to Ingra. "Assuming they are not poisoned."

Joulette scowled and stalked back into the shop, slamming the door behind her. Ingra tentatively nibbled at one of the plums. As they walked on, she whispered to Laithan, "Well, they don't taste poisoned. Juicy and sweet, nicest I've ever had. Try some," and she passed some plums to him and the other two. "I never knew twas that easy for them to make things. As easy as breathing for them, ain't it? But she - oh, Laithan, she weren't friendly, was she?"

Laithan shook his head. Definitely not friendly. He looked at the plums. They were solid, real plums. Strange. Hearing about their gifts was one thing, but to see them in action was a revelation. It was so simple for them! A basket of fruit with no need to dig, prune, weed, harvest or watch the weather. But the scorn with which the woman had said 'dullards'! He hated that word. Talthen, he thought. We are not dullards, we are Talthen.

They turned a corner into a quieter street, lined with autumnal trees, and came to Dernham's city mansion: three storeys high with bay windows, formal box hedges and fading roses in front, with glimpses of wide lawns in the garden behind. As Dernham went up the steps to the front door, Ingra whispered to Laithan, "Tis so grand! Is this really his house?"

The door was opened by a portly butler. Ingra clutched Laithan's arm, and he patted her hand as they went into a wide hall, with wood-panelled walls and a broad oak staircase leading upwards. Porcelain bowls of potpourri stood on polished tables and chests, and a scent of lavender and sandalwood drifted from them. The butler took the two guards to the kitchen to wait, while Dernham led Laithan and Ingra into one of the front rooms. Laithan noticed Ingra gaping again. There were opulent sofas and chairs, a soft carpet, a marble fireplace, vases, pictures and signs of wealth everywhere. A woman, sitting on the sofa, rose to greet them.

"This is my wife, Lady Sarielle Rochale," Dernham said.

She was much younger than her husband, with a glittering amethyst nestled in her curly hair, and she wore a silvery-grey silk dress with a turquoise shawl that highlighted her purple colouring. Dernham's blue skin, dark grey clothes and tall sparse frame appeared sombre alongside her colour and vibrancy.

A young child, a girl barely a couple of years old, stood close to Sarielle, holding her hand and leaning closely into her skirts. Laithan stared at the child. He had never seen a Hued with such intense, almost black, colouring. Her hair, eyes, skin, face were ebony, as dark as midnight, so dark that her features were hard to see. Then she glanced up at Sarielle, looked at Laithan and Ingra, and smiled suddenly. Her ivory teeth and eyes flashed bright against her shadowy skin and hair.

"Sit down, if you would," Dernham said.

Ingra sat gingerly on the sofa, Laithan sat next to her. The child looked at them with cheerfulness, but Sarielle's bright violet eyes glistened with tears as she fidgeted with a lock of her hair. Dernham walked to the window, looked out for a moment then turned back. His face became graver as he looked at the child. He drew in a breath and turned to Laithan.

"Laithan, I have summoned you here to request a great favour of you," he said. "This child is our daughter, Lady Berrena Rochale. She has been labelled a dullard, since she has neither mark nor symbol. The city law insists that she must be exiled from the Hued. We ask if you and your wife would take her as your own."

Ingra gasped.

"Er, my lord!" Laithan stuttered. "Do you mean it? For us, for Talthen, to adopt your daughter? A Hued? How can that be allowed?"

"Yes. We do mean it. She cannot stay in the city. She is not considered to be Hued therefore she must leave. The law permits her to be given to a dullard family. We hope that you will be prepared to give her a home, a safe home, one near my estate. We would support you financially and visit frequently, but she would become your adopted daughter."

"But - but Langron's a week's ride from Hueron. How can you bear to send her so far away?"

"We see no other option. She would not be completely lost to us, she would be safe with you." Dernham glanced at the child, his face grim, then looked directly at Laithan. "Laithan, will you do this for us?"

Laithan thought for a long moment. He had heard that occasionally a non-coloured child would be born in the city and immediately sent away to some remote village, but he had never heard of a child who did not look like a Talthen being exiled. The child was so young, so innocent, yet had such strange ebony skin! He clenched his fists. How could any parent accept sending away their own child? He looked at Sarielle's apprehensive, sorrowful face, then up at Dernham's waiting gaze.

"My Lord, I'm honoured to be asked, but Langron is poor. We will need..." He paused, cleared his throat and continued in a firmer voice. "I insist that we get some relief from the rents and taxes in return for this."

Dernham frowned.

"You don't want your daughter to be raised in poverty," Laithan added.

"Hmm. That is a good point. But, Laithan, I have no power to reduce taxes, you know that."

"Aye, but you can cut rents."

"Of course, Dernham," said Sarielle. "We should do that!"

"Well, I am prepared to, let's say, reduce rents by a fifth until she is adult. And in view of the poor harvests, I will give a year's grace on rents. But only this year, and only to those who, in your opinion, deserve it."

"Many thanks, my lord. Don't think we ain't grateful," replied Laithan, bowing slightly. "Will you also sponsor a school for the town? She will need to be educated."

"By the Powers, Laithan, you demand a great deal!"

"Aye. But tis for your daughter's sake." Laithan said. He glanced at Ingra, who was gazing at the child with blended pity and curiosity. "However, my lord, I'd like to talk to my wife about this, in private."

Dernham nodded.

"Very well. A school too. We will leave you to discuss our request. Tell the butler in the hall when you have decided."

When they were alone, Ingra turned to Laithan.

"I don't understand why they can't keep their child. Nor go with her. Tis cruel! And she's such a pretty little mite, even though she's such a strange colour."

"That's the Hued laws for you. Harsh and cruel to everyone except the coloured people. But, Ingra, do you want to take the girl? I'm willing, and twill make Lord

Sapphireborne help the town more. But tis your choice too."

"Oh, Laithan, love! You know I always wanted children!"

"I know. I did too. And it ain't too late. We could still have a child."

"We've waited eleven years. I don't believe we ever will." Ingra shook her head. "My sister's children are the nearest to my own I'm likely to have. And they live miles away. This could be our only chance."

"But it won't be the same. She won't be ours, and she ain't like us. What if Lady Rochale or Lord Sapphireborne wants her back? And she won't fit in at Langron. She ain't a Talthen."

Ingra leaned forwards and took his hand.

"Where else can she go?" she said. "If we don't take her, what will happen to her? Other towns will be as bad or worse than Langron. Laithan, let's take the little sweetheart. She looked a happy, cheerful child. I'm sure the town'll take to her."

"Mayhap. I hope so. Anyhap, the town can't afford to offend Lord Sapphireborne."

At the city gate Sarielle clung fiercely to her daughter, until Dernham firmly disengaged her arms from the child. As Sarielle turned aside, her hands to her face, he took Berrena, kissed her and placed her in Ingra's lap. He stroked the child's cheek and made as if to speak, but stopped, and turned to Laithan.

"Just go, Laithan. Go quickly. This is unendurable," he said, his face rigid. He turned away, and put his arms around Sarielle.

Laithan shook the reins and the cart moved off, while the two lads followed on horseback. Berrena twisted in Ingra's arms to gaze at her parents, then glanced up doubtfully at Ingra's face.

"Don't you worry, my little one, we'll take care of you,

and you'll see him and your mother again. Hush now, sweetheart, don't you cry," soothed Ingra, for the child's lips were trembling and tears were welling up in her eyes.

"Nay, let her cry," said Laithan. "'Tis best, she needs to have her cry out."

So Ingra held the child close to her while she sobbed. The child did not wriggle or scream, but seemed to find some comfort in Ingra's embrace. She wept, but it was with calm sadness, not the violent grief Laithan had expected. There is something strange about this child, he thought. Why did she not struggle against the strangers taking her away from her parents? Why did she not scream or fight or to try to escape?

On the city wall, high above the gate, Sarielle and Dernham watched their child disappear along the road leading northwards. Sarielle did not weep, not yet. She knew she would later, but for now she kept the tears at bay so that she could see the cart for as long as possible.

"We will go to Langron Manor in early spring," Dernham said. "We will give them a few months for her to settle and then visit. And I see no reason why we can't have Berrena with us at the manor for a month in the summer. There is nothing in the city rules to prevent us having what visitors we please, even ones that are technically dullards. The council will have to accept that."

Sarielle nodded. That was some small comfort, some small hope. And she had another tiny growing source of comfort. She moved nearer to Dernham and he, his eyes still on the distant cart, put his arms around her and held her tightly to him.

CHAPTER 3
RESENTMENT

Laithan saw, as he came around the corner of the lane, three boys circling a small girl in the distance ahead of him. As he came nearer, he heard their chants.

"Dirty Hued freak!" they were crying. "Freak! Freak! Get back to Hueron, you foul cursed runt!"

With a shock of fury, Laithan realised that the girl was Berrena. He started to run towards them. Berrena stood with her arms folded. Her basket was lying on the road beside her.

"Stop it," he heard her shouting back. "Stop it! Go away! Leave me alone!"

The tallest bent down, picked up a stone and flung it at her. It struck her arm. The third boy threw another that hit her on the forehead. Laithan ran faster. But Berrena ignored the stones.

"Don't you dare do that again!" she shouted. "You go away and leave me alone! I ain't doing you any harm!"

"We won't! Tis our town, not yours. You go away! Run away, won't you, you dirty, smelly, little freak! Why don't you run? I'll make you run, I will! I will!"

The boy darted at her with his fist raised. He punched her shoulder. She did not move. He yelped.

"My hand! You've broke my hand. You - you witch!" He looked down at his hand and shook it jerkily. "How did you do that?"

The third boy saw Laithan charging towards them. "Look out!" he called and the boys scattered.

Laithan shouted after them, "How dare you! How dare

you!" then he turned to Berrena. Breathing hard and shaking, he knelt beside her. How could they do this? She was only eight! But he'd recognised them. He'd thrash them for this, or he'd make sure their parents did. Didn't they realise that the only reason their rents were so low was Berrena's presence?

"Berrena! Oh, poor child! Are you hurt? Where did they hit you?"

"Here. On my arm and my shoulder. And my head."

Laithan could see nothing. There was no blood and no mark, although it would be hard to see a bruise on her dark skin.

"Did they hurt you? I can't see anything. Did the stones hit you?"

"Aye, but they didn't hurt. But they called me horrible names! And they made me drop the eggs you wanted."

"Tis only eggs. They don't matter," Laithan said and picked up the basket. "Are you sure you ain't hurt?"

"Nay, I ain't hurt a bit. But they hated me, Daddy! Why? I can't help being – being different. Oh, Daddy, it was funny though. Their faces when you came! They were so scared of you! They ran away! Silly horrible little boys!"

"They're petty-minded stupid boys," said Laithan. "Don't let them bother you. I won't let them hurt you again."

"I know you won't. And I don't care what they think. They're the ones who should go away! I ain't going away. I live here, not Hueron."

"That's right. You do. This is your home. Don't worry, I'll see to them. Tis only three boys. There's lots of folk in the town that know about you and don't want you to leave."

"Aye, I know." She tucked her hand into Laithan's arm. "Tis all right, Daddy. I don't care about them. I know that you like me, Mamma likes me, my birth mother and father and my brother like me. Kianne likes me too. She said we should climb the highest tree in their garden."

"Did she? And did you?"

"Aye! I climbed higher than her then she fell off and she howled! Her mother ran out and was ever so cross with her. But when she saw how high I'd climbed she was frightened. So I came down. I didn't want her to worry about me."

"Good girl!" said Laithan. "No point in worrying people. Come on. Let's have a song as we walk home."

"All right. Let's have the one Mamma taught me last week. Kianne knows it too."

Berrena, holding his hand, started to sing and he joined in at the chorus, as the early summer sun shone down on them both.

When spring was in the air,
He saw that she was fair,
He promised then and there,
To be her hero.
Oh, know your own true love, for wealth's a liar,
Brave men be rare as gold, true hearts as sapphire.

At Langron Manor, a few weeks later, Berrena gave Laithan a firm hug before running to Sarielle and Dernham, crying "Mother! Father!" She embraced them, before looking around. "Where's Vallan?" she said. "Where's my brother? I thought he was coming with you?"

"Darling, of course Vallan's here," replied Sarielle. "But as soon as we arrived he ran upstairs to the playroom to find his toy soldiers and the rocking horse! Come on, we'll go and find him."

Laithan watched them run up the stairs. He and Ingra dreaded the loneliness of the month Berrena spent every summer in the Manor with her birth parents, but it had to be endured. At least it was only a few miles from the town. As Berrena danced along the gallery above them, holding her mother's hand, he turned to Dernham.

"Lord Sapphireborne," he began, but Dernham interrupted him.

"Laithan, as I have said before, you do not need to call

me Lord, nor be so subservient. You have adopted my daughter. That makes us nearly equals. Please, call me Dernham and my wife Sarielle."

Laithan glanced doubtfully at Dernham. Hueds and Talthen could never be 'nearly equals', he thought. But all he said was, "Very well, sir."

"Dernham, not sir."

"Dernham, then," Laithan said, stumbling over the name. "Anyhap, there's something I must tell you about Berrena."

"Yes?" asked Dernham.

Laithan paused, unsure how to continue.

"She doesn't get hurt. Not bruised nor grazed, not even when she falls over."

"She does not get hurt? That is strange! I had not noticed this," Dernham said, frowning slightly. "Are you sure? She doesn't get hurt or feel pain, you say?"

"She does feel pain. She got ill last winter and had a headache, and she's twisted her wrist once. But she doesn't get the cuts and bruises that you'd expect and she never cries when she falls. Tis odd, that's all."

"Extraordinary. Thank you for telling me. I will observe her more closely and talk to Sarielle about this. But I do not understand it."

Laithan wondered if he should tell Dernham about the incident with the boys: the name-calling, the stone-throwing. But if he did, perhaps Dernham would take Berrena away. He could not bear the thought of that.

"Er, Dernham," Laithan said. "There is something else. Now that Berrena is older. The school..."

"You are going to tell me that it is barely adequate, I assume?" Dernham said, raising his eyebrows.

"Aye. It has only one teacher. We need more books too."

"I see. I suppose you want me to pay for another classroom, materials and suchlike, and a salary for another teacher."

"Your daughter should be educated."

"I know! Very well. And I will give the school various books from my library. On mathematics, history, suchlike. Whatever the school needs. As you say, my daughter must be well educated, at least until she is eighteen. Laithan, I have no objection to her doing routine household tasks, learning to cook or garden or look after chickens or suchlike. But she is not to become an ignorant drudge or labourer or farm worker. That would not be suitable for her."

"Mamma, this history book," Berrena said, two summers later. She held up the book that she'd brought home from the school to study. "It only talks about Hueron. Why doesn't it say aught about the Talthen?"

Ingra dusted her floury hands on her apron and stood with her hands on hips as she pondered.

"Don't it? Well, posset, I'm sure I don't know. The book came from your father, so I suppose that must be why. I guess we Talthen are too poor to have any history."

"But there must be some. Why are we called Talthen?"

"Oh, I know that story. I heard it from my grandmamma. It just ain't written down. Well, now, tis a long and sorry tale, but I can tell you quickly, dearie. Let me see, have you heard of the Feorgath?"

"Nay. Who are they?"

"They be all gone now. And they won't be in that book of yourn. Oh, t'were hundreds of years ago, in the great wars. Let me see, there was the fair-skinned Talthen from the north, and the olive-skinned Sarochen in the middle and the dark-skinned Sheiran from far in the south. And they were all peaceful, living quiet-like together in little towns and villages. Then the Feorgath came from over the north-eastern mountains. They were terrible. Strong, cruel; they came south, town by town and village by village. We fought back but they were as fierce as wolves and as relentless as winter frost. Most of us were took over, made slaves, them as weren't killed, that is. Then the Hued came up from the south and they fought the Feorgath. Us ordinary people, we were like field mice trapped between a forest fire and a river, scurrying here and there, trying to escape. The Talthen, Sarochen and Sheiran all got mixed up and driven back northwards as the Hued invaded. They defeated the Feorgath, 'cos of their powers and their gifts, and killed nearly all of them. They hated the Feorgath. Even the name. Yon history book don't talk about the Feorgath, does it?"

"Nay," said Berrena. "You're right, it don't."

"Anyhap, we all be called the Talthen now. And the Hued took over," she said and got a knife from a drawer. "You carry on studying, love, I need to get this pie made. My brother-in-law and nephews are coming tomorrow. They're staying two nights afore going to Reshe, taking horses to the market there. You remember going to see them, in Helsund, don't you?"

"Only a little. It was cold, there was a lake and a woman in bed."

"Oh, well, you were very young. Only four, I think. That was when my sister fell ill," Ingra said. Sadness clouded her face.

"Aunt Brilde?"

"That's right. My poor sister. Twas a sorry shame that the Magi didn't heal her."

"I thought they could heal people? That they had healed her?"

"Well," Ingra said, as she picked up a turnip and started to peel it. "In a manner of speaking, they did. She'd been ill for months. They blessed her and she was better that day, and the next. But it didn't last. She fell ill again, sank as quick as a stone into a pool, the week after they left. Powers give her rest, poor Brilde, she had a hard life. Helsund, tis a grim, starveling place. And the boys were a handful. Little scamps, they were. Fighting with each other, falling off horses, climbing trees, scrumping apples, getting into mischief. I hope they've calmed down a mite."

The two boys didn't seem at all calm to Berrena the next day. They erupted into the house in a boisterous chaos of long legs and shouts and exclamations, followed by their father, Keidun Sulvenor, a thin, bitter-faced man. He frowned at Berrena as he passed her. Within a few minutes the two boys were in the kitchen and being fussed over by their aunt, while Laithan took Keidun round to the back to stable their horses. Berrena went into the front room and sat on the window seat. She knew that, although many of the townsfolk accepted her, others viewed her with resentment or dislike. But she sensed an even deeper hostility from Keidun. He hates all Hueds, she thought. His sons will be the same, I expect.

The door opened and one boy, the tallest and eldest, put his head through. He had a smudge of dirt on his cheek. When he saw her, he stuck his tongue out and rolled his eyes and then, as she stared at him, he pulled another face at her and left. A minute later the door opened again and both the boys came in. The youngest stepped forward.

"Greetings. I'm Jorvund. You must be Berrena. This is my stupid older brother, Felde," he said and gestured behind him to the taller boy who was pulling more faces at her.

Berrena stood up.

"Jorvund. Greetings. Felde? So you're the eldest?" she said, turning to the other.

He stopped his face-pulling, stepped back, and stood looking at her. He said nothing. Then he stuck his tongue out again.

Berrena laughed. "You shouldn't do that, your face might get stuck like it! Don't be such a silly baby. Just how old are you?"

"He's twelve. I'm ten," Jorvund said.

"Well, I'm only ten too, but I've better manners than you, Felde," she said. "Are you sure you're twelve? You're acting like a six-year old!"

Felde glared and stormed out. Jorvund followed him and Berrena could hear bangs and crashes and the sounds of argumentative fighting, then shouts as Keidun intervened.

For the rest of the day Felde ignored her. She didn't mind. She knew he was embarrassed. But Jorvund talked easily to her, asking her about going to school and her parents and Langron Manor and telling her about their home in Helsund.

"Come and see our horses," Jorvund said, next morning. "We've got five we're taking to sell. Father wants to sell them to Hueds for lots of money."

"To Hueds? But I thought they made everything they needed?"

"Aye – 'cept horses. Not even a Hued can make a live horse. And they know nought about training them. They buy them from us."

Felde was riding a dark brown horse around the field, alternatively cantering and trotting. When he saw them come up to the fence he spurred the horse to a gallop and raced round. Sprays of dirt flew up from its hooves.

"Ignore him. He's just showing off," Jorvund said.

"I know," Berrena replied. "I can see that. He's stupid!"

"Come here," Jorvund said and walked to the next field. "See the grey? Ain't he grand? He's the best horse ever."

He called to the horse and held out half a carrot.

"I begged it off Aunt Ingra," he said. "Do you want to feed him?"

Berrena shook her head and stepped back slightly.

"You ain't scared, are you?" he asked.

"Nay, of course not! And I can ride. I fell off once and twisted my wrist, but Daddy made me get back on. And I did. But I don't like them."

"Why not?"

"They're too big. And I can't tell if they're trustworthy."

Jorvund laughed. He held the carrot out on his open palm and the horse ate it while he stroked its neck and mane.

"Of course they're trustworthy! Tis a shame," he said. "They're beautiful animals. I'll miss this one when he's sold.

Let's get another carrot and I'll show you how to feed him."

As they went into the house, Berrena stopped and put her hand on Jorvund's arm. There were angry voices inside the kitchen.

"I don't care how kind you think Lord bloody Sapphireborne is! He's still one of those murdering Hued swine and so's she!" Keidun was shouting.

"Hush now, brother-in-law!" Ingra clucked. "Don't say such things! She can't help her parents and she's a good-natured, sweet girl. She ain't a Hued."

"She is! You should never have taken her in. Those filthy, blood-sucking scum don't need our help. Cursed swine, all of them! Send her back to them, to that bloody great city of theirn. Let them feed her."

"That's enough, Keidun," said Laithan. "That's quite enough! Don't talk of my daughter like that. You'd better leave. I don't mind seeing the boys here, if they can be civil to her, but you ain't welcome. Not til you change your tone."

Berrena could not bear to hear any more. She looked at Jorvund, shook her head, and ran upstairs, leaving him staring after her. He started to follow her, but she turned around and hissed, "Go away! Leave me alone!"

She ran into her room and curled up on her bed, listening to the arguing voices in the kitchen. Eventually they stopped and for a while there was silence, then the sounds of horses being saddled and people riding away. Presently Ingra came up and sat with her, putting her arms around her.

"Lass, I'm so sorry. They're gone and Keidun wouldn't let the boys say goodbye to you."

"What? That's horrible! It's not my fault!" Berrena said. "I can't help it!"

"Of course it ain't your fault, precious, tis him who's wrong. Never thought my own brother-in-law would be so cruel!"

"Why does he hate me?"

"He don't hate you particularly. He just hates all Hued."

"But I'm not Hued. I'm Talthen, ain't I? Ain't I?"

"He don't see it like that, honey. Oh, sweetheart, don't cry. He's wrong. So wrong! My own brother-in-law!" and she started crying too, holding Berrena against her. Berrena sobbed briefly, but felt comforted by the motherly arms around her.

Laithan came in.

"They're gone," he said. "Ingra, love, Keidun shouldn't have said what he said. Tis best that he doesn't come here again. Berrena, I'm sorry if you heard that. Try to forget it. When the lads are grown, they can come to visit. But I don't think Keidun will want to come here, anyhap."

Ingra released Berrena, sat up and mopped her tears.

"Dad, why does Keidun hate the Hued so much?" Berrena asked.

"Tis what happened in Helsund," he replied, his face weary and strained. "Twas terrible and cruel, though it was a long time ago, mind, thirty years. Some of the villagers in Helsund, they were desperate for food and money and it drove them to rob Hueds. A dozen of them set on a group of Hued travellers. They killed two Hueds. But there were three City Guards with the travellers, gifted fighters, and all twelve of the Helsund folk were killed. When the City Council heard about the murders they doubled the taxes and sent more guards. They decimated the village. They killed fifty-three, including young boys and girls barely eighteen. Keidun was only a lad but he saw his father being executed, even though he had nought to do with it."

"That's terrible," whispered Berrena.

"Aye. All them villagers hate Hueds now. Almost the only thing the Helsund folk think about is how to war against Hueds. But they're fools. Only a fool would fight the Hued City Guard and their gifts. Hueron - tis too strong, too powerful for us."

CHAPTER 4
HUERON AND LANGRON

Urns overflowing with blowsy roses, purple-bloomed lavender and tumbling geraniums lined the flagged terrace overlooking the lawns and grounds of Langron Manor. Humming bees and striped hoverflies zigzagged from flower to flower. Sarielle plucked a lavender head and smelt it as she and Dernham paced the terrace in the warm sunlight, looking out at the dark green oaks and cedars arranged on the southern park. On the lawns, Vallan scampered round, slashing and thrusting at the air with a sword; swerving, leaping and dodging to foil imaginary enemies. Around him, darting to and fro like a vicious cobalt-blue wasp, was his symbol, a sharp-pointed arrowhead. Berrena stood on the lawn nearby. Occasionally she clapped or said some admiring word of encouragement and he stopped, bowed and grinned. His skin and eyes and hair were blue; not the deep indigo of his father, but a clear royal blue. His face shone with excitement and pride.

Sarielle and Dernham watched for a while, then walked along the path towards the wisteria arches that framed the benches on the west side of the terrace.

"He is showing-off rather excessively, isn't he?" Sarielle said. "I hope Berrena won't mind him being so ... arrogant? Tactless? Well, you know what I mean."

"Thirteen is a little young to have developed any tact," Dernham said. "However, it is obvious that he needs more scope for his abilities. We should consider placing him in the City Guard for training, when he is a little older."

"Yes, well, time enough to discuss that later. We were

talking about Berrena. She is nearly adult. She's sensible. Visiting the city will not unsettle her. And she has relatives there: aunts, cousins, uncles, my mother, your mother. She should meet them, you know that, Dernham."

"I'm sure some of your cousins would be delighted to make the acquaintance of an exiled dullard."

"Hmm... Well, maybe not all my family. But some! And I was thinking..."

"There's more?"

"Isn't there always?" Sarielle said, giving Dernham's arm a squeeze as they sat down on a bench in the shadow of the yew hedges. "I thought that she could meet Thera too. We could go to a council meeting and cheer her when she speaks."

"Take Berrena to a council meeting?"

"Yes! And, also, did you know that Cairson is witnessing the marking of his youngest niece, next month? Let's go to that. Berrena said she would like to see a marking ceremony."

"But the practicalities, my dear! She will not be allowed to remain overnight."

"I've thought of that. This time of year the gates are open a full fourteen hours. We can stay in the Rising Sun Inn. It's only a mile from the north-east gate and we can ride over in the morning and back in the evening. We'll stay three nights in the inn and have two days – plenty of time for brief visits to everyone."

Dernham raised his eyebrows. "I can see you've planned it all out."

"Yes. It's important! She should see the city. She should know her family, and where she comes from."

Berrena and her parents pulled up their horses at a point where the road curved round the side of a hill and overlooked a wide green plain, dotted with small woods and crossed with the poplar-lined avenues that led to the high walls of Hueron. There were glimpses of bright colour from the flags on the walls, billowing and sinking in the intermittent breeze. Dark green trees speckled the white cityscape of roofs and towers.

"I thought it would be coloured," Berrena said. "Not white. Why is it called the Coloured City?"

"Oh, I'm so used to it having white and grey walls that I never thought about its name before. I suppose it is because of us – the Hued," Sarielle replied. "We are coloured, not the city. Isn't that strange!"

"And it's so big!" Berrena said, looking at the pinnacles, turrets, domes and lofty towers, their gold spires shining against the blue and scattered clouds of the sky.

"Yes," Dernham said. "The city is over four miles across at its widest point and the walls are fifteen miles in circumference. That was one of our greatest accomplishments: using the Hued gifts to rebuild and extend the walls."

"How? How was that possible?"

"The stone makers, that is, the Hueds with that gift, created the blocks in marble and granite and white stone, and we used dullards to build the walls. We can create, but unfortunately, brute force is still required for some things."

"Dullards – I mean, Talthen? Why not Hueds?"

"Yes, dullards. We Hueds, we are not common labourers. For manual labour, we have to use dullards. Berrena, you should know that it would have been slave labour – forced labour."

"Slave labour! Father, that is so wrong!"

"Yes. But it was two hundred years ago. I would hope that now the City Council would pay fair rates for dullard labour, should we need to extend the walls."

Along the road that crossed the plain they could see wagons and carts coming in and out of the city, and white-sailed boats and broad barges floating on the Saroche River as it curved round to the south-western docks.

"Do you see that traffic?" Dernham asked. "The wagons going into the city are empty."

"Really? Why?"

"Because we need nothing from outside the city. There is practically no trade with the dullards. We sell our surplus goods to them, and occasionally buy horses back, but that is all."

"Dernham!" exclaimed Sarielle. "You sound like a teacher. Don't lecture the poor girl so!"

"Nay, tis fine, mother. I want to know," Berrena said. "So the wagons and barges leaving the city are full."

"Of course. We export much of what we create to the dullards, as well as that which goes to the outlying estates and towns. Not as much as we used to, however. That wagon there, the one with the City Guards riding next to it, it is probably going to the garrison town on the eastern border. Carrying cloth and wool, by the look of it. It may even be crossing the mountains to Gathen."

At the gate the next morning, the black-uniformed guards looked with cold curiosity at Berrena as she gazed upwards at the towering walls, turrets and overhanging battlements. Then the morning bell rang and they heard the grinding clatter of the bolts and bars being drawn back. The gates swung outward to show a wide paved street, lined with the grey and white stone houses of the Hued. She looked at the smooth slate roofs, and the gable-ends marked with finials of brass or copper glinting in the sun. The houses were tall, with long windows set in carved embrasures, and intricately wrought iron balconies. The doors were panelled oak or mahogany or pale ash wood, with gold and silver handles and fittings, and with marble steps leading up to them.

As they continued up the street, Dernham and Sarielle nodded greetings to the Hueds that they passed. Many wore silk coats or linen jackets or velvet robes in bright colours that contrasted with their hair and eyes. Others had ornate necklaces and brooches of gold and silver and copper set with glittering jewels. They displayed their symbols at their throats, on the front of their clothes or in their hair: intricate emblems, complex swirls, leaves, spirals, flowers, sunbursts. Some stared with surprise or antagonism at Berrena, others muttered behind their hands to each other as she passed.

At the top of the street, in a wide square, a tall fountain sprayed water high into the sunshine. Stone benches inset with red, blue and orange tiles lined the square, and white marble statues stood at the ends of the benches. Bay trees, magnolias and roses grew in brightly-coloured glazed pots by the fountain, and in front of the houses lining the square. It wasn't anything like Langron. Berrena gazed around and thought how vast was the gulf between the two places.

As Cairson thumped the table, Berrena bit her lip and turned away from the argument.

"It is legal!" he said.

"But she's a dullard," the other councillor said, "She cannot be allowed to watch the marking ceremony!"

Sarielle squeezed Berrena's hand, and Thera gave her a tiny encouraging smile and whispered, "We want you here. Ignore those idiots."

"There is no law against it," said Dernham. "You have no authority to prevent her being here at Cairson's invitation."

"I suppose we don't. But this is going a bit too far, Lord Sapphireborne! Dullards at a marking? Whatever next? Peasants in the council?"

"No more discussion or arguments! She is allowed to witness this," said Cairson. "Now, can we commence, please?"

The child's mother placed the child, a tiny brown-skinned girl called Ezera, on the cloth-covered table.

"Powers above and Virtues around us, by the blood and the life, gift this child," her father said, and the others replied, "Gift this child."

The parents, holding hands, watched intently as Thera cut their daughter's palm. After a moment of hesitation the trembling blood congealed into a solid shape, like a lightning bolt, resting on the child's hand. Thera picked up the symbol to show the mark underneath, a similarly-shaped patch of lighter brown on the child's skin.

"Good," said the councillor. "I will record the ceremony and the symbol. And congratulations. A true Hued," he added, with a glare at Dernham.

Later, as they left, Berrena turned to her father and mother.

"What does the symbol mean? What will her gift be?"

"I cannot say for certain," Dernham said. "The shape of the symbol is not always an indication. Some are abstract; triangles, spirals, squares and so on; and then it is hard to predict the nature of the gift. Oval symbols are usually healers, but others are inconsistent."

"And Ezera's?"

"A lightning bolt like hers can indicate strength, speed and rapid reflexes. She will probably be a gifted swords-woman. As she grows, she will grow in awareness of what her gift is."

"What happened when I was marked? Something must have happened. You both know that I cannot be cut nor bruised. Ain't that a gift?"

"Don't say ain't," Sarielle said. "Please try to speak properly. I hate having to keep reminding you!"

"Isn't that a gift?" Berrena said, suppressing an urge to speak in an even broader Talthen accent.

"We do not know," Dernham said. "The blood sank back into you and left nothing."

"Dernham!" exclaimed Sarielle, turning to face him with an exasperated look on her face. "Berrena should know what happened, and if you won't tell her, I will!"

Dernham looked startled, glanced at Berrena then nodded. "Very well."

Sarielle took her daughter's hand and related how a fine mesh of blood had spread over her then vanished. "So you see, something did happen! Something really strange! Maybe it is some sort of gift – a gift of protection. But now - now that you have grown up and we think about it, it is astounding. And confusing."

"I think I should warn you, Berrena, that this strange protection on you is completely new to the Hued," Dernham said. "And you have no symbol and no mark. It is better for you to accept that you are, as far as the law is concerned, not gifted and not Hued, rather than us hankering after some unreachable goal."

Berrena looked at him and shook her head. "No. That's wrong. I am Hued and you know it, even if the city laws don't recognise me. Hued and Talthen both."

Late the next afternoon, after brief visits to introduce Berrena to several relatives – some neutral, some dubious, some welcoming - they walked down a narrow street towards the north of the city. "We will take a short-cut," Dernham had said.

In this part of the city, the houses were smaller but still newer and smarter than any in Langron. But there was an odd, unpleasant smell. As they turned a corner the smell grew.

"Ugh! What is it? It stinks," exclaimed Sarielle. "It smells like stables or, no, more like drains! It's disgusting!"

At the bottom of the street a group of people with spades and shovels were digging trenches, and emptying buckets into carts. Several City Guards watched them. As they drew closer, Berrena saw that the guards held whips, and that the diggers wore drab grey clothes, with manacles on their wrists and ankles. They were not Coloured, but Talthen. As she stared, a City Guard turned, raised his hand and came up to them.

"You are best not to go this way, sir," he said. "The drains are blocked. We are clearing the blockage, but there is sewage and foul water about. I suggest you go left, there, then take the next right."

Dernham and Sarielle thanked him and turned away. Berrena followed, but not before one of the shovel-carrying men looked up. Their eyes met for an instant. Berrena shuddered. Such weariness, grief, and agony of aching muscles, untreated sores and wounds! One of the guards lifted his whip and brought it down on the back of another of the grey-clad men. Berrena felt him wince with pain. There was no reason or excuse given; the guard whipped the man as casually as one might flick the top off a nettle.

She ran after Dernham.

"Father, what was that? Who were those men? It was awful, awful!"

Dernham looked furious and Sarielle full of pity.

"Dullard prisoners and tax-defaulters, made to work in the city. I have tried to stop this iniquitous forced labour, but the council refuses. It is barbaric!"

"Forced labour? You mean the Hued still use slaves? You said they didn't!"

"They are not slaves, but convicts. Some will be petty thieves, property-wreckers, rebels. But most are there because they cannot pay their taxes. Unfortunate wretches!"

Berrena stared at him. "Unfortunate?" she exclaimed. Did he not recognise the misery, despair and pain that filled those prisoners?

"Berrena, I would have tried to avoid you seeing this, but perhaps it is right that you did," Dernham said. "This is the worst of our city. If a dullard cannot pay their taxes he or she is sentenced to a year's forced labour. Of course, when released he cannot pay next year's tax either. And so he is imprisoned again, in a vicious, pointless cycle."

"Why don't you do something about it?"

"I have! You do not know how long, how strenuously I have tried to end this cruel, futile persecution. It is not even as if the city needs the taxes from the dullards."

"Doesn't it? Why tax them, then?"

"If the taxes were not paid, it would make barely any difference to the prosperity of the city," Dernham shrugged.

"I have argued repeatedly that it is pointless and unfair. The council maintains the tax solely to dominate the dullards and keep them in poverty. Berrena, the injustice and folly infuriates me. But I can do nothing about it!"

Laithan walked to the town square, lifting his head to breathe in the cool morning air. He had a taste of contentment, at last, after a succession of failed harvests, blights, droughts and frosts that had emptied farmhouses, given orchards and fields back to weeds and sparse grass, turned herds of fat sheep into huddles of scrawny ewes. But at least Langron had survived. The folk might be thin, but they weren't starving. Their children might be barefoot, but they weren't in rags. There might be grass and even a small bush growing in the thatch of one of the cottages, but at least it had a roof. He had had to beg help from Lord Sapphireborne, but only once, at least.

They were fortunate that Sapphireborne was well-disposed to them. Other Hued Lords and Ladies would take the skin off a dullard's back for rent as soon as look at him, let alone help. Many towns had been left empty and desolate by death, sickness or because their destitute residents had been carted away to the city prisons. At least Langron was not desolate too. The tiny hope that had grown with each mild winter day, each spring rainfall, each blue summer sky, that had refused to die, had ripened into an unexpectedly good harvest. Nowhere near as good as the harvests of his childhood, and probably next year would be another disaster, but still the best he had seen in his twenty years as town chief, and the first one for years that had sufficed for an autumn feast. A scanty feast, four roasted pigs between a thousand mouths, but still a feast.

He walked into the square where townsfolk were moving the market stalls and awnings to one side and others were building a bonfire in the centre. In a nearby field, people drove poles into the ground then tied ropes to them to create the lists for the fighting contests. Six archery butts had already been arranged on the far side of the field. Laithan crossed the square, weaving around a fletcher with another butt on his back, and then slipped between people who scurried past laden with bunches of arrows and bows, piles of plates, and stacks of linen.

In a corner of the square a stage had been built and upon it a lone musician played 'The Swan Pavanne' with great care and a few wrong notes. In front of him Laithan saw his daughter. Her friend Kianne Deorthsen was teaching her the steps of the dance. Laithan sat on a bench and watched his daughter's grace, as they turned, crossed hands, swivelled, stepped back, rose on tiptoe, circled each other; concentrating on the complex figures of the Pavanne. Then Berrena turned the wrong way and Kianne laughed.

"Nay, you silly! Turn right, not left, then we cross hands again! What'll you do if one of those handsome men asks you to dance? You'll end up treading on his toes! Come on, I'll show you again."

Several people were adding more wood into the fire-pits on the side of the field. A savoury aroma drifted from the roasting pigs as they turned above the flickering red-tongued flames. Besides the pits stood the butcher, in a bloodstained apron, plucking and preparing a few chickens, while other's were chopping apples and peeling potatoes. One of them, sweat dripping down his face, ran over to Laithan.

"Beg pardon, chief, but the pits be running out of wood. Where does we get the firewood? From the bonfire?"

"More firewood? Two of you go to my house. You can use some of the wood stacked round the back. Tell Ingra I sent you."

As he answered, another red-faced man paused from rolling a barrel across the square and shouted across, "Er - chief? Where does you want the beer?"

Laithan stood up wearily. Back to work, he thought.

By noon the square was ready, filled with benches and

trestle tables covered with brightly-coloured tablecloths. Berrena and Kianne crossed the square, each carrying a tray of pasties, followed by the bustling figure of Laithan's wife, red-faced and with flour marks on her cheeks. She was bearing an even-larger tray of cakes and tarts.

Laithan surveyed his realm in satisfaction. There would be food and drink to go around, even if there was only enough for a plateful each, and the warm sun was shining and fulfilling the promise of the early morning.

Someone shouted. Laithan heard the strident voice raised in anger and breaking into the bustling cheerfulness. He glanced towards the corner of the square. A cart was coming up the road from Langron Manor, with two Hued City Guards in black uniforms riding alongside it. The tallest, a coarse-faced man with a deep green arrowhead on his jacket, was yelling at people, "Laithan Veorne! We're looking for Laithan Veorne! The town chief! Any of you ignorant dullard pigs know where he is?"

Laithan stiffened. The City Guard meant trouble. Tax collections or worse. Not today, please not today, no arrests or beatings, please, he thought. He stepped forward.

"Sir, I'm Veorne, the town chief. What can I do for you?"

"About time too. Message for you, from Lord Sapphireborne, and a delivery," the guard snapped back. Behind him, the cart driver, clambered down. Laithan recognised Albis Karne, the estate manager for Langron Manor, a short, scrawny Hued with a doleful face that belied his cheerful barley-yellow colouring.

"Laithan," he said. "Greetings from Lord Sapphireborne."

The two guards dismounted and stood by the cart with their hands pointedly on their sword hilts as if they expected the townsfolk to pillage it.

"You are busy, I see," Albis said. "Preparing for your harvest feast?"

"Aye, sir. What's this about?"

"Letter for you from Dernham." Albis handed him a

sealed envelope. "And the cart. Full of wine, cheese, ale, dried fruit – gifts from him to the town. For the feast. Is Berrena around?"

She crossed the square to him and his lugubrious face brightened as she kissed him.

"Albis! Are you here to join the feast?" Berrena asked. "And where are Mother and Father?"

"Feast? No – not for me. Too busy back at the estate. Trying to get those lazy housemaids to clean the silver properly."

"Oh, Albis. Cleaning candlesticks rather than dancing til midnight?"

"Albis, give Lord Sapphireborne our thanks," Laithan said. "I'll get some people to unload the cart."

He read the letter, nodded, then gave it to Berrena.

My dear Laithan,

I give our apologies, but Lady Rochale and I will not be joining you this evening. We have had word that our son Vallan has been accepted into the City Guard Training School - a year early, on account of his extraordinary prowess. So we are returning to Hueron. I send you a gift of wine and food for the feast, in charge of my manager Albis Karne. I hope it will prove welcome.

My wife is disappointed not to be joining in with your celebrations. For myself, however, I am conscious that, as a Hued Lord and as owner of Langron Manor, my presence would be a constraint upon the townsfolk. I am aware of the resentment many Talthen have against the Gifted People, so I consider that it is best for us not to be present.

My best regards to you, your wife Ingra and my beloved daughter Berrena,

Lord Dernham Sapphireborne of Langron

"Oh," said Berrena, folding it up. "Even so, they should have come. And Vallan too. He'd have loved it."

"'Tis as well Vallan ain't here," Laithan said. "He would have wanted to take part in the competitions. Even our best people wouldn't stand a chance against him, young as he is, let alone with that unpredictable blue arrowhead of his flying around! Nay, tis best he's not here, especially if he's joining the City Guard."

"Mayhap," said Berrena. "You know I dislike the fighting. Tis wrong to train for war. We shouldn't be training to fight Hueds."

"We ain't! But we have to guard ourselves against robbers and suchlike when travelling. And some of the towns further away from Hueron have been known to go raiding or to be attacked by some of the northern tribes. So we've got to be able to defend ourselves. We've got to train to fight."

CHAPTER 5
APPREHENSION

Dernham worked at his desk in his study. Beside him his blue quill danced over a sheet of paper, leaving a trail of black-inked words behind it on the white surface. A slice of sunshine shone through the mullioned window, illuminating the edge of the mantelpiece and casting a bar of light on the figured carpet.

Someone knocked on the door. Dernham looked up from his letters as Albis Karne came in. As he entered, Albis's eyes flicked to the quill as it darted to an open inkwell, like a vivid kingfisher flying across a lake, and dipped its point in the ink before darting back to continue writing. Dernham held out his hand to his quill, which rose and settled in his palm. He laid it on the desk, leaned back and examined Albis's apprehensive expression. He was used to his manager's habitual pessimism, but he had never seen him look so disturbed.

"Greetings, Albis," he said. "Back from Langron? I assume you delivered my letter."

"Yes, sir."

"Thank you. I thought you intended to watch the bouts and join in the feast afterwards?"

Albis hesitated, then said, "I had intended to. Changed my mind. Too much work to do here. And I have something to tell you before you leave. Something that I have been putting off for months."

Dernham waited, turning a ring on his finger, but Albis only stood and gloomily fidgeted with a paperweight from the desk.

49

"What is it, Albis?" he asked. "You had better sit down."

Albis sat and stared out of the window at the sunlight on the lawns and fountains for a few moments. He cleared his throat and spoke.

"Ought to have told you months ago, but I was frightened. But you need to know."

He took his symbol from his pocket and laid it on the desk. It was a perfectly-moulded ear of ripe corn, the same golden-yellow as Albis's hair and eyes. He prodded the symbol with a despondent finger.

"You'd find out sooner or later anyway. And I'd rather tell you myself. You're a fair, just man. And it's not my fault."

"Find out what?" Dernham asked.

"I've lost my gift. My symbol – it does nothing."

"By the Virtues, Albis! What do you mean? Is it dead?"

"No. I still feel it. It's still part of me. But there's no power there."

He prodded the symbol again. It quivered at his touch, moved slightly, and then sank back like an exhausted leaf dropped by the wind.

"It stopped working four, five years ago. I've never had a great gift. Most I could make was a few sacks of grain an hour. Then less and less. And now nothing. Not even a cupful. Not even a grain of wheat. Nothing!"

He laid his head in his hands. Dernham watched him with astonishment. He picked up the symbol and examined it. But there was nothing he could see to explain it. The ear of corn was still pristine.

"How can this happen?" he said. "You say it faded, then ceased altogether?"

"Yes. Over years, gradually. Hardly noticed at first. Sir, have you noticed any lessening of your gifts? Or Lady Rochale's?"

"No. Well, that is not strictly correct. But I put it down to age. After all, I am over fifty. Sarielle has never mentioned any problems using her gift for her jewellery business."

He looked at Albis's lifeless symbol and shook his head in bewilderment.

"I know," said Albis. "Worrying, isn't it?"

"How can gifts fade? They have been part of us for hundreds of years. Albis, you know as well as I do that it is not possible to destroy a gift, or break or interfere with the connection between a Hued and his symbol. This is not possible!" Dernham exclaimed, stood up and went over to the window to stare blankly outside, as if he could see an answer in the green lawns and bright sun.

"Sir," said Albis, after a long pause. "What should I do? Where do you think I should go?"

"Go? Albis, why should you go anywhere?" Dernham asked.

"Sir, you of all people know the laws. Ungifted Hueds have to leave. Suppose I'll have to find a friendly dullard town, if there is one. Do you think Laithan Veorne will help?"

"You are mistaken," Dernham said, as he sat back at his desk. "The law states that a Hued is one who has both a symbol and a shaped scar from the marking ceremony. It says nothing about the power or use of their gift. You still have both your qualifications."

Albis turned his left hand over and looked at the pale-yellow scar on his palm.

"Suppose so," he said. "But I was told losing it meant leaving, meant exile. Are you sure? Is that what the law really is?"

"Yes. Albis, I don't know who told you that, but I have scoured the laws searching for a loophole, any leeway, anything that would have let Berrena stay in Hueron. I know the law," Dernham said curtly.

In the silence that followed, Albis picked up the ear of corn and stared at it gloomily.

"You can stay here. Capable estate managers like you are not easy to come by. You do not need your symbol's power to run Langron Manor as well as you do."

Albis looked up.

"Sir! Thank you!" he said, returning his symbol to his pocket. He stood up to leave but then hesitated, his hand on the doorknob.

"There is something more you ought to know. But can I have your word of honour not to tell the council about the people involved?"

"More? Well, Albis, you should know that I do not gossip or betray confidences. There is no need to ask for it, but you have my word."

"I'm not the only one," Albis blurted out. "There are lots of us. Hueds whose gifts have faded to almost nothing or failed altogether. Many meet secretly in Hueron, to share anything they might find out to help regain their gifts."

"What?" said Dernham. "Are you serious? How many?"

"I know of eight-score, definitely, and I think the numbers are growing. Don't need to tell you what the implications of this are."

"Great Powers and Virtues!" Dernham exclaimed.

An hour later Albis left with a distinct lessening of his apprehensive look. He had convinced Dernham. He had told him how the 'Giftless Ones', as they called themselves, found others in the same straits, and had shown him one of the discrete cards pinned on advertising boards or put in the corners of shop windows around the city, offering to extend and strengthen a Hued's powers.

"Some are charlatans, of course," he'd said. "And one or two go in for blackmail. But we watch them and the people who use them. It's easy to find out if their customers are giftless. They work as cleaners, teachers, grooms, skivvies, waiters — any job that doesn't need a gift."

Dernham had always assumed that such people had chosen their work voluntarily. Now he faced the possibility that many, perhaps the majority, of them had lost their powers. What was happening to them? He turned his quill over and over in his hand with a frown on his face.

He pulled out one of the dozens of bundles of manuscripts that filled the shelves lining one wall, and spread the papers on his desk. It showed a steady rise in prices and a reduction in the quantity of exports from Hueron over the past twenty years. It had always puzzled him. Suddenly he realised that failing gifts might be the explanation.

He thought of the city and sighed. His beloved Hueron - walls and buildings in white and grey, but filled with the rainbow shades of the Hued. The artists, the sculptors, the musicians, the architects and masons, jewellers and artisans, craftsmen and traders. How could Hueron live without the gifts?

Dernham scribbled numbers on a piece of paper. On top of the forty thousand in Hueron, there might be another sixty to seventy thousand Hueds in country estates, like his, with managers and servants living with them. And possibly a further hundred thousand in the remaining Hued domain, from the western seaboard to the eastern mountains, from far southern farms to the remote cold hills of the north, from the Coloured City to the garrison towns on the borders. Two hundred thousand Hued, that was all. And how many dullards? Many more. And how many of them were like those in Helsund?

Dernham had only visited Helsund once. The village huddled at the mouth of a rocky valley between bleak hills ten miles north of Langron. It had been forced into destitution by the doubled taxes inflicted on it. Dernham had heard from Laithan of Helsund's resentment of the Hued and of the villagers' determined training in sword and arrow. What if the Hued lost the ability to defend themselves? He put his head in his hands, a roiling darkness of fear in his mind. If that fear was justified, how could the Hued be safe? Who would help them?

Felde and Jorvund Sulvenor rode along the road from Helsund to Langron. The early mist had cleared from the fields and the hills behind them. The day promised to be warm. Already sunlight tinted the trees with autumn gold and the grass by the road was viridescent in its light.

"You're very quiet," said Jorvund.

"Hmm? Oh, I was thinking about the Langron competitions. Whether we'd win anything. I don't know if I'll do well in the archery, but I'd like to win the singlestick. Anyhap, you're just as quiet as me. What are you thinking?" asked Felde.

"Me? I'm looking forward to the feast afterwards. Good food, ale, music, and mayhap there'll be pretty girls to dance with."

Felde nodded agreement. There were few enough girls in Helsund, and none of them pretty.

They rode on in silence for a while until Felde said, "I didn't think Father would let us go. He wasn't pleased that Uncle asked for us."

"Aye. It doesn't seem right that we should go without him. But he can't stop us. You heard what he said. We're old enough to be our own masters. Well, he thinks you are, though I don't know why. You're only twenty-one, a mere youngster. Course, I'm easily old enough at nineteen to be my own master and I'm catching you up every day," replied Jorvund.

"You think you're old enough? Try to catch me up now!" retorted Felde, putting his spurs to his horse and galloping away down the road. Jorvund grinned and rode after him.

After stabling their horses at Laithan's farm, the brothers walked to Langron square and looked round at the bonfire ready to be lit, the stalls laden with food, the jostling townsfolk, the roasting pigs, the beer and cider arrayed on tables. Felde was the first to see Laithan, at the side of the square, talking to a girl with her back to them. She wore a green dress, belted round a slender waist, with sable hair falling in glossy ripples over her shoulders. Felde thought she seemed to be wearing long dark gloves on her arms. Laithan saw the brothers, and nodded a greeting, lifting his hand to welcome them. Then the girl turned. The sun behind her radiated mahogany and purple through the coronal of her hair. But her face was a dark mask, a blankness, only the white triangles of her eyes visible. Felde shivered. He could not make out any features or expression. Then he remembered – the exiled Hued girl that Laithan had adopted.

But she smiled and the blank mask resolved into a living face, and as she turned back to Laithan the sunlight transformed the eldritch colour of her skin into shades of warm chestnut and deep brown.

"Greetings, nephew," Laithan said, coming forward and clapping them both on the shoulders. "You've grown since last I saw you. I'm very glad that Keidun let you come. Berrena, you remember Felde and Jorvund Sulvenor?"

"I remember Jorvund well," Berrena said, shaking his hand and smiling at him. "I'm pleased to see you again. But I wouldn't have known you, Felde. When we last met, you looked very different. You were sticking your tongue out at me and rolling your eyes."

Felde started to mutter something about it being a long time ago and having been very young. But Berrena forestalled him.

"Aye, I know, you were nought but a silly boy! I'm sure you've learnt better manners since then."

Jorvund laughed. Berrena looked at Felde with a teasing smile on her face, and he dropped his eyes and stared down at his feet.

Laithan looked up at the sun.

"'Tis time to start," he said. "Archery first."

Felde looked around at the scores of people pressed against the ropes. He was relieved not to see Berrena. He could rarely beat Jorvund and he did not want the humiliation of losing to his younger brother in front of her, despite the prizes he'd won in the archery and his victories in the earlier matches. In Helsund men trained with the sullen ferocity of people intent on revenge, and to the brothers the Langron men presented little in the way of challenges. Both he and Jorvund were undefeated. Now it was the last duel of the afternoon. Singlestick, rather than blunted swords – Laithan had said he wasn't prepared to risk serious injuries on a feast day like today.

Felde passed his jacket to one of the audience to hold and rolled up his sleeves. Across the list Jorvund shifted his stick from hand to hand, and stood waiting with his eyes on his brother. Nervous energy coursed through Felde. He gripped his stick, and he took a deep breath. He was ready.

The watchers round the brothers started shouting louder and louder, cheering the closeness and speed of the fight. It had lasted far longer than any other bout: a tense rhythm of attack, block, attack, parry, dodge, block, attack again. One moment Felde was gaining, pushing Jorvund back towards the ropes with fast, successive blows, then Jorvund had seen an advantage, ducked under Felde's stick, stepped sideways and dealt a crashing swipe on his unguarded side. Now they circled each other again, watching for a momentary drop in each other's wariness. Felde breathed hard. Sweat ran down his face and chest, but he barely noticed the bruises and cuts he had received. He had faster reflexes and a few inches height advantage, although Jorvund was stronger, and could usually stop his attacks. He hoped that sooner or later his brother would make a mistake. But Jorvund frustrated him with his careful defence. He left no opportunities and took full advantage of Felde's every rash move. He used his greater strength, now, slamming his stick down hard so that Felde's hands stung as they absorbed the impact, then hitting sideways with all his power and nearly felling his brother.

A slight lull in the voice of the crowd and a movement in the corner of his eye pulled at Felde's attention. He thought he could see a black-haired girl moving through the watchers. The flick of his eye sideways was enough of a lapse for his brother. A hammer blow pounded into Felde's arm. He fell, rolled aside and received another painful thud on his shoulders as he leapt to his feet. Wincing, he stifled a cry, and moved back to regain time and balance.

Words from his father hung in his thoughts: watch your opponent's eyes, not his hands, watch his eyes. The cries of the crowd became muffled as he concentrated on the premonitions of movement in those confident eyes. Jorvund shifted his grip and at that moment Felde knew what his brother would do. That this was the giant's blow, all Jorvund's strength in it, the one that would crush him. Instinct drove Felde, as Jorvund raised his stick over his head ready to power it downwards. He moved forward instead of back and smashed his stick sideways into Jorvund's hands, then followed it with a fast left-handed swipe.

Jorvund clutched his arm in pain and dropped his stick. It lay, a blonde line on the trodden turf, as he staggered back, his face astonished and his hand raised in surrender. The crowd gasped and cheered. Felde held his stick up high, turned round and bowed.

"Impressive," said Jorvund. "As fast as City Guards. Well done, brother."

"Well done yourself, little brother," Felde replied, but Jorvund only laughed.

"Good," said Laithan, ducking under the ropes and shaking their hands. "Keidun will be proud of you."

The watchers dispersed. Some lingered to thump the brothers on the back in congratulations. Felde looked through the scattering people to see if Berrena was there. But she was not. She had not been watching after all.

The feast over and the bonfire lit, the brothers sat with the other young men by the side of the square; discussing the competition, comparing swords and scars, and drinking the excellent Langron ale. Felde was revelling in the attention and boasting of his victory, always aware of the admiring glances from the Langron girls.

Berrena moved among those clearing the tables. He saw her glance at him with amusement on her face as he joked and drank. With her was another girl, who watched him intensely. Suddenly the girl grabbed a glass, filled it with wine and drank it in one draught. Squaring her shoulders, she came over to Felde. The wine and heat from the fire turned her cheeks red as she smiled up at him.

"Will you dance with me, Felde?" she said.

He stared down at her in astonishment. She was a slightly-built, short girl, young in appearance, with a freckled, open face. She wasn't one of the prettiest girls in the town, he thought. Some of the other lads behind him sniggered. He hesitated. He didn't want the embarrassment of being claimed by some unattractive little girl, like a prize won at a fair. No, he'd pick for himself who he wanted to dance with.

"Don't be stupid," he said. "I ain't going to dance with just anybody. Go and find someone else."

There was an appreciative laugh from those watching. Blushing even more, she looked at his sneering face and at the others smirking at her, then turned and half-ran, half-stumbled across the square.

Jorvund frowned at Felde, who felt discomfited for a moment, then shrugged. Across the square he saw Berrena put down the pile of plates she was carrying, and straighten up to look at him with cool evaluation. Then she turned away and walked after the girl.

The fire burnt low and darkness fell, but the musicians still played on, jigs and polkas and old slow tunes. Most of the young men, including Jorvund, had found girls to dance with or to sit and kiss hidden in the shadows away from the firelight, but Felde stood by the fire and idly poked the embers. Laithan came up to him, carrying an empty crate.

"Felde, we're running low on cider. Can you go up to the house and get some from the cellar? Bring back a crateful. I want to give it to the musicians."

At Laithan's house, Felde was about to go along the passageway to the cellar, when he heard women's voices in the kitchen. He paused to listen.

"Good-looking, aye, but he knows it," one said.

"I know. That blonde hair, those shoulders! Powers above, I can't believe I was so stupid," another said. "But you're right. He probably was drunk."

"Drunk and, as I said, afraid of what the others would think. Try to forget it, Kianne."

"I don't think I can. The look on his face!"

"Aye, I saw him. Ever so rude, wasn't he? But did you notice that not one of the other girls dared go up to him, after seeing what he did to you?"

"Serves him right. Arrogant so-and-so. I think I'll ask his brother to dance instead. Anyhap, shall I help you tidy up?"

"Aye. Thanks. I need to get the fire built up. Can you put the dishes into the sink and rinse them?"

There was a clattering of plates and cutlery, and someone started to sing, with a soft cadence.

> *When spring was in the air,*
> *He saw that she was fair,*
> *He promised then and there,*
> *to be her hero.*

> *Oh, know your own true love, for wealth's a liar,*
> *Brave men be rare as gold, true hearts as sapphire.*

Felde recognised the tune. It was one his mother used to sing when he was a child. He had not heard it for years.

> *He thought her love was strong,*
> *But a rich man came along,*
> *And when summer was gone,*

she'd left her hero.

Compelled by the long-forgotten memory, Felde stepped to the door and saw Berrena. She was singing as she built up the fire and in its light her hair glimmered deepest auburn against the green dress. Her eyes opened with surprise as she looked up and saw him. Next to her clear whites her irises shone midnight black with flecks of gold reflected from the fire. Felde thought that he had never truly seen her before. That he saw for the first time her face, her curved lips of deep ebony, her long eyelashes, her sable cheeks. She gazed back at him with intense, wide eyes, the irises black circles against the whites. Her wavy hair hung loose over her shoulder, reflecting the firelight like silk. She was bewildering; her skin like rich velvet, her dark eyes enthralling, her mouth alluring. Felde's heart raced. He could not take his eyes off her and yet he could not bear to look any longer. He stammered, "Sorry... didn't mean to interrupt..." and stumbled out into the darkness.

CHAPTER 6
CONFLICT

When Felde and Jorvund walked into the house in Helsund, Keidun asked them, "Has Laithan still got that Hued freak he adopted?"

"Aye," Felde replied cautiously.

"Laithan's a fool and a traitor for helping those murdering swine," Keidun snarled. "He should be fighting against them, not feeding their cursed children. They as good as killed my wife, working and starving her to death, them and their taxes."

Despite his father's bitter rants, Felde made excuses to visit Langron: taking horses to be shod, going to the market to buy leather and bridles, hanging around his uncle's house. If he couldn't think of an excuse, he took horses out for exercise by riding the ten miles to the town, without feeling it necessary to explain to his father where he was going.

"If you're going to keep visiting us," said Laithan, "you may as well make yourself useful. Not that I ain't pleased to see you, Felde, you know that. But there's a tree blown down. We've got it cut and moved to the yard, but it needs sawing up and chopping for firewood. You can do that."

Felde sawed up branches until clouds of sawdust blew round him and his arms were weary. It was a relief to stand up, lift the axe, bring it down on a freshly-cut log and crack the wood into resin-scented pieces. He threw the pieces onto the woodpile and split more and more, until his hands were stained with sap and dirt. Aching and weary, he straightened up and stretched, then saw Berrena by the door. She had a shawl wrapped around her and the wind shook its fringe and her hair and the skirts of her dress.

"Felde!" she said. "I didn't know you were here."

"I've been here all morning," he replied. It sounded surly, even to himself. "Didn't Laithan tell you?"

"Nay. I came out to get some fresh air and to see what all the banging and crashing was."

"Laithan asked me to chop up the tree."

"What, all that?" she asked, looking at the pile of logs and branches. "You'll be here all day!"

"All day? Nay, I can get that done in a couple of hours," he replied, lifting the axe one-handed and swinging it carelessly. He realised then that sweat was dripping down his face, that he had sawdust stuck to his arms and legs and that he was filthy.

She smiled. By now he had learnt to read her expressions, despite the darkness of her face. To recognise the slight movement of her eyebrows, the tiny creases in her forehead when she frowned, the curve of her mouth shifting: all deeper ebony against her ebony skin. In the clear outdoor light the dark curves of her eyebrows lifted in a mocking, laughing glance.

"Two hours? Well, that would be impressive," she said, and turned to go back inside.

For the next few hours Felde worked until his body burned with tiredness and his hands were blistered from the saw and axe. But he did not let himself stop until the entire tree was sawn, chopped and stacked on the woodpile. Then he went into the kitchen, where Ingra was sewing.

"Dearie me, you look exhausted," she clucked. "Here, wipe yourself down, lad, you're covered in dust," and she fetched him a wet towel. As he cleaned off the sweat and grime she poured him a tankard of beer. He drank the refreshing coolness in one long draught, then asked, "Where's Berrena?"

"Oh, she's out this past hour or more. She's gone to the school to help out with the teaching." Ingra glanced at him. "I don't think she'll be back for a while. She said she wanted to spend the whole afternoon there."

Felde's shoulders slumped. "Did she? Oh. I might as well go home then."

As he saddled up he felt that he was wasting his time. Why should a woman like Berrena, with her Hued parentage, her clever discernment and subtle beauty, look at him? Or be impressed by chopping wood?

Berrena had to smile at Kianne's expert flirting as she swung her market basket under Jorvund's face, so that the scent of honey and caraway rose from the cakes.

"Buy some, then? You know you can't resist!" she said, laughing at him, her hand on her hip and her eyes sparkling. Jorvund grinned back, took a cake from her basket and handed her some coins.

"Thanks. I'm heartbroken, but the horses are shod and we'd better go," he said, glancing back to where Felde stood waiting. "Though it's a long way back without your smiles to warm me as I ride."

He and Felde mounted and rode out of the town square. Kianne hefted the half-empty basket onto her arm. Her eyes narrowed as she looked at Berrena, glanced towards the brothers, then she took her hand and dragged her to a bench.

"Powers above, Berrena! The truth now! I saw you ogling them," she said.

"Ogling them? I don't ogle anyone!"

"Come on. The truth. Which one were you watching?"

"I wasn't watching any of them."

"Oh yes, and I didn't sell him a cake and Felde didn't stand there glancing at you and you didn't try to pretend you didn't notice him. Come on, Berrena. I know you blush when he meets your eyes, though nobody can see it. You're lucky. Everyone can see if I blush!"

"All right. Aye! I do watch him. I can't help it, even though I know what he's like. He's arrogant, self-conscious, he resents the Hued, he's got no common sense, he acts before thinking, he gets bored with horse-breeding. I know he ain't perfect, but I can't help it."

She looked at the distant figures on the road to Helsund and thought, no one should be that handsome. She remembered the week before, when Laithan had asked Felde to stop for supper. As they ate, she had looked up and caught him looking at her, his eyes as brown as fallen leaves in clear water. She had felt the heat rising up into her face and she was the one who had had to drop her gaze.

"Anyhap, Kianne, you like him too," she said.

"Aye, I do. But his brother – he's much friendlier, even if he ain't as handsome. He's sort of calm and strong. I like Jorvund. I like the way he does things. He don't fuss over aught, he just gets on and does it. But I like Felde too. And have you seen the blacksmith's new lad?"

"Kianne! You're incorrigible. You can't have all three!"

"Oh, I don't know. One for morning, one for evening and Felde for bed. Unless you'd rather have Felde for bed yourself?"

"Don't tease me," Berrena exclaimed. "Tis bad enough as it is. I shouldn't think of him, I know. I tried to avoid him for weeks, but it didn't work. He kept coming to Langron and every time he came I could hardly stop looking at him and when he'd gone – it felt empty. He spent hours chopping wood just to impress me, you know."

"He did? And were you impressed? Oh, you should've been. Such devotion, such muscles, Berrena, think of that!"

"Well, I didn't stay to watch him. I never said aught to him. Ain't that terrible?"

"Powers above, Berrena, you don't deserve a man like him!" Kianne exclaimed, rolling her eyes. "Why'd you do that?"

"I don't know! Well, I do. Tis common sense. It says he's only a horse-breeder, he's not well educated or Hued or intelligent. My birth parents ain't going to be pleased with him."

She stood up, and wrapped her cloak around herself. A

sprinkling of faint stars were starting to gleam in a clear evening sky.

"We should get back. But, Kianne, what am I going to do? They aren't going to like it if I encourage him."

"You don't know what they'll think. They might not mind. Laithan and Ingra will be happy, anyhap."

"At least there's that," Berrena said, thinking, it might be all right. I know he's faulty, but he means well. He'd be loyal and kind, I know. But it means being a Talthen wife and schoolmistress, not a Hued. And I'm not sure what I want to be.

"Tell you what, you have Felde, and I'll decide between Jorvund and the blacksmith's lad," Kianne said. "He smiled at me yesterday. I'm going to ask him his name. And you should do something about Felde."

"Aye. You're right. I think I'm going to have to take pity on myself and on him. I want to look at him, smile at him." And forget common-sense and have him kiss me, she thought.

Kianne nodded. "About time too. Tis weeks now. The poor lad needs some encouragement."

Felde stood to one side of Langron square, as his father argued and bargained with two Hueds over the prices of the horses. As Keidun loudly demanded more money, saying, "They be the best thoroughbreds you can get, Helsund trained, they be worth far more than that!" Felde noticed Berrena, carrying a basket of eggs and pies. She saw him, their eyes met for a moment, then she looked down. The Hueds consulted each other, then nodded and handed over several coins to Keidun. As they rode away through the stalls and traders, leading the horses they'd bought, Keidun spat after them.

"Cursed murderous bastards!" he hissed.

Berrena strode over to him.

"What did you call them?" she demanded.

"Nothing," he replied. "Nothing. Nought to do with an

interfering chit like you, anyhap!"

"It is to do with me!" She gestured at the coins he was holding. "You sold those horses for over three times their value, didn't you? Didn't you?"

"Nay!"

"You're lying! I know you are!"

"So what if I did?" Keidun growled. "They can afford it, and we need the money."

"It's still cheating them!"

"Why should you care? I thought you were Talthen?" he snarled. "Or are you a traitorous half-breed after all?"

"How dare you?" Berrena exclaimed. "How dare you say that to me! And how dare you cheat them!"

Felde turned away. Berrena was right, but who cared about cheating Hueds? He knew it was cowardly, but he took his horse over to the side of the square and pretended to adjust the bridle, with his back to them. A few minutes later Keidun joined him.

"Bossy, high and mighty, cursed shrew," he muttered. "Thinks she's better than any of us..."

Felde said nothing.

"Right. I'm going back to Helsund. Are you coming?"

Felde glanced around. Berrena was standing and watching them.

"Er, maybe, I've still got some things I need to get from the leatherworkers. I need a new bridle. This one's wearing thin."

"Curses. All right, take these," Keidun said, handing a few coins to Felde. "Get what you need, then come home. Don't hang around. I'm going, I ain't staying here longer than I have to."

He mounted his horse and rode off, glaring at Berrena as he passed her. Felde leaned his face into the warm, rough flank of his horse and breathed in the leathery animal smell. He wondered if Berrena would say anything to him but she walked past him without a glance. He stared after her, wanting to run after her and explain. They needed, Helsund needed, Hued gold. There were families there on the brink of starvation.

Laithan came into the square, accompanied by three other Hueds wearing the black uniforms of the City Guard and leading horses. His face looked grim. Berrena went up to him.

"What's happening?" Felde heard her ask.

Laithan shook his head.

"They're here to arrest Ruger Lenne. They say he's a tax defaulter. He owes two year's tax."

"But he's been ill!" cried Berrena. "Tain't fair!"

"I know. But there's nought we can do. Even if I could afford to pay it for him, they'll arrest him anyway. I've got to show them where he lives."

"Nay! You've got to stop them!" she cried.

"I can't! Powers above, Berrena, we can't cause trouble. It'll be worse for the town if we try to stop them. Let me pass. We've got no choice."

He pushed her aside and pointed to a ramshackle cottage on the other side of the square.

"That's the house, sir," he replied. "The one with the shuttered window."

"Right. Out of my way, then," replied one of the Hued, who had a captain's badge on his jacket. "Clear the square. We don't want any of you cursed rats trying to interfere."

Laithan turned to the onlookers and traders.

"You heard what he said," he said wearily. "Get back home. Keep out of the way."

The townsfolk slunk away, muttering and looking resentfully over their shoulders at the city guards. Laithan followed them, his shoulders slumped as he walked down the street. Berrena stayed, her arms crossed as she stood and stared defiantly at the captain.

He glanced at her.

"You're a weird one, no mistake," he said. "Never seen a dullard your colour. Go on! Move away! Clear the square!"

"I ain't moving."

"Fancy watching an eviction and arrest, do you? Well, don't reckon a chit like you will cause trouble."

Felde lingered at the edge of the square, unnoticed by the guards. Surreptitiously he tied the reins of his horse to a fence rail and watched. His heart was beating so loud he was sure they'd hear it.

The captain kicked the cottage door open, went in and came out dragging a stumbling man by the hair. He threw him to the ground. One of the other guards knelt on the prone figure, tied his arms behind his back then wrapped a rope around his waist. The captain hauled the man up. Ruger swayed, his face white and beaded with sweat, as the captain attached the rope to his saddle, mounted his horse and handed a whip to the guard. Felde stared, horrified. Where they going to make Ruger walk all the way to Hueron? It would take days. He was already ill. He'd never make it.

Suddenly a young girl, barely fourteen, ran out of the cottage and screamed, "Daddy! Daddy!" She clung to her father, shrieking, until the third guard yanked her away and knocked her aside. Felde couldn't bear it any longer. He ran forward, shouting, wishing he had a knife on him.

Berrena yelled, "Felde! Don't! Don't be so stupid!" but he ignored her and charged, head down, at the guard with the whip.

The guard stepped aside quickly, kicking him hard in his side so that he fell. Felde cried out in pain as the whip cut his arm. The guard stood over him, whip raised high, and the other one rushed up. Before he could move, he was pulled up and pinioned between them. The guard slashed the whip across his face. Blood, sweet and coppery, trickled into his mouth.

Berrena ran forward.

"Stop it!" she cried. The guard laughed and grabbed her arms.

"Hey, captain, reckon we've got a couple of brave ones here!" he said and grinned. "Shall we teach them some manners?"

The captain dismounted.

"Well, well. So is he your boyfriend then?" he said, holding Berrena's chin and looking into her face.

"Let him go!" she cried.

"I don't think so. And as for you..." he said. He leaned forward, seized her hair at the back of her neck and pulled her towards him. His other hand tore her dress open and scrabbled at her breasts as she struggled. Felde tried to wrench himself towards her but their hands held him like iron bands as they laughed.

"That's it, sweetheart, fight back," hissed the captain. "I like a challenge. Especially with your boyfriend watching." He shoved her against the wall of the cottage and pulled up her skirt.

"Don't you dare!" she gasped. "Don't you know who I am?"

"Yes. A black-skinned dullard bitch who needs teaching a lesson."

Berrena stopped struggling. She lifted her head and stared at him.

"You know who I am," she whispered. "And you'll regret it for the rest of your short life if you go any further."

"What?"

"I am Lady Berrena Rochale, daughter of Lord Dernham Sapphireborne of Langron," she said coldly. "You'll have heard of me. The exiled black Hued. Hurt me or him and my father will see you hung."

"No. No, you can't be!"

"I am. You know it. Maybe you'd better get permission from my father before you risk continuing."

"You, you ... vixen. Hell's curses!"

He turned around. His face was furious.

"Release the boy," he snapped. Felde was thrown down to his knees. He looked up as the captain strode over to the young girl lying and sobbing on the ground. He pulled her up.

"You! I'm arresting you too, for evasion of taxes!" he shouted. "Tie her up!"

"No!" screamed Berrena.

He turned on her and snarled, with cold emphasis, "Yes - my lady! I can arrest any or all of the householders. She's coming with us, and there's nothing you or your lordship father can do about it."

"We'll see," panted Berrena. "Do you think I'll let you hurt or touch either of them?" She pulled her dress straight as she glared at him.

"Try and stop me," he snapped back. "Right! Move on!"

They mounted and rode off. Ruger stumbled behind them as the rope around his waist dragged at him. His daughter wept and trembled as she held his arm and tried to help him.

Felde stared after them. Berrena leant back against the wall, breathing hard and pressing trembling hands to her heart. After a few moments, she straightened up.

"You idiot!" she said, furiously. "You stupid, stupid idiot! Don't you ever stop to think? Your thoughtless, pointless interference just made it all worse!"

Felde mouthed, "I'm sorry," but she didn't respond. The whip cut on his cheek stung and the bruise on his side ached as he knelt, feeling the dry dust under his hands and watching her walk away.

CHAPTER 7
THE BINDING

"Keidun's dead? Oh, my poor brother-in-law! Oh, my poor nephews! What happened?" exclaimed Ingra, sitting down suddenly at the kitchen table.

"He collapsed. He was just carrying a sack of oats across the yard and he collapsed. We got him in, got him into bed, but he never came round. He..." Felde tailed off, and turned away with his hand covering his face.

"There, lad, there. Sit down. Ingra, lass, I'm sorry," said Laithan and patted Ingra's shoulder's as she sobbed. She cried, again and again, "My poor brother! Oh, my poor sister! Oh, Brilde, Keidun..."

"Jorvund? How is he?" Laithan said.

"He's stayed back home, arranging the burial. I said I'd come to tell you, ask you to come. The funeral, tis in two days' time."

"Aye, we'll come. What about the horse-breeding? Will you manage?"

"I don't know. I think so. Jorvund reckons we can. We'll have to."

Berrena came into the room and Laithan turned to her.

"Felde came to tell us the news. Tis bad news, I'm afeared. I know we had our differences, but tis past now. Keidun – he's dead."

"Oh! Oh, I'm sorry," Berrena said. Felde turned and gazed at her. She said nothing, merely sat next to Ingra and put her arm around the weeping woman.

"Ingra and I will travel up to Helsund tomorrow, Felde," Laithan said. "For the funeral rites."

"Thank you, uncle."

"And you're sure you and Jorvund will be able to manage the stud?"

"Aye. We'll have to. Some of the villagers will help. It will be hard, even so. Uncle, I won't be able to come to Langron so often."

"Nay, I guess not." Laithan glanced at Berrena who was still embracing Ingra. "But come for the spring-time planting, if you can."

Berrena stood up and came towards Felde, She put her hand on his shoulder. He could not read her calm, neutral expression.

"Felde, I'm sorry. He was a hard-working, loyal, honest man, and a good father," she said.

He could not bear it. He stepped back and her hand fell from his shoulder. He turned away to hide the tears stinging his eyes and muttered, "Uncle, I have to go back. We'll expect you tomorrow."

As he left the room, he turned for one last look at Berrena but she was talking quietly to Ingra. She did not look up. He didn't have the courage to ask her if she would miss him. And he knew that she wouldn't. That she didn't care for him. What would possibly interest her in an obscure horse-breeder from a poor northern village, with no chance of a better future? He had no hope of any excitement or adventure or anything other than being stuck in Helsund for the rest of his life, he told himself. As he rode past the dark pines lining the narrow road to Helsund, he gloomily sang to himself.

> *He went with horse and sword,*
> *Through autumn mist, and swore,*
> *He'd go to die in war,*
> *an unwanted hero.*

> *Oh, know your own true love, for wealth's a liar,*

Brave men be rare as gold, true hearts as sapphire.

A duck up-ended itself. Its tail squirmed as it searched the bottom of the Langron millpond for worms and snails. Felde was tempted to aim for its tail and surprise it, but instead he threw the stone across the water and watched with satisfaction as it bounced several times before sinking. He'd had a strenuous morning planting early potatoes with his uncle, and now he rested on the low wall by the mill and idly skimmed stones over the water prior to riding back. As he picked up another stone he saw Berrena walking along the road towards him. He stood up when he saw her. Was it his imagination or did she smile and walk faster? He tried to flick the stone so that it would skitter across the water to her. But he misjudged it and the stone bounced on the wall and landed in the dust before her. She laughed and picked it up and gave it to him. He looked at her, so intensely beautiful, so sure of herself and with such laughter in her eyes. He felt stupid and clumsy. The ground refused to open up to hide him, so he flung the stone across the road. When would he learn that there was no point?

As he turned away, she came up to him and put her hand on his arm.

"Felde? I'm sorry to have laughed," she said. "I didn't mean it."

He stared down at the ground and said nothing.

"I was looking for you. Laithan told me you were here. I wanted to talk to you. It's been a long time since we've seen you."

"Aye," he muttered.

"It's been three months. We've missed you."

Felde looked up at her in surprise.

"Has it been hard, without your father?" she continued.

He nodded. He could not trust his voice.

"Anyhap, Felde, I wanted to tell you something. I heard from my father. He's been able to get Ruger Lenne and his daughter released. They are on their way home. Ruger was seriously ill in prison but he has survived. Father is helping them get back to Langron and has paid their taxes. And he has managed to get that captain, the guard captain, demoted for his treatment of Ruger and me."

"Oh. Berrena, your father, he is a good man. Berrena, that day ... I shouldn't have done what I did. I am..." He hesitated.

"I know, Felde. You were a brave idiot. But you were trying to rescue them. I shouldn't have shouted at you. I wish I hadn't."

She reached up to touch where the whip had cut his face.

"It's healed well," she said.

Her fingers gently caressed on his face. She let her hand fall and it dropped into his hand as if it was its home. Her cool fingers rested in his. He stroked his hand down the bare flesh of her arm and felt the tiny hairs rise.

"You're cold," he said.

"Nay. I'm not cold," she murmured. She stood with her head bowed, looking at their two joined hands. Please, look up at me, he thought. She raised her face. He could see, as he bent his head nearer, tiny flecks of green and blue and purple in the black irises of her fathomless eyes. She put her hand up to his mouth, traced her fingers along his lips, and she kissed him.

"I ain't surprised," said Laithan, as he shook Felde's hand a few weeks later. "We thought – we hoped - this would happen."

"Aye! We did! And I'm so pleased!" Ingra exclaimed.

"We want to live in Langron, not Helsund, when we're married," Felde said. "Jorvund reckons he can run the stables without me."

"Then I can carry on teaching, and be near the manor, for Mother and Father," said Berrena.

"We'd love you to live in Langron," Ingra said. "I'd hate to lose Berrena."

"You could run my farm with me, Felde," Laithan said, "if you want, or mayhap you could start raising horses here?"

That afternoon Felde asked Laithan to come out to the yard.

"Berrena's written to her parents," he said as they leaned against the paddock rail. "She has asked them to come here to meet me. I've got to formally tell them that I want to marry her. Laithan - come with me. Please."

"Aye, of course. Lord Sapphireborne ain't that bad, not like some of them. He's a just man. He'll listen, he'll be polite. And Lady Rochale is kind and loves her daughter. She will be on your side, I think."

"Mayhap, but what if they say no? How can I ask a ruler of the city if I can marry his daughter?"

"He ain't a ruler, not really. Just on the City Council."

"Why's he called Lord, then?"

"Because he's one of the bloodline families, from the original founders of Hueron. They're always called Lord or Lady. Felde, it may not be as bad as you think. I know your father hated all the Hued, but you've got to think otherwise. Be respectful, but just tell them. You don't need to ask them anyway. Berrena's a free woman and an adult. She doesn't need their permission."

"Aye, but what if they despise me?" Felde asked, kicking the bottom rail of the fence. "They might snub me. They might refuse to see Bee again if she marries a dullard. Laithan, I'd do anything for her, but I don't want her to lose her parents 'cos of me."

"She won't. I know them. I'll talk to them first, if you want."

Felde found that it was not the ordeal that he had feared. Laithan introduced him and he bowed low and kissed Sarielle's hand. She was pleasant and charming, obviously delighted by his cautious politeness. Dernham's grave courteousness overawed him and he could barely stammer out his formal greeting. They invited him into the drawing room and he sat at the edge of the sofa and twisted his hands together as he told them of his desire to marry their daughter.

Sarielle nodded. "Yes, Berrena wrote to tell us," she said and glanced at Dernham.

"I have to say that I was not expecting something like this," Dernham said. "But perhaps that was foolish of me. Berrena is fully grown now and it is her decision. If she wants to marry you, then we will accept it. But it will be a grief to us, to lose her again."

"Lose her?" Laithan said.

"I believe this young man lives in Helsund?"

"Aye, I do. But we plan to live in Langron," said Felde.

"Oh, that is wonderful!" said Sarielle. "That is good news! I am so relieved. Dernham, I'm sure it will all work out wonderfully. And they are in love. Oh, I am delighted! Let's introduce Vallan to his future brother-in-law!"

"Of course. Felde, Laithan, I am glad to give my consent. Not that you need it, of course," Dernham said.

Felde stammered thank you and bowed to them both.

Berrena took Felde to the stables.

"Come and meet my brother," she said. "Apparently he's gazing enraptured at your horse."

Vallan was a young lad, barely eighteen. He had his royal-blue arrowhead perched on his shoulder and he wore the black jacket of the City Guard with youthful pride. Berrena noticed how Felde grimaced as he saw the hated uniform, but she nudged him forward. Vallan lifted his hand in greeting, with a frank smile.

"So you're Felde Sulvenor?" he said. "Delighted to meet you. Berrena's told me about you and your stud. Is this one of yours? What a horse! Looks strong, doesn't he?"

He patted the horse's glossy brown coat and deep quarters.

"What's he like to ride?"

"You can find out, if you want," said Felde.

Berrena had suspected that this might the best way to get Vallan and Felde to strike up a reasonably friendly acquaintance. It seems to be working, she thought, and smiled to herself.

While Vallan was riding the horse around the drive at the front of the manor, watched and occasionally encouraged by the stable manager and by Felde, she went to find her father.

"This is not what we had planned for you when you were born," he said, as he adjusted the position of some of the papers on the desk in his study. "But when one's plans fail, the wise man makes new ones. Felde is hard-working and honest, he is your choice, and that is what matters."

"Aye. He may only be a Talthen, a poor man, with little hope of bettering himself, but he's a good man. Brave, loyal. Despite being Talthen!"

"I do not have any prejudices against Talthen."

"Maybe not. Father, what did you think was going to happen? Were you expecting some Hued Lord to ride through the town and fall in love with me?"

Dernham smiled. "No, of course not. Truly, I had not thought about the possibility of you marrying. Berrena, I accept your rebuke. You are right and I am glad for you - that you have found a good man. There is an abandoned farm on the edge of Langron, some sixty acres, close to the Manor, and we will give it to you both and rebuild the house for you."

"Thank you. And stables?"

Dernham laughed. "Yes! Very well. It will make a good stud. I sincerely hope that you will be happy. And that you will forgive us for your exile."

"My exile? Father, why didn't you come with me? You and mother could have left Hueron to live with me at Langron Manor."

"But the city laws forbid non-Hueds to live in Hued estates," he replied. "We had to accept your exile."

"Oh. But you could still have lived at the manor yourself and been near me."

Dernham was silent.

"Why did you stay in the city?" Berrena insisted.

"Because I have work to do!" Dernham replied angrily. "It needs me. I spend my life fighting for it to be safe, honourable – a place of beauty and justice. I will continue this, whatever the cost!"

"So," answered Berrena slowly, "the city is more important to you than your daughter."

"No! Of course not! That is a terrible suggestion. Berrena, I did the best for you that I could."

"Truly? But you gave your best to the city."

"Do you think that?" He reached his hand out towards her, but she ignored it, and he let it fall. "I thought you were safe and content, Berrena. I thought it was for the best."

She shook her head.

"Perhaps I was wrong," he sighed. "I have never realised it and I do not like to admit it, but you are probably right. The city may have seemed more important to me than you were. I regret it."

"Aye, the city is more important to you than me, or Sarielle, or Vallan. Father, you had a choice, though you didn't see it. You could have chosen to leave Hueron, for my sake."

Dernham slammed his hand onto the desk. "I couldn't!"

"You could! You had a choice. Don't you understand? I am a Talthen, with Hued parents. I am a Hued, with Talthen parents! I want to choose who I am, but I don't have the choice. I have no chance of becoming Hued. Being a Talthen wife, a school teacher, is my only realistic choice. But if you and mother had lived in the manor nearby, I could have spent more time with you. I may have had more choice about my life!" She paused, and looked him full in the face. "Father, I think what you choose was wrong. You should have left Hueron!"

Chatter and laughter filled the town hall. Felde thought that almost all the townsfolk must have come to watch their wedding. Lord Sapphireborne and Lady Rochale had sent flowers, dozens of bottles of wine and joints of beef for the feast afterwards, and were sitting with Albis on one of the front benches. A jaunty Kianne stood behind Berrena as her attendant, and kept glancing sideways to Jorvund where he stood behind Felde. When Laithan asked for the rings Jorvund had his brother's ready, but Kianne managed to drop hers. It rolled away and she giggled. They both chased after it, scrabbling under benches and bumping into each other, with more and louder giggles from Kianne. When it was retrieved she handed it to Laithan with a transparently unrepentant "Sorry", then gave a conspiratorial look at Jorvund as Laithan asked the Powers above for blessings on the couple before joining their hands together. Felde ignored the flirtation going on behind him and kissed Berrena long and slowly. It was finally true. This glorious woman was now his wife.

Laithan asked the newly-weds to come with him and Ingra into a room at the back of the town hall, for The Binding. Another man, the town surgeon, rose to join them.

When the door was shut, Laithan said, "This is the private part of the ceremony. You have become openly joined, and now we do The Binding."

Ingra held out her hand, palm upwards. "You've seen the marks, that we call The Binding, ain't you?"

Felde nodded.

"Listen," Laithan continued, "The Binding marks you for life. The ritual involves cutting your palms and letting the blood mix."

Felde saw Berrena's eyes widen in surprise.

"You have to do this to be properly wed," Laithan said. "Do you both agree?"

Felde would do it, without a moment's thought. But would Berrena do this for him? Go this far? She hesitated, glanced at Ingra, then back at him with trust in her face.

"Aye, we're willing," she said.

"Don't worry, dearie. Laithan and I've done this. Tain't as bad as it sounds," Ingra said. "It stings, but that's all."

Laithan asked Berrena and Felde to hold out their left hands with their palms upwards. The surgeon took out a small knife.

Felde kept his hand as steady as he could. Berrena was calm, her hand still. On her palm the scar from her childhood marking could be seen - a dark grey blur against her ebony skin. The surgeon made tiny cuts and the blood, dark and red, seeped out and pooled.

Laithan said, "Hold your hands together, palms together, for a moment. Let the blood mix. Let the Powers above and the Virtues around us bind you."

They did so. As their fingers and palms were pressed together Felde could feel a faint stinging from the cuts, and Berrena's hand tingling against his as she gazed at him.

"Now put your left hand on each other's hearts. Ingra and I will show you what I mean."

As they stood, left palms pressing against each other's hearts, a prickling warmth grew in Felde's hand: a fierce heat that burned until it was almost unbearable, then stopped. He dropped his hand and stared at Berrena. He expected to see bloodstains on their clothes, but there was nothing. He looked at his hand. The blood had gone, but it had left faint lines, that looped and curved to form an intertwined three-lobed knot. On Berrena's palm was a similar shape in pale grey. He put his hand against hers. The two shapes were mirror-images.

Now Felde understood the marks that he'd seen on his father and mother's hands, and on Laithan's, Ingra's and others.

Laithan smiled at their surprised faces.

"Tis like magic, ain't it!" he said. "Put your left hand on your chest, on the right, opposite to your own heart, and shut your eyes. What do you feel?"

Felde gasped as he felt another heartbeat. It was a steady

beat, unlike his own, which was thumping rapidly. He turned to Laithan in bewilderment.

"Aye," Laithan said. "That's Berrena's heartbeat, and she feels yours."

Berrena looked at Felde with a teasing expression. He knew she was laughing silently at his racing pulse.

"Now, tis done," Laithan said, "you're now bound together, your blood and heartbeats shared. As long as you're both alive you can feel each other's life."

CHAPTER 8
A HISTORY

"Oh, good," exclaimed Sarielle, and turned the letter over. "Berrena says the horse business is going well. Making decent money, at last."

"That is good news," said Dernham. "And her school?"

"Yes, that too. Grown to sixty-three children. She will soon need a third teacher."

"Well, we can help with that."

Sarielle passed the letter to him. As he read it, she stared glumly through the window at the tiny flakes of early winter snow drifting in the cold breeze outside. She sighed.

"What is it, Sarielle?"

"Nothing ... I'm being silly, but every time she writes I'm hoping she'll tell me she's pregnant. It's been two years!"

Dernham took her hand and gently kissed it. "Patience, my dear," he said. He picked up his dark grey cloak and swung it round his shoulders. "I have to go. I told you, didn't I? Yet another meeting... I may be late back."

Sarielle sighed again. She could see he was becoming weary, almost haggard, with the futile and endless discussions as he tried to convince the council to take some action about the gifts fading. "You work too hard! They don't listen to you, do they? Perhaps you should give up."

Dernham shrugged. "I can't. It is too important. So much evidence, so many that will admit - privately, never in public - that their gifts are weaker, or even that have lost their gifts, like Albis! But without any of them being prepared to testify to the council, what more can I do?"

"You can't expect them to, though, can you?"

"No. But I will carry on, Sarielle. Our future..."

He shook his head, and fastened up the silver buttons of his cloak.

"Oh, incidentally... Sarielle, you know Iselle Topazborne?"

"Iselle? Mavretan's daughter? I should think everyone does!"

"She does have a reputation."

"She's earnt it, I hear! What about her?"

Dernham paused. Eventually he said, "To be blunt, Vallan has told me he and Iselle are ... involved. That they have been for some time."

Sarielle leapt up. "What!"

"He's meeting her tonight at the Emerald Restaurant with some of the guard."

"That - that strumpet? Powers above!"

She strode up and down, frowning at the thought. Vallan and Iselle? Oh, he was a catch, she knew. Handsome, one of the bloodline families, Dernham's heir, one of the youngest ever lieutenants in the City Guard at twenty-one. But Iselle? That sluttish flirt, as unprincipled and greedy as her father, flaunting her pink curves and low-cut dresses at her son!

"How dare she? And Mavretan! Oh, the slimy wretch, he'll have plotted this, I'm sure! How can Vallan be so - so silly! To fall for her? She can flutter her eyelashes and simper all she likes but, by the walls, I'll stop her snaring him. Oh, I could - I could bite her!"

"Sarielle! I advise you to say nothing to Vallan. It would do no good. And I'm sure Iselle is not as bad as she's painted."

Sarielle snorted. "Painted! She puts eyeshadow and lipstick on with a trowel."

"I'd better go." He picked up his briefcase and gloves. "Don't wait up for me. And if you come down to breakfast and find Iselle there with Vallan, don't - er - don't eat her!"

After he'd left, she wandered around the room,

straightened the embroidered cushions, drew the thick curtains shut, looked at the paintings and carved furniture and enamelled vases. What use was all this richness to her, with all her worries and fears? She shivered, then shook her head. "Brooding is silly," she muttered, went to her desk, and continued sketching designs for brooches and pendants.

An hour later, Dernham strode in, passed his cloak to the footman, smiled at her and brushed the snowflakes from his hair. Sarielle ran to him.

"What has happened? Why do you look so cheerful? You finished early!"

"Yes. The meeting turned out to be short, and not what I expected at all."

"Oh! Have the council finally agreed with you about the gifts fading?"

"No, nothing so good. To be honest, I suspect it's not something that will please you much, I'm afraid, although I am delighted."

"Well, don't keep me in suspense! What is it?"

Dernham took a letter out of his briefcase.

"This. Theon Meriede, a rich recluse, died recently and he was a great book collector. He has left his entire library to the city and the council have asked me to sort it and catalogue it. Over two thousand books!"

"Two thousand?"

"Some of them unique, some are hundreds of years old. Although I suspect the council have given me this privilege to distract me from haranguing them about the gifts."

He put his arm round her shoulders, pulled her close and bent down to kiss her. She could not help a slight pout as she turned away. He'd be lost in his study, buried in dusty old books, for months now, and she wanted to go to Langron. But at least he'd be happy there, and perhaps it would take his mind off the fading gifts. She turned back. "Well – even so, that is good news. I am pleased for you - a bit!"

Dernham paused at the window of Sarielle's jewellery shop, two months later, and looked inside. She was staring at her palm with her amethyst in her other hand. For a moment he watched her and smiled at the way she stuck her tongue out slightly when she concentrated. A glinting blue jewel appeared on her palm. She looked up as he came in.

"Dernham! I thought you were working on those books?" she said, as she leapt to her feet.

"I was. But I wanted to talk to you as soon as possible. How has business been today?"

"Oh, it's been busy! I've sold seven bracelets – I'll have to make some more – and two of those wide silver rings; the ones set with opals; as well as a tiara and some other bits and pieces. I've bought some more gold and copper wire, as I want to make a necklace for Berrena. I made this for her. This sapphire."

"Very beautiful," he said. "Was it hard to make?"

"Well – yes, a little. Harder than it would have been last year, harder than lapis lazuli or turquoise would be, but much prettier. I'm going to write to Berrena about Vallan's engagement to that slut Iselle, but I'm not looking forward to having to tell her about her possible new sister-in-law. I thought I'd send her a necklace with the letter."

Dernham nodded. "Hmmm. Not too ostentatious, Sarielle. Remember her station."

"I will! Just one sapphire and two citrines, set in gold and copper filigree. It'll be delicate and pretty, not a great thick heavy thing."

"Good. Can you close early today? There's something I found out that I want to discuss with you."

At the house she followed him into his study. He gave her a battered leather-bound book, with ornate but unintelligible gold writing on the cover.

"I have discovered this," he said.

Sarielle opened the book. Inside she could make out the word 'Hueron' on the title page but the rest of the text was archaic and almost unreadable. The paper was thick and yellowed, some of the pages had torn, and it smelt musty and old.

"It's called 'A History of the Founding of Hueron: the Coloured City' and it was written nearly five hundred years ago. This is a copy made about a century afterwards. It is the only known authentic account of the city's origins! I had come across references to it, but it was believed that all copies had been lost."

"You seem really pleased about it! Why? What is so special about yet another history book?"

"It may have some answers for me! You know how frustrated I have been about the lack of records about things that matter. We have archives full of details about gifts, colours, laws, export logs, taxes. Masses of information, but nothing to help me understand the basis of our gifts, hardly anything about where the Hued came from, why we are superior to dullards, where our power comes from, why it is fading - nothing useful! Then this book – finally I have found something! It took me over a week to transcribe it, and there are some passages missing, some words I can't make out."

He paused.

"But first, tell me what you know about the city's origin."

Sarielle thought for a moment then said, "Only the children's story. That seven great lords and ladies came from over the southern mountains to Saroche plain. One of each colour; blue, red, orange, yellow, green, um ... purple and, er ... brown! They fought the local dullards in the great war, even though there were thousands of them. They conquered them and built the city. I've never really believed that – they must have been amazingly powerful for only seven of them to have beaten so many dullards. And who did they marry and get children with? Dullards? It's only a myth, and it doesn't really make sense."

"But there's a grain of truth in it, like many myths," said Dernham. "It's partly true, but only partly. There were nine founders, not seven, and they had spouses and children and others with them, but the most important parts have been forgotten – or deliberately suppressed. Let me read you some of my transcription."

He took some pages from his desk and started to read.

"A History of the Founding of Hueron: the Coloured City. The Hued began in villages far south in the hills beyond Saroche plain. At that time they had no great gifts, only the ability to create water, start a fire, conjure small items of metal or food, and heal minor wounds and illnesses. These powers and their coloured skin made them rejected and persecuted by ordinary people and they fled south in exile. Nine men and women led them. One of each natural colour; red, blue, yellow, green, purple, orange; one brown, which is a mixture of all colours; and one each of the pure hues; white and black."

"Black? A black Hued?" Sarielle exclaimed "Oh, Dernham, like Berrena! Dernham, does this mean that she is Hued after all?"

"Sarielle, I do not know. There is a bit about the black Hued later on..." He shuffled through the pages. "Let me see... ah, yes, here it is... The firstborn children descended from the original leaders were given the titles Lord or Lady Greenborne, Sapphireborne and so on, sons taking their fathers' surnames and daughters their mothers'. But there were only seven bloodlines. The black and white Hued leaders were lost before the great war, leaving no children, and their fate is unknown... That is all it says. And I doubt that this brief mention in an ancient document will convince the council to rescind their decision. Her gift is unusual, and even though we can prove that she has one, she still has no mark and no symbol. Let me read on."

He turned back to the first few pages and continued.

"Magi, wizards from far away, came and offered them greater powers, in return for certain privileges. The nine leaders agreed and a bargain was sealed in the blood of the Magi and the leaders."

"The Magi? A bargain with the Magi? Incredible!"

"Yes. To continue: it says, er, the Magi gave the coloured people the secret of the gifts and the powers, showing them how to cut their palms and how the blood would create the symbols that gave them power. In return the Hued agreed to conquer the surrounding villages and towns and pay the Magi a tax of several uncoloured, young, strong and healthy men every forty years, to be apprenticed as wizards. To the red people the Magi gave the gift of creating fruit, vegetables, wine and beer – this is followed by a rather long list of gifts and colours – but note the importance of the Magi."

Sarielle nodded. He read on.

"The Hued, as they were now called, made war on those who had persecuted them, with the help of the Magi, and they defeated them, making them accept the Hued as masters. The non-coloured people became known as the dullards. As the Hued grew in strength their rule extended over more villages - and so on and so on. From that point on there isn't any further mention of the Magi. It talks about founding Hueron and building the first walls to keep them safe from their former persecutors, how they made the rules restricting dullards from entering the city... interesting to read how they hated and mistrusted them..."

He put the pages down.

"The rest is irrelevant and rather dull, even to a historian like me. But the key point is the role played by the Magi."

"But weren't they those obscure dullard wizards from long ago? How can they have had something to do with the Hued? I thought they were just a legend, apart from that odd city law about them being able to take six dullard men. Isn't this strange! Persecuted by dullards as well? How can our powers have come from the Magi? Why would this have been forgotten?"

"So many questions, Sarielle! The Magi are no legend. Laithan tells me that they, or rather their apprentices, the inheritors of their powers, still travel round occasionally. It is interesting that our official histories have ignored both the part played by the Magi and that we were once persecuted exiles. But that's not why I wanted you to hear it. Do you not see the implications? If the first Magi gave us our power, then the current Magi may know why we are losing it."

"But the original Magi have been dead for centuries!" Sarielle said, picking up the battered, ancient book. "And this, it's so old. It's too long ago to be any help."

"I know, but their apprentices may know about the gifts and know what is happening to them. "

"What do you mean?" Sarielle turned to him with a puzzled expression, and touched her amethyst where it lay in her hair. "Our gifts? How on earth can the present Magi know about the Hued gifts?"

"From their predecessors. They must have some knowledge of them – they must have passed knowledge and wisdom down from generation to generation, along with their powers. They may even have kept records of some sort."

"Do you really think so?"

"Yes, it is possible. And Laithan says they are powerful – far more powerful than the Hueds. Thinking about it now, it is a pity that the Hued have never tried to learn from the Magi, but have simply ignored them."

"Well, I suppose we didn't need their help. Not like the dullards do."

"And Hueds are too proud to go to them," Dernham said. He took the book from Sarielle, and glanced through it before putting it down on his desk. "This book – such a fortunate discovery! It has not only fascinated me, but it has given me hope. It is possible that the Magi may be able to help us. They may be able to restore the gifts or recreate the original bargain, whatever it was."

"Truly? That seems incredible! How?"

"I don't know how, but they may do. They must do! By the Virtues, such knowledge cannot have been lost forever! They may live a long way away, and it may be a tiny, forlorn chance, but I think we should try to find out."

"You sound optimistic, but won't we have to wait until they come round to visit the dullards again? And we don't know when that will be, nor where they will go."

"Yes. We will have to find them, somehow. Maybe by talking to dullards to find out where they come from. That is probably the best way. It will be difficult. But I have determined that I will go and find the Magi and ask them for help. That is the only option I can see."

"What! You will go and find the Magi? You?" Sarielle burst out, stepping back and staring at him. "Dernham, are you serious? That is ridiculous! What about the distance? The danger? Robbers, hostile dullards, who knows what. No!"

"I have to!" he exclaimed. "Something has to be done, and this is all I know to do!"

"Dernham, I don't ask much of you, but I ask this! Don't even think about such a journey!"

"But I have to do something!"

Sarielle reached out and took his hand.

"Dernham, I know! But I can't bear the thought of you going. Send someone else, someone you can trust but, please, don't go yourself!"

CHAPTER 9
PLANS

As the butler cleared away the serving plates and empty decanters, Sarielle exclaimed, "Isn't this exciting? It's like a council of war!"

The five others round the dinner table laughed.

"Hardly," said Cairson, scooping up the last morsels of cream and meringue from his bowl. "I don't expect that war councils usually involve such a delicious meal."

"Well, you know what I mean. Plotting like this," Sarielle responded.

"Anyway, thank you for listening," said Dernham. "Do you understand what I am proposing, and why? And do you believe me?"

Avenessa Lachiare, Cairson's eldest niece, nodded. "Definitely. There is enough evidence, when you consider it. I would like to be involved, even if those fools in the City Council don't believe you."

"Thank you, Aven. Cairson has told me that you are one of the most respected captains in the City Guard, so your help would be invaluable. Remind me. What is your gift?"

She took from her shoulder her symbol, a tiny exquisitely-moulded wren, put it on her palm and held it out towards him. "It's a rare gift, I know. My bird – it can fly ahead of me. Like a scout. And I can transform into a bird myself."

"Good. There are very few who can do that," said Dernham. "That would be useful on a venture like this."

"She is also a capable strategist and a skilled fighter," said Cairson.

"Even better. Would you be prepared to lead this?" Dernham asked.

"Of course," she replied. "I'll take a sabbatical from the City Guard. There will be no problem with that. But I need to know precisely what you are hoping to gain from this. Otherwise there's no point going."

"Ideally, I want the Magi to come to Hueron and renew the gifts," said Dernham.

"Indeed! An ambitious plan. But worth aiming for. And if they won't?"

"At the least, I am hoping for confirmation that the gifts are failing, and also some information about how the gifts work and how to preserve them, even if the Magi do not help us directly."

"If we can get even that, then the City Council should be very grateful to you."

"And to those who go on the mission also. I do not deny that."

"Yes. I'll go anyway, but I intend that, should we succeed, we will gain some recognition of our achievement." Aven leant back and twirled her wine around her glass.

"I hope you do too, Aven. Thera, Headon, what are your opinions?" Dernham said, turning to the others.

"Dernham, anything you need in this, I will do if I can," Thera Redstone replied. "I have given up trying to persuade the rest of the council to listen to you! However, I do not feel I am the best person to undertake a journey like this. But my son, well, Headon?"

"What you are suggesting is difficult to accept but, as Aven says, when you look and think, the evidence is apparent," Headon Alcastor said. His grass-green eyes were serious as he looked at Dernham. "I find it hard to believe that the Magi could have the solution. Though it is worth asking them, if we can. How many people do you want to send, Dernham?"

"I think four or five. That should be sufficient. It is a challenge to decide who to ask and who to trust. I do not particularly intend to hide this from the council, but nor do I wish it to be public knowledge."

"Can you imagine the furore from the council if they knew?" said Cairson. "It's been difficult enough with all the arguments about this issue. Especially with Mavretan blocking us and disagreeing with us at every turn."

"Precisely," Dernham said. "Headon, I know from my son Vallan that you are good with sword and arrow – he says you practise with the City Guards regularly. And having a doctor like you, with your healing gifts, would be helpful."

Headon paused for a moment, glanced at Aven and then round at the others.

"I don't mind the prospect of a break from the hospital work," he said, "and I am curious to travel south of the city. And to find these Magi. I have often wondered how the gifts work, and they may be able to explain it. I think that if Aven is leading, then we have a good chance of success. Give me a few days to arrange it, but I would like to go."

"If you want to go, Headon, I can take over your hospital duties," Thera said.

"Thank you," said Headon. "Excellent!"

"The key problem is going to be finding the Magi," said Aven. "I've seen them once. When I was sixteen. They passed through the village near Marden."

"You've seen the Magi?" exclaimed Sarielle. "What were they like?"

"Impressive," Aven said, and shrugged.

Cairson nodded. "There were six Magi, in splendid velvet and silk robes, jewelled rings, gold chains, holding long staffs, leading a stately procession of attendants, covered wagons, carts, dozens of servants, even more horses. It was an unforgettable spectacle. They were travelling south, apparently, homewards."

"We will have to go south and find a village that they visited recently," Aven said. "From then we will be able to follow their tracks. I have heard that they come from beyond the Crevenne Mountains, maybe from as far away as Sheiran. We should plan for several months journeying."

"We need to arrange this soon, before spring is well under way," Dernham said. "So that you have enough time before next winter."

"You talked of sending five people," said Cairson. "Have you thought who else to ask?"

"I will ask one more Hued – possibly someone from the City Guard, I don't know yet. But I have sent for the town chief of Langron. I am going to ask him to recommend two men, the best fighters that he knows."

"Dullards! Are you mad?" exclaimed Aven. "Dernham, we all know your weakness for them, but why? Scum like them can't be trusted."

"Aven!" cried Sarielle. "You forget that we have entrusted our daughter to dullards! We know they can be trusted!"

"Even so, wouldn't we be better having an escort from the City Guard?"

"No – I don't want to have any interference from the council," said Dernham. "And since you will be travelling through dullard areas, asking questions about the Magi, a City Guard would be unhelpful, to say the least. Having dullards with you to talk to the villagers will be better. And, if you lose your gifts, you will be vulnerable. I have a fear that our gifts may suddenly disappear. Irrational, I know, but if they do, some of the men from Langron would make good bodyguards."

"Let's hope we don't need them," said Aven. "I'm not sure about the idea. You will have to make it worth their while to work with us and not betray us or cut our throats one night!"

"I will!" Dernham said. "And I will ask Laithan to recommend men from his town who can be trusted!"

"Well, it's your mission. I suppose we can cope with two dullards tagging along."

"Aven, since our daughter has been exiled, it has been my aim to encourage dullards and Hued to work together!"

Dernham said. "Fruitless I know, so far, but I am determined to continue!"

"We know, Dernham," Cairson said, and touched his arm gently. "Don't give up."

"I won't." He shook his head. "Anyway, we should consider that there may be a connection between the dullard's problems and ours. Their town chief tells me that their harvests have fallen, with a few exceptions, for the past twenty years. Or failed altogether. And that other dullard towns are experiencing the same. Even after leaving the land fallow, it produces less and less, as if it is weakening as our gifts are weakening."

The fire in the sitting room blazed and warmed the room. Candles had been lit in the sconces on the walls and the room was bright in their light. Dernham fetched maps and Aven studied them.

"Useless!", she said, tossing the parchments aside. "There is hardly anything about towns and places far south. They show the Crevenne Mountains, but nothing past them! We could do with someone from the south coming with us, if we can find someone in the City Guard."

"Yes," replied Dernham. "But it is more important to have someone we can trust."

Sarielle rose and paced around the room. "Wait..." she said, twirling a lock of her hair around her fingers. "I'm thinking..." Then she stood by the fire and turned to face the others. The flames and candlelight illuminated their faces; dark blue, warm orange, deep gold, bright green, chestnut brown; as they looked up at her.

"Dernham, it's obvious. We should send Vallan!"

"What? But he's too young, too..." Dernham started to say, but she silenced him with a gesture.

"No, we should," she said. "I know he's young, but he's the best soldier there is, isn't he, Aven?"

"Yes. He is quite remarkable."

"Well then!" said Sarielle.

"But he has just become engaged to Iselle Topazborne, hasn't he?" said Cairson. "To Ferard Mavretan's daughter?"

"Yes! That's why we should send him!" Sarielle turned to Thera. "Oh, Thera, it has been awful! Mavretan is a blood-sucking, power-hungry, cruel... It's not just the way he continually opposes Dernham in the council. He goes on and on about the marriage settlements he expects from us – first a house, then a bigger house, then servants. And she is no more than a money-chasing pink-faced flirt! I would do anything to prevent Vallan marrying her. This will separate him from her for a few months. Hopefully he'll forget her or she'll latch on to someone else while he's gone!"

When summoned by Dernham, Laithan agreed to help find two bodyguards. The town was yet again, after another poor harvest, under an obligation to the Hued Lord for his generosity.

"I assume that you will provide armour, weapons? Swords - good ones?" he said.

Dernham nodded. "Of course."

"Also - my lord - will you ask the council to reduce the taxes on Helsund?"

"You are asking rather a lot! There is little chance that they will listen. I am getting a reputation as a doom-laden prophet and a dullard-lover and the council have little patience with me at present. But I will try."

As Laithan rode back to Langron, he decided to ask his nephews. He knew that, if the venture succeeded, then Dernham, and maybe even the City Council, would reward those who went, and why not his nephews? And they were, without any doubt, the best fighters he knew.

Jorvund was already in the kitchen of Felde's house. He said that he had taken a horse to the blacksmith, but Laithan wasn't surprised to find Kianne there too, sitting suspiciously close to Jorvund. Laithan took his nephews into the yard to explain Dernham's proposal to them.

Jorvund listened, nodded and said, "It sounds exciting.

Aye, I'll go. When do we leave?"

Felde lent on the fence and shook his head. "I don't want to help the Hued. They should help themselves! Nay, I won't go! Twould be a waste of my time."

"Felde, are you sure?" Laithan said. "You will be doing Lord Dernham a favour."

"Aye, think about that," Jorvund said. "Come with me!"

"Nay! I can't!" Felde said, gesturing at the stables. "Not now – the horses are just starting to make money. And I've only been married two years. I can't leave Berrena and go off chasing wizards to I don't know where!"

"But it's to help her parents," Laithan said. "Her father has asked you!"

"Mayhap... But it would be a waste of time. Why should I go?"

"Because it would be doing something different!" Jorvund exclaimed. "Not just stagnating here."

"And it wouldn't be a waste of time," Laithan said. "It would help us."

"How?"

"Tis good to have Hueds on our side. If we help them, they're more like to help us."

"Felde, you're bored with horse-breeding, like me," Jorvund said. "I know you are. Tired of mucking out stables and cleaning tack and the endless work. I would do anything to escape from Helsund for a while! If you want to do something exciting, then come on this journey with me!"

"I don't know! Let me think about it. And talk about it with Berrena."

That evening, Felde sat by the fire as Berrena marked workbooks and hummed his favourite song,

> *Brought back in winter frost,*
> *Deep wounds sliced through his chest,*
> *She mourned what she had lost,*
> *a valiant hero.*

Oh, know your own true love, for wealth's a liar,
Brave men be rare as gold, true hearts as sapphire.

He gazed at her smooth cheeks, her dark eyes glinting in the lamplight, the intense auburns and rich purples of her hair. How could he leave her just for the sake of being a valiant hero?

"Bee, Laithan - he asked me something," he said. He stammered as he told her. To his surprise, Berrena was acquiescent.

"I can tell part of you wants to go," she said, as she touched the Binding. "I don't have to feel your chest to know that your heart's beating fast at the thought of it."

"But how can I leave you and the stables for so long? It may be months. And I don't like the idea of travelling with Hueds. Even to help your father."

"Felde, I can't pretend that I don't want you to go, though I hate the thought of saying goodbye to you, and not knowing when I'll see you again. But I ain't going to be one of those wives that keep their husbands locked up in cages. You could be be town chief one day. Having helped Hueron City Council will make that more likely."

"Hmm," said Felde. "Mayhap. My father, he wouldn't have wanted me to help Hueds."

Berrena took his face in her hands and looked steadily at him. "Nevertheless, I - your wife - want you to go and have this chance. To gain a little recognition. Powers above, Felde, don't you want more than this - this obscurity!"

Felde looked at her, startled by the passion in her voice. "Obscurity?"

"Aye! This limited, obscure life! You should take this chance to work with Hueds. And remember that one of the others will be my brother Vallan. You like him."

"Aye, he's fine. Tis the others. You know what Hueds think of us. They'll despise me. But anyhap, I don't want to leave you!"

He lay awake for hours, listening to Berrena's breathing

as she slept beside him with her arm flung across his chest. How could he leave her for so long? Just for the chance of adventure and glory? For the chance of doing something heroic?

Next morning, as Felde put more wood on the fire, Jorvund came into the kitchen.

"What have you decided?" he said. "What does Berrena say?"

"I think he should go. Aye, I'm happy – well, not happy, but I can survive while Felde goes," Berrena said, lifting her head from a pile of textbooks. "As long as he comes back."

"I'll do my best to bring him back. There you are, Felde, she agrees. So you should come!"

"Mayhap. I ain't decided yet!"

Berrena stood up, slammed the pile of books down on the table and turned to Felde, her hands on her hips. "You've had the whole night to decide! You should go. When else will we get a chance like this? To put the City Council in debt to Talthens?"

"All right! If you insist – I'll go!"

"Good!"

Felde turned to Jorvund, and poked him in the chest. "Happy now? But I'm surprised, little brother, that you can bear to leave Kianne for so long!"

Jorvund shrugged. "Aye, she's called me all sorts of names. Heartless, seducer, scoundrel, and worse. Burst into tears, slapped me, then flung her arms around me and kissed me. Tis my only regret, leaving her. Berrena, Felde, you know that it may be dangerous."

Berrena nodded.

"Do you think I'm frightened?" Felde exclaimed. "Do you think that's why I didn't want to rush off on this stupid mission?"

"Nay! Of course not. You fight almost as well as I do."

"Faint praise!"

"That's why I want you to come. If it comes to fighting,

99

I'd rather have you next to me than some blue-faced Hued I know nought about."

"Aye, Felde," said Berrena. "If tis dangerous Jorvund may need you."

"Powers above! I've said I'm coming. But if you put it like that, then mind this, I'm only coming to protect my little brother!"

Jorvund laughed. "Good! I'll remember that. But I bet it will be me protecting you, not the other way around."

As Dernham left the council chamber, one afternoon a week later, Mavretan took hold of his arm.

"I need to talk to you," he murmured. "Somewhere private. Away from the other councillors."

"You? You need to talk to me?" Dernham said. "I cannot imagine that we have anything to say to each other. If it's about Iselle and Vallan, I have nothing that I want to discuss with you!"

"No, this is more important than those two silly love-birds. In private! We'll go in here," Mavretan said and pulled Dernham into a side room with a desk and a few chairs. He shut the door.

"Take a seat," he said. "Well - I hear from Iselle that you are sending Vallan and others on a diplomatic mission to the Magi, of all people. Without permission from the council!"

"What is that to do with you? It's not a City Council matter," Dernham snapped. "Where my son chooses to go, and who with, is our concern, no one else's, and nothing to do with you or the council."

"It is to do with the council. A journey to see the Magi on behalf of the Hued! How can it not be? You should have notified the council at least, and you should seek council permission. Sapphireborne, if I told them this, I could have you thrown out, even arrested for conspiracy."

"Conspiracy!" Dernham exclaimed. He stared at Mavretan, trying to ascertain what his rival was intending.

But Mavretan's thin, intelligent face gave nothing away.

"Yes, conspiracy. That is what it looks like," Mavretan said.

"Obviously you haven't told them," Dernham sighed, "so you must want something from me. Money, or my backing for one of your dubious business schemes or exploitative tax proposals, I expect. I'm not going to increase the settlements for their marriage, whatever you threaten."

"I am not so keen on their marriage either. Iselle could do so much better! But I do want something from you."

He paused, frowned and steepled his long red fingers together.

"You may be right about our powers fading," he said, leaning forwards.

"What! Then why have you never supported me? Don't you think this is far more important than our disagreements on the council about our treatment of dullards?"

"I'll support you now. The thought of the Hued losing their gifts fills me with dread."

"So there is one thing we agree on!"

"Unexpected, I know, but true. The safety of the Hued, that is paramount. Given that, I am prepared to help this mission of yours. You should be delighted, Sapphireborne, that I am supporting you."

"I don't know the cost yet. I'm sure you will expect something, knowing you," Dernham snapped.

"Cost? Not much. This mission may be a wild goose chase, but it may not. I hope it succeeds. If it does I want part of whatever reward you are expecting the council to give you. I want to be seen to be involved, and so I want Iselle to go with Vallan."

He waited, eyeing Dernham like a stalking cat watching a bird.

"No," Dernham said, eventually. "I do not want you or Iselle's involvement."

"Ah, but you have no choice." Mavretan smiled. "Accept

my offer or I'll inform the council that you are plotting to get help from the Magi so you can take over the city. That will stop whatever it is you are planning. And you would face a charge of treason. Your son, your friends, your wife too!"

"I knew you were unprincipled," Dernham exclaimed. "But I never understood until now what a cold-hearted, scheming power-hungry villain you were!"

"Compliments, compliments," Mavretan said smoothly, shrugging.

"It's to be hoped your daughter doesn't take after you. So - she may go, provided the council don't hear about my plans. Rest assured I will triple my efforts to frustrate your power-chasing and your plotting. And if you or Iselle double-cross me in any way, I'll tell the council about your offer and we'll face the treason charges together!"

CHAPTER 10
LEAVING LANGRON

Sarielle stormed into Dernham's study at Langron Manor and slammed the door behind her.

"That hussy! That brazen-faced hussy!" she exclaimed. "I can't believe the nerve of her. Dernham, did you see how smug she looked? And her dress! She was practically bursting out of it. With that symbol of hers sitting on her ... her cleavage and grinning at me!"

She strode around the room, gesturing and shaking her fists, then flung herself into a chair.

"Grinning? Sarielle, how can Iselle's symbol grin at you?" Dernham asked.

"Oh, well, you know what I mean. Those intertwined loops on it – it did look like it was grinning. What are we going to do about her?"

"Calm down and accept the situation. You know how Mavretan has manoeuvred us into letting her join them. There is nothing we can do. At least Vallan is pleased."

"Humph! But I'm so vexed! Dernham, why aren't you?"

"I am a little annoyed, I admit."

"A little! Well, I'll show her." She jumped up out of her chair. "I've put her into a tiny little room. One right up on the top floor that's as far as possible from his!"

Dernham laughed. "I doubt that will deter her – or him, for that matter."

"It's all very well for you to laugh, but we have to do something!"

"All we can do is make the best of it. Vallan said she was a good archer."

"All that time spent flirting with the City Guard, I suppose!"

"And you heard what she said about the maps in the library at Peveque House?"

"Yes, but I couldn't see the relevance." Sarielle shrugged. "Where's Peveque anyway?"

"Over a hundred and fifty miles south of Hueron. Mavretan's estate is there. Maps of the southern settlements and mountains would help us. So it would be sensible for them to go to Peveque House and start searching from there. Especially if Iselle can be trusted when she said the Magi passed through Peveque a few years ago."

The evening before they left, the brothers shared dinner at the manor with Dernham, Sarielle and Berrena and were introduced to Aven, Headon and Iselle. Felde had to stop himself staring at their strange colouring. Aven was a mature woman, robust and almost as tall as Vallan; with tawny brown skin, hair and eyes; a square jaw and short chestnut hair. Wearing dark green trousers and tunic, with her symbol, a small brown wren, perched on her shoulder, she looked confident and dauntless, but she stared at him with lifted chin and cold eyes.

However, Headon greeted him as an equal, his hand raised to show a pale oval on his palm. A head shorter than Vallan, he appeared stocky and capable, with intelligent emerald eyes and a short green beard. Felde could not see his symbol, unlike Vallan's arrowhead, proudly displayed below his throat, its blue bright against his black City Guard uniform. Next to Vallan stood Iselle; a young, pretty woman with astonishing fuchsia pink skin and soft, curly hair. Her symbol, an oval embossed with intertwined loops, hung from a necklace at her throat. She nodded briefly to them, then turned back to smile at Vallan and lean close on his arm. She looked too fragile and precious to know anything of long journeys, hard living, sleeping rough, let alone fighting and struggling, Felde thought.

After the meal, Aven spread out maps and took them through the planned route. "We'll follow the Langrest River until it meets the Saroche, cross the plain east of Hueron and continue south through the hills to Peveque. That's about two weeks' riding, and then we'll rest for a day or two and replenish stocks."

"This route is longer than the direct route via the city, but it avoids any possible trouble in Hueron," Dernham added. "If the City Council hear of this, they are bound to interfere. They might even forbid the venture."

"After that we don't have much idea how far we may have to travel," continued Aven. "The Magi might live a further three weeks' journey south, or more, beyond the Crevenne Mountains. Hopefully there will be a pass over the mountains and an obvious route."

She straightened up. "One more thing! Vallan, you are not to wear your City Guard uniform. We are not on duty and it is not an official journey. We go in normal clothes."

The early morning sky was grey and fat raindrops fell in the town square as they prepared to leave. Laithan, Ingra and Berrena huddled in their cloaks, watching, along with three or four other townsfolk, including Kianne. She wept openly as Jorvund put his arms around her and kissed her. But Berrena was still, her face blank. Something about the suppressed pain of her expression tore at Felde's heart. He knew how sad she was at this parting. He took her face in his hands, gazed at her drowned midnight eyes, then kissed her brow and cheeks and lips. "I'll come back. I promise," he said.

The horses waited, saddled, bridled and with their bags loaded with as much as they could carry. Dernham's stable manager had provided seven mounts, but Felde and Jorvund had looked with disgust at them, especially at the two fat and scruffy ponies he had evidently thought were good enough for dullards.

"I ain't riding those slugs," Jorvund had said. "They ain't

even fit for pulling carts. One of them can be a packhorse, but Felde and I will take our own horses."

As the four Hueds, with his parents-in-law, rode towards them, Felde knew a moment of insignificance - he was only an obscure dullard as far as Hueds were concerned. But then he looked at their mounts and compared them to his and his brother's and felt a little pride. The Hueds might be powerful, rich and gifted but they knew nothing about horses. He glanced at Jorvund, who was patting the long, sloping shoulders of his glossy black mare with the same satisfaction.

They gave a brief farewell to everyone. Felde mounted, lent down for a final kiss with Berrena, and then they left. Despite the sadness of parting, his spirits rose as they rode down the valley, travelling towards unknown lands. Patches of blue appeared in the sky and the rain eased. As a breeze shook raindrops from the trees a blackbird flew past, chattering loudly at them. The river splashed along next to the road, the tree trunks shone wet and black against the pale green grass and spring leaves, and the scent of damp earth filled the air. Felde grinned. There was an excitement in the simple fact of going somewhere that wasn't Langron or Helsund.

They rode steadily, stopping briefly to eat, until the sun began to drop below the tree line. Aven, who was leading, pulled up and pointed at a small clearing in the forest a few yards from the road and river. "A good place to camp," she said, and dismounted. She turned to the brothers.

"You two - find some wood for the fire!" she ordered.

"As if we were slaves," muttered Felde to Jorvund. But she also told Iselle to feed and water the horses, ignoring her pouts, and the two Hued men were sent to catch fish, while Aven herself organised the camp.

Her bossy competence irritated Felde, but later, as they sat in a circle round the fire, he relaxed. In the twilight stars glimmered in the east. The firelight shone on their faces; Iselle, pink and sleepy-eyed; Vallan's clear blue eyes gazing at her; Headon writing in a leather-bound journal; Jorvund lying on his back looking up at the evening sky; and Aven cleaning the knife used to gut the fish. Felde took out his sword and started to sharpen it, slowly running the stone along the blade. Dernham had given him and Jorvund long straight city-made swords of folded steel. Un-ornamented, with wooden grips and bronze guards, their only purpose to injure and slash and stab, and a far cry from the blunt swords that he had used in training. The firelight reflected on the polished metal of the sword as he worked on it. He looked along the blade to check no light glinted along the honed edge. He wondered if he would have to kill with it.

Next morning, waking up cold and stiff with his cloak covered in dew and his neck sore from using his saddlebag as a pillow, he felt less happy. Aven was already up and putting her saddle on her horse. "About time too," she said. "We need to get moving. Start breaking camp."

They rode along a widening river valley and headed downwards. The forests started to thin out, occasionally giving glimpses of the Saroche plain south west of them. That evening Aven told them to practise fencing with each other. Felde partnered with Iselle and easily parried her attacks, then knocked her stick out of her hand with a quick upwards flick.

"Ow! That stung!" she said, grimacing at him and sucking her fingers. "Aven, why do we have to do this? I'd rather practise archery."

"You don't need to practise archery. I know how good you are. But you need to use a sword or dagger too."

"Why? It's bad enough having to sleep on the ground outside, but why should I learn to fence?"

"To be ready," said Aven. "We all have to be prepared for anything. We could have to deal with bandits, wolves, who knows." She looked at Vallan who had disarmed Headon in barely five seconds. "However, all we need to do is send Vallan in front. Right. Hmm. You two dullards - you both attack him at once. See if you can give him any sort of challenge."

Angered at the contempt in her voice, Felde flung himself at Vallan. Jorvund watched them sparring for a moment and then joined him. But it was uncanny. Even with them both trying to get through his guard, Vallan reacted instantly. His blue hands moved too rapidly for them to see as he parried their attacks. After a few moments he knocked Felde's stick out of his hand, whirled round, hit Jorvund on his side, and sent him flying.

"Hah!" Vallan said, as Iselle laughed and clapped.

"You're so fast. Strong too," Jorvund panted as he got up. "How do you do it?"

"I don't know – it's instinctive. I know what you are going to do, even if you are behind me or there are several people attacking me. I've always been quick, and the City Guard training has made me quicker and stronger too. But it just seems to work like magic, this knowing. Go on, try to hit me."

Jorvund obliged, but Vallan blocked him as soon as his arm came up.

"See. I knew what you were going to do before you even moved."

"'Tis amazing. How many can you fight at once?"

"I've gone up against seven, in the City Guard, that was the most. And they managed to beat me. I couldn't cover all of their moves, even though I knew what they were about to do. That was single-stick. And they were gifted fighters too. I'm not sure how many ordinary people I could tackle. A dozen, probably. Maybe more."

"Great Powers!" exclaimed Jorvund.

"It's a pity we aren't all as good as Vallan. We'd be invincible," said Aven. "Well, I've decided that we'll ride all day, with a brief rest for lunch or to buy supplies, then set up camp an hour before sunset. We'll share the tasks between us, each doing different jobs each time, and we'll train every evening."

CHAPTER 11
TRAVELLING SOUTH

Felde, Jorvund and the Hued came down to the plain and crossed the Saroche River. A cold wind blew clouds across a pale sky. As they rode over the bridge, they could see the deer parks, walled estates and manor houses of the Hued, nestled among hills crowned with beech hangers, but Hueron itself remained too far away to be seen.

By the time they began climbing the hills south of the plain, Felde found himself weary and bored. Instead of the adventure he had looked forward to, they had done nothing except ride and train and ride and camp. A persistent drizzle had set in, lasting for several days so far. The ridge of hills they were crossing lay shrouded in mist, water dripped from the trees, and the road stretched on for miles through the forests. The rain drove them to spend the night at an inn in a tiny village, where they paid to have their soaked clothes washed and dried.

Next morning dawned drier but still gloomy, with lowering clouds. The road ran along the side of a steep hill, hemmed in by pine trees and a rocky bank, and the only sound came from the clop of hooves and the jangle of bridles. Felde could hear nothing else, not even birds. He nudged his horse forward to where Aven and Iselle were talking at the front.

"It seems too quiet to me," he said. "We ought to scout ahead."

"Don't be so jumpy. We won't be attacked this close to Hueron," Aven said, shrugged, and turned to the others. "Well, we'll humour your nerves. Iselle, get your bow ready.

Swords loose, everyone."

As the road turned a corner, Felde glanced back and caught sight of a blurred shape on the bank behind him. He shouted a warning as a man, carrying a dagger, ran out from between the trees and dashed downhill towards them. Then Felde heard, from Iselle's bow, a soft twang and a whirr, and then again. He turned. More men ran towards them from the rocks and trees ahead, but Iselle had already brought two down. One had an arrow through his neck, the other clutched his shoulder and fell backwards, with the shaft of the second arrow sticking through his fingers. Iselle put another arrow to her bow.

Aven yelled, stood up in her stirrups with her arms wide and her symbol in her hand. Then suddenly she was gone and an eagle, brown and huge, flew at their attackers. Its claws wrenched their shoulders and its curved beak jabbed at their eyes. Felde stared at it, then recalled himself and looked around. Another four men behind him had ambushed Headon, Vallan and his brother. It was all too fast. I've got to do this, he told himself. I have to do something! Breathing in, he drew his sword. He felt a sudden sting in his calf: the first man had reached him, flailing at him and cutting his leg. Felde ignored the pain and brought his sword down hard. He heard a crunching, splintering sound as the blade hit, then the man collapsed in a mess of blood and bone. Struggling against a rising nausea, Felde heard Iselle scream. The eagle flew into the face and eyes of one man. Another man had broken free, and grappled with Iselle. He tried to pull her off her horse as she fought to get at her knife. Felde rode up and struck at him. The man screeched wildly as blood spurted, then he too collapsed. Felde dismounted and ran to where the eagle attacked the remaining man. Its claws gripped the man's head as he swiped wildly upwards at the eagle's wings with a dagger. Felde slashed again. His sword cut through the flesh and bone of the man's legs. He fell. Felde rammed the point of the sword into his chest, then looked around.

Vallan, Headon and Jorvund stood, panting, clutching swords and knives. Three of their attackers writhed and groaned, with red blood pooling around them. The fourth tried to crawl away, still clutching a dagger. Blood poured down Jorvund's arm. Iselle stared at the other five dead men and looked like she was going to start crying. The eagle circled slowly overhead. There were no more attackers. It was over. The sweat on Felde's face cooled, he took a deep breath as his heart restarted. It had all happened too quickly and he felt sick. He'd never even injured someone, apart from minor bruises and cuts, but now he had hurt and killed.

Headon rapidly inspected his and Jorvund's injuries.

"They're not too serious," he said. "They can wait a short while, and we ought to leave, in case there are others. Get the packhorse and Aven's horse. Get clear of here. Aven can fly ahead and scout for us."

They left the attackers where they had fallen and rode as fast as they could. The eagle flew on in front, sweeping from side to side, then, after a couple of miles, it landed on the road in front of them, shimmered in the air and Aven stood there. She looked pale.

"Stop," she whispered, staggered sideways and fell.

Headon leapt off his horse and ran to her. He knelt beside her and checked her breathing and her pulse.

"She's fainted, but there's no injury," he cried. "We'd better move her, then rest and get your wounds treated."

They moved Aven to a narrow strip of grass under the trees on the side of the road and put folded blankets under her head. She opened her eyes, clutched her wren tightly to her chest, and murmured, "I'm fine. Just need to rest...", then her eyes closed and her head rolled back.

"Hmm. She'll come round soon, I'm sure," Headon said. "Right, Jorvund. Let's look at your arm. Take your jacket off and roll up your sleeve."

The cut was long and deep. As Headon cleaned and probed it, Felde could see a glimpse of white bone in the gory and bloodied flesh. Jorvund's face looked grey and taut.

"Head between your legs, Jorvund. Don't faint!" Headon said.

He pulled his oval green stone out from his pocket, put it by the open wound and held Jorvund's arm. As Felde watched, the blood stopped flowing. The gaping slit closed up, the flesh merged and knitted together. Felde stared with open mouth as the wound healed until all that was left was a long red line that then faded to a thin scar.

Headon sat back, wiped some specks of blood from his jacket, and sighed wearily. "Done. You'll always have the scar though. And you've lost some blood so you'll feel tired for a few hours. Lie down, while I look at Felde's leg."

He inspected the cut, then put his stone back in his pocket.

"Small, no longer bleeding, not deep, and not much blood loss. Fortunately I think your trousers and boot got most of the damage. I'm only going to clean and bandage it. That's all it needs."

As he finished dressing it, Aven stirred and opened her eyes. Headon went to her as she sat up.

"You fainted," said Headon. "But you didn't seem to have any injuries. Were you hurt?"

"No, of course not. But I stayed transformed for too long. It drains me. Don't fuss, Headon, I'm all right. How are the others?"

"Fine. Only two injuries but I've treated them. We can carry on in about fifteen minutes or so. Jorvund needs to stay lying down for a short time."

Aven stood up, put her wren back on her shoulder, and turned to the brothers.

"You fought pretty well for dullards. Almost as good as City Guards. And you were right to be jumpy. Though I'm surprised to be attacked so close to Hueron."

"Probably because we're not wearing our uniforms," said Vallan. "So they thought there were no City Guard with us. I recognised one of them from the inn last night. The thin one with the scraggy black beard."

"Strange," said Headon. "For them to take a risk like that - attacking Hueds, even ones without a guard escort."

"We should avoid staying in villages or inns," Aven said. "I think, from now on, we need to keep our journey as private as possible."

Headon and the others nodded.

"Right. And whoever's in front needs to keep a sharp lookout," Aven said. "I'll scout ahead more with my bird. Iselle and Headon, you take it in turns to keep your bows ready, with arrows to hand. Vallan, and you two dullards, swords loose. We'll be in Peveque in three days. I doubt we'll be attacked again before then, but we'll be ready if we are."

When they next stopped, Iselle burst out, "How dare dullards like them attack Hueds! The nerve! Filthy, scabby dirt-rat villagers. Curse them! When I get to Peveque and see the estate manager I'll have them punished. I'll have their village razed to the ground. They'll learn not to attack us."

"Nay!" shouted Felde. Iselle turned, startled. Aven paused from tethering her horse and stared in haughty surprise at him. He flushed. "Didn't you see how thin they were – how hungry?" he said. "They were half-starved and they must have been desperate to attack us with only three daggers and one sword between them! You rich, spoilt..." he paused and shook his head. He remembered the stories in Helsund about the massacre the Hued had inflicted on the villagers. About how the City Guards had arrived with swords unsheathed and sharpened knives. About how all the men and women had been made to line up, their hands bound behind their backs, and, while the children sobbed and the blood stained the earth, every tenth one had been executed. Their heads pulled back by their hair and cold blades slitting their throats.

"Leave it!" he said. "We killed most of them. The injured ones won't be able to work for months. That's punishment enough! Just leave it!"

Aven glared at him then rolled her eyes sky-wards, but the others nodded agreement. Iselle bit her lip, then glanced at Felde. He turned his head away and he pretended to tighten his stirrup. Iselle moved towards him. He saw her lift her hand, as if she meant to touch his shoulder, then she looked back at Vallan and turned away.

That evening, Iselle came up to Felde as he cleaned and honed his sword.

"Felde, I'm sorry about what I said about those villagers. Will you forgive me, please?" she said.

Felde paused then nodded.

"Give me your hand, then."

Her fingers against his tanned skin were like rose petals, warm and soft. She smiled, then went and sat by Vallan, leaning close to him as he put his arm around her. A few minutes later Felde looked up and their eyes met. She gazed at him, with firelight reflected in her eyes and glowing on her fuchsia curls, and her hand held her symbol where it rested below her throat.

Sarielle came into the kitchen of the house in Langron. The fire had died down, even though it was early in the evening, and Berrena sat at the table, gazing into the distance and twisting a strand of her hair round and round her fingers. When she saw her mother she stood up and flung herself into her arms.

"Goodness, Berrena, what is the matter? You're freezing and no wonder. Why is the fire almost out? Why haven't you lit any candles?"

Berrena only clung shivering to her mother. Sarielle held her, rocked her to and fro, murmured, "There, there, it will be all right, whatever it is."

Eventually Berrena released her, shook her head and wearily sat down.

"Right. First things first. Put this around you," said Sarielle, taking off her cloak and wrapping it around her daughter. "Let's get the fire going and some light. I know it's spring, but you still need some light and heat." She fed pieces of kindling into the grate, poked the embers into flames, and lit a candle.

"That's better. Now, Berrena – what's wrong?"

"I slept badly last night. Then after I came back from the school the house was empty and Felde wasn't here and I, well, I forgot how late it was. I'm so fearful!"

"Fearful? What about?"

"Tis Iselle!"

"Iselle? I don't understand. Why are you afraid of her?"

"She's ... she's ... I don't know how to explain it. She ain't trustworthy. She frights me!"

"Berrena! How can she frighten you?" asked Sarielle, too concerned to correct her daughter's Talthen grammar.

"She might ... no, I might be wrong. Mother, what do you think about Iselle?"

"You know what I think. She's just a silly, mercenary flirt – but what can you expect with a father like that? She's had a string of men, mostly older men, cronies of Mavretan. Powers alone know why she's taken up with Vallan. Except it's probably because her father told her too. I'm sure she doesn't really love him. I wish he'd never met her!"

"I think you're right. She doesn't love him. But why is she going with him?"

"Vallan said she wanted to return to Peveque. He said she was really looking forward to going back there. She lived there until she was sixteen, apparently, and she sees it as her home."

"Oh. But even so, I don't like her going with them. She can't be trusted! She won't be loyal to Vallan, I'm sure! But it isn't that that frights me. Tis Felde. Tis her gift!"

Sarielle sat next to Berrena and took her hands.

"Dearest, no one knows what her gift is. She doesn't use her symbol."

"Oh, doesn't she? People think she doesn't. Vallan doesn't know what it is, does he?"

"No, she told him she doesn't need to use it. Like

Mavretan. Maybe they're giftless? They're both really secretive about their gifts. But there are other people like that. My uncle Lauden, for example, he..."

"Mother! That's not the point! Will you listen? I know what Iselle's gift is!"

"Oh! Goodness, how? And what is it?"

"Her symbol – the one that she always wears on her necklace. She can use it to attract men. To make them infatuated with her."

"What? Powers above! Is that how she's trapped Vallan? The – the cunning prim-faced flirtatious money-chasing slut!" Sarielle stood up and clenched her fists. "I knew there was something strange about it! When he gets back we'll tell him. He'll have to break their engagement then. But, Berrena, how do you know? Are you sure? Who told you?"

"Nobody told me. Tis my gift, mother. You know some of it. But you don't know all. I can tell people's characters, if they can be trusted, whether they mean good or evil. I can tell whether they're lying or speaking truth. If they're Hued then I know what their gifts are."

"No!" exclaimed Sarielle, and sat down next to her. "Berrena, that is amazing! Truly? But you never mentioned anything like this!"

"No, I didn't. Tis strange, but for most of my childhood I thought I was normal. It wasn't til I was eleven or twelve that I realised that no one else was like this. And I realised that I couldn't tell anyone. No one wants to know that someone else can read their character, know if they are speaking the truth, just by looking at them."

"By the city walls, Berrena! So you can read me?"

"I know what you are like anyway, mother. I don't need to. But others – I know them inside and out."

Sarielle took her daughter in her arms.

"Oh, my poor, gifted daughter," she murmured. "Why didn't we know this? We could have kept you with us in Hueron."

"Mayhap. But that's a different thing." exclaimed Berrena, striking the table. "The important thing is that I know what Iselle's gift is!"

"Oh, Berrena, but it is so strange! To know all about other people's gifts. I've never heard of anyone with a power like that. But I'm confused. What has Felde got to do with all this?"

"I saw her watching Felde and I could tell she liked him. I knew what that look meant!"

"You mean she liked Felde? That she might try to get him to fall in love with her? But that's terrible! Do you think she will? That Felde will – will become infatuated with her?"

"Don't think I don't trust him! I know how loyal he is and how much he loves me! But if Iselle decides she wants him, what chance have I got of keeping him against her and her gift? That's what I'm frightened of! Why did I persuade him to go? Oh, why didn't I go with them?"

Berrena impatiently dashed the tears from her eyes.

"I should have gone!" she cried.

"You couldn't have, you know that," Sarielle said, soothingly. "And he wanted to go. Don't worry so much!"

"I should be with Felde! I know I've never learnt to fight, I ride like a sack of turnips, there's the school work. It didn't seem like it was my part to go with them, but these are stupid, tiny reasons. I should have gone!"

"My poor darling, calm down! Don't fret so!"

Berrena shook her head. "I tried to warn him, I did. I said, be careful, don't trust Iselle, she's too young, too selfish, too flirtatious. But he didn't really listen. And how could I have said to him: don't bed her? I've got to trust him!"

"Berrena, dearest," said Sarielle, holding her close and stroking her gently. "Don't worry. Felde and Jorvund are Talthen, Iselle's Hued. They aren't rich or important enough for her. She won't be attracted to them."

"I'm attracted to Felde."

"I know, but that's different. You were brought up

among Talthen. Iselle wasn't. Don't worry. He'll come back. He promised. And she won't be interested in him."

She wrapped the warm cloak more closely around her daughter. Berrena leant her head against Sarielle's shoulders, and sighed. "Mayhap," she said wearily. "Aye. Mayhap you're right."

CHAPTER 12
PEVEQUE

The travellers came out from the forests and rode up a steep, gorse and boulder-strewn slope to the crest of a high wind-blown ridge. Ahead a smooth ride led down to a broad valley. Black-faced sheep fed on the grass, while creamy lambs gambolled around them. The afternoon sun came out from behind the clouds and shone on dense woods and rolling hills, and glinted off the ripples of a lake below them.

"Look! You can see where Peveque House is!" exclaimed Iselle. "Oh, I'm so glad to be going home! I was born there. The house is lovely, so lovely!"

"I thought you were a city girl," said Headon.

"No! I lived in Peveque til I was sixteen. That's where I learnt archery, and horse-riding. I'm so looking forward to seeing all the people there! Zarcus, and the grooms, and my old nurse, and the house-keeper...I haven't seen them for years."

"I doubt we'll get there tonight," said Aven. "Anyway, I'm glad to be out of those forests and have an open view and grass at last. Hmm, it's a good road downhill. Tempting place for a gallop."

"Great! I'll race you to the lake!" exclaimed Vallan.

Aven rolled her eyes, but put her spurs to her horse and raced off, leading the way. The other Hued followed her and sped down the hill, scattering nervous sheep around them as they went. Felde hesitated, then glanced at Jorvund.

"Some might still be in lamb," he said. "The Hued don't care, do they?"

"I know. But tis late for lambing here," Jorvund replied.

"Tis further south. Anyhap, the damage has been done now. We may as well catch them up. Show them how good our horses are."

Aven frowned as they overtook, and Felde could hear her shouting and whipping her horse as they galloped ahead. As the ride levelled out they came to a flat lawn between the road and the lake, with a group of ash trees to one side. When they others arrived, Jorvund said, "Campsite here, do you reckon?"

"No!" Aven snapped. "Far too close to the road."

She stalked off, towards a small clearing in the midst of a stand of rowan and alder.

"Better here," she said. "Right. Get unpacking."

"Can't stand losing," muttered Jorvund to Felde with a grin, and grabbed the horse's reins. As he tethered the horses to the trees, Headon said, "That was an excellent race. Both me and my horse needed a gallop."

"Your horses are impressive," said Vallan. "Better than any City Guard horses."

"Yes," said Headon. "How do you breed them so fast?"

"It's our job - our livelihood, ain't it?" said Felde, with a shrug.

As the others set up camp, Felde got the fishing rods and nets out and went to the water's edge, where a sliver of stony beach merged with roots and grass. Fish rose as the sun fell, and Felde watched the rippling circles spread wide and intersect in the dappled water under the reddening sky. Absent-mindedly, he bent down, picked up a flat stone and flicked it over the water. It reminded him of trying to impress Berrena by the millpond in Langron, years ago. He remembered how she had kissed him. With a jolt he realised he had not thought about her for days. How could he have forgotten his wife? When they had first set out, two weeks ago, he had gone to sleep every night with his hand on her heartbeat, but he hadn't for several nights now. Tonight, as he slept, he would keep his hand there. The intertwined loops on his palm, the ring on his finger, were a reassurance and a reminder. He placed his hand on the Binding, listened to the faint rhythm of her heartbeat, and knew she was well.

Late the next morning they rode through the gatehouse of Peveque House. Large beech trees and broad lawns lined an avenue leading to a gravelled courtyard in front of the entrance. The house was a wide, high dignified building in grey stone. Felde counted twelve windows on each side of the column-flanked porch and thought it more like a palace than a house. Langron Manor was tiny compared to this, yet it had always seemed the epitome of luxury and elegance to him and his brother.

As they neared the house a pot-bellied Hued man, with a genial orange face, wearing a tight black jacket with gold buttons, came round the corner of the building. Iselle called "Zarcus!" and he trotted up to them and raised his hand, with a broad smile on his face.

"Iselle, my lady! What a delightful surprise! Ah, such a long time...years, isn't it? You've grown into quite a beauty, you little minx, you!"

Iselle dismounted, shook his hand and kissed his cheek. "This is my friend, Zarcus Trouville, the estate manager," she said to the others, and Zarcus bowed low. He called for footmen and stable boys to take their horses and bags, then conducted them into the house. The butler and housekeeper, both dressed in black but with pale blue skin and hair, bowed and curtseyed low. The hall, with its marble floor and fireplace, carved oak staircase, inlaid tables and gilt-framed portraits was opulent beyond anything Felde could imagine. He gaped at the high, painted ceiling and ornate plaster frieze.

Iselle tossed her jacket onto a burled elm side-table, twirled round with her arms wide, then fell into Vallan's arms. "By the gifts, I'm ready for some luxury after all that riding and sleeping outside!" she exclaimed, and kissed him.

Felde was startled out of sleep by the sound of a

housemaid pulling back the curtains. He sat up in bed and stared at her, as she curtseyed to him.

"Good morning, sir. There's hot water on the washstand for you, and breakfast will be served in the small parlour in half-an-hour," she said and left. Felde washed, shaved, dressed and went downstairs, wondering where the 'small parlour' was. The butler met him in the hall and bowed deeply to him.

"This way, sir," he said and ushered Felde through two vast sitting rooms into a much smaller room. It had a table set out for breakfast. Jorvund was already there.

"Don't know about you, but I can't handle all this bowing and politeness," he said, lifting silver lids from serving dishes. "Look at this! Sausages, ham, mushrooms, smoked fish, bread, fruit, porridge; tis ridiculous, when half the Talthen are nearly starving. And the bed! Did you sleep? I nearly suffocated, twas so soft!"

"Aye, I know. I don't like all these servants treating us like Hued Lords, but I'm happy to eat like one, this once," replied Felde. "We'll be back on short rations soon enough. We may as well make the most of it."

The others joined them while Felde and Jorvund worked their way through platefuls of eggs, toast, mushrooms and bacon. They all ate their fill, then Aven leaned back in her chair, stretching her legs out in front of her and putting her hands behind her head.

"By the walls, it's good to be back on proper food," she said. "But we mustn't forget our mission. I'll give us one day's rest, then we'll leave early in the morning."

"What! Why can't we stay longer?" said Iselle. "We've hardly got here!"

"We have a job to do, Iselle," said Aven. "We're not on a pleasure trip."

"I've had enough of all the riding and sleeping outside. I'll stay behind and wait for you!"

"Don't be irresponsible! We might need you. You're the best archer we've got. I'll consider staying longer on the way back. But we have to keep going. Spring is nearly over."

Felde decided that, despite the overwhelming luxury, Peveque House was an ideal place for recovering from a hard journey. Servants washed and mended their torn and dirty clothes and ran deep baths filled with soothing essences to ease tired muscles. Their horses were rested and groomed and fed the best oats. Sun shone on green lawns as they idled away a couple of hours at the archery butts, supposedly practising but actually doing very little.

In the afternoon they gathered in the library to look at the maps Zarcus had spread out on the table for them.

"Zarcus, get us a copy of the parts of the map south of Peveque," Aven said. "By first thing tomorrow, if possible."

"Certainly. There is a scribe in the town, I can arrange for him to copy it for you this evening."

"Good. So, some of the Magi came through Peveque recently. Where did they go?"

"And what did they do while they were here?" asked Headon.

"They didn't do anything in particular," Zarcus said. "It was five years ago, and there were only two of them. The town wasn't in any difficulty, the flocks and herds and crops were all healthy, and no one asked them for anything specific. The Magi gave a general blessing to everything and everyone and went on their way. But earlier than that, when all six of them came..." He sighed. "Ah, it still makes me feel sad even twenty years later."

"Sad?" exclaimed Headon.

"Yes, sad about it, everyone did. They passed through, just healing a couple of people. Then the next day, the daughter of one of the farmers - a pretty sweet little lass, only twelve years old - she went missing. They searched everywhere, even looking down the well. Someone thought to ask the Magi, so they sent a rider after them. He said they gazed into their rings and whispered strange words, then said the child had gone into the forest and been killed by a bear."

Iselle gasped. "By a bear? Oh, Zarcus, that's so, so desperately sad!"

"Yes. Her parents were devastated. They had younger sons but she was their only girl and they idolised her. Ah, I'll never forget her mother's wailing... They searched the forest for miles but didn't find any trace of her or even any trace of bears, which was odd."

"No trace of any bears?" said Headon. "But the Magi could have been wrong, couldn't they? Maybe it was a wolf or wild boar?"

"Who knows?" shrugged Zarcus. "Anyway, that was twenty years ago. To return to your question. Five years ago the two Magi went south of Peveque, heading home-wards, on the south-eastern road to Tagrinne, there," and he indicated a tiny hamlet deep inside the forests.

Felde and the others bent over to look at the map. After Tagrinne the road ran through two smaller settlements, then south-east through more forests. It ended at a range of mountains, labelled 'The Crevenne Mountains', and then there was only the edge of the map with a tiny arrow pointing south and next to it the label 'To the Sheiran Desert'.

"Any idea what is beyond the mountains?" said Aven. "How far is it to the desert, anything?"

"No," said Zarcus. "No one's been that far and come back. The forests are dangerous and so are the mountains, high and usually snow-covered. If the Magi live beyond them there must be a pass somewhere, but who knows? Also, you need to be wary before the mountains. The area up to the forest edge is controlled by the Hued, and the towns and villages acknowledge them as rulers, but not beyond that. You'll have to be well-armed and vigilant."

"Of course. We'll get our weapons sharpened, and can you get us more arrows and a spare bow?"

Zarcus nodded.

"Oh, and another thing you'll need," he said. "Lots of

water bottles. You should be able to get plenty of water on this side of the mountains, but you don't know how many days you'll have to journey through the desert. Best take as much water as you can carry. I'll go and get that sorted for you."

They left early next morning. Iselle hugged and kissed Zarcus as she said goodbye to him, and pointedly sulked as they rode through Peveque. Headon and Vallan stared, with appalled expressions, at the ramshackle, half-derelict houses and thin, hungry people. Even Felde and Jorvund, who'd known the poverty in Helsund, were shocked at the destitution in the town. Barefoot children in ragged clothes crowded round them, unashamedly begging. Weary labourers, picking stones off fields or pushing ploughs through the dusty earth, stopped to stare at them with gaunt faces and resentful eyes.

"It looks like the Magi's blessing didn't last long," Jorvund muttered to Felde.

"I keep thinking that it's wrong," said Headon. "This poverty, I mean. We shouldn't only be trying to help the Hued. The dullards need help more. Sometimes I'm not sure whether this commission of Lord Sapphireborne's is right or not. Whether finding the Magi on behalf of the Hued is the best thing to do."

Felde twisted round in the saddle to look at him. "Do you mean that?" he said.

Headon nodded.

"Best thing or not, we said we'd go," said Vallan, "and we've got to finish it. Anyway, what can we do? It isn't anything to do with us, and there are lots of other towns and villages equally badly off."

"Well, once we've got help from the Magi, we should be thinking about helping dullards," said Headon.

"But we have to do something to keep the Hued gifts," said Vallan. "First things first. If we lose those, we won't be able to help ourselves, let alone anyone else."

"Yes, but we can do something here," Headon said, dismounting. "I'm not going to just ride away."

Aven tutted. "Headon, this is just a waste of time!" she snapped.

"Perhaps, but we can spare an hour. Iselle, do you know where the town chief lives?"

Iselle shook her head so Headon asked one of the children, who pointed to a slightly less dilapidated two-storey house further down the street. Headon knocked and entered. When he came out several minutes later he said, "Their harvest failed. I've left him money to buy food. There must be some traders passing through that they can get food from. They probably need seed as well. Iselle, when we return, you can get Zarcus to give them something from the estate, can't you?"

"Yes, I suppose so. My father wouldn't be pleased, but he needn't hear about it," she said, looking at the scrawny children around them. "Poor little mites. Yes, I'll ask him."

Felde glanced at Iselle and she smiled briefly at him. It was kind of her to promise this, he thought. Berrena was wrong: Iselle could be trusted. She was generous and thoughtful. And she was very pretty, despite her strange pink Hued skin and hair.

Early morning sunlight slid through the cracks in the shutters on the bedroom window and disturbed Berrena. She rolled over, murmured and reached her arm into the empty space beside her. The void and coldness woke her and she fought to return to her dream, to the memory of Felde holding her, to kisses and caresses and rolling with love in his arms. But the fugitive dream had gone. She sat up and put her hand on the Binding. Was it getting weaker? She couldn't tell. What was happening to Felde?

The doubts and loneliness drove away any chance to sleep more, despite the tiredness draining her and the early hour. She would light the fire, heat some apple juice and honey, and wait until Laithan came to feed the horses.

In the kitchen, she sat at the table, stared at the empty chair opposite her and warmed her hands on the hot mug. Surely this weariness and nausea were unusual? Again, like yesterday and the day before, the sickness rose in her throat and she grabbed a bowl and retched into it. Counting back the weeks, she calculated: two weeks since Felde left, and I last bled seven or eight weeks before that.

It's true.

She laid her head on her arms and wept.

CHAPTER 13
THE FORESTS

The travellers arrived at Tagrinne a few days later. It was
nothing more than a small cluster of houses, a few fields
overshadowed by the trees of the forest, and a ramshackle
inn. Aven, Headon and Felde went into the inn to ask for
news of the Magi, while the others stayed in the yard behind
to stable the horses. Inside the gloomy room smelt of beer
and stale sweat. Three dark-skinned starved-looking men sat
at one of the tables with mugs of beer, and a worn woman
with an apron dried tankards at a bar in the corner. Felde
noticed that one of her eyes was swollen and closed, and a
dark bruise bloomed on her cheek. Aven ordered beer and
bread and food. As the woman went through to the back to
fetch the food, the innkeeper came in. He was a gaunt man,
taller than Felde, with a broken nose and missing teeth.
Pouring the beer, he cursed violently on finding the barrel
was empty and strode off into the back.

Aven, followed by Felde and Headon, went over to the
men at the table.

"You!" she said. "You lot! Do you know anything about
the Magi? Do you know where they live?"

"The Magi? What be Hued swine like thee doing coming
through asking about them? And why should we tell thee?"
one growled.

Her hand shot out. Before he could move, her dagger
was at his neck.

"Dullard scum," she hissed, pressing the edge into his
throat. "You should be more polite."

Felde frowned, but before he could protest, Headon said

"Aven, let it go. We need information, not a brawl."

"Right," Aven said, taking the dagger away and pointing it at his face. "You heard what he said. Then answer me. And if you lie to us, we'll find out so don't try it. And don't even think of attacking us. Some of us are Hued City Guards."

"All right then, my lady. The Magi - all of they - came through here. Twere a long time ago though. We get one or two passing through sometimes. Last time twere a few years ago. Two of they came through. They were going back home, their servants said."

"Where did they go?"

"They went south-east, through the forest."

"Where does that road go to?"

"Dunno. Just through the forest, then over the mountains. Never been that far."

The sound of shouting came from the back and then a thud, as if someone had fallen.

Aven nodded. "Right. You'd better be telling the truth. Where's that food?" she said, and strode back to the bar.

"Did the Magi do anything while they were here?" asked Headon.

"What does thee want to know for? And what be going on – coloureds and Talthen and City Guards all coming through a place like this?"

"We can't tell you, but it's all right," Felde said. "We just need to know something about the Magi."

"Oh, aye. Well, guess there ain't any harm in telling you," one said. "A horse was lame and they cured it. And the innkeeper here, he were sickening with the plague, like to die, and they healed him."

"But I reckon his wife wished they hadn't," another man sneered, nodding towards the back, "and his daughter too. Pregnant and won't tell who the father be, but we can guess."

A young girl came in carrying a tray with bread and cheese and six bowls of stew. She had thin arms but a swollen belly. Her dark hair fell forward and shadowed the most subdued and unhappy face Felde had ever seen. She put the food on the table and scuttled out as the innkeeper came back with the beer. He was a little more help. He told them that the road went through two more villages in the forest and it was about ten days journey to the end of the road and start of the mountains. He also confirmed that the Magi came from over the mountains, somewhere in the Sheiran desert.

Aven nodded to Headon and Felde. "Good. We're on the right track."

The forests after Tagrinne were dark and oppressive, with trees growing close up to the road. They passed through two more tiny settlements, with thin, sullen villagers stopping work to watch them as they rode down the narrowing road. Tall pines and evergreens hid most of the sky and they rarely saw the sun. A cold wind came down from the mountains ahead and shivered the treetops above them. The empty road started to climb, winding through thick woods and tangled thickets of aspen and rowan. They saw no more villages or houses or people and hardly any wildlife; only an occasional deer darting over the road or a swiftly running mountain hare.

On the ninth day from Tagrinne the road widened into a grassy lawn, scattered with patches of brambles and nettles. The clearing was edged with hawthorn bushes and tall chestnut trees, and bluebells glowed indigo in the shade of the forest. Two ancient oak trees spread stout branches over one side of the grass. At the far end three wide paths led southwards into the forest.

"Well? Which path, Aven?" asked Headon.

"I don't know! Look on the map!"

According to the map the road continued to the edge of the mountains. They decided to rest while Aven's bird scouted the three paths. After an hour it returned and Aven told them that all three paths faded away after a mile or so.

"Stuck!" exclaimed Vallan.

"We must have taken a wrong turning somewhere," said Headon.

"No," said Aven. "We've followed the Magi's trail. They had to have come this way from Tagrinne, there's no other route."

"'Tis been twenty years," said Felde. "Mayhap the right path's got overgrown."

"Overgrown? I doubt it. Who has kept the other paths clear? No – they're decoys, to stop people finding the way to the Magi's home. There will be another way. I'll scout further ahead to find it. But it could take hours."

It was a warm afternoon and the quiet glade, flickering with yellow butterflies dancing in the dappled sunlight, was a pleasant place to lie on the grass, watch the clouds drift over the sky, and wait. But sooner than they expected the wren flew into the clearing from between the two oaks.

"There is a fourth path!" Aven exclaimed. "It doesn't start until about a quarter of a mile from here, but there's a way through. Saddle up and follow me. We'll have to lead the horses for a bit."

She led them between the two oaks and they picked their way between tree trunks and creepers and low-hanging masses of ivy. Felde and Jorvund strode in front and slashed at the greenery to make a way through. Suddenly they reached the start of a path that climbed upwards.

"I was right," said Aven. "A good clear path, wide enough for two horses."

"The Magi don't want people to find them too easily, do they?" said Headon. "I hope this doesn't mean they're unfriendly."

They threaded their way uphill through a dark stand of ancient trees, festooned with mistletoe and clematis. The path came out into a sunlit coomb sprinkled with golden-flowered gorse bushes and small birches. A tiny stream ran downwards through the grass towards them. In the brightness the honey scent of the flowers filled the still air. To the south was a high mountain range with cliffs and ridges, white with snow, reaching high into the sky.

"The Crevenne Mountains," breathed Iselle. "They are beautiful. I had no idea how huge they'd be. Look at that snow and the light on those slopes over there!"

"Yes," said Headon, pointing at where steep, rocky shoulders loomed sentinel over a gap in the procession of white sunlit peaks. "Beautiful, but I'm glad to see there is a pass. I don't fancy climbing those, not with horses too."

"We won't be able to cross before nightfall, and there may be higher passes beyond that," said Aven. "We'll go on until the sun starts to drop low, then camp. I can send my wren on ahead so we know what we face tomorrow."

When they stopped she sent her symbol flying ahead. As it returned, Aven held it in her hands for a few moments, with her eyes closed. Then the wren flew up and settled on her shoulder and she told them that there was another higher pass beyond the first, but nothing worse.

"How does it work?" asked Jorvund. "Do you see what your bird sees? Or does it talk to you?"

"How does it work?" Aven echoed mockingly. "You're as curious as Headon. Well, I don't mind telling you. I don't know. I've no idea how it works. It doesn't talk to me and I don't see what it sees. But when it returns to me it gives me knowledge – like pictures or a faint vision – or more like a just-remembered memory – so it's as if I've been there myself a long time ago. Is that enough for you?"

They camped beside a spinney of rowan trees by the stream and lay by the fire. Felde looked across the fire to Iselle. Her eyes glowed in the light from the flames. Vallan put his arm around her, looked fondly at her and kissed her cheek. Like a lovesick blue puppy, thought Felde. He turned away and gazed at the swathes and veils of cold snow on the peaks. Drifts of clouds trailed like blown scarves from sharp pinnacles and as Felde watched them turn from white, to pink, to blood red in the fading light, Langron and Hueron were forgotten.

CHAPTER 14
DESOLATION

They spent the day climbing steadily upwards, over a pass, along an open valley, then up to another higher pass, until they reached the top and paused in a rock-strewn saddle between craggy, snow-dusted peaks. Ridges of wood-covered hills lay below and beyond them they could see a tumbled empty country that faded into grey desert. Flat and dreary, the desert stretched south to a featureless horizon.

"Your friend Zarcus was right, Iselle," said Headon, "We're going to need those extra water bottles. Let's hope there are some streams."

They rode downwards. After an hour or so they came to a spring and followed the trickle of water downhill for several miles before the sunlight faded.

The next day was clear, with a blue sky, and the rising sun shone brightly on their camp. Felde thought he could see where the path started to cross the desert plain. Mid-afternoon the path turned away from the stream and they filled the water bottles and drank as much as they could, not knowing when they'd find water again. But a few miles later they came to a still and reed-fringed lake, surrounded by alder and willow trees with a good clearing nearby for their evening camp. Midges, tiny flies and huge emerald dragonflies, of a sort that Felde had never seen before, darted over the calm waters. There were no signs of people or settlements, and Aven had stopped scouting ahead. The country was desolate, the forests quiet, the winding path the only indication that anyone ever travelled this way.

"Where is everyone?" asked Headon.

"I don't know," answered Aven. "I've never been anywhere so empty. Even the far northern borders, right on the mountains, have more people than here."

No wind blew and, apart from the shrill piping of birds in the trees, a strange quietness surrounded them. Tiny lizards scuttled over the stones of the path and ran to hide in the sparse grass on the side. Presumably, thought Felde, this path was only used by the Magi, and rarely at that. He wondered how it stayed clear of encroaching shrubs and brambles. Perhaps some uncanny power haunted it and kept it open, he thought. As he dismounted, a magpie rose from the long grass and skirred past his horse with its long wings flapping. Startled, Felde flinched and his horse shied, but Jorvund caught the horse's bridle and steadied him with a hand on his shoulder.

"Careful there," he said. "No need to be so jumpy, tis only a bird, not a ghost. Mind your horse."

"You mind your own horse, little brother," Felde retorted.

"Not so much of the 'little brother' now," Jorvund grinned and slapped Felde on the back. "I'll beat you most times, sword or stick, and you know it."

He glanced over to where the others had started unloading their horses, and continued in a quieter voice, "When we've unpacked, shall we try Vallan again? I think I've worked out his weakness. He leaves his right side open too much. If I bear hard towards him on the left, I think you could slip through his guard on the right."

"Do you? Aye, let's try it. Tis about time someone defeated him."

As Felde unstrapped the bags from the horses he glanced across to where Iselle knelt, getting the cooking utensils out. Her jacket was loose, her shirt unbuttoned so he could see her symbol, deep purple in the shadow between her breasts. She looked up and smiled at him with rose-red lips above white teeth, then she glanced downwards. He caught his breath and moved towards her. Then he saw, on the other side of the clearing, the dark shape of a bear lumbering unseen towards the girl. Its ivory teeth glinted above a red tongue, its snout sniffed around the grass. He shouted and ran towards her. She straightened up in surprise. He threw his arms around her, pulled her down and rolled on top of her to shield her. She gasped and looked into his eyes as he lay on her. For a long moment he gazed at her face and felt her breath on his cheeks. The temptation to kiss her was too strong to resist, but a scared cry from her broke the stillness.

The beast was there, its breath stinking as it roared. Its claws swiped down, ripped through his shirt and skin, and sank deep into his shoulder. Hot pain exploded across his back. He could not stop himself screaming. The bear sank its teeth into his flesh and shook him like a dead rabbit. Felde heard Jorvund shouting. The bear dropped him, reared up on its hind legs and roared again and again. Trying to ignore the agony in his back, he twisted over to see his brother run up, holding a sword, and slash at the bear, cutting into its flank. The bear turned and its paw thudded into Jorvund's side and knocked him down. His sword flew aside. Felde staggered towards the weapon as the bear lunged at Jorvund and tore his throat.

Suddenly there was a flash of blue as Vallan's arrowhead symbol appeared and jabbed again and again into the bear's fur, then Vallan ran up and threw his sword hard into the bear's side. Felde, reeling with pain and terror, got to his brother's sword, grabbed it and struck wildly. He stabbed through the black fur of the beast as it lifted its bloody muzzle from Jorvund's neck. The huge body shook and the bear roared again, tried to stand, but fell forward onto Jorvund. Vallan plunged his dagger into its head. Felde collapsed to his knees. Iselle started screaming.

By the time the others had run to the camp and they'd managed to drag the heavy carcass off Jorvund, it was too late. The bear had torn away most of his throat and neck and shoulder. Blood drenched the ground. His body lay crushed and broken.

The realisation hit Felde like a hammer blow, far more painful than the throbbing cuts on his back. All of his remembered life Jorvund had been there; working with him, teasing him, fighting him, annoying him, encouraging him and quietly helping. How could his brother be dead?

They knelt, in the silence of the empty forest, as the realisation settled on them like a shroud. Iselle started sobbing. Aven looked at Felde and said, "Headon, you had better see to Felde. He's wounded."

Headon turned to Felde and inspected his ripped and gashed back. He laid his stone on the bloody mess and bowed his head in concentration. Felde could feel the skin tightening as it started knitting and healing. But Headon shook his head.

"The wounds are too many and they're too deep for my powers," he said, "but I've done the best I can. I'll strap it up, but you'll have a lot of scar tissue and you'll lose some freedom of movement and strength. It's going to be painful for a while."

The others got the horses to pull the dead bear out of the clearing and Felde insisted that they bandage and cover the gaping holes in Jorvund's neck and shoulder. He sat by the body all night, awake and watching, while his back and heart ached.

The next morning, Aven came up and knelt by Felde. "Felde," she said, "We have to do something for Jorvund. We can't bury him, so we will build a pyre. Is that all right?"

He nodded. "Not on the path. The other side of the lake," was all he said.

The others piled dry leaves, brushwood, branches and twigs as high as they could on a grassy area where a stream ran down into the lake. They wrapped Jorvund in his cloak, placed him on the pyre, with his sword in his hands and brushwood piled around him. Aven lit the leaves and twigs. They watched the flames and swirling white smoke reflected in the water.

"He was a brave, strong, capable man. We will miss him," said Aven. "Do you want to say anything, Felde?"

His mind was numb and he could not remember what should be said or done. But at last some phrases from his father's funeral came to him, and he said, haltingly,

> *The Powers above take you.*
> *The Powers judge you.*
> *The Virtue of your strength,*
> *The Virtue of your courage,*
> *The Virtue of your endurance,*
> *The Virtue of your life,*
> *The Powers accept you.*

And they stood, with heads bowed, until the fire died down and all that remained were ashes and charred timbers, a darkened body, and a blackened sword.

They stayed there another two days to give him time to recover. It was Felde who insisted that they didn't wait any longer, so that his brother would not have wasted his life on a pointless journey. If it wasn't for that thought, he would have turned around and gone straight home.

As they travelled on, Felde's back and shoulders throbbed. He would be scarred for life. The blood he had lost left him weary and the misery of his brother's death lay on him like a shadow. The thought of telling Ingra and Laithan and his wife haunted him. And Kianne too. The grief it would cause them! How could he bear to tell them? He put his hand on his chest to feel the rhythm of Berrena's heartbeat, and sadness drowned him. If only they had never started on this long, hard journey. If only Aven had scouted ahead properly. If only he'd seen the bear earlier. If only Vallan had been faster coming to their aid. If only Jorvund had not been so brave. He wanted to revile and hate the Hued for their failure to save his brother. But that would not bring him back. He wanted to stop, fall to his knees and break down into tears. But he kept riding on.

As they rode downwards the sound of water, splashing down rocky pools and over pebbles, accompanied them. They crested a slight rise and saw the featureless desert miles ahead of them, stretching on and on to a distant hazy blur. The next day they came out from the low hills onto level grassy ground covered with tiny yellow and white flowers. The stream continued for a few hundred yards and then sank into the earth and the grass abruptly became rocky, gritty sand. Ahead there lay nothing except grey desert. The path was a faint smudge leading south.

"We'll fill up all the water bottles and drink as much as we can before setting off," said Aven.

"What about the horses?" said Headon. "They have to drink too, and they'll never get across that. We have no idea how far it is."

"It must be feasible to take horses. The Magi cross it."

"Yes, but they are Magi. It's too risky for us. We should leave the horses behind."

"How can we do that? They'll run off. We need them to get home," Vallan said.

"Well, they can't come with us. It's too far and too dry."

"We need them with us. We can't walk all the way back to Langron."

"I'm not walking over that desert for miles, we have to ride."

"Can't you scout ahead, to see how far it is?"

The discussion went on and on. Felde sat apart, gazed aimlessly ahead and wished it was all over, wished he was away from these stupid arrogant Hueds and their selfish plan. But for Jorvund's sake, he'd go on to the end, see these Magi, get what the Hued wanted, then head home as fast as he could.

Eventually the others agreed to ride the horses, but turn the packhorse loose in the hope that it would make its way home. Aven frowned. "We can only carry enough water for a few days. So we'll travel three days before we turn back - unless we reach a well or a settlement or the Magi's home. It's going to be hard. And risky."

Early the next morning they rode over the dividing line where the stream disappeared and the grass turned into sand. Rode into an ordeal of raging heat in the day and bitter cold at night under stars glittering in the void of the sky. The sharp chill of the nights pierced Felde's wounded aching back so that he could hardly sleep. In the morning the rising sun's warmth poured down for a brief time of bearable light and heat, then the fierceness of its glare and the parching thirst silenced them. They rode on and on, along the desolate rocky path and through the empty brightness. Twilight brought a short relief, but they struggled to set up camp and to eat, exhausted by the draining heat. By the third day they were on their knees and panting with weariness and thirst.

"We can't manage another day," Aven gasped. "I'll have to scout ahead."

She lifted her symbol and her wren flapped weakly away into the dust and brightness. They crouched in the shadows of the kneeling, exhausted horses for what seemed like hours until the wren returned. Aven lifted her head. "At last..." she muttered. "There's a haze of green about fifteen miles ahead. We can risk carrying on..."

After shivering through another freezing night, an hour before dawn they set off as fast as the parched, tired horses could manage. As the sun rose and the scorching heat and dazzling light grew around them, they saw the blurred shapes of trees and low hills ahead. Almost fainting with heat, leading their staggering horses, they stumbled towards the greenness.

Then they paused. The dusty grit and rocks of the desert

stopped and fresh grass started, as if someone had drawn a line between the two. The trodden sand of the path became a broad road, lined with trees and paved with cream-coloured stone. The travellers stood in amazement at the sudden transition from dry dirt to lush, verdant foliage. As they reeled over the divide the air shifted. It became cool and refreshing. The haziness vanished. Clouds, little puffs of white froth, appeared in the pellucid sky. There was a lake ahead and a valley between forested hills. Looking back, there was nothing but the unending grey of the desert.

"Wonderful," breathed Iselle.

"We must be nearly there," said Aven. "Powers above, though, I'm glad to see water ahead!"

They stumbled on towards the lake and drank their fill of its cool, clear water. Even Felde's misery lifted when he gazed at the azure water, with the calm lilies floating on it and a graceful heron, wings sweeping, flying overhead. Everywhere they looked it was beautiful, from the tiny flowers in the grass to the rolling hills, fresh green against a deep blue sky. The road led down a valley through beech forests and viridian fields, and they saw, miles ahead, the roofs and windows of some huge building, with sunlight glittering on glass and tiles.

"That must be their house. It looks too far to reach tonight," said Aven. "We'll stop here instead. By the lake. We need to rest after that crossing."

After they'd set up camp, Felde went into the forest on the pretext of finding more wood. He wanted to remember Jorvund and to mourn him somewhere where the others could not see him. Without his brother he felt as if half of him, the better half, was missing. As he walked, not caring where he was going, he heard a sound behind him. Startled, he turned around. Iselle was there.

"Felde, do you need help gathering the wood?" she asked.

In the twilight there was a subtle glimmer about her. He

shrugged. She came close to him and took his arm.

"Felde, I'm sorry about your brother," she murmured. "You must miss him. I do too. He was so brave! He saved your life, and you saved mine. I want to say thank you."

He could smell a faint scent of roses and he recalled that moment holding her, before the bear struck, and he gazed down into her face, feeling unbearably sad and yet touched by her sympathy. She ran her finger down his cheek and he felt the tears brim in his eyes. Unwillingly, but strangely compelled, he bent his head down and put his lips on hers. He kissed her gently and carefully. Iselle ran her fingers though his hair, and without a word or thought Felde was holding her and she was holding him in an embrace that filled his senses. He kissed her mouth, her forehead, her cheeks, her neck, and he pressed his lips into the shadow of her throat.

"Felde, Felde," she whispered, then stepped back and put her hand to his cheek. "Oh, Felde, I'm sorry. I have tried not to..."

"Not to what?" he asked.

"Not to give in like this. But I can't help myself. Felde, when you held me, before the bear came, I realised how much I wanted you. How good we could be together. Do you not feel this pull between us? You do, don't you?"

"Iselle – I don't know!"

"Don't you feel something for me? Felde, tell me truly, what do you think of me?"

She looked up at him. Her eyes gleamed in the fading light and her hair made a fuchsia cloud around her face. He could not deny that she was entrancing.

"I think you're beautiful. And you're engaged to Vallan, and I'm married," he answered slowly.

"Yes, but they need never know. I won't tell them. Hold me, Felde, just once, just this once. You are so handsome and so brave..."

Her fingers were gentle and warm as she traced them down his arms and took his hands in hers. She lifted his hands and put them around her waist, stepped into his encircling arms and leant into his chest. His heart raced as he felt the warmth of her body, the curve of her back; saw the rise of her breasts, the smoothness of her shoulders.

She reached up and stroked his cheek and lips.

"It seems so strange that your hair and your eyes are a different colour to your face. But I like it. I have wondered for weeks what it would be like to kiss you. I know now. Felde, again, one more time?" she murmured, her voice as tender as summer breezes, her lips as soft as flowers as he touched them with his.

"Felde, I want to know - can you love me?" she whispered.

"Aye - nay – I can't say!"

"You want to say yes, don't you?"

Her scent, the contact of her skin, the feel of her curls on his cheek, it overwhelmed him. He surrendered. "Aye," he said. He could not help himself. He kissed her again and again. She undid the buttons of her shirt, pulled his head down to her breasts, and let him kiss them and the hollow between them. He shut his eyes as he felt her body pressing against him. The longing to have her became irresistible. She reached up inside his shirt, caressed his bare skin and whispered his name. As she ran her hands over his chest, he felt her fingers trace over the Binding and he remembered Berrena. His eyes opened and he jerked away.

"Nay!" he exclaimed. "I won't do this!"

Iselle stared at him with wide, startled eyes. She touched her symbol where it rested at her throat, then slowly did up the buttons of her shirt. She whispered, "You want to, though. As much as I do. You said that you loved me. We can't help this feeling between us, you know that, even if we can keep it secret."

She turned and left him, slipping between the trees back to the camp. He gazed after her and every part of him felt bereft.

CHAPTER 15
THE MAGI

Felde avoided Iselle's eyes and hid his confusion and desire behind surly gloom as they rode on the next morning. They passed small cottages and fields of young corn but they saw no other people. The huge building seen yesterday was hidden from view until the road turned round the foot of a hill. Then they pulled up their horses, gasped and stared.

Not even the coloured city was as glorious or magnificent. Wide stone wings radiated from a circular building topped with a glass dome, a hundred feet high and crowned with a shining golden sphere. The glass in the dome glittered in the morning light, flashing vermilion and ruby and emerald and sapphire. Marble statues flanked the balustrades of staircases leading to arched doorways under pediments decorated with bas-relief panels.

"Magnificent," said Aven. "It has to be the Magi's. At last!"

"Very impressive," agreed Headon. "They must have riches and powers beyond counting!"

Behind the vast building they saw a river flowing to a valley between rolling pine-covered hills. The road became a gravelled path leading to a paved area in front of the dome. They rode up, staring at the ornate urns and gilded figures that marched in procession above the elaborate cornices and friezes of the roof lines, and dismounted, Felde wincing as the wounds on his shoulders pulled. A carved oak double door stood open and before it stood six men, wearing robes of different colours and with wooden staffs topped with pale grey stones.

They were younger than Felde expected wizards to be, in their late thirties, wearing embroidered silk and velvet clothes, and with rings set with bright jewels glistening on their fingers. Felde became aware of how shabby and travel-stained he and the others were compared to these richly-dressed, confident and urbane men. A black-eyed and bearded wizard, wearing an orange damask robe and a heavy gold chain round his neck, stepped forward.

"Welcome," he said, "We are honoured to have such visitors. Aven Lachiare, Vallan Sapphireborne, Headon Alcastor, Iselle Topazborne and your servant, Felde Sulvenor." He bowed to each in turn, and they bowed deeply back. "Enter and eat with us."

He clapped his hands. Six servants in grey tunics came and took their horses, and he led them inside.

The travellers paused in awe. The vast room spanned over two hundred feet, big enough to hold all of Langron market, Felde thought, staring around open-mouthed. It was covered by the dome with its arches of thin steel, interspersed with a filigree of copper holding shaped glass in emerald, azure, topaz and ruby. The golden sphere above them gleamed through the coloured glass and the sunlight cast rainbow patches of radiance onto the white alabaster floor. Six wide silver doors led from the room. Between these doors were fireplaces and smaller doors in panelled oak. In the centre a fountain splashed into a black quartz pool.

"We will eat and drink first," said a Mage in sky-blue robes, with a clean-shaven face and deep blue eyes. He led them to a long table, laid with vases of flowers, white linen, crystal glasses and glittering cutlery. "I'm sure you are hungry. The servants will show you where to wash and refresh yourselves. Then sit, eat, and we'll discuss why you have come all this way to see us."

Servants brought fine white bread, creamy cheeses, fruit, fresh juices and pure water. The Magi were courteous and affable, asking many questions about their journey and the country they had passed through. Felde wondered what their names were, but when he glanced at them, so confident, so rich, and looked round at his companions eating and talking naturally, with polite ease, he could not ask their names. Jorvund would have asked, he knew. He looked down at his plate. A servant placed a bowl of fruit on the table near him: clusters of oval, deep red smooth-skinned berries, like giant black-currants. Felde took one and examined it. Aven turned to him. "They're grapes, Felde. Haven't you seen grapes before?"

"Aye, of course I have!" he said curtly, and rapidly ate it, astonished at the sweetness that burst into his mouth. He took a few more, and turned away from Aven. The blue-eyed Mage sat on his other side, bent closely over Iselle and listening to her description of Hueron. He took her hand and kissed it and she blushed and glanced down, showing her long fuchsia eyelashes.

After they'd eaten, the Mage with the orange robes called servants to show them to the guest house.

"We will meet here after you have refreshed yourselves and been shown your rooms. Your bags are unpacked, your horses are stabled and we will arrange for your food and water stocks to be replenished. We are honoured to have some of the Gifted People as our guests and we trust you will enjoy your stay."

He bowed and they returned the salutation. They were led from the dome, between two wings with wide leaded windows interspersed with carved columns, and gargoyles glaring down from the stonework above them, to a plain red-brick three-storeyed house with a slate roof.

"This is the guest house," said the servant. "Your horses are in the stables behind. I will show you to your rooms."

Felde's bedroom was richly furnished and spacious, four

times the size of the bedrooms in the house Lord Dernham had built for him and Berrena. He pulled out his things from his packs, tossed them onto the bed, then checked on the horses. When he went into the sitting room of the guest house, late that afternoon, the Hued were there already, praising the hospitality and wealth of the Magi.

"They must be really powerful," said Vallan. "They'll be able to help, I'm sure! Don't you agree, Felde?"

"Aye, mayhap," Felde shrugged, and flung himself down on one of the brocaded chairs by the windows.

"Oh, I'm sure they will," said Iselle. "I've never seen anything so glorious as that dome, the stained glass, the size of that room. And the food! Even this house, it's just a guest house, but it's still wonderful! So rich! I always thought Peveque was the most luxurious place possible, but this place!"

"So they are even richer than the Hued?" Felde said. "Well, good for them, but don't go on about it!"

"Felde!" snapped Aven. "How dare you talk to Iselle like that!"

Headon came over to Felde, put his hand on his shoulder for a moment, then looked out of the window at the flower-filled gardens, the pools and fountains. "What happens now, Aven?" he said, turning back. "Do we just wait here for them or go to find them?"

"We'll just have to wait. I assume they'll summon us." Aven said.

In the early evening, a servant came and led them to where several red sofas surrounded one of the fireplaces in the room under the glass dome. The scent of lilies filled the air. The descending sun shone scarlet and amber and gold through the coloured panes. Presently the Magi joined them.

"Well, honoured guests, tell us why you have journeyed so far to see us?" asked the tall Mage in orange robes.

Aven explained Dernham's fears about the Hued's

declining powers and why he thought the Magi might help.

The six wizards glanced at each other

"We will not help you," one started to say, but the tall Mage stood up. "We need to consult on this," he declared, and swept out of the room with the others.

The travellers waited in silence for several minutes, then Headon wandered around the room, examining the veined marble mantelpieces, the carved and tapestry-hung walls, staring up at the multi-coloured glass of the dome.

"They have to be able to help. Look at this! These tapestries, the fireplaces – I've never seen such fine marble. Those six doors are solid silver!" he exclaimed. "And the roof!"

He looked up at the huge bronze lanterns that swung overhead, suspended from fine chains.

"The weight of it – all that stained glass, those lanterns, and that huge sphere must be heavy, and yet the supports are so thin. It must be held up by something else, but what? Do you think that sphere is real gold?"

"It can't be. But even so, they must be incredibly powerful," said Vallan.

"Yes, but why is it taking them so long?" asked Aven. "What are they discussing?"

As she spoke the six wizards returned.

"We have considered your request," the tall Mage said, and shook his head. "Sadly, we cannot help you. This is a complex and ancient matter, about which we know little. We..." He paused. "Our precursors taught us much, all they knew, but nothing about the history of the Hued's gifts. We know of no bargain between wizards and the coloured people. That must be a later addition to an old legend."

The other Magi nodded in agreement.

"What?" said Aven. "After all this, you can't help us? No, I don't believe this! No!"

"But you are so powerful. Are you sure? Is there nothing you can tell us?" said Headon. "Are we losing our gifts? There must be something you can do!"

The tall Mage shook his head again. "No, there is nothing. It is true that your gifts are fading. Lord Sapphireborne is correct in his suspicions. The only thing we will say is that the Hued should consider what might be the source of their powers. That is the key, finding the source of the Hued power, but we cannot help you any more than that."

"You cannot help? You must know something! Lord Sapphireborne was certain you'd know what was going on," said Aven.

"I fear that we are unable to offer any help or advice apart from suggesting you investigate where your gifts come from."

"But how do we do that?" asked Headon.

"I cannot tell you," the Mage shrugged.

"Then we have failed," replied Headon.

"By the walls!" exclaimed Aven, flinging her hands up. "This is unbelievable! How can that be all you can give us? Hints about investigating the gifts – what use is that? You must know more than that!"

"No," replied the Mage. "All we know is that whatever gives you your powers is failing."

"How can you be so sure?" said Aven.

"Believe me, my dear Aven, we know." The Mage nodded. "For the same reason that Lord Sapphireborne knows. But our knowledge has limits. We do not know where your gifts come from. I find it strange that you, you Hued, do not either. Has it never occurred to you to find out? No? Well, that is the only help we are able to give you."

"Sir," said Headon, "if that is true, will you come back to Hueron and help us? Powers only knows what will happen should our gifts fail."

"Come back to Hueron? You are joking, surely! No! We are bound only to help the Talthen. We do not expect nor intend to help you further. This problem is something that only the Coloured People can solve."

Aven muttered "Curses!", strode to the fireplace, gazed

down at the flames and bit her lip. Felde realised that his brother had died pointlessly, and turned away. He leant over the pool, staring down at the gold and silver fish in its clear depths. So their mission had been a waste of effort and life. He bowed his head, wincing as the cuts on his back tightened. There was a long silence.

"This is difficult news for you. I can see you did not expect such a disappointment," said the Mage. "But we have no more to say about this matter. Instead, maybe there are things we can do for you personally. We can give strength and healing."

He went to Felde and touched his back. A blaze of actinic light shone from the stone on his staff. The throbbing aches in the wounds from the bear vanished. Felde flexed his arms and shoulders, suddenly free from pain and stiffness, looked up at the wizard and said a reluctant thank you.

"Now we will eat," the Mage said and clapped his hands. Grey-clad servants brought in bottles of chilled wine and dishes of roast meats, herb-covered buttered vegetables, and savoury sauces, and silently served them. The dinner was superb, but Felde and the Hued said little, except for Iselle, who clearly enjoyed the exquisite food and wine, and chatted happily about Hueron and Peveque to the blue-robed Mage.

It was late when they left. The Magi asked that, when they were ready to leave in the morning, they would come to the dome to say farewell.

That night Felde half-feared, half-expected Iselle to knock on his door. But no knock came. In the morning he was furious with himself for feeling disappointed. How could he have even looked at Berrena, if he'd betrayed her? But Iselle was beautiful in a way that seduced him. She said they were meant to be together. She was right. It would hurt Vallan and Berrena, but there was nothing he could do to avoid that, and they'd find other loves. Perhaps he and Iselle should tell Vallan the truth. He'd have to accept it. Then they'd leave and he'd take Iselle back — to where? To Langron? Flaunt his unfaithfulness to Berrena? He fell to his knees, feeling the ring on his finger, looking at the intertwined lobes of the mark on his hand. I can't, he thought. I promised Berrena I'd return to her!

He put his hand to his chest to where the Binding was, to feel the rhythm of his wife's blood beating in him. But the rhythm was strange. It was too irregular, too fast. What was wrong? He stood, his hand pressed to his chest, feeling Berrena's heartbeat, a terrible fear in his mind. Then his senses told him he was feeling two beats. The steady, reassuring beat of her heart and a faster, lighter, 'pat-pat-pat' of some other rhythm, some strange additional dancing beat. He realised with a gasp - it was a baby. A baby's heartbeat! Berrena was pregnant! He was going to be a father. Delighted, amazed, longing to tell someone, aching to see Berrena again, he stood, feeling the double beat, praying for it to keep going, longing to be home.

As they prepared to leave, Felde could not hide his elation. Reluctantly, he told the others Berrena was pregnant. He did not mention the heartbeat, but said that it was a dream that he knew to be true. Aven looked haughtily at him and curtly said, "Congratulations." Iselle flounced away with an irritated look.

"Wonderful news, Felde. I rather like the idea of being an uncle," said Vallan, shaking Felde's hand vigorously.

"Excellent. I am pleased for both of you," said Headon. "You will want to get home as soon as possible, won't you?"

They packed and rode to the Magi's house. Outside, the six wizards were waiting, solemn and stately.

"Your horses have been provisioned and you should have ample food to return home. Also we have taken the liberty of putting a bag of gold coins on each horse. We hope you will accept these," the tall Mage said.

They dismounted and returned thanks, bowing deeply,

and the tall Mage acknowledged their thanks, his orange robe billowing around him. But he continued, "However, we ask one thing. You are free to go, but my colleague has a request."

The blue-eyed Mage stepped up to Iselle and looked into her face.

"I ask that Iselle stays. She is willing to remain here, so you must accept this, and leave without her," he said.

Vallan looked at Iselle in astonishment.

"Iselle! Is this true?" asked Aven.

"I thought you were going to marry Vallan!" Headon exclaimed. " And that you wanted to return to Peveque!"

Iselle nodded and said, "I want to stay here. You go home without me. This is where I want to be, with this Mage," and she moved closer to the wizard.

Vallan seized her arm. "What? Iselle! No!" he cried, but she shook her arm free.

"Vallan, yes. I am staying here," she said.

"Iselle?" Headon asked. " I don't understand. How can you have changed your mind so quickly?"

"I just have," she said, in a firm calm voice. "I want to stay here. You must go home without me."

"You must leave her," said the tall Mage, sweeping his arm around Iselle. "As you can see, she wishes it. We give you our blessings for a safe journey home and send our greetings and regrets to Lord Sapphireborne."

He, Iselle and the other Magi walked into the dome and the door slammed behind them.

Felde stared at the shut door in astonishment. Despite what she had said, now Iselle wanted this wizard instead of him or Vallan? So his choice had been made for him, and he did not have to fear what Iselle might say or do on the way back. Despite this, his feeling of disappointment seemed almost as strong as his relief.

In silence, they rode as far as the forest and then Aven paused, turned in her saddle to look at the distant buildings, stared at Vallan's stunned face, then dismounted.

"We need to talk," she said. "It seems wrong to me. We've got no help from the Magi and now Iselle says she wants to stay behind. There's something strange going on."

"I don't understand it," said Vallan. "She promised she'd marry me. Why has she changed her mind? I'm going back!"

He wheeled his horse round, but Aven grabbed him.

"We talk first!" she insisted. "Then we go back!"

They stood by the road, arguing about why Iselle had said she'd stay. Felde said little, but Aven was convinced that she had not stayed willingly. Headon said that he thought she seemed dazed, Vallan argued that she must be under some sort of spell and that he could not believe she did not love him any more.

"Right! We'll go back for her," Aven said, her hands on her hips.

Felde thought of how he and Iselle had embraced only two nights ago. A revulsion seized him. How could he have been so seduced by her? He could not believe what she had nearly persuaded him to do. Fury filled him, surprising him with its intensity, as he remembered her words and caresses, her looks in the moonlight. How could he have thought she was beautiful compared to Berrena?

"Nay! I ain't going back for her!" he exclaimed.

"What?" said Aven. "Why not?"

"Not for her! She's not worth it! She ain't under any sort of spell! She's..." he hesitated.

"She's...What?"

"I don't know! I just don't think she's under a spell. The Magi – they're rich, powerful. Maybe that's what she wants."

"That's ridiculous, Felde. Of course she doesn't want that. You know she wanted to come back to Peveque with us!"

"How can you even think that?" exclaimed Vallan. "She's engaged to me. She loves me!"

"All right! Mayhap you're right and I'm wrong!" Felde said. "But even if she is under some sort of spell then there's nought we can do! Those Magi, they ain't like ignorant villagers or forest bandits. They've got more power than any coloured person. What can we do against them?"

"I don't believe it!" Aven said. "Are you turning coward on us? After all this?"

"Coward?" Felde exclaimed.

"Felde, calm down. Think," Headon said. "We can do something. We must. She needs rescuing. We can't go home having failed in our venture and having left her behind."

"I am thinking! But either she wants to stay, in which case we'd be wasting our time, or she's under some kind of spell. If she is, what can we do against wizards?"

"We can do something. We've got weapons, gifts; we can work out some sort of plan and go back for her."

"Felde, we are going to need you," said Vallan. "Especially with Jorvund gone. We can't do anything with just three of us. We'll need your strength, your sword."

"My wife's pregnant! I want to go back to her!"

"We know about your wife!" Aven snapped. "But he's your brother-in-law. She's his fiancée. You have to help them!"

"I've already lost my brother! That's hard enough! I ain't going to risk any more deaths. I'm going back! We should all go back!"

"What! Go back? Don't be such a dullard coward!"

Felde gritted his teeth and put his hand on his sword pommel.

"Felde, stop. We've got to go back for Iselle," Headon said, placing a restraining hand on his arm. "I beg you. Come with us."

For a long moment he hesitated. How could he tell them what he knew about Iselle? He shook his head. "Nay. I ain't going to risk my life for that stupid girl."

"Stupid girl?" said Aven. "How dare scum like you call her that!"

"I don't believe it," exclaimed Vallan. "You won't help Iselle? I thought we were friends!"

They stood, the three Gifted people, frowning at him. Felde turned round on his heel and went to the horses. Friends? The Magi had called him their servant and they hadn't contradicted it. He untied his and Jorvund's mounts.

"Mayhap I am a coward," he said. "Or mayhap I'm realistic. I don't think we've got a chance. Do you think those wizards will just let her go? That they won't see you coming? That they can't protect themselves against aught you can do? You can be brave idiots, but I ain't. I'm going home. I don't care about Iselle, Jorvund's already dead because of this pointless mission, and I want to see my wife and child before I die."

He turned back to them, hoping for some relenting, but there was none.

"Go on then," said Aven. "Desert us. If you're too frightened to come with us, then I for one don't want a turncoat like you!"

"Headon, Vallan?" Felde asked, turning to them, but they shook their heads.

They made no effort to stop him as he mounted and rode away, leading Jorvund's horse. They did not say goodbye, only watched him leave. After a mile the road turned a corner and he looked back, hoping to see that they had turned and were following him, or that they were waiting for him to change his mind. But the road was empty and all three had gone.

CHAPTER 16
HUMILIATION

The loneliness and regret of the journey back were more than Felde thought any man could endure. As he staggered over the edge of the gritty sand onto the grass and collapsed to drink great gulps from the stream, the horses blowing and snorting and splashing beside him, he felt broken by the heat and the thirst of the desert. But enduring the turmoil of remorse and shame within him was worse. Every morning he had woken with a jolt of misery, remembering Jorvund was dead and his companions were not there. Every mile he had debated whether to turn back. But he'd think of Berrena; expectant, hoping; and know he had to go on. He could not bear the thought of the grief she'd have if he never returned. Not for that slut Iselle's sake, not even for Vallan's sake. So he rode on. As he left the desert and rode up the mountains, on every ridge and hill he paused and looked back for the others, even though he knew that if they met again they would despise him.

"I ain't a coward," he muttered to himself, remembering Aven's words. But he knew he was.

He reached the place where Jorvund had fallen without seeing anything more dangerous than a deer. Dismounting, he stood and gazed at the scorched patch of soil, the pale bones and the blackened sword lying on the pile of ashes and half-burnt logs, before riding on. At Tagrinne he stopped, handed the horses to the innkeeper to stable and went into the inn. It was empty, but there was the same bruised, weary woman washing mugs and the same lank-haired pregnant girl scurrying to bring beer and food. Her left arm was in a sling. As she placed the stew on the table, Felde gestured to her arm.

"What happened to your arm?" he asked.

She bit her lip, glanced back towards the yard, and said nothing. He remembered what the men in the tavern had said and a cold realisation dawned on him.

"Was it him? Your father?" he whispered.

She shook her head, but there was confirmation in her blanched face and terrified eyes.

He took a long draft of the thin, sour beer, then another, then slammed the tankard down on the table. There was no fairness in the world. The Gifted People had so much, shared so little, yet were prepared to travel hundreds of miles on a quest to keep what they had. A failed quest that had killed his brother and that had branded him a coward. And the Magi were as bad, blessing and healing people, but not truly helping them. Look at this innkeeper: cured by their powers! But as far as his wife and daughter were concerned, it might have been better if he were dead. He gripped the handle of his dagger. He could not pass on, leaving that woman and her daughter to be beaten and abused. This whole journey has been a waste of time, he thought, but perhaps I can do one good thing. Something to correct this evil.

He took out most of the gold pieces in his pocket and put them under the empty tankard, then slipped out to the yard. In the stables, the innkeeper whickered gently at the horses as he rubbed them down. Felde paused. What should he do? He would have to threaten him. Violence would be the only thing that would fight this violence. He took out his dagger. As the man turned, Felde grabbed his shirt at the throat and pushed him against the wall, holding the point of the dagger to his neck.

"Get off me!" growled the innkeeper.

"Shut up and don't move!" hissed Felde. "Your wife. Your daughter. Tell me how they got hurt! Was it you?"

"Tain't none of your business! Get your hands off me, you scum," he snarled back. He tried to wrench his head away, but Felde twisted the point, drawing spots of blood.

"I'll do it, I swear," he said. "You leave them alone. I'll come back and murder you if you touch your daughter again!"

"What's it to you? She's mine! I'll do what I like with her, and no one's got any right to stop me. She deserved it. She ain't nought but a slut anyhap and tis her fault. She asked for it, the little whore. If her mother has put you up to this, I'll kill her..."

Felde remembered the snide remark of the villager. "You... it was you. You're the father. You made her pregnant...your own daughter..." he gasped. He let the dagger point fall for a moment, as the horror struck him. The innkeeper struck his arm away and, before Felde could react, smashed his fist into his side. He dropped the dagger and fell, winded, and then the man's hands were round his throat.

"I'll kill you. No cursed northern peasant is going to interfere twixt me and mine," he said, tightening his grip. Felde couldn't breathe. The stranglehold was a burning iron bar, cutting his life, blinding his sight. He fought to break away and as he twisted his hand found the dagger. He flailed, striking wildly again and again at the man's arms and face. The grip around his neck broke and, choking for breath, Felde staggered to his hands and knees. The man writhed on his back, blood flowing from his arm and neck. Felde crawled over to him but as the redness pumped out, he saw that his blade had caught the artery in the man's neck. The innkeeper groaned and thrashed as Felde stared, knowing that there was nothing he could do. He had killed him.

He got up, his legs shaking and his throat bruised, and he reeled across to the horses. With difficulty, he got the saddle and bridle onto one of them. Then he hunted through the pack until he found the bag full of the Magi's gold. He left that hanging on a hook and led the horses out, stepping around the dying man.

The subdued girl stood by the door to the yard. He realised he had bloodstains on his clothes and still held his dagger. She didn't move or speak, but stood like a statue watching him as he mounted and rode away.

Now I'm a murderer, as well as a coward, he thought, as he travelled back. He rode as fast as he could, swapping from one horse to another and making the briefest possible stops. At night remorse kept him awake. He should never have tried to interfere with the innkeeper and his wife and daughter. He should not have left his companions behind. He should have stayed and helped them, whatever the cost. What might be happening to them?

Without them he felt defenceless and exposed; fearful of ambushes and robbers, and he hid in the forests off the road and catnapped during the day, riding through the twilight and at night when there was enough moonlight and keeping watch over the horses when it was too dark to ride. At least I didn't add adultery to my crimes, he thought in the cold depths of the night. Murder, cowardice, abandoning my friends is bad enough. But at least I didn't bed Iselle as well. Berrena will never know that betrayal.

He was weary almost beyond bearing with the journey and the shame when he arrived at his house. Berrena came out into the garden, saw him and rushed to him, sobbing and laughing. He dismounted, falling into her arms with infinite relief, feeling as if his burden dropped from him as he held her.

"Felde, oh, Felde, at last!" she cried, holding him so tightly that he felt his heart would burst. "Hold me! Don't let me go. Oh, Felde, I've been so fearful and so lonely."

"Bee, you shouldn't have feared. I promised I'd come back," he said. "Twere too long a journey, I know. I should never have gone on it. Powers above, I'm glad to be back!"

He held her close, then pulled her down so that they lay embracing on the grass under the apple trees, and kissed her lips and eyes and cheeks. He put his hand on her stomach. She was just starting to swell round her waist. He kissed her stomach, and looked into her face.

"How do you know?" she asked. "I wanted to tell you, but you know already!"

He put his hand on the heartbeat in answer. Every day since he had left the Magi's house, he'd felt the twin rhythms beating to summon him back to his wife.

"I could feel another heartbeat. When's our baby due?"

"Late autumn, in about five months."

"Bee, Bee. I've missed you," he said, caressing her face, her hair and the smooth dark skin of her neck and shoulders.

"I've worn a thin patch on my clothes, just there, feeling for your heartbeat," she said, putting her hand over her breast. "It was a comfort, but only a heartbeat wasn't enough. Tis been so long. So hard being without you."

"Aye, me too," he replied.

He kissed her hand and her breast again and again. She kissed him back, running her hands through his hair and putting her lips to his eyes, cheeks, neck, throat; starting to undo the buttons of his shirt, then rolling aside, taking his hand and standing up, pulling him to his feet.

"We'd better go inside, shouldn't we?" she said, a teasing joy on her face. "One of my pupils might come along the road and I have to think of my reputation."

As he came in from the stables later that day, Berrena asked the question he had been dreading.

"Felde, I've got to know. What happened? Did you find the Magi? Where are the others? I assumed Vallan went to the manor, and Jorvund to Kianne. But, you haven't mentioned them..."

He sat down and stared at his hands on the table.

"Felde? Are Jorvund and Vallan and the others all right?

Where are they?"

"I don't know, Berrena," he said, slowly, shaking his head. "I left them. I had to come home."

"What? You left them?" Berrena slammed her hand on the table. "How could you? What do you mean?"

"I had to come back! I knew you were pregnant. But they wouldn't come. I don't know what's happened to them. Vallan, Headon and Aven, they stayed to try and rescue Iselle. They'll come back as heroes, and I – I'm the coward who left them."

Berrena sat opposite him and bit her lip. "You - a coward? You left my brother, the others, Jorvund? You left them to rescue Iselle while you came home? How could you!"

"Not Jorvund!" Felde paused. He could not bear the expression of contempt on her face. Words came hard, but he had to tell her, whatever she thought of him. "I would never have left him."

"So what happened to him?"

"It was a bear. Jorvund tried to save me but the bear turned on him. It killed him, Bee. My brother - he's dead."

"Jorvund?" Berrena cried, putting her hand to her mouth. Tears formed in her eyes. "Jorvund is dead? Please, not Jorvund! Oh no, poor Kianne!"

"Aye. Bee, I'll tell you everything, but it's so difficult!"

"Go on then." She took a deep breath. "Tell me it all. What happened to Jorvund, to my brother, Aven, Headon. Where are they?"

"Jorvund is – we couldn't bring him back, and we couldn't bury him. We made a pyre for him, on the southern side of the Crevenne Mountains. It was all we could do. Then we went on. To the Magi. We saw them, but it was a waste of time. They didn't know, didn't have, the answer Dernham wanted. Then Iselle wanted to stay but the others, Vallan, Aven, Headon, they thought she didn't really, that she was, I don't know, under a spell or something. They wanted to rescue her. But I didn't."

Berrena got up, walked away and stared out of the window.

"Bee? Please, Bee..." Felde said.

"And you came back, leaving the others, my brother, behind to rescue her? Why didn't you stay with them?"

"I did it because I knew you were pregnant, and twas hopeless anyhap, they'd never save her, not against those Magi, and I couldn't not come back, not when Jorvund wasn't coming back too..."

"I don't understand. Why were you ... a coward? Just tell me, Felde," she said, turning back to him. "Tell me the whole story!"

"Powers help me, Bee, but tis hard! I've got to tell my aunt, my uncle, your parents as well. And Kianne. Bee, come with me. We'll go to the manor and I'll tell you and them everything. I don't think I can bear to tell it twice."

Felde sat on the edge of the sofa in the sitting room at Langron Manor, staring at the carpet, his head low. Dernham sat opposite, his fingers stroking his chin as he listened. Berrena had moved away from Felde to sit on the other side of Sarielle. As they'd walked to the manor she'd been quiet, her face stony, and she had kept still and silent while he had told them of the journey, the bear attacking them, and how they had found the Magi's dwelling. Ingra had burst into tears at the news of Jorvund's death, and Laithan's gaunt face looked ten years older than his fifty-odd years.

"I am sorry about Jorvund. He was a brave man." Dernham said.

"Yes," said Sarielle, wiping her eyes. "Oh, it is so terribly, terribly sad! Felde, you must miss your brother so much!" She leaned forward and patted his hand.

"But you did find the Magi?" Dernham said. "Good. And what did they say?"

"They said nothing. Nothing of any use. They said they didn't know anything about the history of the gifts."

"What? Oh, no!" Sarielle said. "Dernham, we were so sure that they would know!"

"We were. Was that all that they said?"

"I remember they said you were correct about the gifts fading. That whatever gives you your powers is failing."

"Truly?"

"Aye. And they said that you should think about what might be the source of your powers. Something about that being the key. And that was all. They refused to come back with us either."

"Oh. That is very little help. I am greatly disappointed, greatly," said Dernham, frowning. "At least we have some confirmation of our fears, but what use is that?"

"The source of our powers being the key?" Sarielle said. "By the city walls, what could that mean, Dernham?"

"I do not understand. To be honest, no one understands where our powers come from. But it is clear that the journey was a waste of time and effort and, worse still, the waste of a life. I should never have asked you to go on it. I am truly sorry about Jorvund's death. If I had known ... But, Felde, continue. What happened to my son, to Aven and the others?"

"Yes," said Sarielle. "Please - where is Vallan?"

Felde could not bear to say anything about Iselle's attempt to seduce him and how he had killed the innkeeper, but he told them how Iselle had stayed and how they'd argued about rescuing her. When he said how he'd left the others Sarielle gasped, "Vallan - he's still there? He didn't come back?" and seized Berrena's hand.

"Nay, but - they could be another few weeks," said Felde, shivering at the cold expression on Dernham's face. "I rode back without stopping and they'll probably stay at Peveque. They'll still return, I'm sure. It took me only thirty days to get back - tis faster travelling alone. It had taken us over five weeks to get there. So the earliest they could possibly return is next week."

"I see," Dernham said. "All we can do is wait and hope

that they return."

Outside the manor house, Felde paused. The humiliation of admitting to his cowardice burned. But he realised that he ought to say what had happened with Iselle. It was some explanation for his actions and now that they knew the worst of him, there was little point in keeping that failure hidden. He turned to Berrena but she put her hand up to stop him and stepped away from him.

"There's something more, ain't there, Felde?" she said. "You haven't been completely open. You haven't said everything that happened."

"Aye," he admitted. "There's more. But mayhap - aye, I want to tell Lord Sapphireborne and Laithan first. Bee, can you walk back with Ingra? And you'll have to tell Kianne about Jorvund."

"We will, but I wish we didn't have to," she said. "You know that it will break her heart. But, Felde, you have to tell me everything. The whole truth."

"I will. I'll tell you afterwards, I promise."

She only nodded. As she and Ingra walked away, Felde turned to Laithan.

"Bee's right. There's something more I have to tell you and Dernham. Tis about Iselle."

Dernham gestured for the two men to sit.

"You had better tell me the whole truth, Felde," he said. "What else happened?"

Felde told them, running his hands through his hair as he admitted everything about Iselle, how she'd approached him, how they'd embraced, what she'd said.

"That's why I didn't go back with the others," he muttered. "She didn't deserve them risking their lives for her, but how could I tell them that? It wouldn't have helped and Vallan would never have believed me. And I never wanted to see Iselle again, let alone die in some stupid attempt to rescue her. Not when Jorvund had gone. I'd promised Bee that I'd come back !"

"I see," said Laithan, quietly. "Twas a hard decision."

Dernham nodded, "Hmm, I think I understand. I still think you should have stayed but, as you said, I can understand why you would have been reluctant to risk your life for her."

"I should have stayed for Vallan, for Headon, for Aven's sake. I should have stayed with them!"

On the way back, walking across the fields with Laithan, Felde turned to him. "Laithan, I hate myself! To have kissed Iselle like that! I nearly did worse. What if I had? Laithan, I was so tempted!"

Laithan sighed. "You didn't. At least you stayed faithful to Berrena."

"I was expecting her to come to my room that night. Thank the Powers that she didn't." Felde's voice shook. "If she had - Laithan, I would have lain with her! I would have given in! I was going to tell Bee, but how can I tell her that, when I as good as betrayed her with that - that worthless flirt?"

He dropped his head into his hands. A coward, a murderer and a would-be adulterer. This added worse to what was already bad. Was there nothing good he'd done on that cursed journey?

"You have to tell Berrena," said Laithan wearily. "Tis bad enough as it is without lies too. You have to be honest with her."

In their bedroom, kneeling on the floor in front of Berrena, with a single candle giving a faint light, Felde told her everything. He anxiously watched her face but she was inscrutable. As he said how he'd kissed Iselle she turned her face away.

"I'm sorry..." he muttered.

"Sorry? And is that all you can say?"

He shook his head. "Bee..."

"I knew something like that had happened," she said, turning back to him. "You didn't listen to me. I warned you about her."

"Bee, I should have. You were right. But she seemed..." he paused.

"Seemed honest? Seemed trustworthy? Felde, I know what she was like. And she's gone now. Along with my brother!"

"Mine too! I lost my brother too! But, Bee, do you understand? Is it all right?"

"I don't know."

"Don't - you're not going to leave me, are you?"

She hesitated. "No. We're bound, ain't we? Though I can't forget it. I thought it would be enough that you came back to me. But it hurts. What you did with her, even though it wasn't the worst, it still hurts. And my brother, Vallan – you abandoned him too."

"I know. Don't remind me!"

"How easily did you give in to her, Felde?" she asked, holding his face in her hands and looking straight into his eyes. He could not look back at her eyes, at the tears glistening in the black irises, and he dropped his gaze. Berrena lay down, turned her back on him and pulled the covers over her shoulders. Felde knelt on the floor, still and silent, and watched the flickering shadows cast by the candle, until it guttered and went out.

A week after his return, Felde rode south to watch for the return of the others. As he went through the market square the traders and passers-by greeted him with questions about how his mission had gone, where Jorvund, when would he tell them the story of his journey, was there going to be a celebration feast? He shook his head and rode on silently, hearing the muttering and whispering of the rumours growing behind him. The third time, when he returned, dispirited and alone, Berrena was standing in the garden, watching for him.

"Still nought?" she asked.

"Nay. No sign of them. They should be here by now. Something must have gone wrong!"

"Oh. I wish they'd come back. But - why do you look for them? They ain't going to be happy to see you."

"I don't know! Tis stupid, I know. I never want to see Iselle again and they'll never want to see me. But I want it over, done with. This not knowing is almost worse..."

"You shouldn't have abandoned them, then, should you?" She turned away and strode into the house.

Days, weeks passed, then, as he returned from another futile ride south, shaking his head as he rode into the yard, Berrena greeted him with a look that was less stony, and almost forgiving. As he dismounted, she took his hand. His glance questioned her and she nodded.

"Tis all right, Felde. I'm all right now. Though it does matter, and it does hurt. As far as I know, I've lost my brother. But I can cope," she said, and he put his arms around her.

"Thank the Powers," he said, burying his face into her silky hair. "Thank you."

"I've some news for you." He was delighted to see that she smiled at him. "I know you'll be pleased. I am too. Tis about Kianne. She and Jorvund were very fond of each other, you know."

"Aye, I think everyone did."

"More than fond, it seems. She said that, a few weeks before you left, Jorvund had told her he loved her and asked her to wait for him so they could marry on his return. It turns out that they didn't wait for marriage. Typical Kianne! She always was one who would eat her plum before baking her pie. She's pregnant. Oh, Felde, it is good news, ain't it?"

"Jorvund and Kianne? Jorvund was going to be a father too? Oh, Bee, I can't take it in. Tis too much. He should be here, with her."

"I know, but tis still good news," Berrena said, taking his

hand and placing it on her swelling stomach. "Kianne's baby is due about a month after ours. The two will grow up together. They'll be cousins. Kianne can help us with ours, and we can help her too."

His brother's child and his, together? An unexpected gift, a small consolation for the grief he had wrought and endured in the last few months.

CHAPTER 17
TREASON

Dernham came slowly into the drawing room, holding a letter. "Council business. They want me to return to Hueron. But, Sarielle, how can I? How can I go back, without knowing?"

"I know. Oh, Dernham, it's been weeks," Sarielle exclaimed. "Weeks and weeks...Unbearable!"

"Should we try to find them? I think we should travel south and search for them."

Sarielle jumped up. "What? Should we? But... but what about Berrena? The baby! Oh, Dernham, you know how much I want to be here. To see our grandchild!"

"True. There certainly isn't time to travel past the Crevenne mountains and back," Dernham said, pacing around the room.

"And suppose they come back on a different road?" Sarielle said, taking him by the arm. "We could miss them on the way!"

"You are right. We are better waiting for them at Hueron. Or here."

"Dernham, I've been thinking. Don't you feel it's likely that Iselle decided to seduce one of the Magi? It would be just like her to want all that wealth and attention."

Dernham nodded.

"Well, if she did, than Vallan and the others will return, I'm sure. They can't rescue her if she doesn't want to be rescued. We must still have hope! Honestly, it has been only two months since Felde returned. They may be riding slowly, or have stayed at Peveque for a week or two."

"There is always hope. Sometimes I wish that there wasn't. It would almost be easier..." Dernham said. He feared, but would not say out loud, that Vallan and the others were dead. That they had been attacked and murdered by bandits, or they'd tried to rescue Iselle and died in the attempt.

They left for Hueron a few days later. As they rode, Dernham tried to think of the right words to use to tell Thera and Cairson that their son and niece were missing too, but he couldn't. There was nothing he could say that would lighten the blow. There was not even any helpful wisdom from the Magi to sweeten the bitterness. Dernham pondered the Magi's words, 'The Hued should consider what might be the source of their powers, that is the key', but could get no guidance from them. The phrase tantalised more than it elucidated. Surely the Magi must have some knowledge of the source of the gifts' powers, in order to have said that? Or was it something obvious that they expected him to know? He thought and thought, looking at the marking on his palm, turning his blue quill symbol over in his hands, wondering what gave it its life and power. Was the clue to the whole puzzle staring him in the face? But he could make nothing of it. The whole failed venture had been a tragic waste of four lives, including his only son. Regret was too weak a term for the cutting, wearying sorrow that he felt.

As they rode into Hueron, Dernham noticed cold looks and heard muttered comments in the streets. Rumours about his son and three others being missing, and that he was behind the disappearances, must have been spreading. Cairson and Thera, when he told them the news, were even more hurt and grieved than he had feared, and Thera bitterly, furiously, told him that she would never forgive him for the loss of her son. The council meetings that he had to attend were long and pointless. He tried to persuade the council to reduce the taxes on Helsund, but was voted down. After a few weeks he stopped going, and sat in the living room, idly turning the ring on his finger.

"Dearest, don't give up," Sarielle said, sitting next to him and taking his hand. "Please, don't give up!"

"I can't carry on, Sarielle. When I went out, last week, I could hear the taunts. They are calling me a dullard-lover and a traitor."

"Ignore them! They're idiots: cruel, horrid, wicked idiots! They don't know anything about you!"

Dernham shook his head.

"Shall we go back to Langron?" Sarielle said. "Berrena's baby is due in only a few weeks. Let's go back, let's see her."

"Maybe," he said listlessly, and stared at the fire. Eventually she put her arms around his slumped shoulders and quietly held him. As they sat in silence, the butler tapped on the door.

"Excuse me, sir, but there is a meeting of the City Council and you are urgently required to attend."

"But the council isn't due to meet today," Dernham replied, looking up. "The next meeting is the day after tomorrow. I wasn't going to go anyway."

"I know, sir, but the messenger says it is a formal summons, and you have to go."

"Oh. Something important must have happened. Well, Sarielle, I'd better go."

He kissed her mournfully and walked slowly out.

As he entered the council chamber, the spectators in the balcony stopped talking and leaned forward to look at him, and a susurration of whispers rippled through them. Confused, he looked up at the arena of curious and hostile faces gazing down at him, and around at the three-score councillors already seated. Mavretan was on the front benches, surrounded by his business cronies. He looked at him with thinly-disguised dislike and triumph. What is going on? thought Dernham. Some pernicious plot of

Mavretan's? Revenge for the loss of his daughter? Thera and Cairson were there in their usual seats. She turned her face away from him, but Cairson nodded and raised his hand, and Dernham's apprehension lessened as he crossed the chamber to sit next to him. The murmuring quietened and the president of the council, a stern-faced woman with pale lime-yellow skin and yellowy-green hair, rose and stood at the lectern.

"This is an extra-ordinary session of the council, called by Sir Ferard Mavretan and five other members, under the rules of 417 post-founding that allow a session to be called at short notice to investigate allegations against council members. Specifically, allegations of treason or actions intended to compromise the security of the city," she said, as a junior secretary behind her took notes. "I require Sir Mavretan to state the reason he has called this session."

Mavretan rose and glanced maliciously at Dernham.

"For a very serious reason," he said. "I have discovered that Lord Dernham Sapphireborne, Madame Thera Redstone and Sir Cairson Watergiver plotted to obtain the aid of the Magi, the six travelling wizards who visit the dullards, in order to overthrow the council, take over the city and share power with dullards."

Dernham's heart beat faster as he realised what this might mean. There was uproar in the balcony. Thera put her hand to her mouth and looked horrified. Cairson thumped the bench by his side, stood up and shouted, "Lies, by the seven Founders! All lies!"

"Silence!" the president called. "This is a grave allegation. Anyone in the balcony who disturbs the council will be removed from the chamber. There will be quiet while this is discussed!"

When the hubbub had died down she turned to Mavretan and said, "Continue."

"Yes, he has plotted to give power to the dullards! We all know how Lord Sapphireborne favours the dullards and wants us to share our goods and money with them."

"No! That is a distortion of the truth - a lie!" Dernham said.

"Sapphireborne! Do not interrupt!" the president snapped.

Mavretan frowned at Dernham, and continued. "Sapphireborne and his accomplices cannot deny that they arranged for Vallan Sapphireborne, Aven Lachiare and Headon Alcastor; together with two dullards, cronies of his; to travel south to find the Magi and obtain help from them."

He paused dramatically, and looked around. "Not only has he plotted against the city, he has lost me my daughter! Vallan persuaded Iselle to join them. She was unaware of the plot, thinking they were merely visiting Peveque, but discovered it after they'd travelled south several days. She was able to get a message to me from Peveque and then bravely chose to remain with the conspirators in order to discover more of their plans. Now no one knows what has happened to her, to my daughter, or to the others."

The audience gasped and murmured, leaning forward to gaze at Mavretan and at Dernham.

"Excuse me one moment," Mavretan said quietly, turned aside, put his hands over his eyes and bent his head for a few seconds, then turned back to stare at Dernham with anger and hatred. "My daughter... My only child, and the others, they are lost because of this plot of his!"

Cairson leaned in closer to Dernham, gently squeezed his shoulder and whispered, "Don't worry. He can't possibly get away with this ridiculous suggestion."

Dernham shook his head. Despite Cairson's assurance, his mind reeled at the magnitude and audacity of Mavretan's scheme. With this accusation, he could get them removed from the council or imprisoned or even executed for treason. Dimness came over his eyes and all he could hear was a dull confusion and Thera loudly contradicting Mavretan. The president shouted again and again for quiet then asked Mavretan to finish his statement.

"I have not much more to say," he said. "We all know

that those Hueds have not returned. They are gone. Aven Lachiare, a competent, experienced Hued, one of our best captains. Headon Alcastor, a great and gifted doctor. Vallan Sapphireborne, his own son! Who by all accounts was the finest swordsman in the guard. And my daughter, Iselle Topazborne, an unparalleled archer, whom I loved dearly. All lost, on some treacherous plan conceived in Sapphireborne's ambition, folly and obsession."

He pointed at Dernham.

"Sapphireborne is responsible!" he exclaimed. "For them, for their loss, for their death - if they have died. Or is he still expecting that they will return, with some powerful help from the wizards, to help him take over the city? Either way he should be tried for treason, for conspiracy, for their fate and for the loss of my beloved daughter!"

The council president nodded as Mavretan sat down, his dark red face full of fury and triumph. She jotted some notes, glanced at the law books by her side, then stood. "We will follow the standard procedure for an accusation of this gravity. Lord Sapphireborne, Madame Redstone, Sir Watergiver; you are on trial accused of treason. Sapphireborne, as suspected leader of the plot, you may speak first to answer these charges. We will then debate and view the evidence over the next few days. Finally, the council will vote."

She paused, consulting the secretary in an undertone for a moment.

"On a charge of this seriousness we require a two-thirds majority for a guilty verdict. We will also vote for the accused to remain on the council. This will require a simple majority. Is that understood? And no one will interrupt or they will be ejected and lose their right to vote. Everyone will be given an opportunity to speak!"

As the president was continuing, laying out the conditions and explaining the procedure, Dernham tried to think how to present the truth in order to save them. Treason meant a death sentence. Surely after all he had done for the city he could not be thought a traitor? Surely no one would believe his rival? The mistiness in his eyes grew and it was hard to breathe. The sound of water was rushing in his ears. Was he drowning? He struggled to stay alert against a dark faintness.

The president stopped and motioned for Dernham to speak. As he stood his legs shook under him and dizziness filled him. He stumbled and almost fell, but Cairson came and supported him, walking with him to the lectern. Dernham gathered all his strength and stood upright, his hands behind his back, turning the ring on his finger nervously. His eyes cleared and he looked around at the council members, at the mixture of curiosity, shock and anger on their faces.

"I have served in this council for almost thirty years," he said. "Never have I tried to assume power or control the city for my own ends. You know my reputation. You know that I have worked only for the safety of the city's people and for their benefit, and also for the benefit of the dullards, believing that our prosperities are inter-related. I have not worked for my own good. No one has ever accused me of any plotting or underhanded scheming, of any lies or deceit, of any attempt to subvert the council or damage the city. Not until today has there been any hint of corruption levelled at me!"

He paused. Tightness was clamping across his chest and the misty blackness was coming back. He leaned forward to rest on the lectern and struggled to continue.

"I have dedicated myself to ensuring our safety, prosperity and peace. You all know that I believe we should help dullards, for that reason, even though you call me a dullard-lover. You know that I believe our powers are fading."

The tightness was painful. The faces of the others shifted and floated in a black mist.

"I had evidence, historical documents..."

He stopped to draw breath.

"A document hinting that the Magi gave us our powers."

Another breath, harder now. The whole room was silent now, except for a pounding noise ringing in his head.

"I knew the council would not support me. I sent them, without you knowing, to get help, advice...not to take over the city..."

His head dropped for a moment, then he raised his eyes. All he could see were faint blurs in a growing darkness. His chest was being squeezed by a vice.

"To get help, to regain the gifts... I'm sorry... I failed... Aven, Headon... Vallan... my son... they... "

He could not continue. The vice crushing his chest closed. He could no longer breathe or see. He collapsed to the floor. The raised voices around him blended into a confused roar that faded into silence as his blue quill slipped off his jacket and fell lifeless to the ground.

CHAPTER 18
THE WHITE SON

The midwife bustled in to the bedroom, nodded with satisfaction to Felde, and gave a steaming mug redolent with spices to Berrena.

"Here we be, dearie," she said. "Now you give the babby to his grandmamma, and drink this. Tis my own tisane. Chamomile, coriander and honey. Twill do thee good." Berrena took the mug and drank, as the midwife continued. "Pretty little babe, ain't he? Pale, though. Very pale. But he's fine otherwise."

"He ain't just pale," Berrena said, smiling at the baby wrapped in a blanket and being rocked by a weeping Sarielle. "He's white. I'm black and he's white. Tis strange, but he's beautiful, ain't he, Felde?"

Felde sat by her, stroked her forehead and cheek and nodded. He could not trust his voice. The child was beautiful, but it was white, with light grey eyes and creamy skin. Sarielle handed the bundle to Ingra, who cooed and gurgled and murmured to it, her eyes glistening as she descended into a stream of babbling baby talk. Laithan stood, a calm contentment on his tired face, with his arm around her.

"Well, I'll leave thee all now. Thee'll have to draw up a rota for the grandmammas to share the babby, I think. Anyhap, a good straightforward delivery. Well done, mother, and I'll come back tomorrow to see thee is all right." She patted Berrena's hand. "And thee can tell me the lad's name then."

She turned to go, nodding at Kianne, who was perched

on the end of the bed. "Twill be your turn in a month's time, poppet!" she reminded her.

Felde showed her out, paying her and thanking her. On his return he stood in the doorway, heart bursting with relief. Poor Berrena! But she looked so happy. She had clearly forgotten the hours of labour. Her hair still hung damp with sweat.

"I think Bee needs to rest," he said.

The grandmothers were back the next morning, vying with each other to help bathe and change the baby, cook breakfast for Berrena and give the impression that both Laithan and Felde were very much in the way. When they had finished fussing and the child was feeding, Felde said, "What shall we call him?"

Berrena looked up from the baby at her breast. He was surprised to see tears on her cheeks.

"I wish my father was here to see his grandson! Felde, can we call him Dernham?"

Felde shook his head. "I don't know. Tis a Hued name, not Talthen. And he's going to be different from Lord Sapphireborne. Bee, I'd rather have a name with less memories."

"Oh. Aye, I see what you mean. You're right," she said.

"How about Riathe?" said Laithan. "From the old stories. You know, the hero from the Feorgath, who tried to rescue those being persecuted in the great wars. Neither a Hued nor a Talthen, but he was a good and brave man."

The midwife returned a month later, as she had predicted, to attend to Kianne. "A fine, stout lad," she said, as the baby roared its entrance into the world. "Thee is going to call him Breck? Tis a good name."

Kianne nodded weepily. "Twas my grandfather's name," she said. "Oh, I miss Jorvund! Why ain't he here?" and burst into tears.

A few weeks later, as they sat in Felde's kitchen while the

two mothers fed the babies, Sarielle said, "Well, I can't work out what relation I am to Breck."

"You're not related to him at all, Mother," Berrena said gently.

"Perhaps not," Sarielle exclaimed. "But I'd like to be!"

"A step-great-aunt-in-law, I think?" suggested Laithan.

"What a mouthful! No, I shall call myself an honourary grandmother to him, whatever you say! I rather like the idea of having two such bonny, healthful, lively grandsons."

"Breck seems lively enough, tis sure," Ingra said. "He wants to catch up his cousin, no doubt about it."

"Aye. He's strong. And bonny," Laithan said. "He's ruddy-cheeked, ain't he, compared to Riathe?"

Sarielle reached over and tousled the soft white-blonde hair of her grandson.

"Riathe might be pale, but he's fine! Fine! He's bonny too, aren't you, my little cabbage? Two lovely boys! We are blessed!"

Felde leant back and gazed into the clear flames of the fire. Sarielle was right; they were blessed to have two such healthy babies. He'd sold two ponies in the market and he'd had a long day working: trading, cleaning out stables and tack, and training young horses; but he felt, at last, some peace and some hope. They had hated having to do it, but with Jorvund gone, Laithan and he had been forced to close the Helsund stables and move all the horses and breeding to Langron. Laithan had said, with a grim look on his face, that losing the income from the stables would bring the village nearly to destitution, but they had no choice. Jorvund's loss would always be there; the repercussions, the grief and the shame of that failed venture would never leave, the death of Dernham had only increased it all; but he would be able to bear it.

Sarielle picked up the battered leather-bound book and looked at the ornate gold script on the cover. It seemed like a hundred years had passed since the day Dernham, full of excitement and passion, had told her it was 'A History of the Founding of Hueron'. She lifted it to her face and breathed in the musty, old paper smell, turned the book over and over, then jumped to her feet. It was early spring, but still chilly, and a fire was blazing in the study. She thrust the book into the flames, watched the thick, yellowy pages twist and smoulder and burn. Then she knelt, jabbing at it with the poker until it was burnt away, and let her tears fall freely.

At the sound of a knock on the front door, she stood up, sniffed hard and smoothed the creases from her lime-green velvet skirt. The butler ushered Cairson in. He lifted his hand in greeting.

"Cairson!" she exclaimed. "How lovely to see you! I've been having a gloomy, horrid afternoon trying to sort out Dernham's books and papers." She gestured at the piles of books, papers, folders and boxes scattered around the room. "The library want to have his collection of history books and manuscripts, and his dissertations on them."

"Do they? Well, he was one of our most respected historians. But why waste time sorting it all? Why not simply send everything to them and let them do the hard graft?"

"Oh, you're right. I don't know why I'm doing this. Anyway, Cairson, have a seat, tell me, how are you?"

"Wrinkled and weary, my dear. But never mind me. Sarielle, I have news for you."

"About Vallan?"

He shook his head in sympathy.

"I'm afraid not. By the way, that reminds me, there's something you ought to know. We didn't tell you at the time... Anyway, while you were in Langron last autumn, Thera and I asked the council to send a detachment of City Guards to try to find out what had happened to Aven and the others. But they refused."

"Refused? Why would they refuse? The swine! The heartless, cruel swine!"

"I know. Now the council have threatened Thera and I with a charge of treason if we go south, or send anyone south to the Magi. Idiots!"

"Treason? They are fools!" Sarielle said, lifting her hands upwards in exasperation. "Petty-minded and scared fools! What do they think you are going to do?"

Cairson shrugged. "Powers only know. But I would have liked to have found out what had happened to Aven. She was my first, oldest niece."

He sounded drained. Sarielle turned to him. His concerned, capable face looked old and tired. She put her hand on his arm comfortingly.

"Oh, Cairson. I'm so sorry," she said. "Oh, I've just thought of something. Something I would love to do for you. Give me your hand."

She took her amethyst from her hair, held it in her other hand, and closed her eyes. A tiny point of glowing yellow light appeared on Cairson's palm. It grew, shimmered, and crystallized into a many-faceted topaz, in a deep, clear gold.

"There! For you, in memory of Aven. It ought to have been brown, perhaps, but I thought a topaz would be prettier."

"Thank you," he said, looking at the jewel for a long, quiet moment. Then he shook his head, put it in his pocket, and turned back to her.

"Anyway, on to my real news, Sarielle," he said. "The reason that I called. To be honest, I have had enough of the council. I have insisted again and again that the Hued have to take some action to prevent future disaster, should Dernham have been correct, but they refuse to do anything. Complacent, self-satisfied idiots! I have resigned from the council in protest. That is the news I came to tell you."

"Oh, Cairson!" Sarielle exclaimed. "You resigned? But being on the council was so important to you!"

"Yes. I'll have to find another occupation, won't I?" He fingered his leaf symbol. "I thought about returning to the lumber and building business, but instead, I have decided to apply for the position of the governor of the dullard prison. The brutality there is notorious, and I may be able to do some good."

"Good, yes, for the dullards. The Talthen, we should call them..."

Sarielle got up and paced around the study, twisting a lock of hair in her hand. She pushed the boxes aside impatiently, and went to the window, looking out at the cold sunlight glistening on rain-dewed lawns and bare shrubs. Beyond the gardens the coloured flags of the city billowed in the wind over the white and grey marble spires, domes and walls.

"I would miss the city, this house, the shops... but..." she murmured.

"Sarielle? What do you mean, my dear? What are you thinking about?"

"Cairson, I feel - yes, I know! It has been - simmering, that's the best word for it. But I'm sure now, and what you said has made me surer. Dernham was right about the dullards - the Talthen. So, to be honest - I'm going to leave the city!"

"Leave?" exclaimed Cairson, standing up. "But, Sarielle, where will you go? What about your friends, your family?"

"My family are in Langron! Berrena, my grandson - they are all I have left. You know I was an only child, my cousins and aunts and uncles are not that close to me, most of them disapproved of Dernham's views. Thera was my greatest friend and she won't forgive me, and many of my other friendships have gone - well, cold, that's all I can say. My daughter and her son are all I have left of Dernham and they are miles away!"

She sat back down. "Sit here, next to me, let me explain. What I am planning is this - I will sell this house, my shop, move to Langron and live there."

"Oh. To Langron? Even so, you shouldn't leave the city, not permanently, you know."

"Also, Cairson, I am going to - people will say that I am mad, that it is a pointless flamboyant gesture that is typical of me, but I am determined!"

"Determined to do what?"

"You'll probably think I'm mad too, but I am going to announce that, out of respect for Dernham's beliefs and in order to continue his work, I will stop using my gift. That topaz will be the last jewel I create. It was getting harder anyway. And I want everyone that lives with me at the Manor to agree to stop using their gifts as well. We will try to live simply and off the land. As the Talthen do."

"No! No, you can't do that! You're mad!" Cairson folded his arms and glared at her. "You won't survive. You know nothing of how hard life is for the dullards!"

"I do, you know. And that is the point. That we should share with them, help them. Cairson, I'm not mad! You forget how rich I am. That will help. I can afford to live in the manor, with the servants there, for a few years at least, until we have got the hang of living off the land."

"Sarielle, please!" He took her shoulders and shook her gently. "You, turning farmer? Listen to reason! You belong in the city. Like Dernham did."

She gently took his hands off her shoulders. "Oh dear. I thought you'd understand. But I'm still determined."

Cairson stood up and walked to the fireplace. He paused, staring down at the flames and logs.

"I can't stop you," he said, quietly. "But I can't support you either. You will be missed."

"I hope you'll visit sometimes!"

"I don't know. Sarielle, I won't hide that I think you are wrong. I disapprove absolutely, I'm afraid." He turned away and walked out.

CHAPTER 19
GIFTED

A few weeks before Riathe's first birthday, Sarielle sat with Berrena in the sitting room at the manor, laughing at a kitten that chased Riathe as he crawled round the room, dragging a piece of wool after him. The kitten caught the wool, making Riathe crow with delight and reach out to grab it. The kitten skittered away, yawned, stretched, curled up and started to purr. Riathe curled up on the carpet next to it, pretending to purr too. Sarielle glanced at her daughter and cleared her throat.

"Er, Berrena, there's something I've been meaning to ask you," she said.

"Aye, what is it?"

"Do you remember being sent away from Hueron? And going to live with Laithan and Ingra?"

"I've a blurred memory of riding on a cart and feeling sad, that's all."

"Do you understand why we had to do that?"

"At the time I didn't understand but I did later, when Laithan told me about the gifts and the laws. Mother, if you're feeling guilty about it, don't. I've survived. And I wouldn't have met Felde otherwise."

Sarielle smiled. "Oh, dearest, Felde is wonderful, but even so, I'm so sorry! Looking back, I think we were wrong to not leave Hueron with you."

"Aye, but Father would have hated living away from the city."

"But it must have been so awful, so horrid for you!"

"It wasn't easy. But I felt safe with Laithan and Ingra.

That made the difference. And I know Father loved me, though he loved Hueron more. But how can I resent him for that now that he's dead? I wish – I wish I'd told him that I forgave him!"

Sarielle hugged her daughter, as tears formed in her eyes. "Poor Berrena! But he understood."

"Aye – but I should have told him. And now it's too late."

"I know. And he did love you, dearest. Very much, of course he did. But serving Hueron – it was his life."

Berrena nodded. "I know."

"But, Berrena, about your gift," Sarielle said, releasing her. "I want to talk to you about it. I still can't grasp it. No one can deceive you, and no one can hurt you. Are you really completely invulnerable?"

"Well, my skin, yes. I can't be cut, or pierced, or wounded." She opened her hand and looked down at the intertwined lobes on her palm. "That's why I hesitated, when Felde and I married. I thought they wouldn't be able to do the Binding. But they could. I think the mark on my palm is - is different, somehow. The only spot where I can be hurt. Laithan said it was magic, the Binding. A different sort to the Hued marking, but some sort of strange magic. Anyway, yes, I am, to all intents and purposes, invulnerable."

"Incredible! What about arrows? Or fire?"

"No one's ever shot at me, so I don't know about arrows. But fire doesn't affect me. Look!"

She walked to the fireplace and calmly thrust her right hand deep into the flames. Sarielle stifled a scream. Berrena straightened up and held out her hand.

"But - it's not burnt!" Sarielle gasped. "By the city walls, Berrena, that is amazing. Such a powerful gift!"

"Powerful? Tis a pointless gift for me. I wish that Vallan had had it instead. Then he might have come back. But tis too late. What's done is done," she said, and picked up Riathe, who was lifting up his arms for a cuddle. Sarielle smiled, as she always did, at the contrast between the child's ash-white hair and skin and Berrena's ebony, deep purple and dark blue colouring.

"Mother, I should've done something with my gift," Berrena said. "I feel as if I've wasted it."

"Wasted it? What on earth do you mean, dearest? How can you have wasted it?"

"Of course I have! I've done nothing with it! But what could I have done? Was I supposed to become some sort of warrior? And, it's true, I can read characters. It helps me with the people in the town, it helped me know that I could trust Felde enough to marry him. But, apart from that, what is the point of my having this gift?"

"Oh, darling! I think I see – about the waste. But I don't really know what you're getting at," Sarielle said. "I don't understand why you are so upset about it. Aren't you happy? What more do you want?"

"I don't know! Aye, I am happy. But there is this regret, almost, that I've got this power, and it leads nowhere. But what can I do? I don't even know who I truly am. Although I'm not a Hued, I don't feel completely Talthen either. I still feel linked to the people in the city, somehow. Mayhap I should try to carry on what Father did. So that all his work is not wasted. But I need to think about how to do it."

For a while they were silent, apart from Riathe nuzzling and grizzling quietly as he fell asleep. Berrena gazed thoughtfully at the flames. Sarielle reached over and took Riathe from her.

"My turn for cuddles," she said.

"It always seems to be your turn for cuddles!"

"Privileges of a grandmother, you know. But, Berrena, there was something else I wanted to say. You've got a gift. Riathe must have too. He's clearly not ordinary."

Berrena laughed. "I'm far ahead of you, mother. I've already thought of this, and decided that we should do the marking ceremony on him. But not until after he's two."

"No!" exclaimed Felde. "Never. I'm not having Riathe taken to Hueron, being brought up as a Hued!"

"Give me patience!" Berrena said, her hands on her hips. "That's not what I meant. Of course not!"

"Then what's the point? He's Talthen, ain't he?"

"Aye, but he's also half-Hued. And he could have a gift! He should have that chance!"

Felde turned on his heel and stalked out into the yard. He never could win any argument with Berrena. He knew he'd have to give in. But he would die rather than see his child be sent to Hueron to be brought up as a Hued. At the thought of losing Riathe he kicked the stable door viciously. Laithan had told him once of a family in Brossvik that had had a child born with pale green skin and eyes. It was rare but not unknown for a Talthen family to have a coloured child and most such children were killed at birth, Laithan had said, but this couple had waited seven years for a child and decided to keep the baby. A year later, the Hued lord of Brossvik had seen the child and the next day he arrived at their house with five City Guards and took the child away to be marked in Hueron. No one ever knew what had happened to it. But Riathe wasn't coloured, Felde thought. He looked like a pale, almost albino, Talthen. And there was no arrogant, cruel Hued lord in Langron to abduct children.

Several days later, Sarielle ran into the house, waving a letter.

"Berrena! Berrena, is she here?"

"Nay," said Felde. "She's in the town, in the hall, with Laithan, trying to persuade the farmers to think about rationing the grain stores over the winter."

"Rationing?"

"Twas a bad harvest. She and Laithan want to try to get folks to share the grain. To make sure everyone gets enough. What is it?"

"Oh, I need to talk to her. I'll wait. Is Riathe here?"

"Aye, with Kianne and Breck. In the front room."

"Hooray! Grandmother time!"

Berrena came back a couple of hours later, by which time Sarielle had dishevelled hair and a crumpled dress from playing dragons and giants and horse rides with the two boys. When Felde and Berrena came in, she laughed, got up and hugged Berrena.

"We've had such fun, haven't we?" she said, waving at the children. "Grandmother makes an amazingly scary dragon, doesn't she, my little cabbages? But time for other things now. Berrena, I need to talk to you and Felde. Alone."

Felde led the way into the back parlour.

"What is it, Mother?" Berrena asked.

"I've heard from Thera," Sarielle said, giving her the letter. "I wrote to her asking if she'd forgive me, and if she'd be willing to do Riathe's marking for us. She did yours, you know."

"But we haven't agreed that he'll be marked!" Felde said.

Berrena raised her eyebrows. "We haven't discussed it, you mean. You stormed off when I mentioned it. But, Felde, he is going to be marked. It is his right. If he grows up giftless and knows you refused to give him this chance, what's he going to think?"

"Then let's leave it until he is old enough to decide for himself!"

"We can't! The marking has to be done when he's still a child! For it to work, for him to have the time to learn to use his gift!"

"Ahem," Sarielle coughed. "I'm sorry to interrupt you two, but the point is, this letter! Thera has refused anyway. She says she'll never forgive me for Headon's loss, and she is shocked that I should even suggest she marks a dullard child. She is so curt, so hard. It's awful to read it!"

Berrena gasped and took her mother's hand. Felde stood silently, relieved even though he could see that Sarielle was almost in tears. "I've lost my husband and my son to that pointless, stupid mission, and my best friend too!" she cried.

A week later, Felde gave in. He thought it unlikely that Riathe would end up having a gift, and he could see that Berrena's mind was set on it. Berrena took him in her arms and kissed him. "I know you really don't want this, but thank you. I will ask the town surgeon. He might do it."

"You do that. But let's keep it quiet. I don't want word getting around about us having a gifted son. Sarielle can come, but only her."

As the town surgeon cleaned his equipment and laid bandages and lint out, Riathe lay quietly, his pale eyes watching his mother's face. Felde held Berrena's hand, Sarielle stood biting her lip and twisting her hair in her hand. "I remember yours," she whispered to Berrena.

The surgeon took Riathe's left hand and made a cut in his palm. The child flinched and jerked his hand and the scalpel slipped, slicing deep through the skin and down into the wrist. Sarielle cried out, and Berrena gripped Felde's hand so tightly that her nails dug into his skin. Felde moved forward to pick up his son, but Berrena pulled him back. "Wait one moment!" she hissed. As Felde watched, holding his breath, creamy blood welled up and formed a pool in the child's palm. A trickle ran down his wrist, then he stiffened and shuddered. The blood shook and rolled up into a lustrous sphere, visible for the briefest of instants before his hand spasmed and closed into a fist. Suddenly a pearly milkiness appeared on the child's hand, grew and spread rapidly over him, as if he'd been dipped in shimmering liquid. Sarielle gasped. For a moment the child's body glimmered, then the faint opalescence vanished. The surgeon stood back, doubt and fear on his face. "I didn't mean... my hand slipped when he moved!" he said.

"It's fine," Berrena said. "We saw what happened. It wasn't your fault." She picked up Riathe. "There, my darling. Tis done. Tis over."

Gently she took his hand and tried to lift his fingers. "Let me see, Riathe. Come on, let Mummy see your hand. Show me what is in there."

Riathe squirmed and burrowed his face into her shoulder, putting his hands around her neck.

"You try," Berrena said to Felde. Felde, his hands shaking despite himself, took the child's fist. The milky blood was already drying on his wrist but his fingers remained squeezed closed. Riathe stared at his father, then twisted away. "Hungy. Wanna apple," he murmured. Felde tried again, then shook his head.

"At least he's not hurt. But he won't open his hand."

"What is in there? Baby, let your Daddy see."

"Try this," said Sarielle, taking an apple from the bowl and holding it out. Riathe reached for it, but then took it with his other hand. "Well, you've always wanted to play with this," she continued, took her amethyst from her hair and held it out. Again, Riathe reached for it, but he would not open his hand.

The surgeon tried to prise up the child's fingers, then stared at them, aghast. "I can't do it. They are immovable. I don't understand. It's as if they're paralysed!"

"What!" exclaimed Felde. "Paralysed! My son! Bee, Bee, why did you do this?"

"Felde... I'm sorry!" Berrena said. "Oh, by the Powers above, I'm so sorry!"

"How can he manage with one hand closed up like that? Why did you meddle? Trying to find out if he's got a gift, and now you've made things worse for him! What if he can't ever use his hand?"

"Felde, calm down," said Sarielle. "I'm sure he'll be able to. Something happened. You saw it! It was like when Berrena was marked. We'll just have to wait. Something happened and he's got a gift or power of some sort. His hand will get better and open, eventually, I'm sure, and then we'll see."

CHAPTER 20
THE CITY COUNCIL

Berrena gripped her mother's hand tightly.

"Don't be frightened," Sarielle whispered. "They won't hurt us!"

"But what I'm going to ask them is so - so presumptuous! They're going to be furious, I know."

Sarielle shrugged. "The worst they can do is say no. And they agreed to my request for a meeting. That's a good sign, I'm sure! And at least it's not a full council meeting in the main chamber."

"Nay," said Berrena, glancing around at the bare, windowless room within the City Council buildings. "But this place is like a prison, and we've been here for hours it seems."

They heard the sound of voices.

"At last!" said Sarielle, leaping up.

Several people came in, lifting their hands in greeting. Berrena lifted hers, as did Sarielle. As they sat back at the wide oak table, Sarielle whispered, "The one in the middle, she's the president of the council, that's the city secretary, Thera's on his left."

A few more councillors came in and sat down. Among them was a tall Hued, with a thin ascetic face and deep frown lines on his forehead. Instead of lifting his hand in greeting, he stared down at them and Berrena felt Sarielle stiffen. His dark-red eyes seemed to mock them.

"That greedy, self-satisfied viper Ferard Mavretan," Sarielle hissed. "The murdering..."

"Quiet, please!" The council president said. She folded

her arms, leant back and stared appraisingly at them. "Well, Lady Rochale, what is this all about?"

"Madame, my daughter, Lady Berrena Rochale, has a request."

"Lady?" the president said, eyebrows raised.

Mavretan laughed, and muttered something to his neighbour.

Berrena stood up.

"I inherit the title from my mother. It is legal. But I am not here to dispute that."

She took a deep breath and put a hand on the table to steady herself as she tried to make her voice sound calm and clear.

"I was born in this city, to Hued parents, both from the bloodline families. I have Hued relations in the city. And I am clearly not an ordinary Talthen, a dullard as you call them." She pointed to her arm. "I am as much a Hued as you, more so, in fact. Black Hueds may be new to you, but at least one existed in the city's history."

"I can see where this is leading," Mavretan murmured.

"I want to be given Hued status. To be able to stay in the city occasionally. That is all I ask," she said and sat down.

"That is not a trivial request," the president replied. "The rumour is that you are married to a dullard."

"Aye, I mean, yes, I am. But that is not relevant to my status as a Hued," Berrena replied. "However, that is one reason why you should consider my request."

"I fail to see your reasoning!"

"You know in your hearts that the gifts are weakening. My father, Lord Sapphireborne, gave his life to try to convince you to take action. The Talthen that he sent to the Magi returned with confirmation of his fears."

"Powers above!" exclaimed Mavretan. "Not this same old story! We had enough of Sapphireborne's gloomy dullard-loving prophecies. Now we are expected to listen to more from his freak of a daughter! This is a farce!"

"Mavretan, your comments are noted," said the

president. "Let her finish!"

"Thank you, madame. All I wanted to point out was that you may need help from the Talthen in the future. It would be to your advantage to build better relationships with them. As a Hued and a Talthen, I can help."

"Perhaps. But your offer is not relevant. We have some of the witnesses to your marking ceremony here. Although Jeiran Sabusson died five years ago, the witnesses and the records state that you have no recognisable scar, no symbol and no gift."

"I have a scar," Berrena replied, holding out her hand to show the grey intertwined lines. The president and Thera leaned forward to look, and exchanged surprised glances.

"Is that so? But there was none at your marking."

"It's a fake," said Mavretan. "I witnessed her marking, remember, and there was nothing! Painted on, I expect."

The president seized Berrena's hand and stared at the mark, then ran her finger over it.

"Odd. It looks real. But I warn you, if it is a fake, then you may be imprisoned! Explain this – this discrepancy."

"It was formed from my blood, when my palm was cut as part of my marriage ritual."

"Strange! And interesting. But we will keep to the issue under discussion. Even if you have a valid scar, you have no symbol."

"I am my own symbol," Berrena said. There was a snigger from Mavretan and a muttered "Unbelievable!"

"This gets more and more bizarre," said the president. "Berrena Rochale, is this a joke?"

"No! Symbols are part of Hueds, are they not? Joined, if not physically. My symbol is joined to me. At the marking ceremony, the blood formed an impermeable barrier on my skin. That is my symbol!"

"Really?"

Berrena thought for a moment, then took a small knife out of her bag. She looked around the table, then passed it to Mavretan. "It cannot be damaged, like all Hued symbols.

I will show you. Sir Mavretan, try to cut my skin."

Mavretan frowned and tested the knife on his thumb. "Seems sharp," he murmured. "With the greatest of pleasure."

He seized her hand and pressed the point of the knife into the skin of her arm, then incised downwards towards her wrist, slicing the blade hard into her flesh. Berrena stood still. The other councillors gasped and Sarielle stifled a scream. Berrena took back the knife, and smiled inwardly at the chagrin on Mavretan's face as he stared at her undamaged skin.

"Thank-you, sir," she said calmly. "You have proved my point. I have a symbol, a mark, and I have a gift as well."

"We accept that point," said the president. "It can be argued that you have a scar and a symbol. But - what sort of gift are you claiming?"

"Gifts take many forms. Physical ones – creating bread, vegetables, stone; being fast or strong; these are obvious. But there are others: subtle, invisible. Like mine. I can perceive the abilities, motives and gifts of others. That is my gift. For example, your gift is that you can heal. Yours: to create wood and you make particularly beautiful carved cherrywood boxes; yours: glass," she said turning to each councillor, "yours: cheese, eggs and milk; yours: honey, yours: music. I omit Thera Redstone as it could be claimed that I know her gift from my parents."

"Very impressive. But not convincing, I'm afraid."

"Sir Mavretan. He keeps his gift secret. No one knows what it is or if he uses it."

She heard Mavretan suck in his breath. He stared at her then leant back with ostentatious nonchalance, but she saw that he was gripping hard on the arm of his chair. Time to play her last card, she thought.

"His symbol," she said. "He rarely lifts his hand in greeting. He's never done so to me, of course, and he does not display his symbol, does he? But I know that it is an eye."

"Hmm... Mavretan, your symbol is an eye, is it not?"

"Yes, but what has that got to do with anything?"

"Show it."

Mavretan swore under his breath and put on the table a deep red stone with markings on it like a narrow eye with a striated iris and tiny pupil. The other councillors gasped and whispered.

"Berrena Rochale, how did you know that?" exclaimed the president.

"As I said, that is my gift. And there's more I know about him, about what he has done. He sensed men's desires and motivations, and worked on those desires, so that they believed the lies he told them. Most of his fortune has come from such insight and deceit. That that hasn't come from outright fraud, that is."

"Slander! Pure slander," snapped Mavretan. "You'd better hope you have some proof for accusations like that."

"Perhaps I don't need proof. That was in the past. But now..." She paused, and gazed levelly at Mavretan. "Now - you are terrified. I am almost certain, from things my father and Albis said, that you have been blackmailing the giftless, threatening them with exile if they didn't pay you. But now, you yourself are giftless. You have lost your gift."

"You liar! You lying, dullard witch! How did you know that?" exclaimed Mavretan, leaping up from his chair.

"Well, that wasn't very successful, was it?" Sarielle said, as they walked to the north-east gate to meet their escort at the inn. "After Mavretan lunged at you, I thought we'd be fortunate to leave the room in one piece! Berrena, that was a bit risky, wasn't it?"

"Aye, mayhap twas risky," Berrena said. "But I ain't afraid of risk."

"Berrena! Don't speak like that... like a Talthen peasant! You're perfectly capable of speaking properly!"

"Nay, dost thou think so?" smiled Berrena. "Anyhap, I didn't expect to succeed. Getting the concession to let me to come into the city accompanied and stay one night, and an offer of a second hearing, was as much as I'd hoped for."

"I'm delighted you got that. And you scored a hit on Mavretan," Sarielle said, twirling her ruby and silver pendant. She chuckled. "Did you see his face after the president told him off! He was furious, mortified and frightened all at once! Delightful!"

"Aye, he's not going to find it so easy to deceive and defraud people now, at least."

"And he's really lost his gift? Are you sure?"

"Aye. As soon as I saw him, I knew. And beneath all the scheming and greed: fear. Pure fear. I could almost pity him."

They walked on in silence, then through a wide square into the theatre district. Sarielle pointed out the bright posters that advertised concerts and plays.

"One day perhaps we can go to one," she said. "Berrena, I'm so glad you can stay in the city now! But, that reminds me, you must promise me something," she said.

"What?"

"I know you think you are almost invulnerable. But you aren't really. Not to robbery or kidnap, or worse. Promise me that you won't come to visit the city by yourself without an escort, like we had this time. Get someone from the town to come with you as a guard!"

Berrena smiled. "Of course I will! You're right that I was thinking to come by myself, but I'm not so arrogant as to think I won't need protection on the way."

They turned down a side street and went through a small park. In one corner, in front of a green-painted pavilion, musicians played and groups of people sat, listening and chatting. They paused to listen. Berrena gazed in amazement at the musicians. Three held coloured rods like tiny flutes, and waved their hands from side to side, up and down, gesticulating like fiddle players or trumpet players with invisible instruments. Only one had an instrument, a maroon-coloured woman playing a xylophone, while a drumstick-shaped object - her symbol, Berrena realised - tapped out a bass line on the lower keys. As the others gestured, drumbeats and tunes and counter-tunes poured out from the air in a riotous exuberance. Some of those watching started to dance. Four girls, wearing wide-skirted dresses of bright yellow and green, skipped from the pavilion and formed a moving circle on the lawn. They raised their hands high as ribbons of blue and turquoise flew into the air, arcing around them, then whirling and spiralling high into the sky.

Berrena could barely make out the symbols pulling the ribbons. One was a butterfly, one looked like an arrowhead and another seemed to be a dragonfly.

"Oh, how lovely! I always felt a tiny bit envious of people with symbols that could fly," Sarielle said, touching her jewel in her hair. "Vallan's could, you know."

The music quickened, the dancers speeded up, the ribbons criss-crossed and swirled into a flamboyant chaos, faster and faster, louder and louder, ending in a crescendo of tunes and drumming and foot-stomping and a fanfare of trumpets. The dancers stopped, the musicians bowed and the audience laughed and applauded.

"That is why Dernham loved the city," Sarielle said, as they turned to go. "For things like that. For that sort of careless and beautiful creativity. He said it was the best thing about Hueron."

"I can see why," said Berrena. "It was lovely! I wanted to dance."

"A pity we can't stop. There may be more performances later on. But I assume we are going back to Langron? That you won't take advantage of your concession?"

"Aye, Felde is expecting me back," Berrena said, regretfully, and gazed around at the flower-filled beds, the fountains, the happy groups of people in the park. A woman sat on a bench in a shady corner, a basket next to her. There was something about the disconsolate look on the woman's pale-green face that caught Berrena's attention. She paused, then decided. She would take another risk.

"Mother, wait here a moment, will you?" Berrena asked. She walked over to the woman, and raised her hand in greeting. The woman looked surprised, then lifted her hand too.

"I'm sorry to bother you," Berrena said. "But it seems to me that you are in trouble. Can I help?"

As they walked back to the gate, Sarielle said to Berrena, "What was that all about? That woman you went up to? You were talking for ages!"

"I know, Mother. I kept you waiting. Oh, I forgot! This, this scarf, is from her!"

She pulled a strip of billowing cloth from her bag.

"Oh, it's gorgeous! Silk!" exclaimed Sarielle, stroking the marigold yellows and oranges of the background and the lavender-blue butterflies embroidered on it. "Did you buy it?"

Berrena laughed. "Nay, she gave it to me. I think I've given her a bit of hope in exchange for it. But the council would say I was spreading dissension."

"Dissension?"

"I could tell that she was near to despair. She's terrified of losing her gift."

"Oh! Really? Like Albis was, when he lost his?"

"Aye. She makes silk and flax, and has worked as a weaver for thirty years but she said that it is getting harder, almost impossible some days. It takes her a week to make a few scarves to sell. I could tell that she was poor, lonely and scared. It was risky, and I think the council would be extremely irritated if they knew, but I thought I'd try it. I suggested she consider joining you at Langron Manor. She said she might. I wonder how many others are like her? Giftless, or nearly so, and fearful?"

CHAPTER 21
MAVRETAN'S FATE

Albis stared dolefully at the ravaged lawn at the side of Langron manor.

"Oh, don't look so gloomy," Sarielle said. "Surely you'd rather have plums than grass?"

"Maybe. Less mowing, at least. Ah - looks like visitors. See. Two. Riding up the avenue."

Sarielle turned. "Oh, Albis, they look like Hueds. More giftless from the city, I wonder?"

She stared hard. One had deep-gold skin and hair. "Surely that can't be Cairson?" she exclaimed, and ran round to the front of the house. "Oh, it is! It is!"

Cairson was accompanied by a sturdy Hued who had the air of a City Guard. As they dismounted Sarielle ran to him and took his hand.

"Cairson! I thought you'd never come to see us!"

"Lady Rochale, Sarielle, I have to admit that I have had a change of heart," he said, bowing low and kissing her hand. He turned it over in his own hand. "No rings?"

"No, not any more! Except for the diamond Dernham gave me. Put away or sold, along with the rest of my jewellery. It wasn't really suitable for this sort of life, I felt."

"Ah. I see. But, even so, my dear, I am delighted to see you, looking so well too. Your move has gone according to plan? And you are prospering?"

"Oh, fairly well! Although we've made lots of mistakes. Come and see. If you'd like to?"

"Of course. But first, I need to introduce my companion. This is Devrien Brade. He was in the City Guard."

"Devrien? Pleased to meet you," said Sarielle. The man bowed over her hand and kissed it.

"I have heard a lot about you, my lady," he said. "I am glad to meet you."

"Are you here to join us?"

"No. Sir Watergiver and I have something to tell you."

"Oh. News! Well, come and sit on the terrace, and tell me. Albis, bring some refreshments, please? And then I can give you a tour of the manor and you can see what we are doing here. Cairson, it is so exciting! And I am absolutely delighted that you've come!"

On the terrace, Sarielle could hardly wait for Cairson and Devrien to be seated and swallow some wine before telling them all the events of the last four years.

"And, as you can see, we are digging up half the lawn to make an orchard," she said, waving at the piles of earth ranged on the grass as if giant moles had invaded the estate. "But I've had to buy the saplings from the city. We couldn't get any from the Talthen farms. And we have more people. Nineteen from Hueron! Berrena and Albis visit and find those who are giftless and try to persuade them to come here, you know."

"Do they?" said Cairson. "Fascinating. And how do those who have joined you get on?"

"They take a while to get used to it. But most of them settle in and work hard. I want to try to get some to live in the town, not the manor, but they won't hear of it. The other thing I want to do is take down the wall around the estate."

"Take down the wall? Sarielle, you are out of your senses! What about the safety of your guests?"

"That's what everyone else says! Despite all my persuasions, some of them are still fearful of the Talthen. But at least they are talking to them, going into the town to buy food, listening to Laithan's advice, things like that."

"You've got years of prejudice to overcome. You won't do that quickly," said Cairson. "Now, let me tell you our news. I didn't get the position of prison governor. It has gone to one of Mavretan's old cronies – and I am fairly sure that large sums of money changed hands in the process. It will be extremely hard for the dullards there. The man who has taken the position is known for his viciousness and bad temper. But that is not my main news, though. It's about Mavretan himself."

"Oh! What? Has he lost lots of money? Been thrown off the council at last for corruption? Or got elected president for life?"

"No, none of those. It's bad news - for him, anyway. He's dead. Murdered - lynched to be precise. And, I'm sorry to say, by dullards."

"No! Dullards? I mean, Talthen? Oh no! What happened? Where? Are the council going to retaliate?"

"No. But I think Devrien Brade here can tell you better than me. He was there. That's why I brought him."

"Oh! Don't keep me in suspense! Devrien, tell me all about it."

"Certainly, my lady. Well, three months ago we were asked to provide an escort for Sir Mavretan to go to Peveque."

"You should know that he was becoming very unpopular in the city," Cairson said. "Especially after Dernham's death. People blamed him for that, they called it 'persecution'. Which it was, to be honest. Anyway, as well, some of his more dubious business schemes started failing and he wanted to get away from some of the people he had swindled, I believe."

"True. Well, no one likes doing escort duty for Mavretan. He never tipped – not that we mind that too much, the council pays us well enough for escort duties – but he never said thank you either. He was a miserable tight-fisted swine."

Sarielle nodded. "Oh, I know. Absolutely!"

"But two of us had relatives in Peveque so we agreed to go. Anyway, when we got there, he found out that his estate manager, Zarcus Trouville, had been giving money to the locals instead of collecting the rents. Not only money but seed and bread and wheat flour too. Zarcus said that otherwise dozens would have died; they had had such bad harvests and illnesses among their livestock. Mavretan lost his temper. He shouted at Zarcus, screamed at him. He was raging about Zarcus helping dullards, when dullards must have killed her. I don't know who he meant."

"Oh. I do," Sarielle said, shaking her head sadly. "He meant... he meant his daughter. Iselle."

Devrien looked at her. "Of course, his daughter. That explains it. Mavretan shouted that Zarcus should have stopped her going. That it was his fault she was lost. Then, suddenly, he drew his dagger and stabbed Zarcus, killed him, right in front of all the servants and estate workers, before I could stop him."

"That's terrible! Murder!" Sarielle cried. "I never liked him or trusted him, but to do that! How could he?"

"He was a skulking, vicious, whining piece of scum and I wouldn't waste my spit on him. You can't imagine how satisfied I was when I saw his red fingers scrabbling at the noose, and him squirming and gasping as he hung there."

Sarielle shuddered. "Noose? You mean he was hung?"

Devrien nodded. "That was later. I was - well, Zarcus was my uncle, and the guard with me, he was married to Zarcus's daughter. So you can imagine what we felt. We nearly killed him then and there, but I thought we'll get him back to Hueron, tell the council, and he can go to trial, and be damned to him. But Mavretan insisted that we both went with him to the town. He had the chief fetched to the square, and all the local men, and started demanding the money back. The chief tried to explain how they had nothing, but Mavretan wouldn't listen. He ordered me to kill the chief, there and then, as a lesson to the town."

Devrien paused and smiled bitterly. "But I refused. A crowd had gathered: hostile, shouting. I didn't know what they'd do so I told the other guard that I'd look after Mavretan myself, and that he should get back to the house and make sure everyone there was safe. When I refused to obey Mavretan, he pulled his dagger on me too, but I wrenched it off him. And then the crowd grabbed him. I watched, but I didn't interfere. They dragged him to a tree by the square, and they hung him. He was terrified, crying and begging for mercy, the yellow-bellied rat. They just watched. They looked grim. I rode away then, before they turned on me too."

"Goodness!" exclaimed Sarielle. "I'm not going to waste a single tear for Mavretan, even if he was lynched. He killed my husband as surely as if he'd stabbed him too. He was a ruthless and wicked and greedy bastard! Anyway, why isn't the council going to retaliate?"

"Because officially Mavretan is facing a charge of murder, and it is assumed that he has gone into hiding," said Cairson.

"The other guard went back to Hueron," Devrien explained. "He told them about Zarcus's murder and that Mavretan had not returned to Peveque House. I came back after him, told the council that I was another witness to the murder, but I'm not going to tell the council what I saw in Peveque! I just spun them a story about Mavretan getting the money from the town and riding off."

"Devrien knew me, and he knew where my sympathies lay," said Cairson, "He came to me in secret and told me. No one else knows. Even his cousin doesn't care what happened to Mavretan. He just wants to inherit his estate."

"Well, of course. No one liked Mavretan!" exclaimed Sarielle. "Devrien, thank you so much. Both for telling me, and for protecting those poor Talthen!"

"My pleasure, my lady," said Devrien.

"This has started me thinking," said Cairson. "If Dernham was right and we lose our gifts we will be helpless against the dullards and they have ample cause to resent us. The council will never agree to help the dullards more. I have revised my opinion of your plan. You have set us an example and showed what is possible. I am considering leaving Hueron myself and going to my estate at Marden and to try to build up better relations with the local dullards. I will try to call them Talthen. Devrien is going to join us. Maybe some of the giftless will come too."

"Cairson, that is encouraging!" said Sarielle. "Maybe we can start a revolution!"

CHAPTER 22
RIATHE

Berrena wandered aimlessly around the city. Yet again, she had failed. The council refused to grant her Hued status. It was clear that her plans to persuade them to reduce the taxes on Helsund or shorten the forced labour sentences would never succeed. She was becoming notorious. People turned to watch her, with curiosity, sympathy or hostility. The captain of the company that guarded the north-east gate knew her well, and had greeted her with bantering friendliness, saying, "Morning, my lady. Yet another attempt to persuade us that we are all doomed?"

And now, another failure. She wondered if it was wise to ask Kianne to look after her children, to leave Felde and Riathe for days at a time, on these fruitless trips to the city. But what else could she do?

A young, ardent-faced man ran after her, calling, "Lady Rochale? Lady Rochale?"

She turned and said, "Aye?"

"I hoped it was you," he said. "I've heard about you. Can we talk?"

He led her to a bench by the side of the street. In a quiet, intense voice, he continued. "Is it true? That there's somewhere that those who have," his voice dropped to a whisper, "lost their gifts can go? I have a friend..."

"Aye," Berrena responded, equally quietly. "Tell your friend to go to Marden. About a hundred and twenty miles east. Cairson Watergiver will welcome him. He's turning his estate over to farmland and needs help from those prepared to live, like him, as Talthen."

Not a complete failure then, she thought, as the young man walked away. That makes nearly three-score giftless who have left the Hued. Perhaps there is some hope that, in Marden and Langron at least, the gulf can be bridged.

As Felde came into his front room, shaking raindrops from his hair, he saw Berrena breast-feeding their youngest child, a dark-haired baby boy, his scrunched fist pink against her ebony skin. Their family had grown in the ten years that had passed since Riathe was born, and their two daughters and second son sat on the rug, Breck perched on the window seat behind them, and Kianne sat on a chair in the corner, carefully knitting socks. Riathe leaned against the wall, his left hand clenched shut and held to his chest as he listened intently to Berrena's story-telling. Despite the lingering regret that Riathe's hand had stayed paralysed, Felde looked with pleasure at the scene. Berrena smiled up at him then continued.

"They travelled for many days through dark pine forests, always climbing upwards, until the forests ended and they saw before them the Crevenne Mountains. Higher than you can imagine, as high and white as the clouds. How can we cross those? asked Headon. But Aven sent her wren to search for a way through..."

"Nay," Felde shouted. "Nay! You can't tell them that!"

Berrena stopped. He stormed out of the room, slammed the back door, and strode to the main paddock. He leant against the fence, his head bowed against the top rail, and the rain drenched him as he tried to calm his rage.

He felt a hand on his arm and turned. Berrena was there.

"I won't tell them the whole story," she said.

"Why tell them at all?" he demanded.

"Breck and Riathe asked. Breck has a right to know how his father died! And they need to know what you did, how you fought alongside Hueds, how you rescued Iselle from the bear. They need heroes to look up to."

I'm not a hero, Felde wanted to shout. But he shook his

head and stared across the paddock at the horses enduring the sullen rain.

"Felde, I was going to tell them that the Hued asked you to return while they stayed. In case their rescue attempt failed. And that you agreed, for my sake and so that the Magi's message was delivered. Tis a half-truth. Can you accept that?" she asked.

Felde nodded, but kept his head turned away.

"You made the right decision," she said.

"Nay. I didn't. I should have stayed," he muttered.

She paused for a few moments. "I can't remember what Vallan looked like..." she said quietly. "I don't know, I'll never know, what happened to him. But if you'd stayed then perhaps no one would've returned... Tis better as it is."

For a long time they stood, as the rain fell. Eventually Felde turned back to her.

"You're right. You're always right, Bee," he said. "But it ain't easy."

The downpour soaked her dress and flattened her hair. He still had his jacket on, and he took it off and wrapped it around her.

"I came in to tell you something," he said.

"What?" she asked.

"Laithan has resigned as town chief."

"Oh! Oh, good. He needs to rest. He's worked so hard," she said, "for so many years. He is exhausted, drained by it all."

"They asked me if I'd stand for election."

"Felde!" she exclaimed, turning to him and putting her hand to his cheek. "Oh, Felde. I'm so pleased. You agreed, I hope."

"Nay. I couldn't."

She took her hand away. "You refused?"

"I can't be town chief. Not having done what I've done. I ain't good enough, Bee. I haven't got Laithan's patience and wisdom. You'd be far better than me. Mayhap you should stand, not me."

"Me? Felde... should I? But would they accept me?" She stared into space. "To be the town chief...Powers above! That could help so much. Felde, we need to talk about this with Laithan."

"Aye, but later. See what you feel about it first. Anyhap, you're soaked. Go in, get dry, finish the story. I'll go and clean the stables out and feed the horses."

The rain eased off as he carried buckets of oats to the stables then started brushing out the stale straw and muck. As he worked Felde thought of his old ambitions of glory and heroism - all unachievable. But at least he could pass his fighting skills on.

The next day he took the cousins out to the paddock to teach them the basics of singlestick. Riathe listened with serious attention to Felde's explanations, while Breck jumped up and down in excitement, wanting to start immediately. Felde showed them the basic defence moves and let them practise against him. His son was hampered - unable to grip the stick with his paralysed left hand - but managed well enough. Afterwards Felde got them to fight each other. He was surprised how fast Riathe's reactions were. Eventually, after losing his stick several times, Breck lost his temper and charged at Riathe. He was sturdier and heavier and he wrestled Riathe to the ground. They rolled in the dust, struggling and flailing. Fighting just like Jorvund and I used to do, thought Felde, as he pulled them apart.

"Tis enough for today," he said. "Go inside and get cleaned up. You did well."

As they ran inside, arguing and boasting to each other about what they'd learnt, he watched them. Both were covered in dirt, mud and grass. Breck was bruised on his arms and legs, had a scrape on his elbow, and a bleeding cut on one knee. But Riathe was unhurt. Felde smiled. One of the things he loved about his wife was that she understood him well enough not to talk overmuch to him about her gift. But he knew it. You couldn't be married to someone for fourteen years and not notice that they never got cut, grazed, bled or even bruised. And it looked like Riathe had inherited her impervious skin.

He felt a sense, not of optimism, but of a contented acceptance. Training his sons, running a farm, breeding horses - this would be his future. Maybe his children would have a better future. And his son, Riathe, surely he would do something, be someone more than ordinary. In the meantime, Felde resigned himself to an obscure life.

Years passed, marked by the rhythm of seedtime and harvest, summer and winter. Eight years passed with their small triumphs and celebrations: Berrena becoming town chief, the horses trained and sold, the birth of another son, the autumn feasts, Kianne's marriage to the blacksmith, Alef Ciard. Eight years of pride in his children as they grew and learnt and thrived. Eight years with their grind of perpetual toil, becoming harder each year for less reward, and their passing griefs: the late frost on the orchard, the wheat ruined by overmuch rain, the favourite mare that died, the lines that formed on Laithan's face as his hair whitened and his strength faded so that he needed a stick for walking. The longer-lasting griefs: Ingra falling sick and the bitter sadness of her long sinking and death. Eight years of the daily struggle of Talthen life: the weakening and shrinking flocks, the soil becoming poorer and poorer, the Hued taxation, the people lost to illness or taken by prison and forced labour, the increasing resentment in the town against the Gifted People.

Riathe grew almost overnight, it seemed to Felde. One year he was an earnest boy, the next year he was eighteen and had grown into a slender young man, as tall as his father.

They walked through the town one late autumn day, as the trees writhed in a leaf-stripping gale and grey clouds fled across a cold sky. Felde glanced at Riathe with a father's admiration at his son's striking appearance and the skill he had gained with both horses and weapons, despite his disabled hand. His other children were treasured, and he would die for them, but Riathe was the special son, the first-born, the one who had cost him the most and whom he loved the most.

As they passed the market stalls, Riathe paused and laid his hand on Felde's arm. He gazed across the square to Breck, who had his back to them as he talked to a slightly-built girl with golden hair and a bashful appearance.

"Who's that?" asked Felde.

"Aleythe Fross," replied Riathe. "From Cathron."

"Oh, aye, I remember. Weren't she and her father thrown out from their house when they couldn't pay the rent?"

"Aye. They came to Langron a month back to live with his sister."

A gust of wind blew between the stalls, shaking the awnings and scattering leaves around them. The girl's cloak billowed out and the pale blue scarf she wore was seized by the wind and swept away. As Felde and Riathe watched, Breck ran after the scarf, caught it, and returned it to the girl. She smiled timidly at him as he gently put it back around her.

"She looks pretty, but quiet," said Felde. "Does Breck like her, then?"

"Aye. Oh aye, he does. And she likes him back," Riathe said.

Felde was startled at the intensity of his son's voice and expression.

"What about you?" he asked.

"Me? Nought! She doesn't like my closed hand and she thinks I'm thin, weak and too ... strange," Riathe answered, glancing down at his paralysed hand. He walked rapidly away.

Felde looked back at Breck and Aleythe. He could see why Aleythe would see only strangeness in his son. Breck was broader and stronger than Riathe, curly-haired and blue-eyed, with a wide cheerful mouth. His skin was tanned by outdoor work and he looked a healthy, sturdy boy. Compared to him, Riathe's creamy paleness was paper-white; his chalk-white hair, sparse frame and pointed chin gave him a fey, ethereal look. There was little he could say or do, Felde knew. If the boy had fallen in love with Aleythe, and Breck had too, then it seemed Riathe would be disappointed.

Felde strode quickly to catch up with Riathe. They walked down the lane to the house. The sun glinted through gaps in scudding clouds. Rooks soared and tumbled in the air above them, cawing raucously as they circled the high elms in the wooded clumps behind the fields.

"Riathe? Wait. Riathe, stop a minute. There's something I need to tell you."

"Aye?"

Felde paused. He took a deep breath.

"Before we go in, now that you're eighteem, I need to talk to you about that mission I went on," he said. "We'll walk a bit further, then I can tell you."

"The mission? To the Magi? I know about that, father."

"You don't know all. Bee's told you about it, I know. But..."

Felde stopped. He turned aside for a moment and stared at the flying rooks and grey clouds above.

"Powers above, tis hard. But you have to know the truth," he said, turning back. "Your mother told you that I was a hero. Well, you should know that I wasn't."

"You weren't?" Riathe stared hard at him.

"I was a coward. I left my friends and ran away. They must have been attacked and killed on the journey back and I wasn't there to help them. Vallan was your uncle, Headon was a good friend, Aven was just trying to do her job, and Iselle was only young and thoughtless. She was only nineteen. I left them and I can hardly bear, even now, not knowing what's happened to them."

Riathe said nothing. Felde could not bear the serious, disappointed expression in his cold grey eyes.

"Don't tell anyone, not even Breck," Felde said, but Riathe only nodded and turned away.

CHAPTER 23
THE MAGI ARRIVE

Sarielle, humming an old song, looked round at the study. She had to admit it was both untidy and shabby. The curtains had been bleached by sunlight, the neatly-arranged books were replaced by crooked piles of papers and ledgers, the brass fire-irons were tarnished and the carpet was worn down so much that the pattern hardly showed. But she wasn't going to waste money on the dilapidation. All that she had she'd use to buy food, seeds, tools, and labour. It was probably cheating, she thought. The help that the manor got from Langron, now that Berrena was town chief, was probably cheating as well, but at least they were surviving.

It was a heavy, warm morning and the window was open to let in what little breeze there was. Sarielle sat at the desk and twirled a lock of her hair between her fingers, as she opened up the estate ledgers and wrote in the numbers for the sacks of dried, stored beans, then tried to work out how many sacks to keep for sowing next year. She rubbed her fingers and hands to soothe the twinges of arthritis that had started last winter and made writing hard. Book-keeping had never been her strongest point. I wish Dernham was here doing this, she thought, pausing to stare out of the window. Or Vallan. He should be here, running his manor himself. With a tiny shake of her head, she looked back at the ledger and stared determinedly at the figures.

The estate manager, his barley-yellow face as doleful as ever, came in.

"Ah, just the person I wanted to see! Albis, did you see

213

the honey from the beehives? One of the new women, I can't remember her name, she's getting ever so good at looking after the bees. Isn't that wonderful?"

Albis nodded reluctantly.

"And, oh, yes, I know what else it was I needed to tell you. Two more people have arrived from Hueron to join us! Persuaded by Berrena on her last visit. Two more! I am so pleased!"

"Two more?" Albis said. "Humph. Don't know where they'll sleep. Hope they're happy to work hard. Those last three complained endlessly, even about little things like cleaning out the chickens. Was glad to see the last of the one that went back to Hueron. A right moaner, he was."

Sarielle repressed a smile.

"We can have people sharing rooms, we'll find space," she said. "And there will still be enough chickens and pigs, just about, to last us through the winter. Of course the new people will be happy to work, they're giftless – they're used to hard work."

"More giftless? That's ominous... We've already got fifty-seven. Have to turn more of the lawns over to vegetables. But I came to see you about something else. The Magi. They are travelling round, selecting their apprentices. Two are in Brossvik. It's only seven miles away. Knew you'd want to know."

Sarielle leapt up, knocking pens and papers and her chair to the floor.

"The Magi! Oh, Albis! I can ask them what happened to Vallan! Quick, get my horse," and she dashed towards the door.

"No need, my lady. Knew you'd want to see them. And I want to see if they'll bless the estate and can do anything about the well – you know – the one in the farmyard that has dried up. Sent a messenger the moment I heard. One of them has agreed to come here this afternoon."

"Oh, thank you. Oh, Albis, it is so ... so frightening," she whispered, sitting back down at the desk. "After all these years. Finally I may find out what happened to my son. Berrena too, please, send for her!"

By the afternoon it was sweltering, but the north-facing drawing room felt pleasantly cool, the heavy silk curtains providing welcome shade. The furniture and carpets had dulled with age, but the cushions and sofas still had a pale remnant of their original blue-green colour. Sarielle had kept many of the enamelled vases from her house in Hueron, and these glowed with patterned richness where they stood in alcoves and on tables. A large bowl painted with swirling flowers held pot-pourri and she ran her fingers through it to release its perfume into the room.

Albis ushered the Mage in. He was tall, black eyed, with flecks of grey in his hair and beard; dressed in orange robes and an amber-lined silk cloak. He barely glanced at the faded splendour of the room, but put his staff down and bowed to Sarielle, who curtseyed and gestured for him to sit. It might have been her imagination, but she thought he gave her an admiring look. Even though she was in her late sixties, her hair faded to a pale lavender, both laughter and frown lines on her face, she felt a hint of satisfaction that she was wearing her favourite azure dress and that she could still be thought charming. She adjusted the position of her amethyst in her hair as she sat down.

"Welcome to my home, sir," she said, "and thank you for your help on my estate. We are grateful to you for restoring the well and blessing our fields and gardens."

"Your thanks are appreciated, Lady Rochale," said the Mage. "We are always glad to help those in need. It is rare for us to meet, let alone help, the Gifted People. Usually it is only Talthen who require our help – the Hued have their own powers. But I understand that you and your household have renounced your gifts?"

"Yes, that is true," replied Sarielle. "We are endeavouring to live as Talthen, because we fear that our gifts are fading. My husband, Lord Sapphireborne, sent a group of friends to you to ask your advice on this. Sir, I must ask you, as my son was with them, do you know what happened to them?"

The Mage looked perplexed.

"It was almost twenty years ago that they visited you. Four Hueds and a Talthen," Sarielle continued.

He nodded. "Ah, I remember now. A young man, very handsome, with blue colouring, a bearded green man, a pretty little pink lady, and they were led by a mature brown Hued woman. They had a Talthen servant with them."

"Yes, that's them!" cried Sarielle, leaping up. "Please, sir, can you tell me what happened to them? The blue Hued was my son and the Talthen my son-in-law. He left them to come home, but the Hueds went back to see you again. Did you see them? Do you know what happened to them?"

"Hmm. Ah, yes, I remember. The girl fell in love with my colleague and wanted to stay. The three Hueds tried to persuade her to leave with them – I believe your son loved her too?"

"Yes, he did, they were engaged to be married," she said.

The Mage sighed and stroked his beard thoughtfully.

"That is sad. I'm afraid she was a very fickle girl. There was a lot of argument, but it was clear that the girl, Iselle, was adamant about remaining. So your son, Vallan Sapphireborne – was that the name? Vallan and the others eventually decided to return without her. We gave them money and provisions and one of us travelled with them to the foot of the Crevenne Mountains. That is all I can tell you. There are, unfortunately, many robbers and violent men in the villages the other side of the mountains. If they did not return then the chances are that they were attacked and did not escape."

Sarielle collapsed onto the sofa and burst into tears, burying her face in her hands.

The Mage leaned over and put his hand on her shoulder.

"My dear lady, I am sorry for your loss. Your son was a fine, brave-hearted man. As we return we will investigate and do all that we can to find the truth for you. We will send a messenger back to you with what news we can discover. I wish there was more I could do for you."

"Thank you," sobbed Sarielle. After a moment's silence she asked, "Sir, is Iselle still with you?"

"Yes." He smiled. "She is well, and lives in a small cottage. She stayed faithful to my colleague for several years and then indulged herself with an affair with one of the grooms. Her former lover was furious and deeply hurt and threatened to turn her into a slug." He chuckled. "I almost wish he had, but we persuaded him to restrict himself to turning her out. She lived with the groom for a few more years and then moved on to another servant, and then another, causing much unhappiness among our staff. Now she is on her own."

Despite her tears, Sarielle smiled at this. The thought of Iselle living alone in a humble cottage was a small compensation, although she would much have preferred her to have been turned into a slug.

"Sir, I must ask you another question," she said. "Our gifts - are they failing?"

"Yes. They are. But do not worry, dear lady," he said, patting her hand and smiling at her. "It will be many, many years before the Hued notice any significant diminution of their powers, and many more before they will need to take any action."

"Oh! But Dernham noticed!"

"Yes, but your husband was, from what I have heard, an exceptional man. What you and he have started will provide hope for the Hued in the future. But I estimate that you have at least a hundred years to prepare yourselves."

As he said this, Berrena came in. Both Sarielle and the Mage stood up and Sarielle felt a glow of pride in her daughter. Even though Berrena was wearing her ordinary household clothes, a simple cream tunic and blue trousers with a plain gold necklace, she was striking, her skin as black as sable against the cream and her hair deep ebony. Sarielle glanced at the Mage to see what he thought. He gazed open-mouthed at Berrena, and turned visibly pale.

"Sir, may I introduce my daughter, Berrena Rochale," Sarielle began, but Berrena stood still, gazing at the Mage. The Mage stared back at her. Neither moved for a long, silent moment. There was a repulsed look on Berrena's face and she lifted her hands, palms out, in a gesture of rejection. Her arms trembled. She shook her head as if trying to dislodge some unpleasant thought, then lurched sideways and fell to the floor. Panicked, Sarielle knelt beside her, frantically rubbing her daughter's hands and calling out to Albis to fetch water. She turned to ask for help and to apologise to the Mage but he forestalled her.

"This is your daughter? Strange, but I assure you, she has only fainted. There is no illness, no sickness, no need to worry; she will recover soon. It is probably the heat," he said in a harsh voice.

He paused but Sarielle was too distracted to reply. He picked up his staff, bowed and continued, "I can see you wish to attend to her and so I will take my leave. Madam, thank-you for your hospitality. No, do not trouble yourself, your estate manager will show me out," and he swept out of the room. As she chaffed Berrena's cold hands, Sarielle could hear him calling for his horse. He sounded disturbed, almost angry, and she had a momentary fear that she or her daughter had offended him, but forgot it as Berrena's eyelids fluttered and warmth came back to her hands. Within a minute or two, she sat up, and leaned in to rest her head on her mother's shoulder.

"What happened? Do you feel better? What made you faint?" Sarielle asked.

Berrena shuddered. She looked intently at her mother.

"That man, that Mage ... what did he do here? Did he hurt you? What has he done?"

"What?"

"When I came in there was a foul smell," Berrena said passionately. "It was like rotting meat and then I saw him and knew it came from him! It was so foul I felt sick, and I knew he was lying and cruel. I couldn't bear it - it was like a darkness swallowing me up. He's done something terrible, I'm sure! Tell me, what has he done to you?"

"Don't be so ... so melodramatic! He's a Mage, not some horrid evil villain. He's done nothing but good; blessed the crops and fields and restored the dry well in the farmyard. He was a bit dignified, but perfectly charming and helpful."

Berrena was silent, shaking her head.

"I don't understand. You must have imagined it!"

"You remember how I knew what Iselle was like, before Felde's journey? Well, tis the same thing. I tell you, he is evil!"

"Evil? No, he can't be. He told me what they thought had happened to Vallan. He was really concerned..., well he seemed to be..."

"Vallan? He knew what had happened to my brother?"

"That's why I wanted to see him!"

"What did he say?"

As Sarielle told her, she cried a little, but shook her head.

"I don't believe him," she said. "He's a liar, all surface and falseness. I wouldn't believe him if he told me the grass was green. He knows something else, something more, about what has happened to Vallan. Did you say he restored the well?"

Sarielle nodded.

"Don't use the well!" Berrena said. "Don't drink from it! Please! Is there an animal you could test it on? One that's going to slaughter anyway?"

"There are some piglets Albis is fattening up."

"Give the water to them but don't let anyone else drink it or use it. See what happens to them. The Mage has done something to the water, I'm sure!"

CHAPTER 24
APPRENTICED

Storm clouds piled up in the east as the stifling warmth increased. Riathe worked in the garden, rapidly digging up as many potatoes as he could before the coming storm broke, when Aleythe ran sobbing through the house into the garden, calling for Kianne, Felde and Berrena.

"What's wrong? They ain't here, Mother's at the Manor, Kianne's with the blacksmith, and Father's taking some horses to Shraive's farm. Why're you so upset?"

She wept uncontrollably. Riathe took her to the kitchen and fetched her a glass of water, trying to ignore the growing knot of fear inside him. She sipped the water. For several minutes all she could say was "Breck, he's gone," and sob and gulp.

The knot of fear twisted. Riathe sat down next to the trembling girl and took her hand.

"Aleythe, calm thyself. Tell me what's happened," he said sharply and authoritatively.

She took a deep breath and looked at him. Her face was so sad and lovely, even smudged with crying, that he wanted to take her in his arms and kiss the traces of the tears on her cheeks. He controlled himself and waited, willing her to become quiet. Under his gaze she stuttered, "Breck. He's gone. A Mage has taken him!"

"What?"

"We were ..." She hesitated and blushed. "We were sitting, on a bank, outside the town. Then a Mage came along. I knew it was a Mage. He had jewels, rings, a blue velvet cloak... and a staff. He stopped and stared at us. Then he got off his horse and came right up to Breck. He frightened me."

"Why? For the Powers' sake, Aleythe, what happened?"

"He asked Breck how old he was, if he was healthy. Then he put his hands on either side of Breck's face. He said something, in a strange language, and the stone in his staff - it glowed. Like a star! Then he said Breck had magic in him and had to become his apprentice!"

"Breck - magical? Becoming his apprentice? Nay! Nay, that's not possible!"

"Breck said no. He said..." She hesitated. "Riathe, I'm sorry, we hadn't told you, but you must have guessed. He said that he wouldn't leave me. We - we love each other."

Riathe turned away. It was what he had known all along would happen, but he still wanted to curse and weep.

"It was awful, Riathe! The Mage said that if Breck didn't go then he would be executed! And the town fined thousands! That it was a Hued law so Breck had to go. I wanted to go too, but he said I couldn't, but Breck would come back for me. He promised me I'd see him again, within two years! But two years! Tis so long!"

Riathe turned back to her. Mechanically, he patted her arm. "Well, two years... that ain't unbearable, is it?"

"It is! It is!" She burst into tears again. Riathe stood up, strode around the kitchen then went out into the garden to stare at the darkening clouds covering the west. For a moment he hated Breck. His cousin had got Aleythe and was going to become a wizard. He returned to the kitchen, poured another glass of water and drank it. The coolness steadied him.

"Where is Breck now? The lucky boy gone back to pack?" He couldn't suppress a hint of sarcasm in his voice, but she didn't notice.

"No, they wouldn't let him. They wouldn't even let him say goodbye. That's why I need to find Felde, Berrena, Kianne. Because he's gone, without even telling them!"

"Gone?"

"Oh, Riathe, I don't understand it. The Mage asked Breck where his house was and said he'd meet him there in the morning. But then another Mage rode up. He leapt off his horse. He seemed furious. They shouted at each other. The other Mage was talking about there being a black Hued, in the manor, and so they had to leave. So the Mage grabbed Breck, pulled him away from me, they rode off, they made Breck run with them. All the way to Brossvik. Breck! Oh, Breck!" Her voice broke again as the tears returned.

"A black Hued? They must mean my mother, but why? Why does that mean they had to leave? I don't understand! And if Breck didn't want to go, why would they take an unwilling apprentice?"

He stood and began to pace up and down, thinking and frowning, as Aleythe watched him.

"Riathe, what am I going to do? I love him, and two years is so long, and what if he never returns? Or he's changed and don't love me anymore? I don't want to marry a wizard! I just want my Breck back!"

For a moment Riathe wondered what might happen if Breck didn't return. But he pushed the thought aside. He knelt in front of her and lifted her face, staring at her, as if trying to memorise every feature.

"Do you know that I love you?" he asked.

She only looked at him, her eyes brimming.

"I'll go after the Magi and Breck," he said.

"What will you do?"

"I don't know! Try to persuade them to let him go, try to delay them, kidnap him, try to stop them – whatever I can."

She looked doubtfully at his sparse frame, disabled hand and pale skin.

"Aye, I know. I ain't like Breck, but I'm stronger than I look. When I'm gone you must find Kianne and Laithan, get messages to my mother, and get my grandmother to find out what the law really is, and send someone to get father, and when he comes tell him..."

Riathe paused, remembering Felde's words to him last winter, "I'm no hero!" But Felde's flaw wasn't cowardice, he realised, only that he loved his family and son more than his friends. Riathe knew Felde would give his life for his son and nephew.

"Tell father everything. Tell him I said I trust him – that is really important. Will you do that?"

Aleythe agreed, looking hopefully at him. She's got such confidence in me, thought Riathe, still kneeling in front of her.

"Before I go, give me one thing," he asked.

"What, Riathe? If I can I will. What do you want?"

"Some of your hair to take with me. As a reminder."

She nodded. Riathe took his pocket-knife and cut a short golden tress. Aleythe gave him her handkerchief to keep it in, and he folded it up, kissed it, and put it in his pocket.

"Goodbye," he said. "Remember me," and leant forward to kiss her and wipe away the tears on her cheeks.

A short while later Riathe rode north. He had taken his dagger, food and water, and some money, not knowing how far or how fast the Magi would travel before he caught up with them, although as far as he could work out he was only two or three hours behind them. It was still hot and humid, but blue-black clouds veiled the sky from the east. The threatened storm was closing in.

When he arrived at Brossvik the village chief told him that the Magi had left 'in a tearing hurry' and had gone down the east road. He did not know where they were headed. He started to complain about the loss to the village and the suddenness of their removal, but Riathe cut him short and went east. After several miles the road led downhill to a bend in the river valley and forked, one branch going northwards through forests and the other continuing south and east. He paused, doubtful, but he thought he could see tracks leading south-east. There were about two hours of daylight left, but there would be no moon that night.

Hopefully he'd catch up with them within an hour or two. If not, he'd have to backtrack and try the other route. Praying he'd made the right choice, Riathe turned south-east.

Storm clouds darkened the sky as he rounded a bend in the road and saw a group of a dozen horsemen ahead in the trees. He recognised Breck and spurred his horse faster. As he neared them, a vile smell of decay made him gag and fling a hand over his nose. His heart beat faster as a premonition of danger flooded him. He felt as if he was riding headlong downhill, through stinking heaps of rotting meat and a rain of sewage, towards a huge cliff. Visions of falling, of injury and pain filled his head. Trying to clear his thoughts, he focused on his cousin, who had reined in his horse and turned. But the nearer Riathe came, the worse the stench and the feeling of dread grew, till his head reeled with blackness and a sense of impending horror. Breck leapt off his horse and dashed to him. Riathe swayed and almost fell as he dismounted, but Breck grabbed him.

"Riathe! Do you know? Did Aleythe see you? They've chosen me, Riathe, and I've got to go with them. I couldn't even say goodbye," Breck said.

"I know, Breck, aye, I know. But you can't go, that's why I came. To rescue you, to do something. Aleythe is going to tell the others. I'm sure Felde will follow us," Riathe whispered.

Two of the horsemen had turned and now rode towards them. Unlike the others, who wore grey, they had long, coloured cloaks. They must be the Magi, Riathe realised. His head ached and throbbed but the closeness of Breck steadied him. A strange heat from inside his paralysed fist spread through him. It helped. Breathing deeply, he clenched his other hand into a fist as the Magi dismounted and walked towards them. His body trembled and his mind swirled with an immense terror of approaching danger, but he stood as tall and firm as he could.

He realised then how unimpressive he must look; wearing dirty working clothes, with sweat and grime on his face and hands, and how thin and pale he would seem to those powerful men. I must try to look impressive, try to be persuasive, he thought, not a scared boy, but someone they need to listen too.

"Breck, these Magi, don't go as their apprentice! Promise me you'll go back to Aleythe," he whispered. Breck looked startled, but mouthed agreement.

A perilous idea came to Riathe. It would be pain almost beyond bearing go back with Breck and see Aleythe's joy and watch them together. What if he were to go on with the Magi? As their apprentice? He imagined being a white wizard; a powerful and benevolent Mage; and he stepped forward.

"Sires, I'm Breck's cousin, Riathe. I've come to ask you to release him and to take me as your apprentice instead."

Behind him, Breck gasped, "Nay!" but Riathe turned and glared at him. "Be quiet!" he hissed.

"For the sake of the girl he loves, for Aleythe's sake, for your sake, please take me," he continued, "I'm better than him, more intelligent, quicker to learn."

A Mage in a blue cloak came close to Riathe and examined him. Riathe held his head up high and kept his fists clenched, the warmth from his left hand filling him, his grey eyes meeting the narrowed eyes of the Mage. As the Mage neared him the scent of blood and rottenness assaulted him, and sickness rose in his throat. The wizard circled him. Riathe thought, almost prayed, with desperate resolution, please let him prefer me to Breck. Don't let him notice my hand or my thinness. If there is a good Power above, make him accept me.

"Well, well. So you want to swap? You think you're better than him? You have unusual looks, boy. Nothing like your cousin. Those high cheekbones and that pale blonde hair – are you an albino? A weakling runt?" the Mage asked, walking around him.

"Nay, sir. Pale, I know, but I'm no runt. I'm strong and," he started to say, but the Mage interrupted.

"Yes, strong, brave, clever – I know, of course you are. Well, you certainly look the part of a wizard."

He stopped in front of Riathe and looked him full in the face. The black sickness and fear drowned Riathe and he briefly staggered, blinking to try to break the terror from that compelling blue glare.

"Tell me, this Aleythe, this blonde doll, is she that special?" the Mage asked.

"Aye, sir," replied Riathe. "I don't want her to be hurt."

"I see it all! How boringly romantic. You are both in love with her and she loves your cousin, not you, so you gallop off to rescue him and sacrifice yourself."

The orange-cloaked Mage had been watching with a sardonic smile. He stepped forward and grabbed the other's arm.

"It's getting late and we need to move. Finish this, will you! I would prefer to get there before the storm breaks."

"All right! Don't pester me!" the first Mage replied, shaking off his grip. "It's not like I'm choosing something as trivial as a wine for dinner. You know very well how much this matters!"

Suddenly a huge crack resounded above them and a white flash of lightning flared against the blackening sky. The riderless horses skittered and neighed in fear, as a fierce wind roared, shaking the trees above them. Heavy raindrops started to splatter onto the road. Some of the grey-clad servants dismounted, ran forward and seized the horses' reins. A sudden panic filled Riathe at the thought of going with these two unknown and powerful wizards. Every instinct told him they were evil and dangerous. He bit his lip and reminded himself that he didn't know of anything bad they'd actually done, and all the tales were about healings and blessings, not curses. Mayhap tis this place, not them, he thought. He stood, his legs and body shaking, willing the Mage to decide quickly and choose him, and to stop staring at him.

After a long moment the Mage turned to Breck.

"You can go. I'll take your cousin instead. I'm afraid you'll have to walk — I have a fancy to take your cousin's horse as well. And remember," he seized Breck's chin, "we are merciful and generous, sending you back to your pretty sweetheart," and he released him.

CHAPTER 25
LOSS

"Felde!" cried Berrena, leaping up and running into his arms, as he strode into the house. "Where were you? It's been hours!"

"Over at Shraive's. I came as soon as I could," Felde said, looking around the kitchen. Kianne, curled up on the window seat, sobbed uncontrollably, Aleythe sat at the table with a tear-smudged miserable face, and Sarielle stood beside Laithan, twisting her hands together. His daughters and two youngest sons stood in a group, holding hands, their faces solemn and scared.

"What's happening? Bee, you look terrified. What's going on?"

But she stayed wordless, holding on to him and weeping into his jacket. He put his arms around her and looked the others in consternation. "Why are Aleythe and Kianne here? Where's Riathe and Breck? Laithan, what is going on? Tell me!"

Felde listened, opened-mouthed, as Laithan explained what had happened to Breck and how Riathe had gone after him towards Brossvik.

"Breck's been chosen to be a Mage?" Felde exclaimed. "Great Powers above! Breck? But that's good, surely?"

"No! That's why Kianne's upset. Aleythe too," Berrena said, lifting her head. "Aleythe says they'll take him away for years. Riathe's gone too! But we can't let them go – not with the Magi!"

"Berrena thinks the Magi are evil," Sarielle exclaimed and told him about the Mage's visit and how Berrena had fainted. When she had finished, Felde shook his head.

"Nay, I don't understand. The Magi evil? Nay, that can't be right," said Felde. "But they've taken Breck, and Riathe's gone after him? When?"

"Several hours ago," replied Laithan. "Aleythe had to find Kianne, and me, and send after you."

"Well, don't worry, Bee, they'll come back," Felde said. "There's no reason to worry. I'm sure the Magi will let Breck come back. I'll go after them tomorrow. They'll still be in Brossvik."

"Nay! You have to go now!" cried Berrena. "Felde, please!"

"Why? What's the hurry? Tis getting late, a storm's coming, and they won't come to any harm."

"Powers give me patience! Felde, listen! You've got to listen to me!" Berrena exclaimed, standing in front of him and shaking his shoulders. "Think! Remember what you told me about Peveque! What did the Magi do there?"

"They blessed the crops and herds," answered Felde slowly.

"And did they look like they'd been blessed when you were there?"

"Well, nay..."

"When they left, what happened?"

"A girl went missing ... surely that was just chance. They can't have had aught to do with that."

"And the innkeeper at Tagrinne? The Magi healed him, but do you think they didn't know about his cruelty to his wife and daughter?"

"I don't know. Mayhap they didn't."

"They took Iselle! And the last that we know of my brother, and Headon and Aven, was that they were going back to the Magi. Powers above, Felde! Can't you see? Believe me, please! I met one this afternoon, I know what he's like. He'd kill Riathe and Breck for sport. Felde! You're a fast rider, you've got to go after them!"

Felde took her in his arms again. She trembled against

him.

"I will," he said. "Right. Teiga, can you get the grey saddled?"

"'Tis already done," his eldest daughter replied. "I did it while we were waiting for you. Shall I come too?"

"Nay. Numbers won't help. I'll travel fastest alone, and I'll need to go now."

He put Berrena's hand to her chest, so she could feel his heart beating within her.

"That'll tell you I'm still alive. You wait here til morning, then come to Brossvik after me, if I ain't back. I'll, well, I don't know what I'll do. Beg them for mercy, I think. They did heal my back, Berrena. They can't be all bad."

Aleythe stepped forward and timidly touched his arm.

"Sir, Felde, there's something Riathe told me to tell you. He said it was important. He said to tell you that he trusts you. That's all," she said.

Felde understood and, in the middle of the panic and desperation, felt a hint of encouragement.

Dark clouds rolled across the sky. The light faded. A flash of blue light dazzled Felde as lightning shot through the clouds and then an echoing roll of thunder made his young mare start.

"Easy, boy, easy," said Felde, calming the horse and riding on through the flashes and thunder. By the time Felde neared Brossvik the rain hit him, the flooding downpour of a summer storm, drenching him within minutes. The lightning was moving south and there were fewer thunderclaps, but his horse remained twitchy.

As he neared the village he saw, through the sheets of rain, someone running towards him, yelling "Felde! Uncle!"

It was Breck; soaked, horseless and breathless. He staggered to the horse and leant against it. Felde dismounted and held him steady.

"Breck! Aleythe told us – we feared we'd lost you – that we'd never see you again. What happened? Where's Riathe?"

"Riathe - he's with - the Magi," Breck panted. "He wanted - to go with them."

"Raithe's gone?" Felde exclaimed. "Tell me what happened - no, best get your breath back first, lad."

Breck paused, leaning over, taking in great gulps of air. Finally, he lifted his head.

"They let me go, Uncle! He'd said if I didn't go with them then I'd be executed and I'd been selected, so it was fate and I'd no choice. But Riathe offered to go and they accepted him, when they heard about Aleythe," he concluded, then paused.

"Uncle, you know about Aleythe, don't you? You know how I feel about her. She loves me back. But Riathe, he was thinking of her too... he's gone..." Breck tailed off.

Felde looked up the road to Brossvik, then at the soaked, exhausted boy, and frowned. He didn't know what was best. He didn't want to leave Breck alone to walk the seven miles back through the rain and dark while he rode on.

"Breck, is Riathe all right?" he said urgently. "Did they hurt him? You said he wanted to go?"

"Aye, he did. He said he'd be a better apprentice than me and so they took him instead. They didn't hurt him, why should they have?"

"Where did the Magi go? Where were they headed?"

"South-east, Uncle. We went on the east road and then took the right turn to go south-east. Riathe caught us up about eight miles past Brossvik. They must have been going to the next village."

The sun set behind the storm clouds. The heavy rain showed no sign of stopping. Felde knew he'd not catch up with the Magi before dark. The sensible thing would to be to take Breck home and leave at dawn next day. This horse was fast and their lodging could only be a few hours away. They'd probably not be in a hurry to leave the next morning. He walked slowly home in the rain, leading his horse with Breck sitting on it, feeling as if he had abandoned his son.

Berrena insisted that Felde left at first light the next morning, though he felt that there would be little he could do to bring Riathe back, short of kidnap or murder. He suspected the Magi would not be easy to persuade, trick or frighten. But if he couldn't rescue Riathe, at least he could see him, journey with him part of the way and reassure himself that Riathe was truly determined to go. In the end perhaps all that he could do was say farewell.

He reached Brossvik and took the east road. By the time he reached the bend in the river the sun had risen and there were clear blue skies above him. The trees and grass were fresh green after the storm and the river was full, splashing down little waterfalls and over rocks.

Glancing in the mud on the side of road, he saw faint traces of hoof prints, almost obliterated by the rain. He took the right-hand road. After four miles it crossed the river over a small stone bridge and branched. Felde hesitated. He knew the south road followed the river before coming to a small hamlet, but it was too tiny for an inn or guest house. The east road let to a larger village that had an inn. The rain here had washed any tracks away and there was nothing left to guide him. He chose the east road.

But there was no sign of the Magi at the inn and no one in the village had seen them. He cursed to himself and turned back to try the other road.

CHAPTER 26
THE TRUTH

While Berrena was talking with Laithan, Sarielle dashed into the kitchen.

"Oh, Laithan!" she exclaimed. "I didn't know you were here!"

"He's trying to arrange someone else to help with the horses, while Felde and Riathe have gone," Berrena said. She paused, sat down, and put her hand to her mouth to suppress the swelling terror that threatened to rise and drown her in tears.

"If I weren't getting on so much, I'd do it myself," Laithan said, and put his hand gently on Berrena's shoulder. "But I think Alef can help, and we'll manage. Breck definitely can't do it alone."

"Alef?" Sarielle said.

"The blacksmith. Kianne's husband."

"Oh, of course. Thank you, Laithan. Anyway, Berrena, I came to tell you something. And Laithan should know, too, of course. You were right about the Mage! The evil, wicked fiend! He had poisoned the well! One of the piglets died, and the others are very sick."

"Piglets! What piglets?" Laithan asked in bewilderment.

"I asked Mother to get Albis to give some piglets water from the well," Berrena sighed. "The dry one at the manor that the Mage said that he'd restored. I wanted to test the water. I knew the Mage had done something to the well, something wicked. And I was right!"

"So the Magi ain't the good, white wizards we thought, after all?" said Laithan, sitting down on a stool by the fire, and leaning on his stick. "I don't understand it. They poison wells?"

"Aye! They do! And worse!" exclaimed Berrena. "It's horrible – horrible! They are terrible! They are evil, evil beyond imagination, I tell you!"

"But how can we have been fooled by them for so long?"

"I don't know. But I think that every time they come, saying that they are blessing the towns and people, they are lying. Do things really get better after they have gone?"

Laithan scratched his head. "I don't know. They've never visited Langron. I've heard that they've healed people, restored crops. But, then there was Ingra's sister..."

"Ingra's sister? What about her?" asked Sarielle.

"They healed her, and she did get better. But twas only for a short time, for a day or so. Then she became worse, far worse, and died. Aye..."

"Don't you see?" said Berrena. "They didn't heal her. And now they've poisoned the well at the manor. Not restored it – poisoned it!"

"But why? Why pretend to bless people? Why do they do it?" said Laithan.

"I don't know! But they do! Laithan, you've got to believe me!" Berrena exclaimed, her hands on her hips.

"I do, Berrena, I do. It's only that tis so strange. Tis too much to take in."

"I know. But tis true and we've got to do something about it. Something to stop them!"

"We'll have to warn others. I'll send messages to the chiefs of the nearby towns and villages. If the Magi are often doing things like this, we can find out, and tell people not to trust them, to avoid them, to not to ask them for help."

"Will people listen?" asked Sarielle. "The City Council never listened to us."

"Whether they do or not, we've got to try," insisted Berrena. "They are killing people, I'm sure."

"Tis worth it if we can spread a warning that the Magi might not be what they seem to be," said Laithan. "I ain't going to let them harm any more Talthen if I can help it. But... Riathe is with them..."

"Aye. Tis been so long," Berrena said. "I can't bear this..."

She went to the window and looked out at the back yard and the single horse standing patiently in the paddock. Her hand moved to her chest to feel Felde's heartbeat. He's still alive, she thought. But why is it taking so long? It's been four days since the Mage came. She remembered that moment, when she saw him, before the revulsion had overcome her.

"There's something else," she said, turning back. "Something – well, Mother, do you remember what the Mage was saying when I came in?"

"Um, wasn't it something about Dernham being right about the gifts fading? He said not to worry, it would be a hundred years."

"He was lying!"

"What? Really? Are you sure?"

"Aye! Lying – wickedly, cruelly lying to you! Of course I'm sure, mother! You know my gift!"

"Powers and Virtues! So what does that mean? Does that means the gifts aren't fading at all?"

"It means the opposite, mother. It means that you should worry! Think! He must know, somehow, that they are going to fail altogether, and soon!"

"Oh, great Powers help us! No!"

"Are you sure, Berrena?" said Laithan. "This is almost as bad news as that about the Magi being evil. The Hued will lose all their gifts soon? How soon?"

"I don't know! But, unless he knows of something catastrophic that is going to happen soon, we must have a few years left, at least. Oh, Mother, I don't want to lose my gift, but I'd survive! But the city, the Hued people ..."

Sarielle leapt up and walked around the kitchen, twisting her hands together. "Dernham was right. Oh, if only the council had listened!" She turned to the others. "Powers alone knows what will happen to them. No food, no city guards! The Talthen, when they find out... people will die! The whole city might be destroyed! Oh, Berrena! Oh, it's awful. Terrible!"

"There's still time," said Berrena. "If we can get the council to change the laws, get people to move out and live with Talthen, get them to trade and share the gifts, while they last. Use their riches to buy some goodwill."

"As much chance of that as of getting the Saroche River to run uphill!" exclaimed Sarielle.

"Why do you care so much, Berrena?" asked Laithan. "They exiled you. They're greedy, selfish, lazy. Be they worth it?"

"Don't you see that if the gifts fail, the Talthen will attack the Hueds and it will be war. Felde will be seen as a traitor, as will you. Don't you realise that we'll be the first to be attacked? My husband, my children, my mother, you – everyone I love will be the first to be murdered!"

"Oh, Berrena!" exclaimed Sarielle, taking her daughter in her arms. For a while, there was silence. Berrena gently moved away from her mother's embrace, sat down at the table and sighed.

"There is another reason. Tis hard to explain. Mother, you know that I never really forgave father for his staying in Hueron, and he knew it. I wish, now, that I'd made some peace with him about it. All I can do now, as a recompense, is continue the work that he started, to go to Hueron and try to persuade them to change their attitude, before it is too late. Maybe that is why I was exiled. For this purpose."

Laithan leaned forward and took Berrena's hand. "You don't regret coming to us, do you?"

"Nay! Of course not! I have you, Felde, my family, everything I want and love is here in Langron. But I still have to do something about this! This danger! There are forty thousand people in the city, mostly thoughtless and innocent, people related to me, my kin. Not to mention all the other Hueds in the towns and estates. There are children who don't know anything about what is going on. I don't want to see them starve to death or be destroyed." She paused. "I have gifts too, that I've barely used. I'll be safe. And I'm known and trusted there – partly because of my father. No one else has that advantage. But I'm not doing aught until Felde returns!"

One cloudy afternoon, three days later, Berrena's eldest daughter ran into the house, calling "Mother! Breck! Father's back!"

Berrena, the other children and Breck came rushing out, then stopped. Felde was alone. He dismounted, tied his horse to the fence, then hugged them one by one.

"I'm back, and I ain't found them," he said. "I failed. I lost the trail somehow. I've been riding round from village to village, town to town, trying to find a trace of them, but there was nought. They must have doubled back or something. I can't just ride around at random, when I've no idea where they are. So I came home. But I haven't given up, Bee, I'll do something!"

Later that day, Felde took Berrena with him into their back parlour.

"I need to talk to you away from the family. Bee, do you think I'm a brave man?" he said with serious intensity.

"What do you mean, Felde? Of course you're a brave man!" she said with exasperation.

"Nay, I ain't, Bee. If I was, I would have gone back to the Magi's house after Riathe was born. I wouldn't have stayed here. I kept making excuses. But I should've gone to find out what had happened to the others. To your brother."

"I know, Felde, but we've been through all that! You did what you thought was right. Mayhap I should have asked you to go back, but we had Riathe, and Kianne and Breck... There were always reasons to keep you here. And I think you're brave – you went after Breck and Riathe, didn't you?"

"Well, aye, mayhap. But I know what I've got to do now. I can't find them in the nearby towns - they could be anywhere. But I do know one place I can find them."

"One place?" She paused as she realised what he meant. "Their house..."

"Aye. I've got to go back. It may be twenty years too late to find Vallan and the others, but I'm going back. I may meet the wizards and Riathe on the way, but I know how to get to the Magi's house. So, if I don't find them on the way, I'll go on and find them and Riathe there."

Berrena seized his arm. "Oh, Felde! Tis such a long way!"

"I know. It'll take me at least two months, maybe three if I've got to go as far as their house. That's why I came back first. You need to know where I'm going, and I need food, money, spare clothes, a horse for Riathe, weapons; everything for a long journey. But I want to leave as soon as possible."

"Oh, great Powers. Three months!" Berrena cried. "So long! I wish - should I go with you?"

"Perhaps you could? But what about the children?"

Berrena shook her head sadly.

"Nay, you know I can't. We can't risk them losing both parents and their elder brother, or leave them for so long. And I'm still a poor horsewoman. I'd slow you down. Tis best that I stay here." She took a deep breath. "I've realised that I've work to do in Hueron."

"What do you mean?"

"I need to go there again. I've got to get the Hued to change before tis too late. Tis all I can do. Nay, I won't come with you."

"Mayhap you're right. Bee. You always are. I won't make any promises to come back. Not after last time. But you know that I want to, don't you?"

"Of course," she said, and tears filled her eyes as she remembered his youthful enthusiasm for that mission. He had grown more confident and steadier since then, stronger too, but his hair had faded and thinned. She stroked the lines on his careworn, tanned face.

"Maybe you'll find what has happened to my brother,"

she murmured. "I hope so."

"Twill be harder for you than me," he said. "Waiting for me to come back."

"Aye, with only a heartbeat to tell me you're still alive. But the Magi, they are dangerous and cruel. Be careful!"

CHAPTER 27
SOUTHWARDS AGAIN

The Saroche plain lay shrouded in haze as Felde came round the last bend in the road before it descended to the flatter land below. The air felt heavy and black clouds rolled in from the hills and covered the sky. He rode down to the plain, as wind and rain swept across the wide fields towards him. He got out his cloak and put it over him, pulling the hood up, but within minutes the rain drenched him and the horses. He remembered riding on this road twenty years ago. He had been so young, optimistic and foolhardy then! Now he felt old. Old, wary and full of forebodings.

When he reached the ford over the Saroche, he, all his clothes, and both horses were cold, drenched and filthy from nights spent in the open and days spent riding through the continual rain. He spent one night in the inn at the ford and paid to have his cloak and spare clothes cleaned and dried, remembering a similar night in a tiny village inn, with his brother and the Hued, the day before they were attacked and he had killed for the first time.

The weather cleared over the next few days and Felde saw ruined harvests in the fields; drenched, flattened crops; grain rotting and mildewed. He passed several abandoned farms and homesteads. In many of the towns and villages south of the river men and women begged openly, their faces tired and starved. Felde asked for news of the Magi but no one had seen them. He stayed another night in an inn in a small town and overheard a group of angry and drunk men cursing the Hued for their greed and indifference. Not wanting to be drawn into the aggressive talk, he ate and paid quickly and returned to the quiet of his room.

When Felde arrived at Peveque, the town looked poorer than ever. Felde did not linger, but pressed on to Tagrinne. At the inn he hesitated. Suppose someone recognised him and accused him of murdering the innkeeper? Well, if they did, he'd deny it, but he loosened his sword and dagger in case he had to fight his way out. Inside the inn it seemed cleaner and lighter than before. A thin woman with long dark hair sang as she sliced bread. Two farmers sat eating greedily from bowls of stew in a corner. The stew smelt good and Felde was suddenly hungry. An energetic young lad, of about Riathe's age, came forward and offered to stable Felde's horses. Felde stared at him as he left, then at the woman - clearly his mother; they had similar faces and eyes. She looked up at him, stopped singing, and gazed at him with a puzzled look. He bowed. There was a moment of recognition, of indecision, then, glancing at the other customers in the inn, she came up to him.

"'Tis you, ain't it?" she whispered. "Thank you!" and she took his hand and pressed it.

After eating, Felde asked about the Magi. She told him that all six had passed through Tagrinne heading north about four or five months ago and they had not seen them since.

I must be in front of them, thought Felde. He debated waiting for them, but only for a moment. Now he'd come so far, the desire to go on was irresistible.

He asked about Vallan, Aven, Headon and Iselle, but they had not been seen at all. Even though it was so many years ago, the woman was sure she would have remembered them.

At the clearing in the forest he had some difficulty finding the path beyond the two oaks, but eventually, after much hacking to and fro, he came upon it, more by chance than judgement. A few days later he rode over the mountain pass. He stopped at Jorvund's pyre by the lake. It was overgrown by grass and shrubs and he did not linger. At the desert he decided to wait until late afternoon before attempting the crossing. The woman at the inn had given him several water bottles. He filled them at the stream, then drank and tried to persuade the horses to drink. Then he turned to face the emptiness and heat ahead. He knew it was possible. He'd done it twice. It was only forty or fifty miles to the other edge. He trudged along the rocky, gritty path, with the blazing sun sinking towards the west. Powers give me and the horses strength to endure it, he thought. But I must go on. I must find Riathe.

Three days later, exhausted and desperate with thirst, he and the horses staggered over the divide into the cool greenness of the Magi's land, stumbled on to the lake and drank and drank and drank. He rested overnight, behind the hedge of a meadow nearby. In the morning, he rode past the beech forests and corn-filled fields but he saw no one. The land was quiet and empty. There didn't seem much else he could do, so he continued up to the Magi's house and tied up his horses. Feeling apprehensive and without any plan or idea in his head, he knocked on the door. It was opened by an old man in a grey tunic, with a lined face and hunched shoulders, who was hurriedly wiping his mouth. When he saw Felde he stood and gaped, until Felde said, "Are the Magi here?"

"Nay," the servant replied, "they left months ago to visit the Talthen. What'd you want with 'em?"

"To see them. Can I wait here for them?"

"I dunno. I'll have to ask the steward."

"Can you do that, then? Let me come in. I've travelled a long way and I've got to see the Magi."

Reluctantly the servant led Felde inside. The glass dome rose above him, as glorious and radiant as he remembered. The fountain played still, splashing white and silver water drops into the black pool, and the red sofas were ranged by a blazing fire. A small table held a glass of wine and a plate of bread and cakes. Clearly the servants were taking advantage of their masters' absence.

"I'll go fetch the steward," said the servant.

"Wait! Before you go," said Felde, "do you remember me? I came here nearly twenty years ago. You were here then, I think, you showed us to the guest house. There were five of us, four Hueds and me. Do you remember them? Do you know what happened to them?"

The old man stared.

"I'll get the steward," was all he said, and he scooted off through one of the carved oak doors, leaving Felde to flop down on a sofa and wait.

Two hours later the servant returned, followed by a stocky man, also in grey, with a grey-green beard. The man limped noticeably. His face was dull green and scarred, his hair had thinned, his eyes were those of one who had lived through nightmares, but Felde recognised him. He sprang up.

"Headon! Headon, you're still here? You're the steward?" he exclaimed.

They both stood, looking at each other. Felde remembered the harsh words they'd said when they last saw each other.

"Felde!" Headon shouted, and suddenly rushed forward. Felde was expecting a blow, but Headon flung his arms around him, crushing him in a fierce embrace before releasing him and looking into his face with his wide emerald eyes. "It really is you! Felde! Felde ... what... Why are you here?"

Headon grasped Felde's hands in both of his. One of his hands felt strangely papery and knotted. Felde looked at it. The hand looked twisted and scarred, with fragile dry skin. Headon had a long pale scar running from the middle of his brow, around his temple and across his cheek to his chin. One of his feet turned awry, the leg crooked at the knee.

"Powers' sake, Headon, what's happened to you? And

what about the others? Vallan?"

"If you knew... Felde, you were right to have gone. I wish we'd listened to you. Aven is dead. Vallan and Iselle are still here."

"What? Aven dead? Vallan...Iselle... they're still here! Why didn't you come back?"

Headon shook his head.

"We can't leave. We're prisoners here. It's terrible. The other two, they've been through - no, I can't say, but at least they've survived. Felde, you don't know the risk you've taken coming here. Whatever you do, don't stay! You must go back! Stay tonight and then you'll have to leave tomorrow, before they return."

He turned to the servant. "This man is an important Talthen chief. Prepare a meal for us here, bring some wine - the good bottles! - and get the best guest room ready for him. Look after his horse too. He'll be leaving tomorrow."

"I'm not leaving!" Felde said. "Not yet, not without you. I need to tell you why I'm here. But first I've got to know, what's happened to you?"

CHAPTER 28
THE MAGI'S HOUSE

Headon gestured to a sofa. "We can talk here," he said. He stared at Felde. The Talthen looked as though years of hard work had strengthened him, but had also left their marks on him too, on his lined tanned face, on his strong hands marked by scars and callouses. Headon could hardly believe that Felde had returned. And he wanted to know what had happened? It would be a long and painful tale, but Felde had to hear it. Headon remembered his fury against Felde's desertion, although now, after what he had endured here, he was glad Felde had escaped. It had been craven to leave, but in hindsight, it was right, and Felde should know that.

Nearly twenty years ago, watching Felde leave, Headon had thought he could never forgive Felde's betrayal. He had stood silently, furious and resentful, glaring at Felde riding away. Vallan had turned and thumped a tree trunk in rage and frustration. Aven, a disdainful look on her face, stared after Felde then looked back at the Magi's house. "Bloody dullard coward! I knew he'd be a waste of time!" Headon heard her mutter, then she said out loud, "So, it's just the three of us. We'll go back. We need to find out, first of all, if Iselle does need rescuing."

They mounted and rode back. Anger kept Headon from turning to see if Felde had changed his mind. When they reached the Magi's house, they saw the orange-robed Mage standing outside.

"Well, you three are becoming a nuisance," he snapped, his black eyes glaring at them. "Don't you realise your amorous little friend wants to stay? She has no desire to see you again. Nor do I, to be honest."

He swept into the building, his robes billowing behind him. The door slammed.

They looked at each other in doubt and confusion, then rode back. There seemed no other option. In a clearing in the forests by the road they stopped.

"I still can't leave Iselle," Vallan said. "I've got to see her face to face and ask her, without that wizard around, if she really wants to stay."

"Right," Aven said. "Of course. Best plan, I reckon, is for me to send my wren to scout round, find Iselle, see if she's there freely, or if she's a prisoner. That will help us know what to do."

Vallan nodded slowly.

"I'm not sure," Headon said. "The Magi knew our names, knew that we were coming."

"They won't notice a bird! And when we know where she is, we'll creep up at night, and – well - we'll make the rest up as we go along."

"Darkness isn't going to make any difference. Not with these Magi! We should get help. We could go to Tagrinne, Peveque, and get help."

"What?" Vallan exclaimed. "And leave Iselle, for days, weeks?"

"Out of the question," Aven said. "For something like this, the fewer the better. Stealth, secrecy. And what could they do anyway? Invade? And what about the desert? Not like you not to think it through, Headon. Anyway, we'll send the wren to search, and go tonight."

After a brief lunch, they rested on the grass. Headon stared up at the bright sun-lit clouds, and wondered how the Magi had known both of their arrival and their names. Did they hear what the trees heard? How could the three of them creep up to the house without their knowing? Their plan was hugely risky, but what else could they do? Vallan honed his sword, while Aven stood, watching for her wren through gaps in the trees to the distant roofs.

Suddenly she screamed, a long agonizing scream. She stood stiffly, her whole body shuddering, then collapsed on to the grass, sobbing and writhing and wailing in pain. The two men rushed to her, but Headon could see nothing wrong.

"My bird, my bird," she howled, clutching at Headon with trembling hands.

"Aven! What's happened? Where's your bird?" cried Headon, wrapping his arms closely around her. She leant her head into his shoulders, shivering and moaning.

Vallan jumped up and looked around.

"I can't see her wren," he said. "Where is it? What's wrong with it?"

"My bird," she whispered. "It's gone. Dead. They tore it to pieces." Her face distorted with pain.

"No," gasped Vallan, turning pale. "That's not possible. Powers help us. No one can do that."

Headon's heart started thudding, and sheer terror brought sweat out on his forehead. The symbols were indestructible. How could the Magi have done that?

"What are we going to do?" said Vallan.

"I don't know! Can you ride, Aven? I think we should leave, now, before worse happens."

But as he tried to lift Aven, a score of the Magi's grey-suited servants strode into the clearing. They jabbed swords and spears towards them. Before Headon or Vallan could even pick up their weapons, men grabbed them and pinioned them. Aven staggered, and her captor wrenched her arm behind her. She screamed and sagged to the floor. He yanked her up to her feet.

"March!" he said.

At the house, all six Magi stood outside. The servants released Headon and the others, and stepped back. Aven fell to her knees. Iselle dashed out from the house. There were smudges of tears on her face, and Headon noticed her symbol was missing. She ran to Vallan as soon as she saw him, crying, "He made me! I didn't want to stay!" again and again. He wrapped his arms around her.

"You fools," the orange-robed Mage said. "You should have left while you could. Folly! To think you could rescue your friend! And sending birds to spy on us!"

"We don't like being spied upon, not even by Hueds," said the blue-robed Mage. "Not even for the sake of that pretty bit of flesh over there."

"A lesson, I think. Give me your symbols," the orange-robed Mage said.

Slowly Headon took out his green stone and offered it to the Mage. He could not stop himself. Vallan did the same. The Mage held his hand out and the symbols floated over to him. He held Vallan's up to the light and examined the sapphire-coloured arrowhead. Vallan's face went pale and Headon saw that he was trembling.

"Such a waste, but we can't have something as sharp and dangerous as this flying around, can we? Someone might get hurt!" the Mage laughed. He squeezed his fingers around the symbol, opened his hand, and a trickle of blue dust fell to the ground. Vallan groaned. His face distorted in agony, and he sank to his knees. Iselle knelt by him, sobbing. "I'm sorry, so sorry," she kept saying.

Headon held his hands together tightly behind his back. He shifted his feet and lifted up his head, trying to brace himself for what was coming.

"Hmm, interesting," the Mage said, turning over his stone. "You, green-face, what does your symbol do? Healing, is it?"

"Yes, I'm a doctor, that's all," Headon said, wanting to add 'Please, don't destroy it!' but he was determined that he would not beg.

"Well, I have a fancy to keep this. Relax, I'm not going to destroy your symbol, not yet, anyway, but what will we do with you?"

The blue-robed Mage pointed at Vallan and Iselle. "I'll take these two love-birds. I can have some fun with them. This way!" He walked into the house. Vallan, with Iselle's arms around him, reeled after him. At the door they both turned and looked back briefly, their faces terrified and imploring, to Headon and Aven, before disappearing into the shadows of the house.

"Anyone got any use for the brown woman?" said the Mage, turning to the other four. "No?"

He looked appraisingly at her pain-distorted, pale face. "Well, I can't risk letting you go back," he said, "and, unfortunately for you, we don't want to keep you."

He snapped his fingers. Aven gave a tiny sigh then slipped sideways to the ground. Headon called her name, shook her, but she was motionless and unresponsive. He felt for her pulse but it had gone. He laid her down, closed her eyes and whispered goodbye. For a moment he knelt by her, then he blinked the tears away, leapt up, and ran at the Mage. The Mage held up a hand. Headon couldn't move.

"Oh, what passion!" the Mage laughed. "I think I'll keep you! You amuse me!"

He stepped closer and his black eyes pierced Headon's green eyes.

"You are mine now. You will not leave this land. You will not hurt nor kill yourself, nor your friends, nor any of the other servants here."

He gestured to one of the servants behind Headon. "You - find a room for our new slave," he said. "And get rid of that woman's body."

CHAPTER 29
CAPTIVITY

The room was large and comfortable for a prison; with a bed, washstand, a carved chest, and a desk below the window that overlooked the garden. A butterfly, with clear yellow wings, fluttered fruitlessly against the glass of the window. Headon walked over and opened the window. As the butterfly drifted away, Headon leaned out and looked around at the gardens, the distant fields and trees, the house. It would be a simple matter to climb down: the room was only on the first floor. He went to the door. It was not locked but opened to the corridor outside. But he paused. There was no point in going anywhere with no weapons, no friends, no symbol and no plan. He sat on the bed to think, but Aven's death, Felde's desertion and his apprehension of what might be happening to the others overwhelmed him, and he turned onto his side and let the tears fall.

Before nightfall a servant came in and tossed a pile of grey clothes and a satchel onto the bed.

"Here. Your luggage," he said. "The Mage didn't say you weren't to have it, so I thought I'd better give it to you. And you're to have this."

He gave Headon a hexagonal badge made of orange crystal.

"You've got to wear the grey uniform, and the badge shows which Mage owns you. It goes on the tunic, just there, see," and he gestured to his own orange badge, turned and walked out.

Headon looked at the tunic and trousers, wearily took

off his travel-stained clothes and put the others on, then pinned the badge to the tunic. He unpacked his bandages, scalpels, journal, comb, pens and ink bottle from his satchel and arranged them neatly on the smooth gold-tooled leather of the desk. Opening the journal, he dated a new page and wrote, 'So I'm a captive now. A slave. I need to find the others and work out how to get out of here. The Magi will have weaknesses - there will be a way to escape.' Dropping the pen and folding the journal closed, he pondered for a long time as darkness fell. But all he could think of was to try to discover as much as possible from the servants about the wizards and the house.

Next morning a different servant brought him breakfast.
"Do I have to stay in this room?" Headon asked.
"Nay. You can go where you like, more or less. They know you can't leave."
"What am I supposed to do?"
"I dunno! Wait until he tells you. If he wants you, he'll summon you and you'll hear him, wherever you are. Tis best not to be too far away, though, he gets mighty cross if he's kept waiting."
"Who?"
"The Mage, of course! The orange one, your owner," and he pointed to Headon's badge.
"Don't they have names?"
"Names? Nay, I don't think so. I never heard them use any names for each other. We just call them by their colours. But come on, I'll show you around, show you where the privies are, and the kitchens, then I don't need to fetch your meals to you."

Over the next few days, Headon half-expected the Mage to summon him and give him duties, but he heard nothing. He wandered around, exploring, trying to find Vallan and Iselle, considering what to do, and asking questions from the grey-clad men and women. Many snubbed him, but there were a few who were prepared to talk to a Hued. He learnt that each Mage had their own wing of the building and that there were dozens of servants, all dullards. Some had been born in the Magi's land, some came from towns and villages, taken by the Magi when they were young and now prisoners. Most went about their work with a sullen endurance, but some were cheerful, despite their enslavement.

"Well," said one, a cook in the huge kitchens belonging to the yellow Mage, "everyone's a prisoner of something. You Hued - you hardly ever left that great city of yourn. You were just as much prisoners, in a manner of speaking, as we are here. Anyhap, the food's good, we eat better than most, and the land's large and pleasant enough. They've got so many of us that we don't need to work too hard. Tain't such a bad life, as long as you keep quiet, keep your head down and don't annoy them. A few of us have even got families, in little cottages in the south."

He started chopping shallots and mushrooms with enthusiasm.

"I'm lucky. I've got a wife and kids, I like cooking and I can cope. Now him, see, in the corner. He can't cope."

The cook pointed to a figure, curled-up in a dark alcove. He was quiet apart from a low moaning, and his whole body shook.

"What's wrong with him?" Headon asked.

"Been here eight months and gone to pieces. He's supposed to be washing saucepans."

"Can't anyone help him?"

"Nay! What can we do? He'll be one of the lucky ones, anyhap."

"What do you mean?"

"See his yellow badge? The yellow one's as lazy as he's fat. When he finds out, he'll just kill him. It'll be quick, at least. The red one would use him for hunting or target practice. The green one for experiments. Powers only know what the green Mage does with the ones he takes into those laboratories of his."

Headon searched again and again for his friends but he could find no trace of them. He did not dare explore all of the blue Mage's wing and many of the doors in it were locked. Gradually he found his way around the orange Mage's wing, the gardens and the vast estate. He ventured to explore further, one day going north along the road to where the verdant greenery ended and the desert began. Standing at the divide, he tried to step over, but his body would not obey him. His legs refused to move. He started to walk faster and then broke into a run. But as soon as he reached the sand, he stopped as if he'd run into an invisible wall. No matter what he did, he could not persuade his feet and legs to step off the grass and onto the desert. Eventually, baffled, he turned back. As he neared the house, he heard the strident voice of the orange Mage.

"You, green-face! Headon, isn't it? Get yourself here, to the dome. Quickly!"

Startled, he looked around. He could see no one, but his legs started running of their own volition. When he got to the dome, the orange Mage was lounging in one of the carved dining chairs, staring down at a young man in grey who lay curled up on the floor, whimpering. Broken glass, red blood and spilt wine spread on the floor around him.

The Mage tossed Headon's green stone to him.

"This clumsy idiot dropped the wine bottle. But I feel merciful. I'll give him a second chance. You, Headon, you say you're a doctor? Well, fix him."

Headon felt the familiar cool smoothness of his symbol in his hand, gripped it tightly, then knelt by the boy. He cleared away the jagged glass from around the lad, turned him onto his back and looked at him. There were deep slashes on his face and arms and chest, and he was deathly pale from loss of blood. Headon used his gift to close up each cut in turn and start the skin knitting together.

"That's all I can do. He'll be weak for days and scarred for life, but he'll survive," he said, standing up.

"Interesting," the Mage said. "You have a possible use. A Hued doctor slaving for me. I'll have your stone back."

Headon slowly gave the stone to him.

"Well, you've learnt a lesson now, haven't you?" the Mage said, looking down at the white-faced boy. "Don't be so clumsy next time. I don't want the effort of thinking of a worse punishment for you."

He turned back and appraised Headon, turning the stone over and over in his hands, then he threw it back to Headon.

"You can keep this for now. You can't do any harm with it. You can use it. Saves us having to bother dealing with injured servants. Now get this fool out of here, and find someone to clean up this mess!"

Day after day, from then on, Headon treated accidental injuries, cured sicknesses and healed the beatings and wounds received by servants who had annoyed the Magi. Occasionally the orange-robed Mage would summon him and interrogate him about Lord Sapphireborne's fears, about the city and the garrison towns, about the Hued. Headon didn't want to say anything, but under the gimlet stare of the Mage's black eyes he could not refrain from telling him everything he knew about the Hued, their colours, their gifts, how they were trained and used, and about why they thought they were fading.

But at last, after months, he heard news of the other two. A faded, thin woman with a blue badge, who had sprained her ankle falling downstairs, knew where they were.

"They're in the dungeons underneath the blue one's quarters. He keeps a whole harem there: mostly women, some girls, some boys. But you shouldn't go there," she cried, as Headon leapt up. "You won't be able to get in or help them, and he'll know if you even go near them. He'll kill you if you try. Just wait. He gets bored and he lets them go. Or he goes away and he tells us to empty the dungeons. He doesn't kill them, not often anyway. I know, I was there for a few years. When he'd had enough of me I was released."

"Thank you," Headon said, and turned his face away for a moment. It was as terrible as he'd feared, but at least they weren't dead.

She stood up, tentatively putting weight on her injured ankle.

"Thank-you too. For this." She pushed her soft brown hair off her face, turned to go, then paused and looked back.

"Er... I might be able get a message to them," she said quietly. "If it would help."

"Yes. Tell them I'm still alive, but Aven's – tell them she's dead. And tell them that I'm trying to find a way to rescue them," Headon said.

CHAPTER 30
DISCOVERIES

Headon stood at the border and stared northward. The Crevenne Mountains were too far to be seen, he knew, but he could almost imagine that he could see glimpses of their peaks. He thought of the city, his mother, of Cairson, Dernham, Sarielle, his colleagues at the hospital, shook his head and turned back. As the months passed, whenever he had a rare, quiet day, he would take a different route, walking to the edge of the land, but the invisible barrier was always there, no matter where he went.

"Oh, we've all tried that. It don't work, though. Tis the commands, ain't it?" said a servant. "He ordered you not to leave, didn't he? Tis their power – you can't disobey them, once they've looked into your eyes and told you summat."

"Bastards," said another servant. "They're all bastards. Callous, selfish bastards. But the orange one's the worst. Those black eyes sneering at you!"

"Aye. He's relentless," agreed the first servant. "The others punish you, but tis only pain, and tis over quick. Tis nought compared to what the orange one'll do. He's cruel. I warn you. He'll torture you physically and mentally for days, weeks, and laugh in your face while doing it."

The quiet sound of a grey-clad slave trimming privet hedges in the garden drifted into the room as Headon sat at his desk, writing his journal. He turned the pages back to look at the dates. Two years and eleven months spent in captivity, he realised, and drummed his fingers on the surface as, yet again, he tried to think of a way to rescue the others and escape. He heard a knock on his door and then the thin, faded woman came in.

"Sir, the blue Mage, he's travelling north for a few months," she said.

"Is he? Some respite for them, at least."

"More than that. He's told us to clear out the dungeons, 'cos he'll be bringing back 'fresh meat' - as he calls it." She shuddered. "But tis good. Your friends - there's an empty cottage in the south-east, they can go there. He won't care."

"Thank you! At last! It's been so long. Are they - are they in good health?"

She looked down, twisting her hands together.

"What about the others in the dungeons?" Headon asked, after a pause. "What will happen to them?"

"Oh, most of them are well enough, after a few months, to become regular servants like me," she said matter-of-factly. "Some are too weak and die, some are broken or half-insane. The Mage kills those."

"How can you be so cold-hearted about them?" exclaimed Headon.

"Cold-hearted! If I cared I'd go mad. Tis the only way I can cope. I can't go home, I've got no hope, but if I start caring about all the others suffering too, I'd be a broken-hearted wreck. I do what I can to help them, but I try not to think about what they've been through. I've been through it myself, remember?"

Headon looked closely at her worn sweetness. She was in her mid-thirties; faded soft brown hair, pale skin and light blue eyes.

"What is your name?" Headon asked.

"Loira. Loira Faure."

"Where were you from? How long have you been here?"

"Over twenty years," she said in a subdued voice. "I came from Peveque. He took me from the town when I was only twelve."

Headon gasped at Iselle's changed appearance, when she

and Vallan were released. Her thin body shook. She gave Headon a brief embrace, shook her head mutely and clung to Vallan's arm. Her pink skin had a greyish pallor and her hair hung in dull violet tangles beside sunken cheeks. Vallan's blueness had faded too, his face etched with faint lines, above a straggly beard.

"I can't speak of it, Headon," he muttered. "Just get us away from him."

The next day, the orange Mage beckoned Headon aside. He chuckled.

"You've set the love-birds up in a little nest, haven't you?" he said. "Well, when he returns, their owner will be pre-occupied, no doubt. He may forget about them. Or I may choose to remind him, if you annoy me. But for that you'll have to wait. I'll be travelling myself soon. Don't look so downcast, my dear fellow! I know exactly how much you'll miss me!"

Later in the year, when the Mage returned, he had a self-satisfied air as he swept off his cloak and tossed it to Headon.

"Well, you green rascal, you'll be pleased to hear that I had a delightful trip," he said, rubbing his hands together. "No news of Hueron, but the Talthen are struggling. Lots of plagues, droughts, starvation, that sort of thing. Plenty of demands for blessings and healings, and plenty of rewards. Nine new servants and some fine horses. Get them sorted out, there's a good slave."

When Headon came back he found his master lounging on the sofa, glass of wine in hand.

"Sir, may I ask you a favour?" Headon said, standing straight as he could, with his hands clenched behind his back.

"Hah! The slave wants a favour! Think I'm in a good mood, do you? Well, what favour?"

"That you would give us all leave to return home. You can have no need of us anymore, surely?"

"What a small favour for a slave to ask! But you are so useful. Having a tame Hued doctor around is so convenient."

"Sir, please? We want to go home. Please, let us go." Headon hesitated, then knelt.

The Mage chuckled.

"You always amuse me! Let's see, seven years is the traditional time to work for your freedom, isn't it? Well, I will promote you to steward as a reward for entertaining me. Yes, I think you deserve that. Then you can work another four years, and I'll let you and the love-birds go."

Headon worked until he could barely stand, some days: managing and training servants, healing, and overseeing the farms and kitchens. Occasionally he was ordered to prepare the guest house whenever some Talthen visited the Magi. They were unsavoury-looking characters, with dirty shirts and sharp swords, who talked in whispers to the Magi. Headon heard the chink of coins passing between hands. Vallan and Iselle recovered somewhat, to his relief, but the years crawled by like slow-worms.

"Sir, our agreement?" Headon said, one day, as the Mage was giving him orders about repairs to the ice-house.

"Is it four years already?" the Mage said. "No doubt your enjoyment of them has made them pass quickly. Well, don't just stand there gaping. Fetch your love-birds friends!"

But when the three of them stood, meek yet hopeful, before him in the dome, he laughed.

"Hah! Did you really think I'd let you go? And have the whole country, Talthen as well, know the truth about us? Headon, it's been a delight to see you working so hard for your freedom!"

Headon could not bear to look at the others, but he heard Iselle sob and Vallan gasp. He would gladly have died rather than have brought this disappointment on them.

"Your expressions! Priceless! Oh, you fools," the Mage said. He leant forward and jabbed his fingers towards them.

"No. You cannot leave. Not now, not ever. I expect you to continue working as diligently as ever. Any slacking and I'll remind the other wizard about the two love-birds here. The pink one has regained her looks. He may like to know that."

This is a nightmare, Headon thought, and I have to find the weakness in this trap. He knew that the source of the Magi's power lay in the dull grey stones on their staffs: he had seen them flare with light as the Magi used them. One evening, while the corpulent yellow Mage was almost unconscious in sleep after a long and gluttonous meal, he managed to steal his staff. But he could do nothing with it. There was no rush of supernatural strength, no power to command, nothing. Disappointed, he laid it back next to the somnolent wizard and crept away.

One morning, as Headon entered the Mage's bedroom with his breakfast tray, he found the wizard soundly asleep and snoring loudly. It was late autumn and a fire was blazing and crackling in the fireplace. The white staff, with its grey stone held in a carved wooden claw, lay on the carpet next to the tapestry-hung bed. Headon knelt by the staff. Perhaps the stone could be destroyed. But how? He could try to smash it with a candlestick, but the noise would wake the Mage. Fire, perhaps? It was worth trying.

Stepping cautiously on the thick carpet, he thrust the tip of the staff into the hottest part of the coals. The flames curled round the wood and the grey stone. For a few moments the only sound was the crackling of burning wood, then there was a chuckle behind him. He whirled round. The wizard was standing by the bed, his black eyes laughing.

"You cunning green rascal. But you haven't thought it through, have you?" he said. He stretched, then settled luxuriously into an armchair. "I've slept well. And now I fancy some entertainment. Get me my stone back."

Headon picked up the tongs.

"That would be a bit too easy, wouldn't it?" the Mage

said. "Your hand, slave. Get it out with your hand."

Terrified, flinching, Headon watched as his hand moved to the fire. He could not stop it. His fingers reached into the blazing flames and his flesh bubbled and charred as it grasped the grey stone. A stink of burnt meat filled his nostrils. His hand clenched in agony, he sank to his knees and dropped the stone, clutching his wrist, moaning as the pain hit him and his hand smouldered before his eyes.

The wizard watched him writhe for a moment then touched the burnt flesh.

"Enough. I don't want you to completely lose your usefulness."

The smouldering stopped, but Headon's hand was a black claw of singed and ruined flesh. The wizard bent down to pick up the stone. It left a dark oval of burnt wool on the carpet. He tossed it high into the air, caught it and examined it.

"Undamaged, of course," he said. "You don't know what these stones are, do you? They are ancient. Made with the blood of the Magi and the nine Hued leaders. And indestructible. Oh, you fool, you! You're a nuisance. You've wrecked my staff. Have you any idea how long it will take me to make a new one? Well? Answer me!"

Headon could only groan as he knelt, cowering, on the floor.

"Not long at all! Watch this!" the Mage laughed, picking up the half-burnt staff.

He clicked his fingers, the stone flared white, and the burnt wood paled and hardened. The Mage held the stone above it, and the prongs re-appeared and curved around the stone, gripping it as it darkened back to grey.

"See! Perfect!" he said, tapping the restored staff on Headon's shoulders. Headon gazed hopelessly at the carpet, clutching his arm as the pain jabbed along it. The Mage stared at him for a few moments.

"Now, give me your stone," he said.

His head bowed, Headon gave the green oval to the

Mage. He threw it into the heart of the fire, smiled and stood up.

"Hmm, a good morning so far. Let's hope breakfast is up to the same standard," he said, lifting the silver cover from a dish of kedgeree. "While I eat, slave, get your stone out and heal your hand. But not with the tongs. Use the same hand. You don't want to lose both hands, do you?"

As he staggered back to his room, holding his wrist and moaning softly, Loira came down the corridor and saw him. She gasped, took him to her room, put salve and bandages on his burnt hand, and tried to comfort him, sitting on a stool in front of him and holding his other hand between hers. Tears fell from her weary, pale blue eyes. He no longer noticed her Talthen colouring, only her pain-marked patient face and warm, soft hands. He leaned closer to her and rested his head on her shoulder. She stroked his hair, caressed the lines etched on his face and kissed his bandaged hand, as he put his arms around her.

CHAPTER 31
BROKEN

Firelight and candlelight lit up the marble pool, and reflected off the alabaster floor and silver doors. The wizard sat by the fire with a bottle of wine beside him. Headon stood respectively near him, his hands behind his back, and stared up through the glass dome at the distant stars above. The fountain splashed cheerfully behind him, as if it had never heard of torture or imprisonment. He rubbed at the aches from the paper-dry, twisted scars on his palm.

"I think, my dear slave, it's time you know some truths about your gifts," the Mage said, swirling the wine round his glass. "You can't leave, so why not? And I'm bored and idle..."

Headon nodded. "Yes, sir, if you wish to."

"Oh, I've trained you well! So delightfully subservient!" he said, gulping down a mouthful of wine. "But, well, your gifts. You don't know the source of the Hued powers, do you? The irony of it! You're so proud of yourselves and your superiority over the Talthen. You're even arrogant enough to call them dullards. But you're worse than thieves, stealing food and life from them. The very people you despise."

"What? No! The Hued are not thieves! We're honourable, noble..." Headon said, but the wizard held up a hand.

"Noble? Do you know what your oh-so-noble ancestors did to get your gifts? They became thieves, leeches, parasites. Fool! Open your eyes! Your leaders made a bargain with the Magi and created these." He indicated the stone in his staff. "Oh, granted, they could, in a small way, exploit the virtue of life from the land around them. But the bargain they made increased that. It gave them and us vast powers. Powers to heal and to create and to protect ourselves."

"I don't understand. How does that make us thieves?"

"You fool, the Hued symbols and our stones are linked by blood, and through that to the virtue. Using the symbols to create anything drains the land of life's virtue. Every time a gifted person uses his power to create something even as small as an apple, then there is one apple taken from a Talthen orchard somewhere. And some of that life's virtue goes into you. That is why you live longer, have fewer illnesses, than the suffering Talthen. You understand?"

Headon nodded. It made sense, he thought bitterly.

"Your so-called noble ancestors knew this would happen," the Mage continued. "They made the stones in order to starve and punish the Talthen."

"To punish the Talthen? Why?"

"For betraying them. But that wasn't the only reason," replied the Mage. He poured another glass of wine. "It was the only way the coloured ones could save themselves."

He fell silent for a long moment, then turned back to Headon. "Do you know about the Feorgath?" he asked.

"Feorgath? No. What it is?"

"Not it. Them. Of course you wouldn't know. The Hued destroyed them, every remnant of them, even the name. The Feorgath came from the north-eastern mountains. They conquered everywhere. And they hated the coloured ones. They ordered every coloured person to be killed, and the Talthen helped."

To Headon's astonishment, there was a trace of sadness on the Mage's face.

"They tried to escape but they were betrayed by the Talthen. For money, for power, for their own safety. Their friends, people in their villages, their families, anyone coloured: the Talthen sold them to the Feorgath. Sold them, slave! Even children, even babies. Even tiny babies."

The Mage turned back and gazed into the flames and coals of the fire.

"Every one, almost. A few fled south, led by the nine – the leaders who made the bargain. To give themselves the power to destroy the Feorgath, and to punish those Talthen who had betrayed them. For revenge," he said, then added quietly, "Sometimes revenge is all that is left."

He continued staring into the fire. The flames crackled in the silence. Suddenly he stood up and threw his glass towards the fireplace. As it shattered on the marble, he advanced on Headon, sardonic harshness on his face.

"Of course, that was hundreds of years ago. But now you know the reason behind the original bargain, and the consequences. Which you Hued have conveniently forgotten."

He laughed, leaned forward and seized Headon by his ear.

"Do you know why I am telling you this, dear fellow? So that you can see your oh-so-beautiful Coloured City as it really is." He tugged at Headon's ear, then released him and picked up his staff. "A huge and ugly leech, sucking the life from the lands around it. And giving us our power too. As the Gifted People feed on the lands, we feed on them, on their gifts. Now that there are so many Hued we have almost unlimited powers. That's why your gifts are fading. The land is being drained, the Talthen are starving, the crops and herds are dying, and there is less and less power for you to use. You are sucking the world dry, like I might suck the juice from an orange."

The stone in his staff flared briefly, he held out his hand and an orange appeared on his palm.

"See! One less orange on a tree for some poor southern farmer. Imagine the a thousand greedy people in the coloured city all creating oranges. No wonder the Talthen are suffering!"

From then onwards, if Headon was called to heal some injured or beaten servant, his master would remind him that he was weakening or killing an innocent Talthen hundreds of miles away. "Use it while you can, slave," he said. "The Hued gifts are fading away. By fifty years there will be nothing left."

Headon stared with hatred at the chuckling Mage as he swept out of the room, his orange robes billowing behind him.

"I'll kill him," Headon muttered. "Murder him while he's asleep, then run for it. I might be able to get through the border if he's dead. I think that Vallan and Iselle could survive while I'm gone. I'll get to Hueron and persuade people to stop using their gifts. Then come back here with City Guards. Surely not even the Magi could fight off a thousand Hued soldiers."

The obstacles were like a range of high mountains blocking his path. But the first step was clear. He packed saddlebags with food, clothes, his journal and pens, water bottles and knives purloined from the kitchens. Then he waited. His opportunity came one summer evening. The Mage had been hunting all day, and on returning ordered two bottles of wine to be served with his meal. On the pretence of fetching the wine Headon ran to the stables and ordered a groom to saddle up a horse, then took out a sharp, fine-bladed knife from the saddlebags. Hiding this inside his grey uniform, he dashed to the cellars and fetched two bottles of the strongest red wine and a bottle of brandy. He poured one into a decanter and added a glassful of brandy before taking it to the Mage's private dining room.

"I'm sorry, sir, for the delay. The wine had some sediment and I thought it best to decant it," he explained.

To his relief the Mage hardly responded, merely gesturing for his wine glass to be filled. As he dined, Headon kept the glass topped up. When the Mage demanded the second bottle, Headon added even more brandy to the wine.

It was clear that, whatever powers the wizard had, he still

got drunk like ordinary men. An hour later he lay slumped in an armchair, head lolling and mouth open, dribbling into his beard. Headon deliberately dropped a serving spoon, but the wizard slept on.

He slipped the knife out, but paused. Could it be this easy? If so, why had his master omitted to command him not to hurt the Magi? And how best to kill him? Stabbed through the heart would be most satisfying, but it would not be quick enough. Instead he drove the point of the knife hard into the temple of the sleeping Mage.

The knife blade buckled like foil. A jarring shock ran up his wrist and elbow to his shoulder. His fingers stung. His nerves rang, insistent with pain, as if he been stabbed himself. He dropped the knife and clutched his throbbing hand, staring at it, half expecting to see blood pouring out of it.

The Mage stirred and woke. His eyes gazed at Headon blearily.

"Eh, what? Why have you woken me up?"

He saw the knife, its blade bent and crumpled.

"Ha! I see! Another attempt. Damn you, you rascal, I was asleep. Oh, stop whimpering, you idiot. Get your stone, sort yourself out."

Fighting to calm himself, Headon took out his symbol and managed to reduce the pain. But his arm felt as useless as if a horse had trodden on it.

The Mage picked up the knife and ran his fingers along the blade, straightening the metal as if he was pulling flat a folded piece of paper. He gave the restored knife to Headon, saying, "You fool. You still don't realise, do you? There's no point in trying to kill us. We're invulnerable. I don't think any Hueds are left with this gift, but the black and white Hueds had it, and so do we. Nothing hurts us. See for yourself. Cut my arm."

As Headon ran the sharp blade along the wizard's arm, he could feel the pain of it on his own skin, but the knife made no impression.

"We cannot be hurt. We turn any attack against the attacker. That's why your arm hurts. Well, how shall I punish you this time, slave? I think I'll slice your scheming face off. Come here and keep still."

He grabbed Headon's hair and placed the point of the knife on his forehead. Headon could smell the wine and brandy on the Mage's breath. He could not look away from those black eyes. The Mage frowned with concentration as he pierced the skin and slid the knife along the side of Headon's face, scoring down to the bone at the temple, cutting deep into his cheek and chin. Pain flooded through Headon but he could not move. Green blood poured down his face and onto the Mage's arm and hand. His master paused, looking vaguely at his wet and stained hand.

"Look at that mess. Hued blood. What a strange colour."

He belched.

"Too much wine. You're a lucky fool, slave. I'm too drunk to bother with you now. Get out!"

Headon kept out of the way as much as he could the next day. When he was summoned and the Mage saw the long, deep wound around his face, he roared with laughter.

"Did I do that to you? I have a faint memory of punishing you for something last night. Did you spill the gravy or drop a fork or something?"

As Loira rubbed salve onto his wound that evening, he slammed his fist onto the table.

"Curse them! They can't be wounded or stabbed, Loira. How can I kill him? I need to do it without him knowing, so he's got to be asleep. Maybe I could smother him or strangle him."

"Nay, don't! He'd wake up," she replied. "One of the servants tried to strangle the green Mage, but he woke up. Beat him so much that he died."

"Oh. But there's got to be a way. Fire? No, the stone was fireproof. He picked it up with his bare hand, even though it was hot enough to burn the carpet. No, I can't risk fire."

"I don't think you should risk anything," she said. "You've suffered enough. Look at your hand and your face. Just put up with it all, like I do. Keep quiet, get on with the work, stay out of the way. Tain't worth the punishment."

The eleventh year of their captivity arrived and, yet again, Headon's hope grew with the leaves and flowers. The Magi's land was at its most beautiful in spring, with crocuses and anemones in the woods, white clouds in an azure sky, bright green shoots on the hedges and shrubs. Headon had taken Loira's advice and worked diligently, been quiet and obedient. But as soon as the snow on the far southern peaks began to melt and he knew that the high passes would be clear, he decided he'd make one more attempt. He told Vallan and Iselle what he was planning.

"But - I'm not sure we can," Iselle said, placing a trembling hand protectively on her stomach.

"Headon - you don't know. We were about to tell you. She's pregnant," Vallan said, putting his arm around Iselle's shoulders.

"Oh," was all Headon could say. Conventional congratulations seemed unsuitable. "When is the child due?"

"Early autumn."

"So we have to escape as soon as possible. We don't want to be crossing the mountains with you about to give birth or carrying a new-born. I'll start preparing tonight."

Holding a single candle, Headon searched through the laboratories of the green Mage late that night. The flickering light shone on benches, jars, shelves of flasks filled with orange and ochre and pale blue liquids. The rooms stank with the smell of chemicals and blood and vomit. Rows of skeletons, ranging from that of a rabbit to a horse, stood against a white-washed wall. Other rooms had tables holding trays of scalpels, clamps and surgical equipment, next to beds with strong leather straps and buckles. Headon tried not to think what those were used for. In a storeroom he found a glass-fronted cupboard containing rows of labelled bottles. He searched them, reading the labels; arsenic, strychnine, cyanide, belladonna; until he found the one he wanted: zocadine. Odourless, colourless, tasteless and deadly, if I remember correctly, he thought. He tipped some into a small phial and put it in his pocket.

A few days later all the Magi dined together. The table in the dome had been laid with white damask, gold candlesticks, crystal and silver epergnes, vases of lilies, and decanters of wine. Headon tipped a few drops of zocadine into the wine glasses. Holding one up, he examined it. The crystal glittered and refracted the light, and it was impossible to see the tiny pool of liquid inside. He tipped the rest of the zocadine into the decanters, straightened the silver cutlery, smoothed flat the linen napkins, and waited.

The meal seemed to go on forever. It had not been a convivial occasion. The other Magi had complained about the food and wine that the yellow-robed Mage had chosen. The orange Mage had a long quarrel with the red Mage because one of his horses had been ridden too hard last week, then two others argued about who owned one of the women brought back from their recent travels.

Headon cleared the used glasses and bottles himself, tipping the dregs away before the servants drank them. He started to pace up and down the room. But his master glanced at him with a suspicious look and Headon stood still, tense with mingled fear and hope. Zocadine took about an hour to work. As far as he could tell, each Mage had drunk enough to kill several men, but by the time the cheese and fruit had been eaten, the brandy swallowed, the final plates cleared and the Magi had begun to rise from their chairs, he had to admit it had failed. His last, best plan had failed.

His master turned to him. In the golden candlelight his robes were amber and his face red from the meal, but his eyes glittered as black as night.

"Thank you, slave, for serving us so well," he said

ironically. "Before you retire, would you like a glass of wine?" and he held one out to Headon.

Headon stepped backwards. The Mage knew! But how?

"No, thank you, I have more duties to do," he stammered. The other five wizards watched, eyes narrowed in anticipation. The chief Mage advanced on him, holding the wine, smiling.

"You rascal, I know you've been plotting again. Tell me. Why won't you drink?"

Headon could not stop himself replying.

"There's zocadine in the wine."

The Mage threw the wine glass down and it shattered. He pressed his fingers onto Headon's forehead and stared into his eyes.

"I knew you were planning something, pacing up and down like that. But I told you we were invulnerable, so why did you bother? Shame I can't read your thoughts," he hissed. "We can read men's feelings and motives like open books, but not thoughts. I would so enjoy knowing what you are thinking. No doubt you are terrified." His fingers bored into Headon's forehead like gimlets. "Suspense is almost as bad as pain, isn't it, my dear slave? But if I could read your thoughts, your fears... Oh, how I could torment you."

He paused for a long time. Then he clicked his fingers. There was a snapping sound and Headon felt his leg break. He fell to the floor, collapsing sideways onto the shards from the broken glass. He gritted his teeth to stop himself screaming. The bone had shattered so badly that he could feel fragments sticking out through his skin. Emerald blood spread in a pool on the floor to join the dark of the wine. The Mage stood looking down at him.

"You're lucky your pink friend is expecting, otherwise my colleague here would be visiting her," he said. "But sadly he doesn't find pregnant women at all attractive."

He turned to the other servants in the dome and said, "No one is to touch him or help him, not even to give him a drink of water, until I say so. Understand! Tell the other servants too."

The blue-robed Mage glanced down at Headon.

"Why do you bother?" he drawled. "Kill him and have done with it. And don't use me as a threat. I'm not your tool, I'll make my own decisions about women."

"I don't care what you do about that woman, but he does. And I keep him because he amuses me. You have your pleasures, I have mine. Which reminds me." He turned back to Headon. "I don't think you've been punished enough."

He clicked his fingers again. Headon's other leg broke. He moaned as the pain flooded him, then blackness overwhelmed him.

CHAPTER 32
RESPITE

Three days passed in a daze of pain and fever and thirst. Headon could smell his own blood, urine and sweat festering around him. On the fourth day, through the darkness edging into his sight, he saw the Mage standing above him, gazing dispassionately at him. Someone else was there. Headon turned his head slowly. It was Loira, sitting on the floor by his side.

"Sir, I think he's dying," she said expressionlessly.

"We can't have that, can we? Not that it's any concern of yours," said the Mage, seizing her chin and looking at her face. He gestured at the blue badge on her tunic. "You're not one of my servants. Get out of here. Go and do whatever it is you're supposed to be doing!"

She scuttled out. The Mage bent over Headon.

"Well, my steward, you must be thirsty. I have a choice for you. Water - or zocadine?" He held up a glass and a small phial.

Headon stared at the wizard. After a long pause, he whispered, "Zocadine."

"I can't quite hear you. What did you say?" said the Mage.

Struggling to draw breath, Headon croaked, "Zocadine."

"Sorry, dear chap, you don't get that. You made the wrong choice - you get to live. Get your symbol. Heal yourself."

"I can't," said Headon. "Too faint..."

The wizard tutted, then poured some water into Headon's mouth. He placed his hand on Headon while a pallid light glowed from the stone in the staff. Headon felt strength returning to him, but his legs were still smashed into agonising fragments.

"I'm not going to heal you," the Mage said coldly. "You'll have to get some of the servants to put splints on your legs, then do the best you can, for your own sake. I want my steward back, obedient and penitent, remember!"

He called for some servants.

"Get this fool out of here – he stinks. And get this mess cleaned up!"

In the autumn Loira brought Headon news that Iselle had had a baby girl. He limped to the cottage, trying to feel some gratitude that he could still walk. After his failure, he had struggled to heal himself, while Loira stroked his forehead and comforted him. "I can't do it, Loira!" he had cried, collapsing back onto his bed, and striking the splints on his ruined legs. "There's just not enough power in my stone. My gift - it's fading..." It took him weeks of willing all his power into his legs, determinedly forcing his aching, twisted limbs to move, before he could take even a few trembling steps, and every time he used his stone, he heard the Magi's words about killing or weakening Talthens.

At the cottage, Headon held the baby with careful awe and smiled at the child's wispy hair and tiny hands. She was the rich scarlet of holly berries.

"We've decided to name her Avenessa, after Aven," said Vallan. "But we'll call her Nessa for short. If only we could show her to my mother and father, or even get a message to them, somehow, to say that we're alive and they have a grand-daughter."

"I'm sorry, Headon, more sorry than I can say, that your plan failed. And your legs – oh, Headon," exclaimed Iselle. "How you must have suffered!"

"At least I can still walk and I'm still alive," said Headon. "Your daughter is beautiful. Think about her, not me."

"Yes, isn't she beautiful? If only we can keep her from falling into his hands!" said Iselle.

Headon did not need to ask who 'he' was.

The next morning the Mage ordered Headon to fetch the others and their child to the dome. As they stood, waiting in fear and suspense, the Mage swept in and took the baby from Iselle. She tried to snatch it back, but he held up a hand.

"Well, it seems your friends have a very low opinion of me! Relax, I'm not going to hurt her. But I want to see her."

He held the child in his arms, as a father would a newborn baby, and gazed at her sleeping face. He stroked the scarlet hair back from her forehead and lifted her hand. Her tiny fingers clutched his finger. He turned away and went towards the fountain in the centre of the dome. Headon had a moment of fearful horror and leapt forward. But the Mage walked around the fountain and came back to them. The minuscule red fist was still trustingly holding his finger as he gazed at her. Carefully, he prised open her other hand.

"I'm glad to see you haven't cut her palms yet," he said.

He handed the child back to Iselle.

"She's to wear an orange badge and be mine. Understand! And I will see to it that the blue Mage has nothing to do with her. But you are not to perform the marking ceremony, or I will give her to the blue Mage, I promise you."

They nodded.

"Now go!" he snapped and they scurried out, relief lightening their hearts.

But Headon had noticed lines on the Mage's face, crows' feet round his eyes, white hairs in his black beard. He remembered when they had first seen the Magi. Then they had been men in the prime of life. Now they were beginning to look older. They were invulnerable, but not immortal. It seemed that they would grow old. And die, perhaps? He hoped so. He had given up trying to escape. All he could do now was endure and hope for some miracle as the years passed.

Leaning against the mantelpiece, a few years later, the Mage told him that all the wizards would be travelling that spring.

"We are getting old as, no doubt, you have noticed, my dear rascal. Time for us to select our apprentices, so we are leaving in four days time."

Headon nodded respectfully. "Do I go with you?"

"Oh, I'm sure you'd love to. But of course not! We expect to come back to a decent feast and well-managed household, understand! Til then, you and the other servants can have a holiday. I don't care what you do as long as the harvests on the servants' farms are gathered in."

"How long will you be gone?"

"At least six months. When we return we will be bringing apprentices and more servants, girls, horses, treasures and so on. We will send a servant on ahead to give you few days' notice."

Headon stared at the floor to hide the joy in his heart.

The Mage chuckled. "Don't be so downcast, my dear fellow! Although, who knows? I may bring back another tame Hued doctor as a replacement for you. But I know exactly how sorry you would be to leave my service."

That summer was warm and balmy. Larks sang high in the blue skies, showers of soft rain greened the meadows and gardens, oranges and lemons in the trees ripened, bright sun sparkled on the lakes and streams. Headon and Loira rode south-east past fields of barley, oats and corn that spread for miles: acre after acre of green ripening slowly into pale yellow.

At the cottage, he gave Nessa a ride on his shoulders through the rows of geraniums and runner beans, while Loira and her parents sat laughing at him. He knelt down so the child could get off his shoulders, picked her up, swung her high in the air as she giggled, then caught her. She ran to Loira and her mother.

"Come on! Come and play dancing with me!" she insisted, grabbing the hands of the two women and imperiously tugging them to their feet.

Headon sat down on the bench next to Vallan and, wincing slightly, stretched out his legs in the sunshine. From the cottage the southern mountains could be seen beyond the encircling desert. In the morning light the peaks were clear and sharp. He sighed.

"Blessed, blessed respite..." he said, flicking a scarlet petal off his tunic. "In this sun, in this peace, I could almost forget the future, the danger to the city, to my mother..."

Nessa danced round in a ring with the two women, whirling them faster and faster. Suddenly she sat down and laughed as her mother stumbled and sat down too, Loira tumbling on top of her, as white butterflies rose up from the cabbages by the side of the path.

"Yes, I know," said Vallan. "To be here, growing vegetables like peasants, watching sunsets, idling, while the city is in danger. Frustrating. But I worry more for Nessa. When they return, if the blue Mage takes her..."

"Perhaps they won't return. Perhaps he'll have forgotten about you," Headon said, but was interrupted by one of the other servants, an old, hunched man. He came round the side of the cottage and paused.

"Yes? What do you want?" said Headon.

"'Tis a visitor, a stranger. He wants to see the Magi. He wants to stay here until they come back. So I said I'd fetch you, 'cos I dunno what to do with him."

The others glanced at each other, puzzled.

"A visitor? Probably one of those Talthen bandits that came last year. Well, I'd better go. Nessa, give me a hug before I go, please?"

She trotted up to him and gave him brief hug and a perfunctory kiss, before skipping away.

When Headon limped into the dome he saw a tall, vaguely familiar figure, a broad-shouldered muscular

Talthen, resting on a sofa. The man sprang up as he entered.

"Headon! You're still here? You're the steward?" the man exclaimed.

For a long moment Headon stared, doubt and confusion struggling in his mind. The man's blonde hair had darkened and thinned, there were faint creases on his tanned face, he looked broader and older, but Headon remembered him.

"Felde!"

The evening sunshine shone gold on the scarlet hair of Nessa, as the Hued and Felde sat in the cottage garden. Iselle leant against Vallan, holding her child tight, with her tears overflowing.

"Lord Sapphireborne dead, Mavretan dead, Zarcus dead, mother estranged from Lady Rochale, giftless people leaving the city," Headon said, his head bowed. Then he looked up. "It's not good news. But I'm grateful to learn even that, Felde."

"Aye. 'I don't know any more. But I'm sorry that twas me that had to tell you, Vallan, Iselle, about your fathers' deaths," said Felde. "Don't cry about Mavretan, Iselle."

"I'm not crying about him!" she gulped. "I'm crying for Zarcus! Not my father. When he took me to Hueron I was so excited! I thought it was because he loved me, but he didn't. Not much, anyway. He wanted to use me to charm his business cronies, to seduce them. He didn't care about me that much, but Zarcus did!"

The others were silent. Vallan held her tighter as she hid her face in his shoulders. Eventually she turned round, wiped her eyes, and looked up. "Felde, thank you. I should apologise for what I did to you," she said. "I was so selfish, so thoughtless."

"Did to Felde?" Headon exclaimed.

"Don't talk about it, Iselle," Felde muttered, looking downwards. "'Tis done now."

"No. Powers above, after all we've been through here, I don't want anyone to blame you for leaving us. It was my fault. Do you think I haven't spent years thinking about it? Headon, Vallan, there's something I ought to tell you." To Headon's astonishment, she explained how she had tried to seduce Felde, before they had met the Magi. Headon stared at her. So that was why Felde had refused to return for her. And he had thought it was cowardice.

"Iselle? I can't believe that... We..." Vallan gasped, looking thunderstruck.

"I'm sorry," she said, after a long pause. "What I did was terrible. I can only say that it was like a habit, with me, then. It's all different now. Vallan and I... Anyway, Vallan, Felde was right. None of you should have come back. Vallan, I'm so sorry!"

Vallan took her in his arms, saying, "Iselle, it's all right, it's all right."

Headon put his hand on Felde's shoulder, and said, "I understand now. And you have come back for us."

"But I've come back for my son too," said Felde.

"Even so...It's good to see you. But what are you going to do?"

Felde got up and strode to and fro, saying, "I don't know! What you've told me about the Magi - it's terrible. I've got to stop Riathe coming here and you need to get out too." He stopped, stared at the distant mountains then turned to Headon. "I don't understand why you can't leave."

"Believe me, Felde, we've tried everything," replied Headon.

Vallan nodded glumly in agreement. Nessa squirmed out of Iselle's arms, saying, "I want to play. I'm going to see if I can find some worms," and ran off down a path to a vegetable bed.

"What about the child?" Felde said. "You've got to get her out! There must be some way. Can't she leave?"

"She might be able to leave," Headon said. "She's not been commanded to stay. You could take her and go back to Langron."

Iselle and Vallan both cried "No!"

"Nay, I can't! Look, I know you want to save your daughter, but that would mean me having to leave my son. I can't do that," Felde exclaimed.

"And how can we bear to lose her?" cried Iselle.

"But if Felde can save her from the blue Mage," said Vallan, "it's worth it. We couldn't save you, Iselle. Do you want Nessa to go through what we went through? Felde, please. Don't let us down again."

Headon saw Felde clenching his fists.

"He didn't let us down," he said. "If Felde had stayed, he'd be dead now. Like Aven. And we can't ask him to abandon his son for your daughter."

"Wait," said Felde. "There may be a way. How long have we got before the Magi return?"

"I would estimate about two months. It's over four months since they left, and they said six."

"There may be time enough," said Felde. "I could take the child to the inn at Tagrinne and come back. The woman who runs it would look after her, I'm sure. She could hide her from the Magi when they pass through."

"Hmm. It's possible," said Headon. "You could come back and find your son. You might even be able to rescue him, go to the inn, get Nessa and take her back to Langron."

"Aye. And even if we can't get out, the innkeeper would take care of her. She might be able to get a message to Lady Rochale."

"But we'd never know if she was all right or not," Iselle cried, "Surely it's better to keep her here and pray the Mage never remembers her?"

"No," said Headon. "No! If I know she's safe, I can bear this place. And if the blue Mage did take her, what would we feel, knowing we'd turned down this chance? Vallan, Iselle, for her sake, for my sake, let's try it. Even if she doesn't get to Langron, but stays with this innkeeper, it's worth it."

Nessa came up to them, crowing, "I made pretty leaf patterns by the beans! Hands dirty now," and proudly held out soil-encrusted hands to her mother.

"Felde, what's this woman like?" asked Vallan. "Can you be sure she'll take care of Nessa?"

"I think she will. I think she was grateful for what I did," said Felde and he explained, reluctantly, how he had accidentally killed her violent, abusive father.

"I can't bear to lose her, but I can't bear the fear for her if she stays!" Iselle cried. "Give me a little time to decide, just a little more time with her! Please? Just two more weeks? Before I have to let her go for ever!"

At the northern edge of the Magi's land, a fortnight later, Iselle knelt and held Nessa tightly while Vallan stood still, gazing on the child as if trying to memorise every feature.

Felde murmured to Headon, "Iselle's changed. I never thought I'd feel sorry for her."

Headon nodded. The careless and flirtatious girl she had been was barely visible in the thin mother kneeling and weeping over her daughter.

"Years of suffering, of fear, of imprisonment," Headon said. "We have no idea what she has endured. She won't speak of it, and I hardly dare imagine it. I hope we can save her daughter from going through the same ordeal."

He turned to Vallan.

"Are you sure about this?" he asked.

"Yes. Even if Felde can't get her to Langron, to mother, at least she'll be safer in Tagrinne than here. I've gone over it again and again in my mind. Iselle agrees. We can't trust the orange Mage to keep his word. If we kept her and the blue Mage took her we'd – well, anything is better than that. But these last few days, getting ready to send her away for ever..."

"It may not be for ever. The Magi will die eventually. We may be free one day to follow her," said Headon. There is always hope, he thought, and gazed at the faint line of the path heading northwards. He thought he could make out a faint smudge where the path faded into the distant haze. It was growing, changing into a tiny cloud of dust. A dark spot appeared in its centre.

"What's that?" he asked.

Vallan said, "I think it's someone on a horse, riding fast this way."

"The Magi!" gasped Iselle, clutching her daughter close.

"Powers above, please, no! No! Surely it's too soon to be them?" said Headon.

They waited. The darkness at the centre became a rider wearing grey, coming towards them. He rode slowly up to them and stumbled off his horse. He was caked in dust, his mouth was cracked and dry, and the horse looked spent. It collapsed to its knees.

"Steward?" the man croaked, glancing at the others with weary curiosity. "The Magi sent me on ahead. They will be here in three or four days. You're to get the house ready for them and the apprentices and the new servants, fifteen men and twelve women. And they want a feast prepared."

The Hueds and Felde looked at each other, then Vallan turned away. He kicked a stone on the path hard, then said to Iselle, "You may as well take her back. It's too late now."

Headon asked the servant, "Three days' time?"

"Aye, they're following me, but going slower. Have you got any water? I'm parched. My horse too, poor beast."

They gave the servant and his horse some of the water loaded on Felde's horse. He emptied the water bottle into his mouth, pouring the last few drops over his head. "Powers above, that's good," he gasped. "I nearly died of thirst. That bastard Mage! He said the horse was too good to risk, so he'd provide us shade for the crossing. A cloud over us. It lasted one day. One day! Is there any more water?"

When he'd finished drinking, Headon said to him, "Go on to the house. Tell all the other servants. We'll follow you shortly."

Felde gazed towards the horizon. "The Magi," he said in a stunned and awestruck voice.

"We'll go back," said Vallan. "Maybe the Magi will forget about Nessa. It's a pity we were too late. But at least we haven't lost her yet..." his voice trailed off as he lifted Nessa onto her pony.

Iselle, tears pouring down her face, kissed Felde, and whispered, "Thank you."

"I'll wait until I hear from you, Headon," Vallan said. "You'll be busy. Felde, I hope you can save your son. Goodbye." They rode off.

After a pause, Felde turned to Headon.

"What do I do now?"

Headon replied, "I don't know. I don't think you should go to meet them. They'd see you coming and you wouldn't stand a chance. Your only advantage is that they don't know you're here."

"I don't know what to do. I can't even be sure that Riathe is with them," Felde said. "'Tis weeks since he was taken."

"I think we'll try putting you in grey - as a servant. Then perhaps you can get to your son without them knowing."

"And then what?" said Felde.

"I don't know!" replied Headon with exasperation. "I've been trying to escape for years – I have no answers! Do you think I don't long to get back to the city, to my mother, to my friends? You might be able to, but I don't know how! Just pray you can rescue him before the Magi get to you. Get him away from them and then run for it."

CHAPTER 33
WITH BRIGANDS

It felt as if Riathe had been with the Magi for months, although by his reckoning it was only five weeks since he had stood, in the shadows under the trees, and watched Breck walk away. They had ridden through incessant rain, as dusk fell and thick clouds covered the sunset. The Magi stayed dry, but Riathe and the others were drenched within minutes. I want power like that, Riathe had thought, cold rain dripping down his neck and his hands so chilled that he could hardly hold the reins.

After several miles they left the road and turned onto a rough track going eastwards. Riathe had a sudden thought. His father would surely be on his trail. He was determined to continue on this journey, to become a wizard's apprentice, whatever it took, but he longed to see his father again, even if only to say goodbye. But Felde, even if he had tracked them this far, would never know they had taken this track.

Cautiously, Riathe allowed the others to get ahead of him, and dismounted, hoping the deepening twilight would hide what he was doing. Taking out his dagger he tore a strip of cloth from his shirt. The track was lined with simple posts and rails, and Riathe stealthily tied the cloth strip to a rail near the road, as quickly as he could. Then he mounted and rode on to the others, praying that his father would see the ripped cloth and realise what it was.

After a few hundred yards, he looked back. A curious cow, attracted by the flapping strip, had seized the fabric in its mouth. It tugged. The cloth ripped and the too-hastily tied knot came undone. The cow chewed the strip for a moment, then dropped it into the field where it lay sodden in a puddle.

Riathe turned away, his shoulders slumped, and rode on.

The rain eased, and they came to a sheltered limestone gorge. Servants scurried round setting up spacious pavilions for the Magi or small canvas tents. As Riathe stood, unsure what to do or where he'd sleep, a hardy well-favoured lad came up to him.

"You're an apprentice, ain't you?" he said. "I'm one too. The one with the orange cloak picked me. I'm Halke Beorse. From Thulron."

"Riathe Sulvenor. From Langron," Riathe answered. "Aye, I'm an apprentice."

"Both of us picked, eh? I was amazed when he told me I had magic powers. I mean, you'd think I'd have noticed something."

"And you hadn't?"

"Nay! I'm just a farrier's lad! No-one special. Anyhap, I wanted to say, you can share my tent, if you ain't got one."

"Thanks."

The blue-robed Mage came out of his pavilion, looked around, saw Riathe and walked over to him. He took hold of Riathe's shoulders and stared at him. As the Mage's blue eyes met his, he shivered as the dread came over him again.

"You are mine now," the Mage said softly. "That means you do everything I say. Firstly, you stay with us. You may not leave us nor return to your families or homes. You are not to kill or hurt the other servants or other apprentices or yourself. When we go through towns and villages you will keep silent. Understand?"

Riathe nodded. The Mage released him and strode away. Halke shrugged. "The other one did the same to me," he said. "It gave me the shivers."

They travelled east for three days, staying at inns in

Talthen towns, with Riathe and the other servants camped in fields or back gardens. Late one evening they turned into a narrow track that ran past fields then uphill through sparse forests. Riathe saw, through the gloom, a tall hedge of holly. The leading Mage pointed at it with his staff and the hedge divided, revealing a wrought-iron padlocked gate. The Mage waved his hand over the lock and it sprang open. Gesturing for the others to go through, he followed them and locked the gate, as the holly trees merged behind it. They rode through trees and onto a grassy meadow surrounded by forest and sloping downhill to form a wide bowl-shaped clearing. In the centre stood a two-storey, gabled house, with ivy twining up the brickwork and smoke rising from tall chimneys. Riathe stared. This house looked almost as grand as a Hued manor. It was a wide house with many windows, with stables and outhouses behind it, and a front door flanked by carved stone wolves. Candlelight shone through the windows and Riathe could hear laughter and loud talk over the steady sound of the rain.

The leading Mage dismounted, flung the door open, and strode inside. The others followed him. Riathe paused on the doorstep and looked around curiously at the large quarry-tiled hall, with plain brick walls, bare rafters and wide stairs twisting upwards. Several dirty-looking men lounged on benches, with tankards and plates of bread on tables in front of them. One shouted, "Oy! We've got visitors!" towards the back of the house. A richly-dressed fubsy man, with a gold chain round his neck and fine lace trimming a crumpled linen shirt, scurried into the hall. His bald head shone in the lamplight as he scowled at them with suspicious eyes. He saw the Mage and his frown changed into a smile, revealing several missing teeth.

"Sires! You're most welcome!" he said, with an oleaginous bow. "We were hoping you would honour us with a visit."

"Ulban, you old rogue! Still here?" said the Mage. "Still prospering? We will be staying with you for a few days, until our other colleagues join us. Get our usual rooms ready for us, and stabling, servants' quarters, as before," He clicked his fingers. A gold coin appeared in his hand and he tossed it to the obsequious man, who bowed even more deeply.

"Don't overdo the grovelling, my dear fellow," said the orange Mage. "We are under no illusions about what you really respect." He flicked another gold coin high into the air, then laughed as Ulban tried to catch it and stumbled backwards.

The blue-robed Mage walked over to the empty fireplace. He raised his staff, the stone shone for an instant, and blazing logs appeared.

"That's more civilised," he said. "Ulban, get your men to work. We have servants, luggage, women, horses, all to be sorted out!"

Ulban called for men to stable the horses and the Magi's servants ran in and out, unloading the horses' packs and taking bags inside. Riathe and Halthe stood unsure amidst the bustle of competent people. The orange-robed Mage turned to them.

"Ah, the new apprentices!" he said. "Don't dither on the threshold like that. Ulban, get these two peasant lads a room!"

Riathe and Halke were led upstairs to a large room with several bunk beds. A gaunt man wearing a grey tunic, with a blue hexagon-shaped badge, spread blankets on the beds and folded towels and clothes.

"Oh dear, dear. More work," he snapped, glaring at Riathe. "I'll get a change of clothes for you. You can't wear those filthy rags. Right. Sleep on those bunks. Then s'pose I'd best take you down to the kitchen to eat and show you where to wash and where the privies are."

Halke started unpacking his saddlebag onto one of the bunks.

"What house is this?" he asked. "And who's Ulban? He's too rich to be a farmer, but he ain't a Hued."

The servant laughed. "Farmer? Don't be daft! The

Talthen farmers are all poor as starving sparrows, but not Ulban Hirshe." He paused from folding clothes, and looked with faint mockery at them. "You greenhorns don't know what you're getting into. Ulban? He's head of a band of cut-throats and brigands, and this house is their base. The north road passes through forests and gorges about ten miles away, and they get rich ambushing travellers."

They stayed at Ulban's headquarters for several days before any of the other Magi arrived. Riathe had no duties and time hung heavy. He had thought that he'd start training to be a wizard straight away, but the Magi ignored the apprentices. Instead they went riding out with Ulban and his men, or inspecting horses, or eating and drinking, or doing very little. The debilitating terror and vile smell had faded, or Riathe had got used to it, but even so, he was relieved not to have to go near them. He spent his time helping in the stables, talking to the other servants in the kitchen, and finding out as much as possible about the Magi and where they were going.

Two more Magi arrived, one a balloon-shaped wizard, enormous in yellow robes, and the other a serious wizard dressed in green. By now Riathe knew that the Magi had no names and had learnt to call them 'the blue one', 'the orange one', like the other servants. They brought two lads to be apprentices, looking both proud and apprehensive. Riathe was passing through the hall when the two wizards greeted the other Magi.

"Hmm, it was annoying, but we are here now, so don't go on about it!" said the yellow-robed wizard. "Two weeks earlier than we planned too! Fortunately we were able to come straight away, despite some unfinished business. So, what was the urgent reason? It had better be good!"

"A black Hued woman! That was the reason. We need to talk. This could change everything," said the orange Mage.

"A black Hued?" exclaimed the green-robed Mage.

"That is serious news."

Riathe paused, just by the door, to listen. He expected the Magi to order him away, but to his surprise, they ignored him.

"So what?" said the yellow Mage.

"Think with your brain and not your stomach, for once!" said the orange Mage. "There are two problems. Firstly, she met me, and knows our little secret. Suppose she tells the Talthen and they start putting two and two together?"

"Suppose she does? It won't harm us."

"Don't be a greater fool than normal! You know the deal. We bless the Talthen and they are suitably subservient and grateful. If they realised our blessings were curses in disguise, that we infect their cattle, poison their wells, steal their horses and children, do you think they'd be appreciative? No! I don't want to go to some Talthen town and be met by an angry mob, nor do I want to be trapped skulking south of the mountains."

"You are over-reacting. We can deal with angry mobs. We could go back and silence this black Hued," said the yellow Mage, settling himself into an armchair by the fire. "Ulban, a glass of wine! Now! It's been a long ride."

"We can deal with mobs, yes," said the orange Mage, "but that's not high on my list of pleasures. I'd rather be welcomed by grateful and deceived Talthen!"

"Well, we all know your odd tastes," drawled the blue Mage, "but I agree. The alternative is too much work. How do you propose we silence this Hued?"

"We can't," said the green Mage. "You know perfectly well there is nothing we can do against a black Hued. We have to hope they don't talk to the Talthen about us, which is feasible, given the Hueds' attitude. And we should also keep away from that area for a while. A few genuine blessings, next time we visit, would be a good move."

"But there's another issue, don't you realise, you fools?" said the orange Mage, slamming his staff on the tiles. "Oh, you were so sure that the black line had died out. So where did this black Hued come from? And what if there are more? We don't know enough about the Hueds and what is happening in Hueron city!"

"I don't know where she came from! There were no children. The bloodline had died out. We made sure of that. You must have been mistaken. Maybe she was dark blue or brown?"

"I'm not mistaken! And she understood me. She knows!"

"Calm down," said the yellow Mage, swallowing the remainder of his wine and hauling himself out of the armchair. "There's no advantage in quarrelling over this. We'll keep out of the way, lie low for a few years. And get Ulban to tell us as much as he knows about the Hued. I'm going to my room. I need to have a nap before we eat."

That afternoon, as a bored Riathe lay on his bunk and wondered what he was supposed to do and if his father would find him, the gaunt servant came in, muttering to himself and looking perturbed.

"What's happening?" asked Riathe, starting up. "Anything I can do? Give me something, a job, something!"

"A job for you?"

"Aye! Anything! I can't stand this waiting to start training!"

"I can't. Tain't no business of mine to sort your training, or find stuff for you to do. I've got worse worries..."

"What?"

"Oh, nought you and I can do aught about. The green Mage brought a slave girl. Pretty and terrified, barely thirteen. He's given her to the blue one in exchange for a horse. A horse! That's all! So now I've got to find a badge and uniform for her, and I ain't sure I've got aught small enough. I hate it when they go to the blue one. Still ain't used to it, even after all these years," he grumbled, pulling grey tunics out of a pack.

"Why, what does the blue Mage do?"

The servant straightened up and looked at Riathe with

pitying contempt. "What do you think he does? Welcome to hell, lad."

Stung into action, Riathe ran downstairs. He heard the blue Mage's voice, low and murmuring, coming from one of the parlours that opened off the main room. He pushed open the door and went in. The Mage sat on a bed, holding the arms of a fragile childish girl who pulled away from him, terror on her face. Riathe ran to her and knocked the wizard's arms aside.

"Leave her alone!" he shouted.

The Mage scowled at him. "What? Get out! This is my slave girl and my business. I'll teach you to interfere, filthy Talthen runt!"

He struck Riathe hard and knocked him to his knees. Then he hit Riathe on the side of his face, so forcefully that he fell to the floor. Riathe felt no pain from the blows. He was about to leap up and retaliate, when he saw the Mage stare at him and shake his fingers as if they stung. Riathe realised that the blow had hurt the Mage more than him. Instinctively, strangely, he knew that he must not let the Mage realise this. He yelled and rolled on the floor as if in pain. The girl screamed too. The Mage pulled Riathe up and pushed him outside, shouting incoherently at him, then slammed the door. Riathe heard a bolt slide across. He tried to turn the handle but it was locked. The girl's screams stopped. Riathe pounded on the door, but heard nothing. Suddenly someone grabbed him and pulled him away from the door, clapping a hand over his mouth,

"Young idiot!" hissed the servant. "There's nought you can do and if you disturb the other Magi you'll be in worse trouble, and I'll be too. Luckily for us, they're out somewhere. Leave it!"

Late that evening the blue Mage summoned Riathe to his room.

"That was impressively noble of you," he said in a soft, sneering voice, "trying to rescue the damsel in distress, but

I can't have you interfering with my games. Apologise!"

Riathe longed to rip the gloating eyes out of that debauched face, but he stood as still as he could, with his hands clasped behind his back.

"I'm sorry for angering you, sir," he said, through gritted teeth.

The Mage put the tankard down and lifted his staff. He stared measuringly at Riathe.

"Hmm. Apology accepted. I ought to punish you," he said, waving the staff, "but I'm unwilling to damage your looks and, frankly, I've had such a good afternoon that I'm in too cheerful a mood. Consider yourself punished enough, knowing you failed. The girl's fine, you'll be glad to know. A pretty, delicate morsel of frightened innocence. And you - I advise you to keep out of my sight for a while!"

The final two Magi arrived with their apprentices. Like the other three, they were strong, broad-shouldered boys, tanned from outdoor work, and they exuded health and high spirits. Riathe knew he looked unhealthily pale and thin beside them. None of them seemed particularly bright or educated, and they were all surprised to have been chosen to be wizards.

The Magi shared a feast with Ulban and his men that evening. The other five apprentices were asleep, but Riathe lay awake, listening to Halke snoring and looking forward to the prospect of being on the move the next day. He heard loud voices from downstairs. It sounded like an argument and he thought he heard the word 'Hued'. He threw off the bedclothes, slipped out of the bunk and crept part-way downstairs until he reached a point where he could hear without being seen. The argument was over. One Mage was saying, in decisive tones, "Well, as he says, we'll avoid Langron, and hope she doesn't discuss us with the Talthen."

There was a clatter of plates and cutlery, and the sound of servants going to and fro.

"We should stay away from the Hued," said another.

Riathe thought it was the green Mage. "They're too unpredictable. You don't know what powers they may have."

"Yes. Anyway, we have more important things to discuss," said the orange Mage. "Ulban, your men and the servants are to go."

Riathe ran back to his room as two or three men came up the stairs. When they had passed he opened the door and, seeing no one around, tiptoed back. The orange Mage was still speaking.

"You know the problem. There's no way to stop the Hued draining the land except by breaking the connection."

"Are you mad! Break the connection? We'd lose everything!" the red Mage shouted.

"Idiot! We are going to lose it anyway! But if we are in control, if we destroy the gifts at a time of our choosing, we can plan."

"Oh, sure. Destroy the gifts, you say. How, precisely?" said the blue Mage.

"It is feasible. We destroy the stones by turning their power back on themselves. That destroys the gifts," said the green Mage.

"But why, by all the Powers?"

"Because we can plan ahead," said the orange Mage. "Destroy the gifts. Start a war between the Talthen and the City. Rescue some Hueds, use them to recreate the connection, the gifts, and so on."

"But without the black and white Hueds we lose our greatest gifts!" said the green Mage.

War? Between the Talthen and the Hued? thought Riathe. He shook as he imagined it. His grandmother, his mother, his brothers and sisters, what would happen to them?

The discussion turned into a raucous argument and Riathe could no longer make out individual voices in the clamour. Then suddenly there was a crash, as if someone had slammed the table. The green Mage shouted, "Stop! Be quiet! Listen to me, you ignorant scum!"

There was a sudden hush.

"Scum?" said the blue Mage. "A tad harsh, I think. Unprincipled, selfish, powerful, evil - yes, but not scum, please."

"Ignorant, anyway! None of you know as much as me about the connection, the gifts, the powers. And I have a suggestion that solves all our difficulties. I have considered this for the last few months, while seeing for myself how the land is being drained. It needs at least thirty, if not forty years, to lie fallow and recover."

"Go on then," said the orange Mage.

"My plan is that we travel round the Talthen, fomenting their resentment of the Hued. We promise to help them attack the garrison towns and estates, and we ensure that the garrison towns fall and that news gets back to Hueron. We also ensure that thousands, on each side, die."

Riathe gasped and put his hand to his mouth.

"Then we persuade them to besiege Hueron; giving them weapons, protection, whatever they need. Ulban and his men will support us, with the incentive of looting the city."

"Uncivil war between Talthen and the Gifted People, and us involved," said the red Mage. "I like it."

"No surprises there," said the blue Mage.

"To continue," said the green Mage. "At the height of the siege, we call a ceasefire and enter the city under a flag of truce."

"Enter the city? Are you mad?" exclaimed the orange Mage.

"No! Hear me out! We meet the Hued City Council. They will be desperate and afraid. We tell them that we have come to help them. We offer to renew and double their power. We spin some yarn about a complex incantation being required and tell them, all of them, to put their symbols on a table or altar or in a hexagon surrounded by candles. Something impressive. Any hocus-pocus will do.

Then, when we have most of the Hued symbols together, we destroy them all."

There was a murmur of surprise.

"Not all the Hueds will be in the city or will give us their symbols," he continued. "As long as several of each colour, preferably a few hundred Hued in all, keep their symbols, then the connection will continue to work. And the gifts from the black and white Hueds will remain in us. But enough Hued will lose their gifts to allow the land time to recover. And our power will fall, but only temporarily. We leave the city and the powerless Hueds to their fate, letting the Talthen massacre the Hueds and fight between themselves for the city."

A babble of raised voices started questioning and arguing.

"Why involve Ulban?" the purple Mage said. "He could warn the Hued what we are planning."

"I wouldn't, sires, on my honour," bleated Ulban.

"Don't be a dunderhead. Who can he tell?" snapped the orange Mage. "The Talthen? The Hued? No doubt the Hued would execute him as a robber, wouldn't they, my dear fellow? And he'll make a lot of money. Men like him always do well out of war."

"And how do we escape the city?" said the yellow Mage. "The Hueds will attack us!"

"Of course not," said the green Mage. "You've seen how it affects them when their symbols are destroyed. They will be too weak. And we won't lose our invulnerability."

"It's far too risky. Suppose they don't believe us?"

"You're an idiot!" said the orange Mage. "The ones we speak to directly will believe us. The rest will be greedy enough and frightened enough to swallow the bait as well."

"But how can we be sure enough Hued symbols are left?"

"That's perfectly feasible," said the green Mage. "We just 'rescue' a few dozen, maybe a hundred or so beforehand, and offer them sanctuary. There are many Hueds that have left the city for their country estates already, and will flee further. Probably enough."

"But what..."

The orange Mage interrupted.

"It's a good plan, very good. We'll do it. As soon as possible. We'll go straight back, work out the details and prepare, then, let me see, next spring we'll return and meet you, Ulban. You can prepare too. Start recruiting now, getting stocks of weapons, that sort of thing."

He paused. Riathe heard him push his chair back and stand up. "Raise your glasses, everyone. Drink to a summer bloodbath, the ruin of Hueron, the destruction of the gifts and the recovery of our own power!"

There was a clink of glasses and a cheer. Riathe slipped back to his room. He lay awake on his bed until dawn, raging inwardly at the Magi and trying to think what he could do. How could he get to Langron in time and warn the Talthen and the Hued, how could he get them to listen to him? But if he left the Magi he wouldn't be made into a wizard, and if he was a wizard, maybe he'd have some chance to stop them. And perhaps the other apprentices would help. He turned over and over on his bed, unable to decide on anything, full of desperation at his own powerlessness.

CHAPTER 34
FATHER AND SON

As they travelled south, Riathe noticed how villagers passing them on the road stopped and bowed, how exhausted workers in the sodden fields straightened up and wiped the rain and sweat from their faces to watch, how even the occasional Hued rider paused to stare at the Magi and their procession as they passed by. The wizards led; riding thoroughbred grey or dappled horses; dressed in rich velvets, linens and lace; adorned with jewels and silver and gold; and staying dry despite the persistent rain. Behind them were two dozen grey-clad servants, spare horses, several women, boys and girls in covered waggons, and the apprentices. Riathe rode as near to the back as possible. He looked for the fragile girl that he had tried to rescue, but he never saw her. Every time he saw a tall horseman on the road his spirits would rise, then plummet as he saw that it wasn't his father.

They travelled at a steady pace, south through the rain and wind, stopping at inns or overflowing into Talthen houses if the inn was small. The Magi paid well, and the Talthen gratefully received them and their money and would beg the wizards to "bless my harvest, it's been ruined by storms and mildew" or to "heal my son, he's sick with plague". Always the Magi would smile benevolently, mutter strange words, and a blue-white light would blaze from their staffs.

Without incident they continued, through Peveque, past Tagrinne and on through gloomy pine forests, then across the mountains. As they came down the pass, they passed a lake with willow trees and pale green reeds reflected in still water. Riathe remembered Felde's brother, but he could not see any trace of Jorvund's pyre. At the base of the mountains, the Magi sent a servant ahead to tell the steward to prepare for their arrival. Ahead of them Riathe could see the desert, and with a thrill of mingled fear and excitement he thought of the Magi's land beyond it: the rainbow dome, the vast house. There he would become a white wizard. He'd stop the evil plotted by the Magi, and save his family, the Talthen and the Hued. His clenched left hand tingled.

The desert crossing, under dense clouds summoned by the Magi to shelter them, was easier than he had expected. Three days later they rode over the demarcation between the sand and the lush grass. Riathe, at the end of the cavalcade, paused for a few minutes and looked back northwards. He could see no one. He could ride back, but that would be the act of a coward. Feeling that to take one step over the divide would be irrevocable and would have terrible consequences, Riathe took it anyway.

As he followed the others along the winding road past a lake, down through beech woods and fields, he heard someone whisper "Riathe!" He turned to see a tall man in grey standing in the trees. With a shock of relief, Riathe recognised his father. He rode back, dismounted and threw himself into his father's arms.

"Thank the Powers you were at the back and I could get to you without the Magi knowing," Felde whispered. "Quick, get off the road, out of sight, before they see us."

Riathe followed Felde a mile or more deep into the wood to a glade where a horse was tethered.

"I'd given up hope of seeing you," he said.

"I lost your track. But I knew where you'd be going to. I got here several days ago. Riathe, you can't go on. These Magi, they're the worst men you can imagine, the most evil, cruel ... anyhap, trust me. We've got to leave, now, while you can."

"I know what they're like!" said Riathe. "But I won't go

back. I promised. And I want to be a wizard. They're not going to hurt me. They're going to teach me."

"They ain't teachers! Whatever they've got planned for you, it won't be good. Don't risk it!"

"I don't care about the risk. I ain't going back as a coward and a failure!"

"Like I did?" Felde said. "Mayhap I did, but, Riathe, there's more at stake. Please...You wouldn't be a failure. You'll still have saved Breck, and we can warn people about the Magi. Tell them the truth."

"Nay! I'm going on, to stop them, before they destroy everything. I'm the only one that has a chance, from what I heard them say. I ain't a Talthen. I'm a white Hued."

"A white Hued? Mayhap, but what difference does that make?"

Riathe remembered how the blows from the blue Mage had not affected him.

"They can't hurt me. I'm invulnerable to them." He held up his closed left hand and glared at his father. "I have a gift and I'm going on!"

Felde turned away for a moment, his head bowed. He took a deep breath, and turned back.

"Then we go together," he said. "I'll stay with you, unless they kill me or tear me away."

"Nay! What about mother? You've got to go back to her!"

"I ain't going back as a coward either! Berrena will know why if we don't return. We'll face the Magi together. I won't leave you!"

"Brave words!" said a voice. They spun round. The orange Mage, and several servants, rode into the clearing.

He dismounted, strode up to Felde, and tapped on the badge on his grey tunic.

"I noticed we were missing someone. But you - you're not one of my servants. Ha! A spy! How intriguing!"

"Nay, sir," said Felde. "I'm this lad's father. Felde Sulvenor. I followed you, hoping to persuade him to come home."

"Your powers of persuasion haven't achieved much, have they? Looks to me like the lad's made his choice. But I'd hate you, my dear Felde whatever, to miss out on the fun. Come and watch your son be made into a wizard. Follow us!"

Inside the dome the blue Mage trailed his fingers through the pool under the fountain. He flicked the water from his hand and swirled round as Riathe, Felde and the others entered. Riathe stared up in astonishment at the rainbow glass and around at the vast room.

"I've found your errant apprentice," the orange Mage said. "And a bonus: an over-fond father who can't bear to let his son become a wizard."

"Really? How absurd. Doesn't the fool know what an honour it is?"

"Apparently not. And our tame Hued doctor's been plotting again. Headon!"

A green-skinned man, with a short beard and a scarred face, limped into the room. He glanced at Riathe and Felde, turned away and stood, expressionless, looking at the Mage.

"I'm intrigued as to how this man got a uniform and an orange badge. I can see I'll have to think of yet another punishment for you, slave. You tax my ingenuity, you really do."

He turned to Riathe and Felde.

"Listen! You are to stay in this land. You may not leave, nor hurt yourself, nor kill yourself, nor the other apprentices or servants here. Understand? Headon, find a room for these two, and then we will eat. I hope you and the servants have prepared a suitable feast, for your sakes!"

Headon left them in an upstairs bedroom, saying that he would return as soon as he could. A servant brought a tray with cold meat, a flagon of wine, bread, apples and cheese. Riathe tried, but the apprehension gnawing at him meant he could only swallow a few mouthfuls of the wine.

"You should eat," Felde said, "We will need all our strength."

"I can't!" Riathe exclaimed. "The waiting, the not knowing... The wizard talked about punishing that man, that Headon. How can I eat?"

Felde bowed his head. "I know. Riathe, I need to tell you about Headon. And my friends. About what they have been through."

Riathe paced around the room, pausing only to look out of the window at the darkening gardens, then flung himself onto the bed, while Felde briefly told him Headon's and the others' stories. As he finished, Headon came in with candles. He looked grim. He turned to Riathe and said, "Greetings - Riathe, is it? You are clearly Felde's son. I wish I could say that I was pleased to see you. But I'm grieved, very grieved, that they caught you."

"Aye," said Felde. "The one in orange, he caught us where we were hiding in the woods. I don't know how he found us so quickly."

"He is the worst of men! Nothing seems to escape him! But, Riathe - I have news for you."

Riathe stood up expectantly. At last, he thought.

"The Magi want you both in the dome tomorrow morning. They say they will be making you a wizard, and Felde has to be there. I don't like it. They are too cheerful, curse them!"

"Cheerful?"

"There's nothing that Mage enjoys more than tormenting people. It's a shame you're too late to leave."

"I'm going to stay anyway!" Riathe said fiercely. "I want to be a wizard!"

"You have no idea what that is!"

"I do. I'm determined!"

"A pity... Anyway, there's something I need to ask. Riathe, Felde didn't tell me that you weren't a Talthen. Your colouring is - unusual," Headon said, staring at him.

"Nay, I'm Hued, like my mother!"

"Ah. Do the Magi realise that?

"I don't think they do. They think I'm an albino, very pale blonde – something like that."

"Strange. Do you have a gift, a symbol?"

Riathe shook his head. Felde told Headon how the surgeon's knife had slipped at Riathe's marking.

"He didn't expect Riathe to move," he continued. "Riathe jerked his hand and the knife cut into his wrist as well."

"I was only two, I couldn't help it," exclaimed Riathe.

"Twas our fault. We shouldn't have done it."

"Hmm. Interesting," Headon said. "Riathe, give me your hand, your closed one, please."

He turned Riathe's hand over and over, and ran his fingers over the closed fingers, the muscles and joints and the faint scar running down the wrist. Riathe could feel the papery, burnt skin on Headon's hand, he looked at the pale mark of a slash on his face, and wondered what had happened to him. Clearly there were more things - horrors - that his father hadn't wanted to tell him about this place and these Magi.

"As I thought," Headon said eventually. "The tendons and nerves are damaged. Can you feel anything or move anything?"

"Only my thumb and my little finger, a tiny amount. But I can feel things."

"I think I can heal it. Let me try."

Headon took his stone and placed it on Riathe's wrist, then cupped his hands around Riathe's hand. He bowed his head.

"Can you move your fingers now?"

"Nay," said Riathe, though he could feel a tingling warmth spreading through them. "But there's something..."

"Wait," Headon said, shutting his eyes and breathing deeply for a moment. "Try now."

"They're stiff, and tis painful, but I can move them! Only

a bit, but they move!"

"It will be painful. The muscles and tendons haven't moved for years. Open your fingers as far as you can. Carefully. The pain will ease."

Riathe's fingers felt strange and aching, like the twinges in his legs after a hard day's riding. Slowly he opened his fingers. On his palm an iridescent white sphere nestled on a circular scar of paler skin.

"What's that?" said Felde.

"I knew there was something there!" Riathe exclaimed.

"It's your symbol," Headon said. "Don't let the Magi know about it. Hide it!"

Riathe closed his fingers around the pearl-like orb. He shut his eyes and tried to concentrate. Surely he ought to be able to feel something, some tingling, some power, something, anything?

"Can you feel it? Anything? Does it do anything?" Headon said.

Riathe's eyes flew open. "I don't know! But tis vital I know!" he snapped. "Headon, how did you learn what to do with your stone?"

"I don't remember. I was two when I started, and I learnt quickly. It's instinctive now. I can't help you! And I've never seen a symbol like yours. It is tiny. So small..."

Riathe opened his hand and they looked in silence at the white sphere. Eventually he shook his head. "Tis hopeless. I don't know what to do with it and you can't teach me."

Headon got up.

"It's no help," he sighed. "Anyway, it's late. You should try to sleep. All we can do is pray for some miracle. Powers and Virtues help us!"

A servant brought them breakfast the next morning. Felde had grey shadows below his weary, fearful eyes. Riathe paced the floor, feeling like a condemned man.

"I couldn't sleep. I can't eat," he said. "I wish Headon would come. The suspense is unbearable. I feel sick with dread. I wish I knew..."

"Knew what?"

"What they're planning! What this symbol is!" Riathe shouted back.

Felde stood in front of his son. "Riathe, Riathe," he said, and put his arms around him. "Twill be all right," he said, meaninglessly, adding in a whisper, "Great Powers above, keep him safe!"

When Headon came in, his face taut with apprehension, he was carrying an embroidered silk and velvet robe.

"You are to wear this, Riathe," he said. "So the servants know you are a blue Mage."

CHAPTER 35
THE PEARL

When they entered the dome they saw a low bier-like table occupying the centre of the vast room. The six Magi stood by it, holding their staffs and smiling.

"Headon, you can stay to witness his transformation - as your punishment. Come here, apprentice," ordered the chief Mage.

Riathe, his hands clenched by his side, reluctantly stepped forward.

"He's a bit thin and weak looking, pale too," remarked the yellow Mage. "Why did you pick such a runt?"

"I like his height, his thinness, his aloof, unearthly face. I've never seen a Talthen look so mysterious. Makes a change from all those stout bucolic peasants," replied the blue Mage. "And he offered himself, instead of his friend, to save the girl he loved. Reason enough for me."

He came close to Riathe, and his blue eyes pierced Riathe's grey ones. Riathe stepped back.

"Don't move! Listen to me! You think you are going to become the next blue Mage? Well, in a way, that's true. Your body is. We can't stop ourselves growing old, so we take new bodies every forty years. Your spirit dies, and I take your body."

"What? Never!" roared Felde, charging at the Mage. But the wizard held up his hand, the gesture knocking Felde to the floor. Headon ran to him. Riathe turned to go to his father, but the wizard grabbed his arm.

"Stay put," he hissed, and then turned to the orange Mage. "Do we have to have those two here?"

"Oh, Headon can endure this," said the chief Mage. "And it will be easier to destroy the lad's spirit if he can see his father's pain."

He lifted his staff and drew a circle in the air with it. A high glass wall appeared around the six Magi, Riathe and the low table, encircling them. Felde rose up and hammered on the glass.

The orange Mage seized Riathe's shoulders and stared at him. Riathe stared back, helpless and terrified, shaking. He wished he could keep still, at least look brave, but his body was beyond his control and black dread threatened to overwhelm him.

"When he's taken your body, your first act will be to kill your own father. You'll feel the power, and the delight in using it. Well, you won't, he will," said the orange Mage. "And it will be an act of mercy, you could say."

Riathe turned to his father, who was kneeling, shouting, striking the glass again and again. Headon had grabbed a candlestick from the mantelpiece and was frantically smashing it at the wall.

"They won't be able to break it," the orange Mage said. "It's made of the virtue of protection. No one can rescue you and you have to obey us. It's hopeless."

The blue Mage came closer to Riathe.

"It is, you know," he whispered. "Nothing can save you. And your friend and his sweetheart - Breck and Aleythe are their names, aren't they?"

Riathe gasped, "Don't you dare hurt them!" but the mage only smiled.

"When I'm in your body I'll go back, as I promised the girl," he said. "She's just the sort of delicate, young, fair-haired girl I like. I'll enjoy taking her. Breck will think she's gone off with you. He'll be broken-hearted. And she'll join my harem, until I'm tired of her."

"No! No!" screamed Riathe, hurling himself at the Mage, who moved aside and held out his hand. Riathe fell to his knees. He sobbed.

"Oh, enough!" said the orange Mage. "Let's get on with it."

He hauled Riathe to his feet. "We like to observe the traditions, so there is an altar ready for the sacrifice. Lie down," he ordered, looking into Riathe's scared eyes.

Shivering with fear, but unable to stop himself, Riathe lay on his back on the cold hard table. Above him the multi-coloured panes of the huge dome glittered from the sunlight shining slantwise through them. He could see glorious patches of emerald, topaz, amethyst and deep red, shimmering through the tears in his eyes. He had thought to stop them. How stupid that seemed now. He'd failed, after all. The Magi were too strong for him. He thought of Aleythe and what would happen to her and what Breck would think of her and him, and it broke his heart. Blinking away the tears he looked sideways to see Headon and Felde, their faces filled with despair and grief, standing against the glass wall, eyes fixed on him. I wonder if I'll see him again after we're both dead, Riathe thought. He stared at his father's face, wanting the moment to last as long as possible, wanting that face to be the last thing he saw, and Felde stared back, holding Riathe in his eyes.

But the blue Mage moved to Riathe's side, coming between him and Felde. He placed his fingers on Riathe's temples and leaned forward. The touch of his hands made Riathe shudder. As he looked into the Mage's eyes dimness fogged his vision. All else faded and darkened, and the sharp blue irises, with the jet black holes at their centres, were all he could see.

"We are going to destroy you. Your mind, your spirit, your will and your soul. Despair will kill you, leaving only your body. There is no hope left now. Firstly, these are my memories. Over seven hundred years of cruelty and vice and triumphs; of people who have tried to fight me and lost again and again," his subtle voice hissed.

Riathe shut his eyes to escape the intense blue gaze, but picture after picture, vision after vision flooded into his mind. Countless memories of violence and rape, of subtle deceptions and vicious tortures, of children stolen and wells poisoned and herds cursed and fields blighted. Vision after vision, picture after picture. He had not thought that one man could do so much evil. Revolted, horrified, he fought to stop the sickening images from branding themselves into his mind. But he could only accept them. The Mage was too powerful.

The sibilant voice of the Mage broke the stream of memories.

"Receive our desires, our feelings, our lusts."

The other Magi drew closer and placed their fingers on his temples as well. Tormenting pain pierced his head. He opened his eyes and saw again the black pupils inside the sapphire circles, and he felt horrible yearnings rise in him. A lust for strength and power, a fierce and strong joy in wanton destruction and suffering, a longing to violate and murder and destroy, to hunt and to kill and to consume, to torment and hurt and deceive. The desires drowned him. He was in hell, loathing himself and sinking down into a deep and endless horror.

The blue Mage put his hand on Riathe's heart and he and the others raised their staffs. The stones shone with a blue light, then arcing threads of black shot upwards from each stone. The arcs met above Riathe and fused into a whirling, ebony mass, hovering above him. The room grew dark as light was sucked into the blackness.

"Now," said the blue Mage.

A thick ribbon of deeper darkness snaked down from the fused arcs and struck Riathe on his forehead. He arched and writhed in an agony like scorching fire running through his bones, and then the pain was quenched as if he was falling into black, fathomless water.

"Riathe! Riathe!!" shouted Felde.

Deep in the darkness, Riathe heard his father calling him. He could see nothing, sense nothing, feel nothing. He heard only the faint echo of a familiar voice. A flash of gold flickered in the dark. It moved, turning into the golden hair of a quiet girl. Riathe remembered the earthy scent from his spade as he stood in the garden listening to Aleythe. He had loved her once. No more.

In the emptiness, he heard Felde calling his name again and again, his voice growing fainter with each cry. There was one tiny good thing left, he realised, the ghost of a desire to save Felde and Aleythe. He saw an image of the pearl on his palm and another memory came into his mind. With it came hope.

Riathe opened his eyes. Above him brooded the ebony shadow, feeding and growing from the dark arcs writhing upwards from the stones. Riathe's hand suddenly tingled with the power in his gift. He summoned strength into his arm and punched his fist into the ebony arc above his head. Opening his fingers, he released the white sphere. The tiny speck floated up into the snaking black ribbon. It hung, a serene point of light against the turbid cloud. Felde, Headon, the Magi and Riathe himself gazed at it for a moment. Then it shone silver, turning and glistening in the gloom.

"You fool! He's a white Hued!" howled the orange Mage, abject terror on his face.

The pearl grew as it turned, flashing silver and gold and dazzling white, becoming larger and brighter, swallowing up the whirling black globe. Black veins flickered over the iridescent surface and sank into the pearl as it glowed many-coloured, outshining all light. Like sunshine through the stained glass above, its coruscating radiance flooded the dome. The Magi shrank back and covered their eyes against the glory. Jagged lines of white shot from the pearl along the black arcs, spearing through the darkness and piercing each stone, bursting them asunder. Deafening thunder echoed around the room. The white bolts flowed on, striking the Magi. They staggered and fell as the lightning hit them, stabbing into their bodies, splitting their hearts, burning their robes and flesh away piece by piece, morsel by morsel, blazing out from them in a searing glow of brightness, until they were gone.

The light dimmed. The echoing thunder faded. The pearl shrank and floated down into Riathe's hand. As he took it, the fading silvery light from it spread over his hand and arm and skin, rippling over him like shimmering mercury. His hand fell by his side and he lay still.

CHAPTER 36
DESTRUCTION

The glass wall vanished. Headon threw the candlestick aside and ran, with Felde, to Riathe's side. Against the deep royal blue of the robe he wore, Riathe's face was paper-white. His eyes were closed, but he was breathing.

Felde pulled his son into his arms. Above them the overarching metal ribs of the crystal dome creaked. They glanced up as a piece of turquoise glass fell and splintered on the floor.

"We'd better get out of here!" Headon exclaimed, and limped as fast as he could, ignoring the stabbing pains in his damaged legs, towards the doors. Metal buckled and groaned as coloured glass plummeted down around them. A fragment struck him and he staggered, dropping to his knees. Felde had reached the door. "Felde!" Headon called as he struggled to his feet. The metal ribs overhead sagged and cracked. A massive bronze lantern splintered and crashed to the floor next to him. Felde ran back and seized Headon's arm and, carrying Riathe one-armed, dragged him through the fusillade of sharp-edged shards and slivers of metal. Razor-edged pieces of glass hit them, sliced their arms, drawing blood from their skin. The roaring and crashing noise surrounded them.

They hurtled through the door and threw themselves onto the lawns. Headon, his heart pounding, his breathing fast, stared as the dome collapsed and the golden globe on top hurtled down in a storm of noise and dust, flying metal and crystal. The walls collapsed with a chaotic rumble and the thundering of falling masonry and woodwork. He covered his face as a choking cloud of dirt and grit rolled forth from the rubble, enveloping them, and the cacophony of shattering glass and falling metal deafened them.

Gradually the noise faded and the dust cleared. Headon gazed around, astounded at the destruction.

"Headon..." Felde whispered, laying his pallid, motionless son on the grass. A strange mercurial opalescence shimmered on Riathe's skin. "Headon - is he...?"

Headon crawled over to Riathe.

"No. He has a pulse, he's breathing," he said, in a shaking voice. "But - by the city walls, what just happened?"

"I don't know!"

"How can the Magi have vanished? What did Riathe do?"

"Headon, I know they're gone, but what's wrong with my son? Riathe, wake up! Riathe!" Felde cried frantically, as he shook the boy's shoulders. Servants came running towards them from the surrounding buildings. Seeing the shattered remains of the golden globe lying on the ruined dome, they stood, open-mouthed, pointing and gasping, then stared at the three men on the grass, stained with filth and blood and fragments of metal. One came over.

"Headon, sir, what happened?" he asked.

"Wait - no, get some water!" Headon said to him and turned back to the boy. "Riathe! Riathe, wake up!"

"For the Powers' sake, Headon, get your stone, heal him!" Felde cried.

"My stone...where is it?" Headon searched his pockets, pulled out the green oval and stared blankly at it. "It's gone..."

"What? Headon, use it! Heal him, do something!"

"I can't," Headon whispered. "It's gone. My healing gift, it's gone."

"Gone?"

Headon looked at the ruined dome, realisation filling

him. "It's because the Magi's stones are gone. I don't know how, but Riathe destroyed the Magi and their stones. That must have destroyed the Hued powers too. That's why my symbol is dead. Felde, the implications! All the Hued... By the Seven Founders, what will happen to us?"

"Headon! Remember Riathe? Do something! Even if your stone's gone, you're still a doctor, ain't you?" Felde shouted.

"Headon ... water, sir?" said the servant, coming up and holding out a jug.

Headon turned, tipped water into Riathe's mouth and sprinkled some on his dust-covered face. Riathe stirred and opened his eyes.

"At last...Riathe? Is it you?" Felde asked, a trace of doubt in his voice.

"Aye, tis me," Riathe whispered in a shaking voice. "Not a Mage."

Felde pulled his son into his arms. Dozens of the servants clustered around them, questioning them and staring at the father clutching his son. Headon looked around at the frightened and confused faces of the servants, then up into the unbounded heavens. Late summer sunlight poured down on him in blazing glory. The miracle had finally happened. He looked up at the azure clearness and white clouds. Nothing and no one could prevent him leaving. He did not need to walk to the boundary to know that he could walk over it. Despite losing his gift, every inch of him exulted that he was free.

"They're gone," he whispered, and, walking to the low wall around a fountain, he stood on it and shouted. "The Magi are gone!"

A susurration of excitement rose from the servants. Headon yelled above the rising sound of wondering voices. "Go and get everyone! Get Loira, get them all here, quickly, so we can tell them. And get the prisoners out of the dungeons and the other five apprentices. Tell them the Magi are dead and we are free!"

He returned and knelt beside Felde and Riathe.

"I have to tell Vallan and Iselle," he said. "Their child - she is safe now. I'll ride down there, tell them and come back with them. But before I go - Riathe, what happened? How did you destroy them? And - you are altered. Your skin, it's shining like silver."

"Tis strange. I feel different. Weakened but more alive," Riathe said, in an urgent, elated voice, his eyes glittering. "But I'm not wearing these foul wizard robes any longer. Headon, can you get me a grey tunic?"

"Yes, but later! Tell us what happened. Your pearl - what did it do? How did you know how to use it?"

Riathe opened his palm. The pearl glowed. Strange lights swirled on its opalescent surface and reflected on his shimmering skin.

"Because the blue Mage gave me his memories." He laughed. "Tis ironic. When you called me, Father, I'd almost gone, but I remembered you and the gold of Aleythe's hair. Then I remembered something else. How, hundreds of years ago, I... no... the blue Mage, he gave the Hued leaders their gifts. How we made and connected the stones, and shared our gifts with the Hued in exchange for theirs."

"Ah. I knew some of this already," said Headon.

"Do you? Anyhap, the Hued were weak, but they could take power from the life around them and control it and create with it. We had the power to read men's characters and desires, we could control men. It was easy to persuade them. Connecting their blood and ours together in the stones increased the powers and created new powers and gifts. Like this."

He looked at the pearl in his hand.

"The green Mage knew how to create the shared connection. He knew that the Hueds, by cutting their palms and symbolically sacrificing the blood of their children, would continually renew the connection, and their powers."

"Sacrificing?" Headon exclaimed.

"Aye. Symbolic, but still powerful. Evil, foul black evil!"

Riathe shook his head. "Anyhap, I remember - there were two Hueds, one black and one white. They had rare gifts – they were invulnerable. In order to be invulnerable ourselves we, I mean the Magi, had to share that gift with them. And they wanted the power to defend themselves from any attack, even a gifted attack, and the white Hued had the ability to do this, though it was weak. Her symbol was a pearl like this."

"Oh!" exclaimed Headon. "I'm beginning to understand."

"Aye! I remembered teaching him how to turn attacks back onto the attackers. Then I knew. How to make the pearl take their power and turn it, so that it destroyed the stones and them. It nearly killed me and my pearl. But it didn't..."

He gestured at Headon's twisted legs.

"Let me try something."

He knelt, the pearl hovering mid-air above him, and put his hands on Headon's ruined legs. The shimmering iridescence spread over the distorted joints. Headon felt them move, then twist. Something wrenched, he gasped, and suddenly the relentless aching had vanished. He took a few tentative steps, then more, then stopped. "This is beyond belief, this is..." His voice broke and he fell to his knees.

A few hours later, Headon came back to the front of the house, with Vallan, Iselle, and Nessa scampering elatedly around them. Telling them about the Magi's death, seeing the expressions on their faces, embracing them, even crying with them, had been the greatest joy that he had ever known.

As Nessa and her parents ran with exclamations of delight to welcome to Felde and a grey-clad Riathe, Headon gazed around. It looked like all the servants, all the apprentices, everyone from the dungeons and the farms, were on the sunlit lawns: laughing, dancing, exclaiming, or wiping tears of joy from their faces. Headon was pleased to see that someone had raided the cellars; bottles of wine were being passed around. Among the crowd was Loira. She dashed up to him.

"Oh, Headon, is it true?" she cried.

"Yes, it's true. They've gone."

She grabbed his hands and whirled him round, then stopped, "You're not limping!"

"No! More miracles. Riathe - he healed me."

"Who?"

"Loira, so much has changed! I'll tell you - on the way home."

"Home?" she gasped, her hand to her heart. "Oh, Headon, does this mean I can go home?"

Headon thought of her family, of his mother, of Sarielle, of Berrena, and smiled. Despite his apprehensions for the powerless Hued in the city, despite his fears of what the Talthen might do, there was joy ahead.

"Yes," he said. "We can go home. We can all go home."

The End

Their story continues in The City, to be published soon

ABOUT THE AUTHOR

Cathy Hemsley is a radical Christian, software engineer and author. She writes a blog about Christian fiction called 'Is Narnia All There Is?', is involved with various charities to help people in her home town of Rugby, and to help rebuild houses and lives in Beira, Mozambique.

This is her second book: the first is a series of short stories, called 'Parable Lives'

https://isnarniaallthereis.wordpress.com/

Printed in Great Britain
by Amazon